ON
THIN
ICE

ON THIN ICE

S. RENA

FOREVER

New York Boston

This book is a work of fiction. Names, characters, places, and incidents are the product of the author's imagination or are used fictitiously. Any resemblance to actual events, locales, or persons, living or dead, is coincidental.

Copyright © 2026 by S. Rena

Cover design and illustration by Daniela Medina.
Cover copyright © 2026 by Hachette Book Group, Inc.

Hachette Book Group supports the right to free expression and the value of copyright. The purpose of copyright is to encourage writers and artists to produce the creative works that enrich our culture.

The scanning, uploading, and distribution of this book without permission is a theft of the author's intellectual property. If you would like permission to use material from the book (other than for review purposes), please contact permissions@hbgusa.com. Thank you for your support of the author's rights.

Forever
Hachette Book Group
1290 Avenue of the Americas, New York, NY 10104
read-forever.com
@readforeverpub

First Edition: April 2026

Forever is an imprint of Grand Central Publishing. The Forever name and logo are registered trademarks of Hachette Book Group, Inc.

The publisher is not responsible for websites (or their content) that are not owned by the publisher.

The Hachette Speakers Bureau provides a wide range of authors for speaking events. To find out more, go to hachettespeakersbureau.com or email HachetteSpeakers@hbgusa.com.

Forever books may be purchased in bulk for business, educational, or promotional use. For information, please contact your local bookseller or the Hachette Book Group Special Markets Department at special.markets@hbgusa.com.

Library of Congress Cataloging-in-Publication Data

Names: Rena, S. author
Title: On thin ice / S. Rena.
Description: New York : Forever, 2026. | Identifiers: LCCN 2025048739 |
    ISBN 9781538775264 trade paperback | ISBN 9781538775271 ebook
Subjects: LCGFT: Romance fiction | Sports fiction | Novels | Fiction
Classification: LCC PS3618.E574 O5 2026
LC record available at https://lccn.loc.gov/2025048739

ISBNs: 9781538775264 (trade paperback), 9781538775271 (ebook)

Printed in the United States of America

LSC-C

Printing 1, 2026

Author's Note and Content Guidance

If you're reading this book, thank you. Truly. Thank you for giving Sam, Alex, Kane, and Bryden "Mountain" a chance to wreck you.

This book was probably the hardest for me to write for several reasons. It's raw and often unfiltered. This was a lot of firsts for me, a new subgenre and new tropes.

Their story is harsher than any characters I've written before them. It won't wrap you in warmth; it's not soft, clean, or polite. You'll hate these characters, but you'll love them, too. You'll judge them, root for them, scream when they get it wrong, and maybe, just maybe, you'll see pieces of your own broken humanity through them.

This is for readers who aren't afraid to feel all their pain and rage. To question where the line between love and destruction begins and ends. It shows the truth in the way trauma often feels...ugly, complicated, and sometimes cruel. It's about survival, and what happens when the people who break you become the ones who help you stand again.

They're not heroes. Not yet. Maybe not ever. But they're trying. And sometimes, that's the most honest kind of story to tell.

This won't be a story for everyone, but for those who resonate with it, thank you for letting me share it with you. It touches on heavy and sensitive topics, so please take care of yourself FIRST.

XO,

Sade

This content contains depictions of bullying, dubious consent, verbal and psychological abuse, abuse of power, sexual harassment (off page) and coercion, physical assault, past sexual assault, mention of self-harm, suicide (off page), parental death, mental health struggles, profanity, violence, sex, alcohol, and emotional manipulation. It also references past and current trauma.

If you or someone you know is struggling with suicidal thoughts, please know you are not alone. Help is available. In the U.S., call or text the Suicide & Crisis Lifeline at 988.

Resources Used

When writing outside of my lived experience, it is important to do so with care and as much accuracy as possible. Below are the resources used in writing Bryden's character. Thank you to the Mille Lacs Band of Ojibwe for your help.

- The Ojibwe People's Dictionary by Nora Livesay and John D. Nichols with support and collaboration from the University of Minnesota's university libraries and Department of American Indian Studies
- The Tribal Council of Mille Lacs Band of Ojibwe
- "5 Stereotypes to Avoid When Writing Native American Characters" by Sarah Elisabeth Sawyer
- "Writing POC 101: Native American Characters" by TalkThePOC
- "How to Write Indigenous Characters Without Looking Like a Jackass" by Reanimated Courier

CHAPTER ONE

SAM

Goodbye.

God, that word fucking sucks.

"See you later, little bro."

Desmond clings tighter to my legs without answering.

I'm never good at saying the G word. The only people I held dear left, never to return. I won't do that to Desmond, but I have no idea when I'll return.

Standing in the doorway of this run-down house, I tell myself that this goodbye is only temporary. The paint is chipped and peeling. There are holes in the walls, some from water damage, others from fists. The carpet is stained, and there isn't a single piece of furniture that doesn't have a tear in it somewhere. No matter what, I'll be back for him... for us.

"Don't leave me, sissy," Desmond pleads. I give him a squeeze and lean down to rest my chin on the top of his head, fighting back tears. I hate that seeing me walk out the door frightens him like this.

We've lost so much... first our mom—our lifeline—and now it must feel as if he's losing me, too. We're the only good left in our fucked-up world. One day, he'll realize that I had to leave for him. I have to do what's needed to save him from this dump. Even if it means the first step is damn near abandoning him.

I lift his head, forcing him to look at me. Tears stain his beautiful brown cheeks, and his chest heaves with each sharp inhale.

"Look at me, Des. I'll be back." I suck in a breath, blinking back my emotions. Being strong for him is the only thing that matters.

Who am I kidding? I also need to be strong for myself. Otherwise, I won't make it in the real world without him. Since I was twelve, and he was only two, we've been holding each other when the nights felt like they would never end. Especially the nights that Gary, Des's father and my stepfather, decided to take whatever anger he had from the day out on me after having too much to drink.

My eyes land on the bike leaning up against the tree. A small smile tugs at the corners of my mouth as I think about how happy Des was when I gave it to him for his birthday last year. I saved every penny I made from babysitting other kids in the neighborhood. With Gary finding my stash every other month and using my money to feed his vices, it took me almost two years. But the look on my brother's face was worth every sacrifice.

"I have to do this so that I can come back for you." I keep my voice down, barely at a whisper.

He sniffles and dries his face with the sleeve of his shirt. "You promise?"

I force a smile. "What do we say?" I watch his shoulders rise and fall in rapid succession. "Through shadows and storms—"

"It's you and me forever." Desmond swallows, nodding as if to remind himself.

"That's right. I'll only be on the other side of town, but I'll call and come to see you every chance I get. You just need to be strong for me. Can you do that?"

"Mm-hmm." He nods again, his breathing finally settling.

"I know you can." I kiss his head and hug him some more.

"Hurry up and close my damn door," Gary barks.

Desmond flinches as I peer up over his head at Gary without breaking our embrace. His tall frame stands there menacingly, a beer in one hand and a lit cigarette in the other. He seethes, staring at me with nothing but hate in his heart. A monster that poisons everything in its presence.

That stops with us. I'll free Desmond from this hellhole if it's the last thing I do. Luckily, he's never made Desmond the subject of his physical torment. No, this asshole reserves that for me. Just like he did Momma, up until the day she left this earth.

That's the one thing keeping me sane. There's no way I could leave if I thought he might hurt Desmond. Gary may not have laid a hand on Des, but that doesn't stop the yelling or the nights where he'd show up with no dinner but had enough money for a six-pack.

I turn my attention back to my brother, refusing to let Gary take more from me than he already has. So, with another peck to Desmond's head, I lean down to whisper into his ear. "Be brave. And go to Evan and Mrs. Holmes if he gets too upset."

I hate this, but I know it's for the best.

The sound of a horn blares outside. Reluctantly, I back away. The tears I fought so hard to keep at bay pour down my face, and I don't bother to wipe them.

I drag my luggage out the door. With a quick look back, I pass my brother a tight smile.

"I love you, little bro," I choke out, my heart pounding.

"I love you, too." He sniffles.

Gary has lost his patience. "That's enough, dammit. If you're going to leave, get the hell out."

My teeth grind together as I bite back the words I want to say to him. They would be useless and would only give him what he needs to justify his actions. Not that it takes much to set him off these days.

I won't give him that satisfaction.

I shake off the anger and step away from the doorway. Walking toward the small passenger bus, my eyes fall on the name stamped on the side in bold, gothic script. **SOVEREIGN KING'S UNIVERSITY**. This is it. My chance to make something of myself for both our sakes. Momma would have wanted it that way.

When I reach the end of the driveway, the driver is waiting by the luggage compartment. He's a tall Black man with streaks of gray peppered throughout his hair, reminding me of my late grandfather. He smiles at me, but I can't find the strength to return the gesture. Thankfully, he doesn't seem to be bothered by it. I allow him to take my luggage, and I sling my small backpack over my shoulder before climbing the steps of the bus.

It's empty except for two other students. One is in the first seat with her eyes glued to the book in her hand. The other is in the middle with his head up against the window. Both are in their own world, hiding within themselves from everything around them. A behavior I know too well.

As I move through the aisle, I can't help but wonder what brings them to SKU. Did they also miraculously receive a scholarship to the most prestigious university in the county?

The guy glances at me and smiles. "Hey. I'm Xavier."

I tip my chin. "Sam."

"You transferring in, too?"

I nod.

"Cool. Maybe I'll see you around."

I don't bother answering. He's being nice, making small talk so that the twenty-minute ride across town isn't so awkward.

And it's nothing against him. I'm just not interested in making friends, even with cute guys with freshly styled locs and warm eyes.

I settle in and peer out the window as the bus pulls away. Before long, all the houses with overgrown sidewalks and assorted trash on their lawns whisk by until there's nothing but open roads and fields of grass. Still focused on the world outside, my mind wanders, thinking about these past eight years of pain and neglect. And for what? Because my mother fell in love with a man who turned out to be nothing more than a nightmare?

One day she decided death was better than living another moment with him.

That same day, I was forced to grow up before I was ready. To become a parent to a child who wasn't mine. I've spent most of my life trying to convince myself things weren't as bad as they were. But none of that matters now.

This isn't the time to dwell on the past. I may be arriving at SKU a semester behind, given that my initial scholarship application was denied, but I'll bust my ass and prove that I deserve to be there. Scholarship or not. The only thing that matters is moving forward... and then doing everything in my power to get my brother out.

CHAPTER TWO

SAM

The ride to SKU is quiet. Peaceful. Something I'm not used to. The sounds of Melanie Martinez flow through my headphones, and I let myself zone out while listening to the lyrics.

Opening the messaging app, I tap on a thread with my best friend. The first friend I made when we moved in with Gary. We were eleven at the time, and when none of the other kids could be bothered to talk to me, Evan swooped in. He's always had my back from day one, and when Mom died, Evan helped me through. Now we'll be worlds apart.

Sam: I'm going to miss you, bestie.

I hit send, and a second later, he replies.

Evan: I know.

I laugh.

Evan: Love you, babes. And remember, you're a badass.

A smile parts my lips, his words speaking life into me. As we pull off the main road, the entrance to the university looms up ahead. I sit up straighter, my heart pounding as I take in my surroundings. Students walk along the sidewalk, some with backpacks, others carrying books. A group of girls stands near the fountain laughing.

I imagine myself there with them, getting to live my life the way I want to—the way I deserve to.

The bus comes to a stop, and we get off to gather our things. The driver hands me my two suitcases and duffel.

I meet his gaze. "Thank you."

"You're welcome. Good luck."

I nod and turn to face the quad.

A wave of nervous energy washes over me, a numbness that pricks its way through every limb. Historic buildings tower over me, their weathered stone architecture a reminder of this university's age. I can't help but stare in awe, my gaze moving from one end of the campus to the other. The grounds are perfectly manicured, with lush green lawns and flower beds.

It's beautiful, even more so than what I saw online. And suddenly, I'm reminded of how out of place I am here. The unfamiliar opulence reflects the fact that I'm from a different world. I don't come from a big, happy family or have a rich daddy to fund all my needs. While my peers have been rocking Prada and Fendi since infancy, I've learned to use my creativity to upcycle *vintage* clothing. No one bought my way into this school, and I damn sure don't have a legacy that ties me to this place.

I shake away those thoughts, square my shoulders, and inch toward the central part of campus. My two suitcases and duffel bag weigh me down, but I press on, ignoring the pain in my arms and the stares from the students passing by. They probably had help from loving family members while moving into their dorms at the beginning of the school year.

I focus on the path ahead, doing my best to navigate the crowded sidewalk. Every few seconds, I have to dodge someone who isn't paying attention. And each time I do, I stumble, nearly dropping my bags in the process.

After a while, I give up trying to avoid them, bumping into people who turn to give me nasty looks. I'm not winning any friends yet, but I like it this way. The fewer people I have to talk to, the better. The strap of my duffel bag digs into my shoulders, and the broken wheel of one of my old suitcases scrapes against the concrete.

And as my luck would have it, others notice, too. Their faces tell me what I already know... that I'm not welcome here. It's in the way they look at me. How their eyes linger just a second too long. And maybe I don't. I don't know what it feels like to live with an excess of money instead of bruises. To not be broken.

I ignore them because, frankly, I've got enough on my plate to worry about. But one particular group of people catches my eye. Students are in a circle near the steps of the main building. The girls are all smiles, their eyes focused on the boys standing in front of them.

They're wearing navy blue jackets like a badge of honor, the hockey team's logo stitched on the back. That red and light blue armored knight is easily noticed. SKU is known for its D1-level sports teams, but the hockey team is their pride and joy. Given that they've won the last four championships, it makes sense. I only know that because Gary, along with many of the people in this town, sports the team's jerseys as if they're gods. The fandom here is almost cult-like, and I'm the odd woman out when it comes to how ritualistic the people of this town are when the season rolls around.

There's an air of authority around the athletes, and it's clear they command respect. It's evident not just from the way they carry themselves but also from how everyone seems to hang on to their every word. I can't say that I blame them. They're fine as hell—too fine, if you ask me. It's apparent that the three of them are friends, but they couldn't seem more different.

The blond guy is clearly the ladies' man of the group. His cockiness is evident in every movement, from the way he leans casually against the railing to the confident tilt of his head. He's got that classic look, a mix of polished elegance and raw masculinity. His olive-toned skin glows in the sunlight, and his perfectly styled hair highlights the sharp angles of his chiseled jaw. He's old money meets magazine cover sex symbol, but it fits him.

I'd bet everything I own—*not that I own much*—that he's the king of this campus. Or one of them, at least. The way he engages with the girls—it's all calculated, designed to draw them in and keep them hooked.

And it's working. They lean in closer, their eyes wide with desire, laughing at his jokes—probably even the ones they don't find funny. It's as if they're under a spell. He knows exactly what he's doing, and from the looks of it, he's loving every minute of it.

I slide my gaze to another—an absolute mountain of a man—and can't help but focus on how beautiful he is with his strong jaw and smooth, tawny brown skin. His long, black hair is in a single braid that falls over his broad shoulder. But it's the way his T-shirt hugs his thick, muscular frame under that jacket that truly holds my attention.

In addition to his powerful arms and a wide chest, there's something about his presence that does it for me, a quiet intensity that sets him apart. Despite his commanding physique, he doesn't seem as involved as his friend. He's obviously utterly uninterested in the poor girl trying to get his attention. His eyes focus on his phone, his expression one of mild boredom.

The girl finally moves away, but he doesn't glance up. It's as if he's in his own world, unaffected by the attention and happy to let his friend be in the limelight. He's not here to impress anyone, and from what it seems to me, he doesn't need to.

And then my eyes fall on the last guy, and my heart stops.

It's him...

The only boy I've ever connected with... *aside from Evan.*

When my mother first attempted to take her life, in the psychiatric ward, *that* boy was there. We were alike or, at the very least, we bonded over the shared trauma of loving someone through their mental demons. He was a few years older and my first crush.

He was kind when the world was cruel and got me when everyone else failed, when nothing felt right in the world. He made me laugh and made sure I ate. When Gary caused a scene, he shielded me. Mature beyond his years, he made dealing with my mother's attempt easier to stomach. New emotions grew in me like flowers in a barren land.

But it all ended when Gary forced Momma to check out and closed that door forever. Sometimes, I wish she would have fought harder to stay the course with her therapy. Maybe then I wouldn't be doing life without her.

It's been years, and if I'm honest, I never expected to see him again. We were young and had no way of keeping in contact. We weren't old enough for emails back then, and Gary and Momma could never seem to keep a landline on at home.

So that was it, and I often wondered what became of him.

Everest.

My skepticism has been at an all-time high since I received the scholarship. Knowing someone here makes me feel less alone going into this new journey. Maybe things won't be so insufferable after all.

He stands out from the rest. His stance is rigid, his shoulders tense as he stares out at the crowd. Then, his gaze shifts, and suddenly, he's looking right at me.

His eyes trail the length of my frame before meeting mine again. A small smile meets my lips as I stop to give him a half wave that immediately falters when he doesn't return the sentiment. He only stares at me coldly—angrily, I might even say.

Confusion knits my brow.

Realistically, he probably doesn't remember me. I don't know why, but it stings. Why would he remember that sad little girl? I've outgrown the barrettes, and he certainly looks nothing like the scrawny boy who loved anime and superheroes.

Now he's Mr. Tall, Dark, and Handsome. A certified pretty boy, that's for damn sure. His preteen acne is gone, and he has the smoothest light brown skin I've ever seen. The cornrows have been replaced by a tapered fade on his curly, dark hair.

His jaw looks like it's been cut from glass and molded into pure perfection. I remember the soft flecks of green in his brown eyes and wonder if that's at least the same. He's filled out, every muscle evident beneath the fabric of his shirt. He's solid, not as buff as his big friend, but solid all the same. And the way he stands, with his legs apart and arms crossed, gives off serious Big Dick Energy.

Back then, he was the kindest person I knew, yet the guy I'm staring at seems everything but. Nevertheless, there's this invisible pull that is making it extremely difficult to look away. His gaze is intense, almost as if he's challenging me. It's as if it's some sort of game of who will blink first.

Turns out he wins because I nearly run into someone.

"Watch where you're going," the guy seethes.

I stumble back a bit, then quickly regain my balance. "Sorry."

He grumbles something under his breath and storms off. I shake my head, somewhat thankful for the distraction. Everest doesn't remember who I am, and that could be a good thing. The thing I need least right now is to find myself caught up in a childhood crush with some hot hockey player.

Hell, I don't even like hockey.

CHAPTER THREE

EVEREST (KANE)

"Ready for the championship, Kane?" Vanessa asks, batting her eyes and fishing for attention.

"As ready as I'll ever be," I say unenthusiastically, then pull out my phone.

"I can't wait to see you play. You always crush it," she continues, stepping closer to me. But I ignore her, much like I have every day since the start of the season. She's not a quitter; I'll give her that. Don't get me wrong, she's bad as hell with perky tits, long curly hair, and a fat ass. And I certainly remember what her mouth does—but that's as far as it'll ever go.

She and every other girl here are the same...puck bunnies looking for their label of WAG one day. They can miss me with that. I have bigger things to worry about, things that none of them will understand, so there's nothing she or anyone else can do for me. Unless they can solve all my problems and make them disappear, I'm good.

Vanessa eventually gets the picture and turns her attention to Alex. I smirk because he thrives on the love we get around campus. With a new girl in his bed every other night, I'm sure he can fit Vanessa into the roster.

The sad thing is, she'll wait. They always do. As long as they can attach themselves to the hottest player with the best chance of making it big, they'll do whatever it takes. Including letting us run through them whenever and however we see fit.

Play a sport on this campus, and you can pretty much have your pick of the litter. And the better you are, the more pussy you get. There's barely a chick at SKU that the boys and I haven't had, save for the nerds and rejects.

Except for maybe Mountain. He's all respectful and shit, staying to himself and keeping his focus on the game. Hell, I can't even remember the last time I've seen him smile. It's scary how focused he is. His ability to set aside all the bullshit and hone in is why he's one of the best damn goalies I've ever seen on the ice. He's big and burly, which makes it easy for people to assume he's slow. But then the six-foot, two-hundred-pound fucker will block your shot before you even realize it.

If anyone is good under pressure, it's him. No matter how aggressive the girls get, he's got nerves of steel. He's the complete opposite of Alex, the biggest man whore you'll ever meet.

Which is fitting. You can tell a lot about a person by the position they play.

While Mountain is guarded and dependable, preferring to stay in the background, Alex is a charming motherfucker. That and the confidence he possesses makes him the perfect center. He's quick on his feet and can read people better than anyone I know.

Meanwhile, I earn my reputation of being as ruthless off the ice as I am on it. I hear all the shit the other students on campus call me: aggressive, scary, and rude as fuck. All perfect traits for a defenseman. I've been told I'm unapproachable more times than I can count. You'd think that would steer the bunnies away... It doesn't.

And while getting my dick wet is always fun, that's the last thing on my mind right now. With only three games left in the season and NHL scouts dropping in, all I'm trying to focus on is the game.

Well, trying to, at least.

Lately, I've been distracted, and it damn near cost us our last game. The fucked-up part of it all is there's no reprieve. Nothing can make this better, and I'm reminded every damn day just how unfair this world is. The corrupt remain untouchable, poisoning everything in their path, while the people they hurt suffer in silence.

I glance at my phone and open the email from my mom's doctor. For what feels like the millionth time, I read the single paragraph as if maybe the words will change this time. But they don't. It makes me angry every time her doctor tells me that she's spiraling and needs her meds adjusted or that her account is past due because my asshole of a father likes to make us beg for help.

He's the reason she's in that place. He's the reason everything about my life is so royally fucked.

"So I was thinking maybe we can hang out," Vanessa proposes. Damn, this girl doesn't quit. Her eye for Alex was short-lived. "It's been a while. I figured we could catch up."

I open my mouth to tell her I'm not interested, but I'm distracted when I hear the bus screech at the end of the sidewalk and three passengers step off. The new students are easy to spot with their wide eyes that try to take it all in.

It's like this every semester. A bunch of kids from the inner city with big dreams and a scholarship come from different backgrounds but somehow always seem the same. Damn near carbon copies of the batch from the previous season.

Then I take in the last girl, and every muscle in my body tenses.

Sam?

It's not her... it can't be.

But the closer she gets, the clearer I can see. It's been nine years, and the dorky eyeglasses have now been replaced with large, stylish ones that accentuate her face. She's no longer the little pipsqueak who followed me around the hospital.

She's all grown up, and the way those tattered jeans fit on her, every guy with a heartbeat will see just how filled out she's gotten. Her outfit sticks out among the crowd, a sore thumb next to the Gucci loafers and Prada backpacks. She's just a simple pair of jeans and an old Adidas hoodie, but it works for her.

She drags behind her two large suitcases and a duffel, and something tells me that's all she has with her. Why else would she take the bus instead of being dropped off with all her things?

If the pinched brows are any indication, she's lost. I take her in as she glances between her phone and the buildings. She looks innocent, a feeble fawn in a den of lions.

She's also the only other person who knows about my mom. Not even my best friends know what I've been dealing with all these years. I never wanted them to, and I did everything possible to keep it that way. I never invited them over to play video games or watch a movie. It was easier when I started playing hockey. All the practices and games made it so that I was rarely at home anyway. And if we wanted to hang out, we did it at Alex's place since he had an entire game room in his house.

But now, with her here, they could find out. And once they learn about my mother's condition, it'll lead to more questions that they could never know the answers to.

I struggle to tear my gaze away, but it's dragged back against my will. Our eyes lock.

Her face shows shock at first; then she waves. I don't respond. I stare at her, my mind racing a mile a minute. Her sweet smile slowly gets pulled down into a frown, and I force myself not to care.

Her face twists into a grimace, and I know it's because of me.

It's for the best. I'm not the guy she used to know. My world is dark, and she needs to be far away from me.

But right now, she's close enough that I can't help but notice the small details about her. Like the way the halo of tight, dark curls frames her face. Or how flawless and soft her golden-brown skin appears from here. Her expressive, almond-shaped eyes are framed by perfectly arched brows, and her full, glossy lips add to her allure.

Hell, she even looks like she smells good—like vanilla and cocoa butter or some shit. And even though she's wearing glasses, they don't hide the sadness in her stare.

For a brief second, I want to know how she's been. But then I remember I don't care—at least, I'm not supposed to—about her or any of the other students on this campus.

"Think they're freshmen?" Alex's voice slices through my consciousness. I don't even bother looking at him. Instead, I continue to watch Sam as she turns and walks away. I shrug. She's only two years behind us, so she would be a sophomore, but I agree anyway.

"Probably. They usually are."

He nods in agreement. "That's true. Are you ready for the new semester?"

"No." The word comes out more like a growl than an actual response, but he gets it.

"Yeah, well, neither am I, but at least we have some fresh meat to play with." He smirks and wiggles his brows suggestively.

I roll my eyes at his antics. If there is one thing you can count on when it comes to Alex, it's that he never misses an opportunity to make things about sex. It's how he's always been, and I doubt he'll ever change.

Not when every girl on campus throws herself at him. And who could blame them? He's the golden boy and captain of the hockey team. Not to mention, his father runs the school.

"Have fun with that," I tell him, not bothering to hide the lack of interest in my voice.

"Oh, come on, Kane. Don't act like you won't be trying to get a piece, too. Last time I checked, you were pulling just as much ass as I was."

I shrug, unsure how to answer him because he isn't wrong. We both ran through our fair share of women last year, so I can see why he'd assume that nothing had changed.

But it has. At least for me.

I've spent the break trying to figure out who I am outside of this life I've been handed.

"Seriously, bro, what's up? You've been a little off lately."

I suck in a breath, glaring at him for not letting this go. The truth is, shit changed for me, and he can never know why. I can never truly let him in because that would mean blowing up everything either of us has ever known. It would mean ruining lives and reputations. It would mean my mother no longer gets the care she needs.

It could mean the end.

So while it may disappoint my best friend that chasing ass isn't on my priority list, he'll just have to take it as it is.

"I'm fine." My gaze lands on the girl again, and everything stills for a beat. "Look, man, I appreciate the concern, but I'm good, okay? Whatever happens between me and these girls, or lack thereof, is my business. So how about we focus on what's important, huh?"

"Yeah, and what's that?"

"Winning the championship."

He grins. "Fair enough."

Thankfully, he turns his attention back to the girls. Unfortunately, I know that's not the end of it—it never is with him. But a win is a win.

I glance over at Bryden, or Mountain, as we call him. He's been standing a few feet from us with his back turned. If it isn't about hockey or schoolwork, Mountain wants nothing to do with it. And that includes girls. It's one of the many reasons the team thinks he's weird.

But in reality, he's probably the most normal out of all of us.

"What about you, Mountain?" Alex pries. "Do you plan on getting any this semester? We have fifteen weeks left before college is over."

Mountain glares at him. "Why are you so concerned with where the rest of us put our junk?"

I laugh. Mountain rarely engages, but when he does, it's always hilarious.

"I'm just saying. This is prime time, and there are way too many girls around to not be getting some."

"That may be true, but unlike some people, I have nothing to prove."

Alex nods, knowing his friend is just teasing him and seemingly satisfied with Mountain's answer. Even if he did care, he couldn't do much about it. Everyone knows Mountain does whatever he wants when he wants, and no person on this campus could convince him otherwise.

"Well, now that I've killed your little peer pressure campaign, I'm going to go. I have things to do tomorrow, and I'd rather not spend my night listening to you two." Mountain pats me on the shoulder and walks off.

I use this chance to get lost. "All right, man. I'm out, too. See y'all at the crib."

"Yo. Where are you going?" Alex asks with his hand out at his sides.

"Away from you, Captain."

CHAPTER FOUR

SAM

When I finally make it to my dorm, the sun is setting. My keys rattle in my hand as I struggle with the lock, but after a few seconds, it finally gives way. With a grunt, I push inside, dragging my bags across the threshold.

"Shit," I huff, dropping everything so that I can massage my neck where the strap of my duffel bag dug into my skin.

Toting all of these bags around campus while lost was no picnic. Now, I'm a tired, panting mess by the time I close the door behind me. Once I do, I turn around and come face-to-face with who I assume to be my new roommate. She stares at me, her mahogany eyes wide.

She's cute in a bubbly kind of way, with long, brown hair that she wears straight, and brown skin that's a similar complexion to my own. She smiles, immediately takes one of my bags and brings it farther inside.

"Hi," she says, her voice high-pitched and full of excitement. "I'm Gracie Martinez."

For a moment, I stare at her, taken aback by how friendly she is. I've only been at this school a few hours, but I can already say that she's drastically different from everyone else I've encountered.

I clear my throat. "Sam. Sam Collins."

She's dressed in pink socks with polka dots, shorts, and an oversized T-shirt that hangs off one shoulder.

"Nice to meet you." She sticks out her hand for me to shake.

I glance down at it, then back up at her before accepting her offer. "Likewise."

She nods, sets my suitcase next to my bed, and then glances around the room as if unsure of what's next. The air around us is awkward, but that has probably more to do with me than it does with her.

I'm not exactly the friendliest these days, and meeting new people has always been a struggle.

Gracie steps away, moving farther into the room. I watch her momentarily, then drop my bag on the edge of the bed. Finally, I take in my surroundings, mentally accepting that this will be my home until graduation.

It's an upgrade from my room back home, even with having to share with a total stranger. The walls are intact, and the stench of cigarette smoke isn't stinking up the place. In fact, Gracie has at least two wax burners going with a subtly cozy aroma.

It's nice.

And the more I take in, it's obvious she comes from money. Her side of the room reeks of spoiled rich kid. It's not enough that she seems to have brought her entire bedroom here. Her perfume collection alone could pay my tuition for an entire year, and that's not including all the expensive makeup brands she owns. Even her bedding is top-notch, with pink and yellow decor everywhere.

Then, there is my side of the room, akin to a prison cell with bare walls and a single desk. Not that I expected there to be more. After all, this is college. And I didn't exactly expect them to roll out the red carpet for their students who don't come from wealthy families.

At least the school splurged and provided us with a full-size bed, but the bedding is a dreadful beige. It's better than nothing, so I'll make do. But I can already tell this is going to be a long two and a half years as one of the few students born without a silver spoon.

I know it's wrong to judge people. For all I know, she's the sweetest person on campus, but it's hard not to make assumptions when life has dealt you a shitty hand. Plus, if I've learned anything from my experiences back home, it's that overly friendly people are masking something. Those are the ones you need to watch out for.

But I put my apprehension behind me and suck in a breath. If there's one thing Momma taught me, it's not to be rude when the person has been nothing but nice to you.

"So, you're all moved in, I see," I say to help break the silence.

Gracie chuckles and looks at her area. "Yeah. I'm sorry. I know it's a lot, but I just wanted to feel at home."

I unzip my duffel bag and shake my head. "No, I totally get it. We'll be spending a lot of time here, so why not make it your own."

"Exactly. I'm glad you get it." Gracie smiles and sits on her bed with one leg beneath her.

"It must have taken you hours to set all that up. What time did you get in?" I remove my satin pillowcases from my bag and begin to cover the pillows. If I do nothing else, I'm going to protect my hair.

"It did. But that was two years ago, so I barely even remember it."

I frown, taken aback by her response. "You aren't a sophomore? I thought they assigned sophomores to the same room."

Gracie shuffles in place. "Oh. Yeah, well. Usually, but I guess they made an exception for you."

"Mm," I mutter.

It seems they've been making a lot of exceptions for me. First, the scholarship, which isn't such a surprise. They've given out hundreds of scholarships over the years, so that's not out of the ordinary. But they didn't stop there. Not only is my tuition covered for the next three years, but so are my housing and meals.

"So... Sam. Is that short for something?" she pries, her voice hopeful.

I feel bad because I get the sense that a friend is what she's looking for, and that's not really a part of the plan. Then I remember Momma's words again.

Kindness takes you a long way, my pretty girl. Always kill them with kindness.

Sometimes I wish I could ask her where kindness ever got her.

"Samantha."

"That's pretty."

"Thanks," I quip.

There's more awkward silence as I empty my suitcases and put my clothes in the dresser they have for me.

"You didn't bring much with you. Is this everything you have?" she asks, her eyes wide.

I stop and look at her. My chest tightens, and my heart starts to race. And now the judgment begins. *That didn't take long at all.*

Though I expect nothing less from people at this school, it still makes me uncomfortable. Not just because of what she thinks about me but more so because of how true the statement is.

This really is all I have.

All I've ever had.

With a sigh, I force a smile. "Yeah," I say, holding her gaze. "It is."

She nods, her expression softening. "I'm sorry." Her voice wavers as if she's embarrassed by her actions. "That was rude. I didn't mean—"

"It's okay," I cut her off. "Don't worry about it."

We stay silent for a moment, staring at each other. Neither one of us moves, nor do we attempt to speak again. Instead, we just let the awkward silence fill the room while we both try to figure out what to do next.

"Wait." Gracie finally hops down from her bed and saunters over to her closet. The door creaks as she slides it open. A moment later, she pulls out a square-shaped bag and inside it is a comforter set. One of those expensive ones that cost at least a few hundred dollars.

"Here."

"What?" I ask, my brows pinched tight.

"You can have it."

I shake my head, pushing the bag toward her. "No. You don't have to do that."

"Sam, I want to. And trust me. You'll want these. The bedding they give us feels like steel wool. These will be much better."

I glance down then back up at her. "But these are yours. I can't take them."

"Sure you can. I keep two extra sets in my closet anyway. Plus, we're going to be friends, and last I checked, friends look out for each other."

I stare at her for a second, studying her face. I'm speechless from her sudden act of kindness.

"Thank you." It's all I can say past the lump in my throat. Taking the bag from her, I turn to face my bed. The comforter does look like it's made of the hardest fabric in existence.

"Let me help." She gets to work stripping the linen from my bed.

I don't even bother to stop her. What's the point? I can see now that she would only insist. *Maybe I was wrong about her.*

"What's your major?" Gracie asks while taking the bedding set from my grasp and removing the fitted sheet. I jump in to help, taking one end from her and stretching it onto the top portion of the mattress.

"Psychology," I answer, my voice low and strained. "Yours?"

"Kinesiology. What classes are you taking this semester?"

I shrug. "I'm not sure yet."

"How do you not know?" She pauses to look at me.

"There was some kind of mix-up with my schedule," I explain. "I tried to get it worked out when I went to pick up my key earlier, but they were busy with only one person working and a line of students waiting. So all she cared about was making sure we got our dorm assignments."

"Yeah, that sounds like something they'd do." She sighs and continues toward the other end of the room. "Well, you should go first thing in the morning. It'll be less crowded since most people won't be getting up that early."

"Thanks," I add with a grateful smile.

When we finish dressing the bed, Gracie takes the old linen and tosses it in the bag the others came in before throwing them at the back of my closet.

"Have you eaten? I'm about to head down to the food hall. Did you wanna come with?"

I blow out an embarrassed breath. "That's another thing I need to get tomorrow. I haven't received my meal card yet."

"They're so unprepared this semester," Gracie chimes.

"Yeah. Tell me about it. You go ahead. I brought ramen from home."

"Come. I'll cover you."

I shake my head, sensing I'll be doing a lot of that where she is concerned. "Gracie, really. I'm f—"

"Are you really going to make me eat alone? What a way to start off this budding friendship," she teases. "Really. It's not a big deal."

"Fine. But tomorrow's dinner is on me."

She laughs while slipping on a pair of low-top sneakers. "Deal. Now let's go, I'm starving for some tacos. They aren't nearly as good as my abuela's, but they aren't bad."

When we get to the dining area, my eyes roam over the room. Students are everywhere, most of them seated at tables or walking through the aisles with their trays full of food.

"Come on." Gracie tugs at my arm.

I follow her lead, weaving through the crowd while staring at the walls. Everything about this place screams rich, from the marble floors to the flat-screen televisions mounted high above our heads. The chandeliers hanging from the ceiling look like they cost more than a person's entire life savings. Not that I have a life savings, but that's beside the point.

This doesn't even feel like a college cafeteria. There's no long line leading up to a buffet-style counter. No lunch ladies serving mystery meat on plastic trays.

This feels more like something straight out of a movie. Like those private schools for kids whose parents have too much money and not enough time. It's set up like a mall food court, complete with different options of cuisine and beverage stations. You could probably find anything you want here. Hell, you might even be able to order a steak if you ask the right person.

"It's crazy, huh?" Gracie says after clearing her throat to break my trance. "I know how overwhelming SKU can be, especially when you first get here."

"Yeah," I say breathlessly. "This isn't what I'm used to."

"Where did you transfer from?"

"The junior college." I let out a puff of air. "It was nothing like this, that's for sure."

Gracie moves to the front of a taco station that has an assortment of options to choose from.

"Three steak tacos, please. Lots of onions and cilantro," she tells the guy behind the counter.

He nods; then he looks over at me with his eyebrows raised.

"Can I do the same?"

"Sure thing." He flashes me a smile.

A few seconds later, he hands us two plates. These aren't those cheap paper ones that most schools use. They're real and have gold edges. After grabbing drinks and checking out, we make our way to an empty table.

We sit in comfortable silence while we eat, only speaking when one of us wants to know more about the other. The conversation is easy now, no longer awkward like it was earlier. I find myself relaxing around her—and if I'm honest, that's a little weird for me. I guess that's what happens when you make a new friend. You become vulnerable.

"This is your third year, and your sanity still seems to be intact. So tell me, how does one survive here?"

She doesn't speak right away. I notice her eyes are darting between me and whatever—or whoever—is behind me. I turn to see Everest and the guys he was with earlier.

My heartbeat picks up against my will at the sight of them. There are different girls with them this time, and another guy with dark hair and just as attractive as the rest of them.

One of the girls is sitting on the table, with her friends all around her. She stares in our direction, her gaze shooting past me and straight to Gracie. She's blond and gorgeous, with a tan that says she just left the beach even though there isn't a body of water for hours. She flips her wavy hair, a smirk playing on her lips.

I stare between them, both confused and concerned by the sudden change in Gracie's demeanor. There is clearly bad blood between them, and whatever it is, Gracie's probably got the bad end of it. Why else would she be over here with an unknown new girl instead of over there with the other popular kids?

Gracie doesn't break, though. She holds the girl's gaze with the same venom, and I can't lie...it's impressive. But then the dark-haired guy the girl is sitting next to turns in his seat to see what she's looking at. With his attention on Gracie, all the life seems to drain from her face.

He smirks, too, and it's almost as if they're taunting her. Turning back to face Gracie, I slide over so that all she can see is me.

"Who is that? What was that all about?"

"Christina Lindsey." She seethes, her bubbly persona an afterthought. "You wanna know how to make it at this school? Stay away from them."

I frown, my curiosity stronger than ever.

"The girls or the guys?" I question with a glance back at their table, my eyes connecting with Everest.

His jaw ticks, and darkness flashes in his eyes. He really is different from the boy I knew. The sound of Gracie's plate scraping the table grabs my attention, and I turn to see her standing to leave.

"All of them."

CHAPTER FIVE

ALEX

"There's plenty of me to go around. I'm a lover, baby. The more the merrier."

And just like that, they're putty in my hands. It never fails. Show them a little attention, and the panties practically melt off. It doesn't hurt that I'm a beast on the ice.

"And why would we say yes to a threesome?" Maria asks in return, a flirty smile tugging at her lips.

"Don't you have a lineup of girls already?" Erika adds.

I smirk, staring at the taller of the two directly in the eye. "The only girls on my mind right now are you. So, what do you—"

"Ahem." A throat clears behind me, stealing my attention away from the girls.

I glance over my shoulder to find Ms. Johnson standing in the threshold of the administrative office with her arms folded and a stern expression on her face. She's unimpressed if the pinched lips and cocked brows are any indication. It's that way every time she sees me. Hell, at this point, we should be best friends.

"Ladies." I smile and back away. "Think about it."

With a wink, I spin on my heel and give Ms. Johnson a nod. The sound of the girls' whispers are followed by their shoes clicking against the marble floor as they walk away. And I'd bet a grand they'll be taking me up on my offer.

They always do.

"I'd like to get this meeting going. Is that all right with you, Mr. Williamsburg?" Ms. Johnson asks.

That's the most personality I've ever gotten out of her. Which isn't surprising since she's garnered the name Ice Queen for her sunny disposition. I personally think she needs to get laid. Maybe some good dick would loosen up those tight-ass laces.

I turn to face her, taking in every line on her face and each gray hair on top of her head. Unlike everyone else here, she hasn't changed much since my freshman year.

As far as staff goes, she's probably the only person who still looks the same. Everyone else has either aged rapidly or moved on to jobs elsewhere. Even some of my old professors are gone now. That's what happens under my father's tyranny. People get tired of his shit.

Except for my mother. Somehow, she manages to see the good in him. She's the only one, that's for damn sure. Don't get me wrong, he provides designer clothes, can open any door with just one phone call, and kept us in a lavish mansion that was more like a golden cage. But those things are all for show. A show for others to see him as untouchable.

Actual parental support from him only comes in the form of suspended accounts, constant lectures, and emotional abuse. He's a powerful man with a penchant for treating the people who work for him like second-class citizens. He's managed to go through his forty-five years of life unscathed by consequences. There should be a course on how a person can be an utter asshole and still be so successful. But it'd probably be summed up with one word: *money*. I'm honestly surprised Ms. Johnson hasn't dipped out like the rest of them.

"Of course." I shake away my thoughts and brush past her. "So, Tanya, how are the kids?"

She makes a sound and scrunches her nose, telling me without words that I should watch it. So I do what anyone would do—I egg her on by holding up my hands defensively. If I were anyone else, I'd be kicked out before this meeting ever started. But because I am who I am, there won't be any repercussions.

There never are.

I can feel her gaze burning through me, but I ignore it, knowing exactly what she wants to say. I also know she won't dare speak those words aloud. Not unless she wants to lose her job. And despite everything, I wouldn't want that for her.

She shakes her head at me and proceeds to walk around me to lead me over to her tiny cubicle—one of the many smaller spaces located inside the administrative office. There aren't any doors on the cubicles, which are separated by tall glass walls and a cutout to give the illusion of an office. That's why I always come first thing in the morning, before any other students show up.

I don't want anyone hearing that I, the chancellor's son and captain of the hockey team, am failing. It's not a good look and certainly won't go over well with dear old dad.

Her space is bare save for the essentials—a desk, chairs, a computer, and a printer in the corner. You can tell she tried to spruce up the place with pictures of her family on her desk and a colorful calendar on the left wall that is from two years prior. I don't know if she just forgot or simply gave up. This place—the people—can suck the life from your bones.

"Looks like somebody is stuck in the past," I tease.

She frowns and then follows my eyes to the outdated spread. "Focus, Mr. Williamsburg."

I tip my head. "Yes, ma'am."

She pulls up something on her computer screen and then looks me dead in the eye. "I'm just going to get straight to it. The makeup exam—"

"I know, I know. I missed it. But practice ran late and, with national championships on the line, it was kind of important that I not dip out early. It was unavoidable," I explain nonchalantly.

"And so is graduation," she deadpans. "Now, you promised me at the end of the last semester that you would turn it around. I've pulled strings to get last term exams rescheduled so that you can walk with your class. And I've kept this from your father in favor of that promise. This only works if you do, Mr. Williamsburg."

"Okay. So, I'll take the test." I shrug. "No big deal."

She breathes in again, this time closing her eyes, seemingly to settle whatever I've stirred up inside her. "It's a very big deal, and you need to start seeing that."

"Fine."

Ms. Johnson only stares at me with a look of discontent. Damn, maybe she's survived working here this long because my father rubbed off on her. I swear she is staring at me with that same deadly look he gives me.

But I'll take her over him any day. And a part of me believes that she knows that. Otherwise, she wouldn't have helped me this far, going out of her way to bend the rules for me. Maybe she knows just how ruthless our esteemed chancellor gets when it comes to these types of indiscretions.

All he cares about is the image, keeping up appearances, and making sure the Williamsburg legacy lives on. The last thing I need is for him to find out I've fucked up yet again. Especially after throwing an unsanctioned Selection Sunday rager to await the NCHC announcements. Even more so because said rager resulted in a trashed estate, cops, and wild accusations.

If he knew his only son was failing, he'd kill me, and they'd never find my body. Maybe in death, he can ensure I never stray from the path he's forged for me.

"You have another test scheduled for tomorrow."

There's a *ding* in the distance, one that says someone has entered the office, but I can't be bothered to check. The only thing that matters is getting Ms. Johnson to type on her little computer and make this all go in my favor.

"I can't. Practice."

"You have practice at four." She stares at me. "That's why this one has been scheduled for the morning. Since this time seems to work best for you."

I let out a sigh. "All right."

She shakes her head. "If your grades get any lower, my hands will be tied, and I'll have no choice but to recommend academic probation."

I tune out everything but those two words—academic probation. Just the thought lights a fire under my ass.

I sit up in my seat, sweat starting to bead above my brow. "You can't do that."

"I can, and I will."

"Come on, Ms. Johnson. There has to be something else."

"This is it."

"I can't go on probation. Probation means being benched for the rest of the season. This is our chance to win nationals. There will be NHL scouts at these games."

"Then I suggest you take this more seriously than you have been. I'll hold off on my recommendation until after your exam tomorrow. If it's reported to me that you didn't show up, I will submit the paperwork, and your father will unfortunately have to be notified."

"You don't understand. This is my future."

She calmly looks at me, and for the first time, there is sympathy in her eyes.

Ms. Johnson sighs. "I understand more than you think I do, Alex." She pauses. "But it's time you understand that rules apply to everyone, even you. Fix your grades or face the consequences."

My career is riding on this. Not pissing off my father is riding on this. My emotions shift to something deeper than anger—something more akin to fear. "Please fix this," is all I say. My hands clutch into fists so tight that my nails bite at the flesh of my palm.

"You're the only one that can control how your future turns out." She shifts in her seat, and I can tell she's trying not to be fazed by the look on my face.

I don't mean to take my frustrations out on her. It's not her fault; she's simply doing her job, but I can't end up on probation. It's out of the question.

Ms. Johnson glances around me, her sights fixating on the waiting area. "Samantha?"

A second later, the sweetest voice fills my ears. "Yes, ma'am."

Ms. Johnson swallows. "I'll be with you in a second." She pauses and looks at me again. "Mr. Williamsburg was just leaving."

"I'm not in a rush. I just need to correct my schedule and get my meal card," the girl answers.

With my nostrils flared, I grunt and punch the desk. "Whatever."

With that, I stand sharply, turn, and exit her cubicle, nearly running smack into the girl. Deep brown eyes and a cascade of curls peer up at me. She's cute—*really* cute, actually—but I couldn't care less right now.

Whoever she is—this *Samantha*—has heard everything that was said. Which means she knows what the people around me never could. The whole point of meeting in the morning is so that no one finds out. It's the safest way of keeping my shortcomings away from not just my father but from the coach.

"Sorry." Samantha attempts to go around me.

Her shoulders go rigid as she stares at me, her eyes widening when I step over to block her path. I don't know why I do it; maybe there is some sick part of me that likes the flicker of fear that flashes in her eyes.

"Watch where you're going," I say while bending down so that we're face to face, so close I can smell the vanilla on her skin.

Something clicks because that flicker of fear is short-lived. I see the moment the defiance builds in her chest. But it's her response that solidifies it.

"Likewise, asshole," she spits.

I continue to tower over her, watching her chest rise and fall rapidly. It's the briefest distraction from the mixture of anger and humiliation running through me.

"You should get to class, Alex," Ms. Johnson says from behind me.

My attention remains on this interesting girl in front of me. She's clearly new to campus because she isn't reacting to me like most do. She obviously has no idea of my status, so it wouldn't be fair to hold that against her.

Instead, I opt for a warning. She may be new to this school, but she better quickly figure out the lay of the land. I scan her from head to toe, noting how out of place she looks.

"Watch that mouth, if you know what's good for you," I warn. My eyes drop to her plump lips for a moment before returning to the venom in her brown gaze.

Without a response, Samantha steps around me toward Ms. Johnson, but not without the last word.

"Jerk."

CHAPTER SIX

SAM

An old counselor once told me that no one is born unlucky. It's all just a series of events that happen as a result of choices made. By her standard, it's simply a little cause and effect. But I called bullshit the moment the words slipped past her thin lips.

My life has been nothing but the unlucky event of being stuck in a never-ending loop of poverty, neglect, and despair. I'm reminded every day that no matter what I do or how hard I try, something will always go wrong.

Like today.

It's only my first day of classes, and I'm late for the first one of the morning. *So much for a fresh start.*

I race forward and yank the door to the lecture hall open. The professor has already started, his voice booming through the room. To keep from disturbing anyone, I slowly close the door behind me, being careful not to make a sound.

But fate has other plans, because while I manage to quietly close the door, the strap on my old book bag snaps and all of my things fall loudly to the floor.

And who said people aren't born unlucky?

The room stills, the only sound to be heard that of students twisting in their seats to see what or who caused the commotion.

Me, that's who. So much for keeping a low profile.

"You're late," the physics professor says after what feels like forever.

In reality, it's been mere seconds, but with all eyes on me, it seems much longer.

I bend down to collect my things, my breathing still ragged. "I know, and I'm sorry. It's my first day, and I couldn't find—"

"I don't care," he says with a huff.

"Right," I mutter while collecting the last item and standing upright.

"Just take a seat and try not to be late again."

I nod, though I'm sure he doesn't see it as his attention has gone back to the front of the class. The students are still staring, and of course I can feel every pair of eyes on me, but it isn't until now that I notice just how many.

Then, like clockwork, the dirty looks come, followed by mean jokes and sharp jabs. People size me up, taking note of my non-brand clothes, the Adidas hoodie that is well worn, my outdated sneakers, and the large backpack. By now, this is par for the course around here.

I've been on campus for less than twenty-four hours, and I've had several people walk directly into me, as if I am just invisible. Not to mention being threatened by the hockey player in the advisory office earlier.

"Eww. What is she wearing?" one girl says to the person beside her. Her voice is low, and she probably thinks no one can hear her except her friend, but she's wrong.

I hear it all.

"How embarrassing!" another person says.

"She must be one of the new scholarship kids," goes someone a few rows up.

"They could have helped her with some new clothes at least," a girl says, followed by laughter from those around her.

Anger bubbles in my chest, and it takes everything in me not to lash out and tell each and every last one of them where they can shove it. Doing that would only draw more unwanted attention, and I'll be labeled as the poor *and angry* Black girl.

So instead, I still my emotions, mentally reminding myself why I'm here. This is all for Desmond.

Just two and a half years. Then, I'll graduate with endorsements that will set me and Desmond on the right path. Yes, I could have stayed at the junior college or gotten a minimum wage job, but it wouldn't be enough to prove to a judge that Desmond would be better off with me instead of his father.

This is the lesser of two evils in the grand scheme of what's important to me. So, if I have to deal with a few stares from some stuck-up rich kids, so be it.

Besides, none of this surprises me, anyway. I knew what I was getting myself into when I accepted the scholarship. I guess I never quite realized how overwhelming it was to be in a cesspool of elitist pricks.

But as long as I keep my head down, nothing will distract me from the goal.

Even Everest...

Nearly every person besides Gracie has treated me like some outcast so far. Yet, for some reason, the reaction Everest had when our eyes met in the courtyard continues to sting.

I finally settle in the seat closest to me. It's only two rows away from the exit—perfect for getting out of here as soon as the lecture ends. The quicker I get out of this class, the quicker I can put the embarrassment behind me. Out of sight, out of mind. Eventually, the stares will fade if I keep to myself, do my work, and stay out of the way. Something shinier will come along, and their focus will shift.

I realize that's going to be easier said than done with this particular class. I recognize the group of girls Gracie warned me about. Christina and her little crew are sitting two rows up on the other side of the aisle, not bothering to hold in their snickers.

I may have been dealt a shitty hand in life, but the last thing I'll do is give those plastic Barbies the satisfaction of knowing they're getting to me. So I do the next best thing and zero in on Professor Wilson. Except my plan fails miserably because my focus lands on another student. He's just a row up, on the other side of the aisle.

I'm not sure why, but my body reacts on instinct. He's one of the hockey players, and it takes a moment for me to remember where we've crossed paths. Then it clicks. He was with Everest yesterday. The huge guy who didn't seem too interested in whatever was happening around him.

God, he's gorgeous.

And though I want to look away, I can't. Not when his eyes seem glued to me. There was no doubt about how handsome he was, but sitting this close, it's undeniable. From here, his jaw seems sharper, and his shoulders broader. He's massive—in the best way—brooding, and unbothered, with dark eyes that peer right through me.

He's Indigenous if his strong, angular features are any indication. Today, his hair cascades over his shoulders as opposed to the braid from the other day. And his lashes are every girl's dream. This guy probably doesn't even realize how lucky he is.

My breath hitches as I note that he hasn't blinked or even appeared to breathe since we made eye contact. He doesn't glare at me like the others, and there doesn't seem to be any judgment on his face. Just a reserved, unwavering stare.

A shiver races down my spine, and I shift in my seat out of discomfort. What's with all the guys in this school peering at me like I'm prey?

I take a deep breath and glance around the room again out of curiosity. Everyone else has gone back to doing whatever they were before I came in. Except for him; he still hasn't moved.

Christina and her group snicker among themselves. I want to ignore them. I need to, but something keeps drawing me to them. Maybe it's self-sabotage, and I enjoy punishing myself.

Either way, I let out a sigh and watch Professor Wilson make his way to the back door to talk to someone outside. When he comes back inside, he stops beside the giant hockey player and says something too low for me to hear.

The guy stands to leave, taking one last look at me on his way out. A wave of relief washes over me after he's gone. My stomach unclenches itself, and I release a breath.

A couple of girls seated behind me whisper to each other.

"I know she doesn't think she has a chance with the Mountain."

The other laughs. "Right. Like he would ever date a girl like her."

Unable to hold my composure, I turn and look them dead in the eyes. "And what kind of girl might that be?"

Their smiles falter, replaced by reddened faces and daggers in their eyes. As expected, they don't respond; girls like that never do. All talk and no bite.

When they don't offer up any kind of rebuttal, I face forward, pull out my notebook, and begin to take notes.

The rest of the class flies by, but the moment I stand to leave with everyone else, the brunette behind me gestures to my backpack and says, "Don't forget your trash."

Her friend cackles. "Good one."

Just when I am about to defend myself, another voice slices through the air.

"Hey, skanks. Why don't you back off?" Christina steps up beside me.

With that, their mouths snap shut, and all the color drains from their faces. And I've got to admit, it feels damn good to witness. I love it when karma is served instantly.

"Because from what I understand from Daddy's files, shouldn't you be more worried about taking those antibiotics to clear up that chlamydia, Taylor?"

All I can do is watch. Christina clearly isn't a person whose bad side you want to get on. But why is she helping me? Especially when just an hour earlier, she was also laughing at me.

"Screw you," Taylor bites out, and the two girls scurry from the room.

"Too-da-loo, girlies," Christina continues to taunt.

I turn to Christina, reluctance coursing through me. That was nice of her to defend me, but why? Girls like Christina don't do anything without reason. There is *always* a catch.

"Thanks. But you—" I start, but she raises a hand to cut me short.

"Before you go saying I didn't have to, stop. I don't like those two bitches, so that was more for me than it was for you."

And there it is.

"Well, thanks anyway," I say gingerly while gathering my broken backpack to head to my next class.

"Don't mention it. It's Samantha, right?" she pries, smiling at me when I look at her again.

"I go by Sam," I answer, somewhat confused at where this conversation is leading.

"That's cute."

"Thanks. But how do you know that?"

She playfully waves my question away. "Oh, girl. I know everything there is to know about everybody. Plus, you're roommates with Gracie. She and I go way back."

Internally, I cringe at that. While Gracie has been very vague about what happened between her and these girls, something tells me there's a lot more to it than them *going way back*. And until I know what exactly, I'll err on the side of caution.

"So, some of us are getting together for a party tonight. You should come."

I shake my head, but she continues.

"It'll give you an opportunity to meet people. I know SKU can be overwhelming, but we're pretty cool once you get to know us."

I scrunch up my nose. "I'm not really the partying type. I just want to focus on school."

Christina saunters up to me and unexpectedly places an arm over my shoulder. I stare at that arm in disbelief of the lack of boundaries this girl has.

"And you will. But you should also have a little fun. Plus, there'll be hot guys there. The Knights are hosting, and you don't ever want to miss one of their parties."

I don't respond, this time only staring at her until she gets the point.

"Okay, how about this?" Christina holds out her palm. "Take out your phone. We'll drop each other our contacts, and I'll send you the address. If you come, great. If not, your loss."

I want nothing more than to be done with this conversation. So instead of fighting her on it, I pull my phone from my back pocket and unlock it.

She takes it from me and eagerly airdrops herself from my phone, then hands it back a few seconds later.

"Perfect," she says while dropping her phone in her purse and stepping around me. "Think about it. It'll be a blast."

The thought of being in the same room with a bunch of drunk, sexed-up college students doesn't sound appealing to me. Especially not when Everest and that asshole Alex will probably be there. Something tells me that would be a bad combination.

The muffled voices of students passing through the halls are the only signs of life on the other side of my room door. It's late on a Friday night, and while my peers are out enjoying college life, I've been holed up in this room for the past two hours. I've lain in bed staring up at the ugly popcorn ceiling.

It mocks me... reminding me just how lonely I really am. It's funny how being in a place full of people can make you feel even more alone than ever.

Maybe if I'd taken Gracie up on her offer to join her in the study hall, I wouldn't be sitting in here sulking. But, after this crap start to my time at SKU, my mind is far too scattered for that.

Light filters in from the sheer pink curtains, the shadows dancing across the ceiling I'm staring at from where I lie on my bed. I glance around the room at the vast difference of decor. My side remains pretty sparse, but with the little trinkets Gracie conveniently had to give so freely, it's really starting to shape up—almost like someone happy lives here.

I chuckle when my eyes land on the yellow and pink lava lamp on her desk. She really does have a big personality. If I'm honest, it's growing on me. I need that kind of positive energy.

I wouldn't go as far as to say we're besties just yet, but she's real and truly sweet. Two traits that are hard to come by these days.

Needing to do something other than wasting away, and too lazy to sit up, I feel around my bed, flailing uncomfortably until I find my phone. I tap the screen to life and scroll social media in a weak attempt to fill the void. Another night of mindlessly swiping, I guess.

If Evan were here right now, he'd tell me to get off my ass and make the night my bitch. This is the first time in my life where I'm not stuck indoors with Desmond because Gary is too high off his ass to actually watch him. I get to be like every other nineteen-year-old—experiencing things, making mistakes.

So why am I rotting away, and passing my time by counting the grooves in the ceiling and aimlessly scrolling?

Because whatever reprieve this scholarship is providing from my miserable life is merely a Band-Aid. In two and a half years, I'll graduate and the fight for custody of my brother will commence. Back to reality I go.

My cell buzzes against my thigh.

Chrissy Lindsey: Image attached.

With a furrowed brow, I open the text. The picture loads on the screen.

Christina's face fills the screen, a champagne bottle tilted toward pouty lips in a sea of too-short skirts and hockey jerseys. She's straddling some guy, his face buried in her neck so I can't see his face, but the jacket he's wearing gives it away that he's on the team. Behind them someone's doing a keg stand in the center of the room.

I'm surprised the party is actually going on. Earlier today, I heard a couple of students say that the team was on curfew and banned from throwing any more bashes. Clearly they make their own rules. I guess when you've won the school as many conference championships as they have, you can do whatever you want.

It may have only been less than a week, but I picked up rather quickly that the hockey team are like gods on this campus, probably because that prick Alex is the captain and the chancellor's son. If there's one thing they care about around here, it's status.

I focus on the image again, and it's fascinating to see. So much is going on in the background. Students dancing, conversing, or making out—living their lives out loud for us all to see.

At the top right corner, I notice Everest sitting on the couch surrounded by girls—completely oblivious that he's been caught on camera. And now, suddenly, I do care a little. I don't know why; it's not like Everest has said a word to me. I've seen him a handful of times on campus, and in each moment, he acts as if I don't exist.

Another buzz.

869023: Your RydeShare is on the way. Douglas is 10 minutes away from your location. Black Mercedes-Benz E-Class. License plate: 8XJH527.

Chrissy Lindsey: Ryde 10 mins out. Wear something slutty.

My thumbnail finds the groove it's worn into the phone case as I pick at the plastic while contemplating her message. I don't even own anything slutty.

Am I really considering going to this party? Should I go?

Don't I deserve an ounce of fun? Evan would tell me yes. I

laugh because I can hear his voice in my head. *"Why is that even a question? Go shake your ass and shake some for me, too."*

"Just for an hour," I try to convince myself.

With newfound determination, I throw my legs over the side of the bed and make my way to the closet. I then dig through my stuff for the sluttiest thing I can find.

Which is nothing...

I can't wear the same old clothes unless I want to be the laughingstock of the night. I've already been nothing but comedic relief for these people—as if my misfortune was designed for their amusement.

Yeah. This is definitely a bad idea.

Girl. Go to the damn party. Evan's voice is like an alarm in my head now.

"Fine," I say aloud to no one and turn on my heel to stare at Gracie's closet.

She's been nothing but generous and has told—more like demanded—me to help myself to her stuff on multiple occasions.

I saunter forward, and hesitation lingers like a lead weight as I pull it open. Rows of high-end blouses, dresses, and skirts fill the shelves while the floor is covered with stacks of shoe boxes. Purses and accessories line both walls, and all I can do is stare in awe. She could dress a village with the number of items she has here.

I spot a black miniskirt that I could pair with my favorite green knitted cropped sweater, fishnet tights, and boots. Wouldn't be my first pick, but we're at the start of spring so it shouldn't be too chilly. Not wanting to overstep, I text Gracie.

Sam: Hey. Could I borrow your black miniskirt? I'll bring it back in one piece.

Roomie 😎: It's totally cool. I told you. What's mine is yours.

I smile, a weight lifting off of my shoulders. Having someone be as kind as Gracie feels surreal. I quickly change into my outfit before styling my hair into a topknot. Costume jewelry—a bangle, large hoop earrings, and rings—complete the look.

869023: Your Ryde has arrived. Douglas is waiting outside.

I grab my ID, room key, and the twenty-dollar bill I've been holding on to for dear life, before locking the door behind me. I pause to shoot another text to Gracie.

Sam: Thank you! You're the best!

I race down the three flights of stairs, and as I reach the bottom, my phone buzzes and I look down to see a reply from Gracie.

Roomie 😎: Of course! Where are you going?

Sam: I decided to go to the Knights' party.

Not bothering to wait for her to text back, I stick my phone into my skirt and head out of the building. I approach the curb where the black Mercedes waits and climb into the back seat. Douglas pulls up the route, and his face contorts into a look of surprise.

"Wow. That's a nice neighborhood. Big night, huh?"

Instead of responding, I give him a tight-lipped smile. Douglas puts the vehicle into drive and slowly pulls away from the campus.

Here goes nothing.

CHAPTER SEVEN

BRYDEN (MOUNTAIN)

Another party.

Perfect. This is exactly what I don't want, to wade through a sea of juiced-up college kids. I turn onto the gravel drive, and my headlights cut through the dark. Cars are crammed haphazardly on the lawn, and red Solo cups litter the steps.

My jaw clenches as I ease into the only remaining spot, the bass pulsing so hard it feels like it's coming through my chest. I kill the engine, but the vibrations don't stop. They're in the air, the pavement, and the bones of this house that was supposed to be quiet tonight.

Someone stumbles off the porch, already drunk out of their mind, and I suck in an aggravated breath. Just once, I'd like to come back to something other than one of Alex's beer-soaked ragers.

Frozen Four are three weeks out, nationals are looming, and the last thing we need is another visit from the cops. We're already pushing our luck with the coach. You'd think a curfew and the threat of a team-wide bag skate would've stuck with Alex after the last time.

But no. Alex and consequences? They've never been on speaking terms. It shouldn't surprise me, he's spoiled, and oftentimes the rules don't apply to him. Kane's no better, always complacent where Alex is concerned. He might not plan for these things, but he certainly goes along with them.

Don't get me wrong, I love my boys. We've been friends since elementary school, and if it weren't for Alex's father buying us this lake house, my folks would be out a lot of money to cover room and board.

But this is idiotic. There is too much riding the line to risk it all for chicks and bad decisions waiting to happen.

A cheer erupts from somewhere inside, sharp and reckless, slicing through the thick night air. My grip tightens, the leather of the steering wheel cool against my palm. A hot shower and the kind of silence only exhaustion can deliver is all I wanted. Instead, I'm about to walk into a battlefield of beer pong and bass drops, plus probably pulling double duty as a bouncer and cleanup crew.

I sit for a moment longer than I should, letting the sounds of laughter and muffled shouting filter through the car windows. The ache in my shoulders from staying at practice longer than everyone else begs me to just turn around, find a hotel for the night, and deal with the aftermath tomorrow.

But I don't.

This is my house, too, and someone has to keep things from spiraling. With an exhale, I grab my bag from the passenger seat and step out of the car. The scent of lake water and spilled beer carries through the air, a damp heaviness clinging to everything from an earlier rain.

A group of rowdy kids spills onto the porch, beer splattering from their cups as they laugh entirely too loudly. I set my jaw and head for the door, bracing myself for whatever disaster waits inside.

Once I step onto the portico, a guy I don't recognize stumbles out the front door and gives me a sloppy grin, holding up his cup in a silent toast.

I ignore him.

Inside, the house is a writhing mass of people packed into the kitchen, the living room, and along the stairs. The music is deafening, and the heat of too many bodies in too small a space makes the air thick.

I navigate through the crowd, sidestepping a couple dancing—or grinding, really—near the doorway. Jackson, my teammate cuts in front of my path, and I pause, turning slightly to keep from running into him.

Someone shouts my name, a voice too familiar to be ignored, as I step into the kitchen.

"Mountain!" Alex's voice cuts through the chaos, drawing more attention than I'd like.

He's propped against the counter with his easy grin and a cup dangling from his fingers. A couple of girls crowd around him, one twirling her hair, the other leaning a little too close. He doesn't seem to mind. Alex never minds.

"Look who finally decided to show up," he chastises.

I don't stop moving, shouldering past a cluster of guys to exit out the other side of the room. "Didn't realize I was coming back home to another party."

Alex laughs, slinging an arm around one of the girls. "Come on, man." He gestures around with his cup. "It's just a few people, nothing crazy."

"Nothing crazy," I echo, glancing at the horde crammed into the living room. A girl stumbles over a stack of beer cans, sending a small avalanche across the floor. "Sure."

Alex waves me off like it's nothing. "Relax, Bryden. No cops this time, promise."

I look at him, deadpan. "You promised that last time."

"That was different." He flashes me that disarming grin he thinks works on everyone. "This time I mean it."

I don't say anything. Instead, my eyes slide past him, landing on the far corner of the room where Kane sits, partially swallowed by the shadows. He's perched on the edge of the couch, a drink resting in his hand—untouched, judging by the thin layer of condensation trailing down the plastic.

His shoulders are hunched, his stare fixed on nothing. He's distant, quiet in a way that's different from my kind of quiet. Alex follows my gaze, but instead of commenting, he just smirks.

"He's fine," he mutters, almost like he's reassuring himself more than me, before shifting his focus back to his entourage.

I hesitate, then decide I've had enough. Leaving Alex to his chaos, I turn and head for the stairs. I move through the living room with a steady stride, my eyes scanning but never lingering on any one person longer that I need to.

A girl sways into me, her drink sloshing dangerously close to my shirt. She grins up at me, oblivious. "Mountain, right? You're on the hockey team."

I step around her, barely offering her a clipped nod as I continue on my way. I can feel her eyes follow me, but I don't turn back. Unlike my friends, getting wrapped up in girls is the last thing on my mind. I don't need the distraction. My life consists of hockey, getting drafted to the NHL, and making my mother happy.

I steal a glance to my left, where Kane sits.

To anyone else, you'd think he's just being his usually unapproachable self, but when you've known someone as long as we have, you can tell when there's something more. What exactly? I guess only time will tell. Secrets have a way of spilling over if you keep them bottled up too long.

The thought of going against my better judgment to check on him runs through my mind, but Alex says he's fine. They've always been closer, glued at the hip. So if anyone would know when to intervene on Kane's doom staring, it's Alex. Besides, Kane doesn't talk unless he's ready, and tonight doesn't seem like the night he'll break that rule.

With a fraction of a breath, I turn away and push through the final cluster of bodies toward the upper level. The stairs creak beneath my weight, and I keep my focus on the landing ahead, threading past a couple tangled in each other at the top of the stairs without so much as a glance. They are so wrapped up in each other that they don't notice me either.

The house quiets marginally as I step onto the second floor. It's not much of a reprieve, but it's enough to ease the edge of frustration. I make my way toward the far end, where my room waits—my one corner of this house untouched by chaos, though it feels farther away with each step forward.

A girl stumbles out of one of the rooms, cup in hand and her hair half-falling out of an unsteady ponytail. I recognize her as one of the puck bunnies that hangs around every game. The same girl that's been all up on my roommates. Vanessa.

A second later, two other girls exit behind her, their voices rising and falling in high-pitched giggles. The first girl makes eye contact with me and brightens immediately, her smile wide.

"Hey, Bryden," she says, her voice lilting like she's known me forever. She reaches out to touch me but I subtly sway to keep her from doing so.

Vanessa steps closer, too close, her words syrupy and blurred. "You're, like... always so serious. So... so... uptight."

Exactly how many drinks has she had tonight? She attempts

to stand upright, her brows knitted tight and her shoulders back in a weak imitation of me.

"Ever think about loosening up?" she slurs while trying to balance herself with a hand on my shoulder.

I dip my shoulder, sidestepping her as easily as I might dodge a wayward puck. "Not really."

"Oh, come on...don't be a pooper party. No, that's not it. A party pooter."

Plucking the partially empty drink from her hand, I say, "And you've had enough for tonight."

Vanessa sways and looks me up and down, her eyes lusty and lazy from intoxication. "Did you just come from practice?"

I turn my attention to her friend. "You need to take her home; she's too wasted."

"I...I'm fine. You should dance with me tonight."

"Dancing's not really my thing." Neither are girls too messed up to consent to anything.

"Boooo," they say in unison.

"Take out your phone and call a rideshare. She needs to sleep it off."

With her drink still in my hand, I turn away. The sound of their voices fades away as I enter my room and let the door close with a soft click.

The quiet hits instantly. The music is still there, faint and distant, but it's muffled enough that I can finally breathe. I let out a long exhale, and lean back against the door for a moment. The tension in my chest loosens, but it doesn't fully let go.

Crossing the room, I set my bag down by the foot of the bed, place the cup on the dresser, and fish my phone out of the side pocket. The screen lights up, and a single notification stares back at me. It's a message from my mother. It's simple, just a few words, but they mean so much.

Mom: Proud of you.

The knot in my chest eases further, a small warmth creeping in to replace it. Nationals aren't just about the game. They're about them. Every sacrifice, every early morning, every extra shift they took on just to make sure I had what I needed. They're about doing something my family can be proud of.

I set the phone down, the message still glowing faintly on the screen as I stride into the bathroom. I flip the switch, and the light flickers as it comes on, casting the small space in a harsh glow. I lean forward with my palms against the edge of the counter. The cool surface presses into my hands as I let my eyes drift shut. When I open them again, my reflection stares back.

I exhale slowly, assessing the person in the mirror. The lines of my face feel heavier tonight, the weight of expectations sitting firmly on my shoulders.

Why can't Alex or Kane take any of this seriously?

Finals.

Nationals.

The future.

All it takes is one bad decision and everything we've worked for can be stripped away.

But as quickly as it comes, I push the thought away. I guess everyone deals with pressure in their own way. Mine is silence and space. Theirs, booze, girls, and noise. I'm not judging—just tired. It's lonely sometimes, but a necessary evil. There'll be plenty of time for girls *after* we win nationals. Until then, I'll keep my head on the game. That's easy enough, or at least it used to be, until that girl showed up in class today, staring at me like she can see right through me. There was something about her, something I haven't been able to pinpoint. Whatever it is, I push it out of my mind.

I peer at the gash above my brows, now healed, yet a constant reminder of the sport I love so much. Roughhousing a little too much during practice with no gear will result in all sorts of bruises. It's just the nature of the game. We play hard, dirty and unrelenting.

Pushing off the counter, I face the shower and turn on the water. Steam thickens, fogging the mirror until I can no longer see myself. I peel off my sweaty clothes, letting them fall into a pile at my feet. What's left of the cool air bites at my skin for a moment before I step into the heat of the shower.

The water beats against my skin, the pressure massaging away the aches from practice. And when I undo my braid and stick my head under the showerhead, all the tension from the day melts.

Nationals isn't just a game—it's our lifeline—so while I want nothing but to catch some Zs and call it a night, I mentally prepare myself to wrangle the mess downstairs. Because another house party turned police report is the last thing the team needs.

CHAPTER EIGHT

SAM

Quick glimpses between an array of trees are all I can make out as we turn down the gravel road, but even from a partial view you can't miss how massive the property is.

Some people have it all, and clearly, whoever lives here has never seen a bad day in their life. How could they? But then again, if I've learned anything these past few days, it's that even rich people can be just as miserable as the rest of us.

Still. It must be nice.

"Whew," Douglas whistles as he pulls into the driveway. "What I would give to live here."

We stare out the front window in awe. Just two people caught off guard by how wealthy some people really are on the rich side of town. The vacation homes of politicians, lawyers, and businessmen, all dispersed around and overlooking the lake.

This particular house sits on a hilltop, and the view is nothing short of amazing. It's a sprawling two-level property with a huge deck that faces Lake Haven and floor-to-ceiling windows that reflect the moonlight.

Douglas brings us to a stop in the sea of parked cars. Students mill about, laughing and shouting at each other. The noise from inside the house spills out into the night, a mix of thumping bass and the occasional cheer. Settled in my seat for a moment longer, I take it all in, my heart pounding in my chest.

What the hell am I doing here?

This isn't my scene. These people aren't my friends. Hell, I don't even like half of them, and I'm pretty sure the feeling is mutual. This world of privilege and excess is so far removed from my own reality that it's almost laughable.

Almost.

"I can do this," I encourage myself, only it feels like a lie. I suck in a breath and let my hand rest on the latch of the door for a painfully long minute.

"Look, kid, I have a long night ahead of me," Douglas says, interrupting my inner struggle.

"Of course. Sorry," I mutter and exit the car.

The world seems more vibrant on this side of the vehicle. The voices are louder, the air feels cooler, and a chill runs through me. I hug myself in a failed attempt to keep warm. It was probably a bad idea for a miniskirt. Too late for regrets now. Besides, what's a night out without a little frostbite in tow?

Taking another deep breath, I brace myself for whatever the night has in store and move ahead.

It isn't lost on me that no one seems to even notice that I'm here. They're caught up in their own worlds tonight, oblivious to what's going on around them. The girl taking selfies is unfazed by another girl puking her brains out by a tree a few feet away. A guy tossing a football nearly slams into someone and couldn't care less.

There's serenity in being unseen, a luxury I unfortunately never get to experience. My whole life, eyes have been on me for one reason or another. So, oddly enough, I welcome the invisibility.

The path toward the door is littered with red plastic cups, and the second I step inside, the heavy bass of the music hits me like a physical force. Bodies in expensive clothes press in from all sides, packed tight like sardines.

The smells of alcohol and weed blend together and make my head spin. I push through the crowd, trying to find a space to breathe. It's suffocating, cloying, and I can almost taste the bitterness on my tongue.

Everywhere I move, there's someone there, bumping me, making it hard for me to maneuver through the space. I've only been here a few minutes, and it's already the kind of sensory overload that makes your eardrums ache.

I take a deep breath, trying to steady myself. I force my feet to keep moving because turning back now isn't an option. Not when I've come this far.

Three girls come stumbling down the stairs, one barely able to stand as her friends help her move toward the front door. I recognize her. We've never spoken, and I don't know her name, but she was talking to Everest when I arrived on campus. She's wasted, head bobbing, and trips over the foot of a guy on the couch making out with some girl. Completely oblivious while the poor girl's friends struggle to get her back on her feet.

Bad things happen to girls every day at college parties, and oftentimes, no one is ever held accountable for it. The scene twists a knot of anxiety in my stomach. She's lucky to have her friends, and hopefully she gets home safely.

"Sam!" someone yells, their voice a loud streak. A flash of pink catches my eye, and before I can react Christina is on me, her icy blue gaze locking me between a blonde and a hard place. "I thought you were going to chicken out."

Gracie warned me to be careful with Christina and her crew.

She's been a little cagey on the details, but I don't usually stick my nose in other people's mess. I have enough of my own. Besides, I can take care of myself. Tonight is about doing something different and trying to make the most of this opportunity.

Christina looks me over, taking in my outfit. "Hot. Love the curly bun."

I force a smile to match her enthusiasm. Not a hair out of place, and her makeup is flawless.

Grasping at straws to return her energy, I say, "I love your dress."

Christina's already chipper expression only grows. She gives me a pose, and turns, poking her butt out slightly in my direction. "I know, right. It makes my ass look so good."

She's not wrong, the dress does make her look good. It should since it looks expensive and will probably end up at the back of her closet never to be seen again.

"Oh. And thank you for sending the Ryde. That was cool of you." I tap her elbow before awkwardly dropping my hand. "You didn't have to roll out the red carpet, a regular Ryde would have been fine."

"Oh, girl... I never ride in anything that cost less than sixty thousand. Besides, we're friends now, so forget about it."

Just as the declaration leaves her pink painted lips, she snatches a drink from some poor, unsuspecting fool who is on his way to the other side of the room.

"Here." She thrusts it into my hand. "And friends don't let friends party without alcohol."

He glares at Christina, the silent anger behind his eyes making me feel bad for him. But by the way he shrugs and turns back toward the kitchen, something tells me this isn't the first time something like this has happened. If I've learned anything about Christina it's that she and her little friends run this school.

The cup is cold and the scent of alcohol immediately floods my senses. I hold it awkwardly, like it's a live grenade.

"Thanks." The word is barely audible over the pounding music. I don't drink at parties. Being aware of myself and the things that happen around me are far more important than getting a buzz. So, while I might have accepted Christina's offering, I won't be drinking.

I glance around, searching for an escape.

Christina watches me, her smile sharp and knowing. She thinks she has me figured out, thinks I'm just another girl desperate to fit in.

"Now that that's settled, let's have some fun." Her voice is bright and insistent, like she's doing me some type of favor. Christina grabs my arm, pulling me close to the center of her world.

My feet move even though everything in me is telling me to turn the other way. As we draw closer to her friends, they close in around me, a circle of polished nails and designer smiles.

Christina gives her friends a devilish grin and tilts her head toward the large mahogany dining table. They return her smile, theirs just as mischievous.

One after another, they hold out a hand for the closest boy to help them use the chairs as stepping stools and climb up onto the table.

"Come, dance with us," Christina suggests.

The guys start to huddle around the table, their eyes glued to the girls. It's perverted the way they stare, pounding their fist in the air and cheering. The girls live for the attention, and they'll obviously take it in whatever form they can get it.

Definitely not my scene.

"Where's the bathroom?" The words come out rushed, a lifeline if I ever needed one.

She waves a hand, dismissive and full of annoyance. "Upstairs. End of the hall, last—"

Her attention shifts as a new song blasts through the speakers, the crowd going wild. The rest of her directions are swallowed by the noise.

I don't bother asking again. Instead, I turn and push through the bodies, each step taking me farther from the chaos. The drink is still clutched in my hand, untouched and unwanted. I leave it on the mantel next to the staircase, where it'll be for the rest of the night.

I take the stairs two at a time, eager to put distance between me and the rest of the party. The air is cooler up here, and the music is a distant thrum beneath my feet. The hallway stretches out before me, quiet, and oddly peaceful compared to the madness below.

It's a world apart from the paper-thin walls of the house I left behind. I heard everything there.

Pushing the thoughts away, I try to remember which room Christina mentioned, but all I can recall is that it was at the end of the hall. I take a chance and continue forward. Pushing the last door open, I expect to see a bathroom but stop dead in my tracks at what I find instead.

On the other side of the door is a nearly naked guy. He's tall and muscular, with a body that screams athlete. But it's the bulge behind his towel that catches my attention, sizable enough like it's got its own presence.

"What are you doing?"

It's not until I make eye contact that I realize it's the guy from my physics class, Mountain. He stares at me, a mix of surprise and annoyance on his face.

"Sorry." The word is weak, almost drowned out by the thump of my own heartbeat. My eyes drop back to his towel.

"Get out." His voice is stern, but more annoyed than angry. A chick just barged in and nearly saw his holy gift, and he's acting like it happens every day.

I close the door, and I don't get more than a millisecond to register it all before a deep voice behind me startles me.

"Why the fuck are you here?"

CHAPTER NINE

EVEREST (KANE)

Sam?

The name alone tightens something in my chest, a coil wound too tight, and ready to snap.

It's her. I thought I saw her downstairs, a brief flicker of familiarity in the crush of bodies, but convinced myself that it had to be someone else. There was absolutely no way the ghost from misery's past was standing in my living room. Surely all the liquor and weed smoke has gone to my head, got me seeing things that aren't real.

But it is real.

Very fucking real.

She doesn't belong here. In my house, at my party, or at my school. But there she is, standing in front of Mountain's room, out of place and out of touch, her head tilted slightly.

The door is open, and she's standing between the doorframe completely oblivious that I'm coming up behind her.

What the fuck is she doing here?

Clenching my fists at my sides, I try suppressing the sudden emotions, my chest heaving as I fail to calm myself.

And why the hell is she talking to Mountain?

I shouldn't care about the latter when the former is far more important.

But seeing her standing in his doorway sets me off in a way I don't expect. My jaw ticks, heat creeping up my neck at the thought of the two of them... together. And all I can think about is how long have they known each other? And how far has this little connection of theirs gone?

Pushing out a breath, I shake away the thought, hating that I give a damn at all. And this is why her being here is bad news for me. Everything I've worked so hard to keep buried could float to the surface.

She's a part of a past I've been killing myself to keep hidden. A past I carry more shame for than I should. Shame I hate myself for having. But it's there, festering beneath my skin. Sam being here, being the only person to know what I've been through, makes it damn hard to keep pretending.

I can't have that. Not with everything going wrong in my life right now. Not when finals and nationals are just in reach. Sam's presence is a distraction—one I can't afford.

For a second, I consider walking away before she sees me, before I have to deal with this shit. But the thought of her existing in my world again, breathing the same air, standing in this house like she has a right to be here—it makes me furious.

She has to go. Now.

My feet move before my brain catches up, and the closer I get, the easier it is for me to hear.

"Get out," Mountain orders.

She doesn't move right away; instead she sways a little almost as if she can't get her mind and body to move as one accord. Finally she manages to stop floundering enough to pull the door close.

"Why the fuck are you here?"

Sam spins to face me, a mixture of confusion and fear written into her features. The moment her eyes land on me, she softens a little. Relief, maybe? All this time and she still looks at me like the girl who followed me around the psych ward, hanging on to my every word.

It's fleeting...that admiration. It's a lie, some false ideology that serves more harm than it does good. It allows people to put you on a pedestal, robbing you of your humanity so that you remain the version of you they've conjured up. It's suffocating having to live up to other's expectations when all you want to do is give up.

The comfort behind her eyes only pisses me off. And I hate her for it. Sam and her kind eyes have got to get as far away from me as humanly possible. I grab her arm, my fingers digging into her skin. She barely gets out a gasp before I yank her into the bathroom, slamming the door shut behind us.

She stumbles forward, twisting to look at me, eyes flashing with confusion, then anger. She jerks her arm, trying to break free, but I let go before she can rip herself away. Her sweater's disheveled, her breath coming faster.

"What the hell is your problem?" she snaps, rubbing at her arm. "You can't just—"

"What the hell are you doing here?" My voice is low, sharp enough to slice through the thudding bass from the party downstairs.

Her brows knit together. "What?"

I step closer. She doesn't flinch, but I feel the tension crackle between us. "This school. This house. This party. Why the fuck are you here?"

She lifts her chin. It's a quiet challenge, like she's daring me to knock her down a peg. "I got invited."

A laugh pushes past my lips, humorless and sharp. "Well, I've uninvited you. Leave."

Sam's spine snaps straight, and I can see the moment she goes from feeling familiar with me to pissed. Good. Maybe if I get under her skin enough, she'll disappear.

"I'll leave when I'm ready." She stands her ground, folding her arms over her chest, plants her feet, and cements herself in place.

I step closer, looming over her, my jaw ticked tight. "Leave or I'll carry you out of here myself."

Still she challenges me, glaring back, her focus never waning. So, I step closer, and that's when this tough act of hers starts to crack. Her face remains steely as she tries to hold on to the control she thinks she has. With each step I take forward, the more nervous she gets. First, she stumbles backward; then her arms fall defensively at her side, until she's pinned between the wall and me.

"Don't you fucking touch me," she manages to get out, her voice shaky.

"Go home, Sam."

"Oh...so you *do* remember who I am? Why do you even care?" she demands to know, her eyes searching mine, pleading with me to answer her. "You've said nothing to me since I've been at this school, damn near treat me as if I got some contagious disease, and now you're so bothered by me. Why? Why not keep pretending like I don't exist?"

"You don't belong here," I bite out.

Something flickers across her face. Hurt. It's quick, barely there, but I catch it before she forces herself to go blank again. That same fucking mask. The one I remember from years ago, the one she used when her stepfather got too loud with the nursing staff. When she'd sit holding my hand as we sat in that sterile family room. When she didn't want people knowing how deep words could cut her.

"Says who?" she challenges.

I don't hesitate. "Me."

She folds her arms again, shifting her weight like she's settling in for a fight. "I don't know what your problem is, Everest. But that's just it, it's yours, so leave me the hell out of it."

My name from her lips makes my stomach turn. I hate it. Hate that it's familiar, that it drags up shit I don't want to think about. Hate that she's here at all, bringing parts of me I buried long ago back to the surface.

"Don't call me that. It's Kane now," I grind out.

"What?" She rears back her head in confusion. Then she exhales, slow and measured, like she's trying not to lose her temper. "I don't know what the hell happened to the *real* Everest. But, out of all the possibilities, this version of you is the worst one I could've imagined."

The words hit harder than they should, settling in my ribs. It's a dull ache, persistent and nagging.

I take another step forward. She has to tilt her head back to keep her eyes on me. "And I'm supposed to give a fuck what you expected?"

Her nostrils flare. She doesn't back down. "No, but you're acting like you do."

That gets under my skin, causing my jaw to tighten further. She sees too much. Always has.

I close what little gap is left between us, daring her to challenge me. She doesn't, though. Instead, she stands there, peering at me, her eyes wide with resentment. My chest brushes against hers, and my muscles twitch as the heat of her frame clashes with mine. Suddenly, I'm violently aware of the feel of her, of the way her eyes say she hates me, but her body softens just a little. Her scent envelops me, and I realize how close my guess was, it might not be cocoa butter that I'm smelling but the vanilla is just as intoxicating.

I roam her features, taking in every little imperfection, tiny dark spots across her forehead, the texture in her skin, the way her lips part ever so slightly. They're full, heart shaped, two-toned, and worst of all, downright kissable. And without even realizing, I find myself wanting to do just that, my body leaning in all on its own. We're dangerously close, breaths now synchronized, gazes competing as we stare from our eyes and back to our mouths.

Her nose flares again. She feels it, too, the unwanted chemistry that's there nevertheless. And just when the tension thickens, Sam shoves past me and throws open the door before I can stop her.

"Fuck off, *Kane*."

CHAPTER TEN

SAM

"Asshole," I mutter as I burst out of the bathroom, flinging the door so hard it slaps against the wall, the sound ringing in my ears like a bell. Every nerve in my body is on edge, my skin still burning from the sting of his words.

You don't belong here.

Those five little syllables cut deeper than he'll ever know. Not because he was some angry beast set on antagonizing me. People are mean every day.

They stung because I already know that. I *don't* belong here, and no amount of miniskirts and hockey parties is going to change that.

I storm forward, not daring to look back. He may be the man around here, and used to getting his way, but I won't give him the satisfaction of knowing he's gotten to me. Even if my pulse races a mile a minute and numbness pricks at my flesh. *Kane* will not know that he's won.

Kane? I huff. *When did he start going by his last name? Probably around the same time he decided to become a Grade A dick.*

I hurry to get as far away from here as possible. At some point he is going to come out of that bathroom, and I don't want to be here when he does. I definitely don't want to be standing in this hallway; my nerves will already be all out of whack when Mountain finally joins the party.

How am I supposed to face him now?

Oh, jeesh. Sorry I walked in on you and your monster dick.

He'll probably just stare at me until I do something stupid to embarrass myself more than I already have. And I've had enough humiliation for one night. For the briefest of moments, I regret not following my gut. The moment my courage turned into hesitation, I should have gotten back in that car and went back to my dorm.

Maybe then I wouldn't be feeling like shit right about now. Maybe then I could've held on to the childhood memories of Everest. But that's gone now, forever tainted, the sweet boy from my past extinct.

The sound of girlish giggles brings me out of my thoughts, and my vision unblurs as two girls reach the top of the landing at the end of the hall. They're talking among themselves, barely sparing me a glance as they pass. And even though it's obvious they're unfazed by my presence, I shrink into myself. From the corner of my eye, I take in the tall, broad silhouette of Kane stepping out of the bathroom.

That nervous numbness returns, the adrenaline building almost instantly, damn near lighting a fire under my ass. But not before I hear the whispers. Not before I feel the very instant the rumor demon got his grubby hands on this moment.

"Was she in there with Kane?" one of the girls says.

"She's one of the new scholarship kids, right?" the other responds. "Lucky slut."

My stomach clenches and I take the stairs two at a time. My senses are immediately bombarded—flashes of moving bodies, laughter, and that overwhelming stench of liquor. All the air seems to leave my lungs in a rush, and I gasp in a breath.

Each step toward the door feels longer, and soon I tune out everything, my sights focused on the exit.

"You're back." Christina's grip is suddenly on my wrist as she pulls me into her space like I belong there.

She's wasted.

Scanning the room, I note the different levels of drunken chaos. Half the people here are a bad decision waiting to happen. The other half are already making them.

Christina leans too far into me, and I grab her shoulders, keeping her upright. "Hey, I was thinking about heading out—"

Her balance wavers, but she doesn't fall.

"You bitch," she says with a high-pitched squeal of laughter. "You just got here and have been in the bathroom the whole time."

If only she knew. If only she had any clue that I was cornered, torn apart, and left raw in that goddamn bathroom. It wasn't exactly some bubbly walk in the park.

Before I can argue, she snatches my phone, holds it up to my face, and taps away, moving through the apps on my screen. "Here, you're now logged into my account. You can order a Ryde."

I blink.

She's serious.

"But only if you hang out first." She grins, waving a hand toward the group of guys gathered nearby. "I want to introduce you to everyone."

Since I don't have the funds to cover that expensive Ryde back to SKU, I'll just have to tough it out.

"There are a lot of cute guys," she continues when I don't answer her. Her arm hooks around my neck, turning me toward them.

Hockey players.

"That's Jackson; he's a winger." She points out the cute guy from the photo she sent me earlier, the one sitting next to her when Gracie warned me. "And off-limits."

"Have at it." I let out a huff and hold my hand up in mock surrender. "He's your guy?"

Christina smirks. "Something like that. We used to date, but he's still obsessed with me. I mean, who wouldn't be."

I chuckle inwardly. *She really does love herself.*

"There is Ryker; he's also a winger, and Jackson's little brother. You have Carlos, a defenseman. Luka is one of the goalies, even though he probably shouldn't even be on the team. And that's Alexander, the captain and center, plus Chancellor Williamsburg's son. You've got to watch that one. He'll try to convince a nun to give it up. Then there are his two best friends—who must be somewhere around here—Kane, our star defenseman, and Mountain, our goalie. You know him, though, since he's in our class."

Little does she know, I needed no introduction of the last three she mentions. Christina continues to ramble off names of the players...all twenty-six of them. Meanwhile, I've tuned her out as Alex locks onto me with dark intent behind his eyes. My stomach twists as his gaze drags over my legs, lingering where my skirt ends.

The girl beside him notices. Her expression hardens as she mutters something under her breath and places her hand on his bicep.

Alex slides her arm off his like it's an afterthought, then strides toward me with that same cocky swagger that makes half the campus swoon and the other half want to punch him in the face. Blond hair perfectly tousled like he just rolled out of someone's bed complements green eyes sharp with calculation above a deceptively easy smile. That effortless charm oozes off him like cologne, intoxicating and intentional. And something about the slight lift of his chin tells me exactly what this is. He's about to try to smooth over how harshly he confronted me in that office, like he thinks a grin and a wink will be enough to make me forget.

Nope. Not happening.

I don't have the patience for another one of these assholes tonight.

Alex stops in front of me, about to take my hand. Instead, I decide to shut him down before he can even get out words.

"No, thank you." I snap my hand out of reach, crossing my arms instead.

His smirk. "I deserved that."

Damn right you did.

Alex turns so that he's standing beside me and leans in so that I can hear him over the music. "I think we started off on the wrong foot."

I face Christina, trying but failing to ignore him. She raises a curious brow at our interaction.

"I was having a bad day and shouldn't have spoken to you like that." Alex cranes his neck to search my face, making it impossible to avoid him.

"Don't worry about it." I step off, walking around Christina.

He follows me, sandwiching me between them. "You really don't like me, do you?"

"What do you want?" I let out, annoyed at the arrogant smirk on his face.

"To apologize."

"Fine. You've apologized. All's forgotten." I roll my eyes.

"Let's start over. I'm really a likeable guy if you get to know me." Alex leans in so close I can smell the alcohol on his breath.

I snap my gaze to his, my brows knitted tight, my frustration only amplifying when I take in the flirty gleam in his eyes. Ugh, he's insufferable, grinning and so sure of himself with his stupid handsome face.

He stares at my lips hungrily.

"Yeah, I'm not doing this with you." And with that, I walk off but can still feel his eyes glued to my ass.

A shift in the room stops me in my tracks, yanking my attention to the stairs.

Mountain looms there, fresh from the shower, hair still damp and clinging to his broad shoulders. I watch him scan the crowd, something akin to bored disapproval etched into his features. An expression that seems on brand for him—always uninterested, never impressed. Then his eyes burn into me, the hard set of his jaw making my throat dry.

My mind betrays me, flashing back to that brief, shocking moment earlier—him carved from muscle with water dripping down his skin. Now that image is seared into my brain, and I can't unsee it.

Suddenly, a large frame blocks my line of sight, cutting off the noise of the room like a slammed door. I blink, focus, and my breath hitches the second I register who it is. Every muscle in my body goes rigid. My hands ball into fists, knuckles aching from the pressure. It's a useless attempt to ground myself.

Kane steps fully into view, his massive frame coiled tight, like he's one wrong breath from snapping. That expression—pure stone, eyes like frostbitten steel—locks on me. No words. Just a look that says exactly what he's thinking.

Like he's trying to figure out why the hell I'm still here. Like if he stares hard enough, I'll vanish into thin air. My fight-or-flight instincts kick in, but before I can react, a guy slides in front of me with a grin that doesn't quite reach his eyes. "Sam, right? I'm Jackson."

"I remember. We have physics together."

"That's right. You're one of the new students," he says as more of an observation than anything else.

And as he continues to speak, Kane's stare burns hotter. Pissed? Jealous? Like I owe him a damn thing. My spine straightens. Fuck that. If he wants to act like we don't know each other, like my existence is such an inconvenience for him, then I'll give him a reason to feel that. I'm tired of people thinking that they can treat me however they want, talking down to me as if I'm just supposed to roll over and take it.

If Kane wants me out, then he's going to have to man the fuck up and do it himself. Something tells me he won't, though. He doesn't want his friends to know he's associated with me. To address me in a room full of his peers would mean answering questions as to why the presence of a new sophomore bothers him so much.

Deciding to get under his skin, I place a hand on Jackson's shoulder. I don't even flinch when he slips an arm around my waist. If Kane has a problem, he can choke on it. I barely hear Jackson's next words. I'm too focused on Kane, and the way his expression darkens, his jaw tightening.

"How about I get us a both a drink," Jackson offers, breaking my train of thought.

I almost refuse, but Kane is still watching, so I let Jackson take my hand and begin to lead me to the kitchen.

On my way out of the living room, I notice Alex leaning against the wall with a girl grinding on him, his eyes locked on me. Mountain remains a silent storm, barely moving, but watching. And Kane glares like I just did something unforgivable.

When I first got here, I was invisible; now it's as if I'm the center of attention.

The second Jackson and I are alone, I try to come up with a plan. I was never going to take the drink. I just wanted to get under Kane's skin. Now that I've done that, I can leave content. I'll just have to find a way to let this poor guy down without bruising another fragile ego.

Christina waves me over from the dance floor. I hold up a finger, silently stalling. I could join her, that would get me away from Jackson for sure, but then I'll have to indulge her drunken stupor. Plus, I'd rather not be within eyeshot of Alex, Mountain, and Kane.

Whatever decision I make isn't being made fast enough because the next thing I know, Jackson shoves a cup into my hand.

"Here you go."

With a fake smile, I take it. "Thanks."

"No problem. You're cute, you know that?" Jackson says while looking me up and down, his eyes lingering uncomfortably long on my thighs. "We don't usually get girls that look like you around here."

I have no idea what the hell that's supposed to mean.

Jackson motions to get my attention, pointing toward the front door. "Now that we have our drinks, come outside with me while I spark up."

Hesitation grips my chest.

"Oh, come on. Keep me company," he pleads when I don't move.

With a slow nod, I follow. It'll be fine since I need to leave in this direction anyway. Jackson leads me across the threshold and past a group of guys on the porch. We descend the short staircase, and I take in my surroundings. There's double the number of vehicles here now than when I arrived. People loiter about as we walk to the side of the house, where the party noise fades into the background. Close enough to still see people, but isolated enough that no one's paying attention.

When I turn to face Jackson, he's already pulling a joint from the pocket of his ripped jeans. The flame from his lighter flickers against his smug expression as he lights up, then takes a long drag. Smoke curls from his lips, slow and lazy, before he exhales into the cool night air like he owns it.

He holds the joint out in my direction. "Wanna hit?"

I frown. "Naw, I'm good. That's not my thing."

"Suit yourself." Jackson takes another puff while staring me up and down, his eyes gluing to my thighs again.

"They don't do random drug screens or something?" I fold my arms, careful not to spill the drink, and watch the cloud dissipate between us.

He chuckles. It's low and condescending, as if I'm cute for being concerned. Like he doesn't have a single consequence in the world.

Which, judging by the way he's looking at me with sharp eyes, and a grin full of challenge, he probably doesn't.

"Why, you plan on telling on me or something?" Jackson smirks.

"No." I glance around. "It's your lungs you're nuking."

He laughs, then his gaze drops to my untouched drink. "You didn't even sip that."

I shrug. "I'm not really thirsty."

"That's kind of shitty to waste perfectly good liquor. Plus it's rude to make me drink alone." His stare lingers too long.

Fine. Just a sip if it'll get him to back off about it. I bring it to my lips as he watches me intently. I glance at the cup, more out of habit than anything. A frown forms along my brow, and I tilt the red cup just to be sure I'm not seeing things.

Turns out, I see just fine.

There's something floating near the surface.

My stomach twists. I frown, tilting the cup under the dim light coming from the floodlights on the side of the house. It's small, but it's there. A film of something.

Jackson moves closer. "It's just foam."

My pulse spikes. I didn't say anything about what I'm looking at, yet he has an answer for it.

My fingers tighten around the plastic, breath coming too fast. "Did you put something in my drink?"

His easy expression cracks, in its place a cold, defensive stare.

I step back but he grabs my wrist.

"Relax. You're overthinking—"

Yanking free, I stumble. Some of the drink sloshes onto the ground. His face twists, frustration boiling over into something ugly. Before I can fully make sense of what's happening, Jackson lunges, shoving me against the house, his breath hot and sour against my cheek.

"I said relax. We're just talking. Getting to know each other better."

I grunt, twisting and turning under his weight, my shoulder scraping against the cold siding of the house.

"You tried to drug me," I blurt out, voice shaky but loud enough to punch through the haze of weed and alcohol between us.

Jackson stiffens; his joint and cup hit the ground with dull thuds as his hands shoot up to silence me.

"Shut the fuck up." His voice drops into a growl that only I can hear but sharp enough to split me open. One hand clamps around my mouth, the other tightens on my arm, and suddenly the party noise fades behind the ringing in my ears.

"Do you know who I am?" he hisses, face so close I smell the whiskey clinging to his breath. "No one's gonna believe you. I run this school, and I take what I want."

My blood runs cold under the bruising force of his grip. I thrash harder, my heart thundering, panic roaring inside me. And all I can think is I've been here before. Trapped. Cornered. Abused.

But not this time.

This time, I scream.

"Get off me."

His fingers grip my neck, squeezing just enough to make my pulse hammer. The music is too loud, so no one seems to hear me. Those fight instincts rear their ugly head and without another thought, I bare my teeth, snap forward, and sink them into his arm. His grip loosens for a fraction of a second. It's all I need.

I knee him between his thighs. Jackson huddles over, grabbing himself, pain staining his face, and that's when I do it: I draw back, and drive my boot into his kneecap with all the strength I can muster. A sickening crack pierces the air between us; then he crumples to the ground with a sharp yell.

"AHHH! You fucking bitch!"

It's either him or me—and it damn sure *won't* be me. I don't stick around, taking off before the words fully leave his sadistic lips. And as I sprint to safety, I hear voices behind me.

"Sam!" It's Christina's voice. "Oh my God! Jackson, what happened?"

I won't stop. Not until I'm far, far away from here.

CHAPTER ELEVEN

SAM

The silence in this hallway doesn't feel normal. There are no footsteps, no murmurs behind closed doors, no staff. It's just me and whatever this summons means.

I shouldn't be here. Not on a Saturday. Not alone.

But here I am, staring down a heavy oak door with my heart in my throat, and every nerve in my body screaming for me to *run*. Coming to SKU was supposed to be a blessing, but right now, it feels more like a curse.

I told myself to forget it, but fate's a cruel bastard with a very long memory. Last night still clings to my skin, and I can't shake the feeling that my being called to the chancellor's office has everything to do with that.

It was just one party. One mistake I felt coming before I even made up my mind to go. The entire ride to that lake house, my stomach turned flips—much like it is now—yet I still went. And now everything I've scraped together, everything I've worked for—the scholarship, the long hours studying, every threadbare hope—is fraying.

It's all going down the drain, and I fear there might not be anything I can do about it. Desmond was counting on me to get us out of this mess we were born into. To rewrite the story no one ever gave us a chance to change. And I might've just burned our only way out to the ground.

I didn't plan for this to happen. It was just supposed to be a harmless little house party. I wasn't supposed to have to fight for my life.

But I did.

I told myself that I could bury this, forget the whole thing. But I couldn't. After I left the party, running until my legs nearly gave out, I used Christina's account to call a Ryde and snuck in while Gracie was asleep. And as I sat on the bathroom floor with the shower running, all I could do was replay it in my mind.

His hand wrapping around my neck, his voice that was all teeth and arrogance, and me suddenly biting down on his flesh, shoving him off me, and hearing the sickening snap.

Now his knee's destroyed, it has to be. I did more damage than I intended, and now I'm going to have to face the consequences.

With one deep, shaky breath, I raise my fist and knock.

The door opens with the slow deliberateness of a horror film. A click. A creak. And then the chancellor's cool, unreadable gaze flicks to mine.

"Come in," he says with no warmth or pretense.

My feet move before I can talk myself out of it. I step into the room—and stop cold.

Jackson is here.

He's sitting stiffly in one of the leather chairs directly across from the chancellor's desk, one leg stretched out awkwardly, the other bent around the thick white cast that encases his knee. A pair of crutches lean beside him. He glares at me, and I can feel the hate swimming just beneath the surface of his stillness.

There are two other people aside from the chancellor, who is now back behind his desk. One of the men is tall and broad-shouldered. He wears a varsity-branded pullover, and the whistle hanging from his neck confirms that he's the coach. That's usually how it happens, right? A player gets injured, and the coach gets involved. Otherwise, why else would he be here?

The other man stands directly behind Jackson's chair, a hand on Jackson's shoulder and the other in the front pocket of his slacks. He's older, harder, with silver at his temples and the same cold edge in his jawline as Jackson. There's no mistaking the father and son relationship.

They all just stare at me like I've ruined something valuable. As if I'm the perpetrator and not the victim.

"You must be Samantha," the chancellor says, his voice clipped. "Have a seat."

Hesitation bites at my limbs, and I glance between the men, my brain telling me to get the hell out of here, while my body freezes in place. The energy in the room is draining. It's dark and cold, and not just from the lack of heat.

It's *them*. The way they watch me like I'm dirt under their boots, like I've dragged filth into a room that was never meant for someone like me.

I make myself move, grabbing the top of the chair and scooting it closer to create space between Jackson and me. I lower myself into the seat and am acutely aware of how small I feel. *How am I the only girl in a room full of angry men?*

My palms press against my thighs to hide the shaking. I won't give them that. I won't let them see me flinch. But still, my chest tightens.

"I assume you know why you're here," the chancellor says, lacing his fingers together as he leans back in his office chair, his gaze never leaving mine.

I swallow hard, my voice stuck behind the taste of dread. "No. I don't."

I do know, but if I've learned anything from watching crime documentaries—you let them tell you what they know first.

A flicker of annoyance crosses his face, like I've failed some unspoken test. "Then let me make it abundantly clear."

And just like that, I am fully aware of what they know, and whatever comes next won't be mercy. From my peripherals, I notice Jackson looking at me. My gaze darts around, searching for something—*anything*—to anchor me.

That's when I spot the paperweight on the chancellor's desk. A knight, wrapped in brass and silver, twin swords crossed over its chest. It's massive, about half a foot tall and several inches wide. And somehow, even knowing it's a nod to the school's mascot, it feels more menacing than the men in this room. Red pearls burn behind the helmet's visor, glinting where its eyes should be. The grate around its mouth looks more like a snarl than armor.

"I don't know what they do where you're from, but we don't tolerate violence at this school, Ms. Collins." The chancellor's voice snaps me out of a daze.

"Neither do I," I bite out. "I'm not a violent person."

"I'm in a cast. You broke my knee in three places. That feels pretty violent to me," Jackson snaps, leaning forward in his chair in an attempt to intimidate me.

"You attacked—"

"Enough. Why don't you tell us what happened, Mr. Kincaid?" Chancellor Williamsburg asks, cutting me off.

Seriously? Why the hell is he asking only him?

"She was drunk, coming on to me," he says smoothly. It's sickening how easily he lies. "But when I told her I wasn't interested, she got aggressive."

A cold prickle runs down my spine. "That's not what happened," I say, forcing my voice to hold steady. "I wasn't drunk. I don't drink at parties because there's always some asshole—"

Coach bristles. "Watch your tone."

"Coach Barrett," the chancellor warns. "Let's allow Ms. Collins the courtesy of finishing her statement before we descend into barking."

I glance at the chancellor, wondering if that was a defense or just a performance of fairness. But his expression gives nothing away and I'm no closer to knowing if he is friend or foe. Although my instincts are telling me it's the latter. The chancellor nods for me to continue.

"Sir. I wasn't drinking. I never drink at parties. I hadn't even been there long before Jackson approached me."

"Tell him how you were all on me, touching my shoulder," Jackson interrupts.

"Young man," the chancellor warns again.

Instantly, I think back to the moment I let my hand rest on his shoulder. What was supposed to be a dig at Kane might just bite me in the ass. *Fuck.*

"Did you touch him?"

All eyes are on me, boring deep, waiting for me to slip up.

I sigh. "I did, but it was a friendly touch, more like a tap. He approached me, even put his hand on my waist. I didn't make a big deal of it because he was being nice. But I did not come on to him. He offered me a drink, and I accepted to be kind."

"Why not just turn it down?" Coach Barrett asks, accusatory.

"Girls don't exactly have the luxury of turning a guy down without bruising his ego," I say matter-of-factly. "We don't know who's a decent guy and who's not, so it's safer to just take the drink and not drink it."

"And you don't see how that could give him the impression that you were interested?" the chancellor adds.

"No. I should be able to take a drink and not have some prick think that means I want him."

The chancellor lets out an uncomfortable sigh and waves for me to keep going. It's a silent apology because God forbid he do so out loud.

"He asked me to go outside with him while he smoked—"

"Richard. You can't be buying this crap. Smoking? Jackson doesn't smoke," Mr. Kincaid blurts out.

"Then you don't know your son very well, Mr. Kincaid," I snap.

Chancellor Williamsburg holds up a hand to quiet Jackson's father before he can say another word and looks at Jackson. "Is this true? You know drugs are prohibited for all players."

Jackson shifts in his seat, the faint rustle of his crutches tapping against the wooden armrest.

"I don't remember much, to be honest," he adds, gaze locked on mine. "But I do remember her kicking me. Pretty hard. After I told her I wasn't interested."

My heart stutters.

"You tried to drug me," I snap. "You pushed me against that house, and—"

"You were drunk," Jackson says with a shrug. "Everyone saw it."

"I wasn't drunk."

"Oh?" His brow lifts. "So you broke my knee sober? Good to know."

"Sir. I'm telling the truth." I swallow to catch my breath, trying and failing to ignore the hateful stares from Jackson and daddy dearest. "He offered me some of his weed, I again said no. Then he encouraged me to drink the alcohol he gave me, and when I said no, he accused me of being rude. That's when

I noticed a white foaming substance floating around in my cup. And before I could ask about it, he told me to relax, that it was just foam. It was spiked punch, and last I checked, punch doesn't foam."

A laugh leaves Mr. Kincaid's mouth, dry and humorless. "You assaulted my son," he growls. "And you think you can sit here and lie your way out of it?"

I turn toward him. "I defended myself. He put his hands on me, and I reacted. I didn't mean to—"

"But you did," the chancellor cuts in. "Didn't you?"

Silence falls like a curtain.

He folds his hands again, leans back in his chair, and looks at me like I'm a stain on his perfectly buffed floor.

"Regardless of whether you 'meant' to, Ms. Collins, the fact remains: a student-athlete has sustained a serious injury that will bench him for the remainder of the season. Witnesses say you were aggressive and that alcohol was involved. This institution cannot afford scandal. Nor can we allow violence to go unchecked."

"And they're lying," I let out, my voice rising before I can stop it. "Was I just supposed to let him touch me, pin me against a wall, and—"

"You've got some nerve, girl," Mr. Kincaid snarls. "My son is on track for the draft. The draft. And you shatter his knee because what—he smiled at you?"

"That's not what happened," I grit out.

"She should be expelled," he growls, turning toward the chancellor. "And arrested. If you don't press charges, I will."

The chancellor raises a hand, quieting the room. His expression stays neutral, unreadable. "That won't be necessary." His tone is calm, but there's something colder underneath it.

"Not necessary?" Jackson's father explodes. "She attacked him! I donate a lot of money to this university, and my son is the only reason this damn team has a chance at National—"

Chancellor Williamsburg rises from behind his desk and tilts his head toward the door. "Sebastion, let me have a word with you outside."

Mr. Kincaid stands there, seething, but he doesn't push back. Instead, he steels his shoulders, shoves his fists into his pockets, and glares at me on his way out the door. The chancellor follows behind him, closing the door, effectively sealing me in a room with my enemy.

Thankfully, Jackson doesn't taunt me, and I'm sure I have the presence of the coach to thank for that. Something tells me that what I saw on Friday night isn't even half the length Jackson would be willing to go. The way he switched from flirtatious to viciously angry in the matter of seconds.

The thick oak makes it so that we can hear their raised voices but not what is actually being said.

It's killing me—the anticipation, the not knowing what's being said or which part of my life they'll rip apart next. They want to strip me down. Not just physically... emotionally. They want to humiliate me until I break.

After what feels like forever, the door creaks open. Mr. Kincaid lingers on the other side of the threshold, that grimace of his looking more and more like a permanent disposition.

"Come on, son," he mutters, not bothering to meet Jackson's eyes, his stare drifting sideways. Almost as if he's detached, resigned, and defeated.

"What about—" Jackson starts but is cut off.

"Now," Mr. Kincaid barks.

That shuts Jackson right up. *About damn time.*

Jackson rises, grumbling under his breath as he grabs his crutches. His father mutters something sharp and entitled, a low growl of money and threats, before the door swings shut behind them.

And then there's silence. It's not a reprieve, not really—more like concentrated pressure now that it's just me and the two men still staring at me like a problem they're tired of solving.

The chancellor folds his hands behind his back and walks slowly to the edge of the desk.

"Let me be very clear with you, Ms. Collins."

Here it comes.

"You are dangerously close to expulsion."

I don't breathe and just wait.

"What you did—what you admitted to doing—could've resulted in a lawsuit, a scandal, a shattered reputation for both you and this institution. And instead of reporting it through the proper channels, you chose to react violently, recklessly, and with no regard for consequence."

"He put his hands on me."

His voice sharpens. "And you broke his knee."

"I defended myself."

He raises a brow. "And you'll continue defending yourself when you're back home, no degree, no options, and no way to afford the life you think you deserve?"

That shuts me up. Because I don't have a comeback for the truth.

"Now, I've convinced Mr. Kincaid not to pursue this, but you can't go unpunished for your actions."

"And what about Jackson? It isn't hardly fair that he gets—"

"You've effectively ruined the rest of his college hockey career and potentially his chances of going pro. I'd say he's being punished enough."

Not even close.

Had I not been observant and had I drank from that cup, there is no telling what that jerk would have done to me. There's no telling who else he's done this to, but I'm supposed to just be grateful that they aren't pressing charges.

And it's not that I expected them to hold him accountable. They never do. The rich boys' club always protects their own. It's just that they somehow think we're even. He tried to assault me, but because I fought back and hurt him, the guilty verdict goes out the window.

It's bullshit.

"You have two options," he finishes, his voice clipped. "Expulsion or community service. After class, you'll report to Coach Barrett until the end of the season."

"I wanted to apply for work study in between classes this semester," I say quietly. "I need the money."

He sighs, long and exasperated, like my words personally inconvenience him. "Well. You should've thought of that before you made such impulsive, self-destructive choices."

I say nothing.

"What's it going to be?"

I blink. "Community service."

"All right." He walks back to his seat. "Coach Barrett will oversee your assignment. You'll assist with the hockey team. Practices, equipment, travel coordination. Whatever he deems necessary."

My stomach sinks. "You're kidding."

"Do I look like I'm joking?" His tone turns icy.

I clench my jaw, eyes burning. My fists curl against the strap of my bag.

"This is absurd—"

"It's your only path forward," he says, cutting me off. "Bury this, keep your head down, do the work, and graduate with opportunities. Or fight back, stir the pot, and I promise you, the Kincaids will destroy every dream you've ever had."

His eyes narrow.

"Make no mistake, Ms. Collins. They have the resources. You don't." He pauses to write something on the notepad in front of him. "You can go."

Just like that. No paperwork. No report. No hearing.

And I'm not expelled.

I guess I should be... relieved? Grateful?

The chancellor should want me gone. Jackson's father certainly does. And yet... he doesn't. He gave me this scholarship with no interview or explanation. Just an offer that felt too good to be real.

And now, instead of throwing me to the wolves like I expected, he's protecting me.

Why?

I gather my bag and rise to my feet. Coach Barrett strolls toward the door and pulls it open. He doesn't look at me as he gestures for me to follow.

The chancellor's voice stops me in my tracks.

"And, Ms. Collins?"

I turn slowly, my teeth clenched, and back straight.

"One more incident... one more anything... and you're gone."

CHAPTER TWELVE

ALEX

Fuck.

My stick barely connects with the puck, sending it scraping haphazardly across the ice. It's a weak shot—one I'd be embarrassed of if I wasn't still hungover from last night. It was all fun and games until we were beckoned at the ass crack of dawn.

It doesn't help that we didn't sleep a lick, aside for occasionally dozing off in the hospital waiting room as we waited to hear news on Jackson.

Now I see what Mountain was worried about. I'll bet my 911 Carrera GTS that he's about to be a major pain in my ass about it.

No one was around to see Jackson get his ass kicked, just the new girl running off. If she wasn't guilty, then why run? I honestly wouldn't give a shit if it wasn't for us being three games away from nationals. Everything is riding on having all of our best players on that ice. I might not like that dickwad, but we wouldn't be this far without him.

I glance around, taking in my team. Everyone looks just as beat up as I feel. Well, almost everyone. Mountain is making the rest of us look like degenerates.

Kane's doing that thing where he skates circles so tight he

might carve up the ice with his rage. Something he's been doing a lot more lately, like there's something eating at him.

A loud clank ricochets off the ceiling as someone yanks open the doors. I turn just in time to take in the snarl stretched across Coach Barrett's mug. Even from here I can see the vein in his temple, his anger loud and glaring.

"Circle up!" Coach roars, stopping near the tunnel and turning to face us. "Now!"

"Hundred bucks says he's about to make us do suicides," Luka says to another player.

He's wrong.

We broke curfew, threw an unsanctioned party, and one of our best players ended up in the hospital. Coach is going to do a lot worse than suicides.

Mountain skates pass, bumping me along the way. A silent *I told you so* if I ever heard one before. Kane and I are the last to join the circle, and when we do, my eyes go straight to the person half-hiding in Coach's shadow.

Sam.

The skimpy skirt is long gone, her thick thighs covered in denim instead. The old hoodie is way too big for her, the sleeves swallowing her hands. She doesn't look nearly as feisty as she was last night. Instead she's tucked behind the coach as if she wishes she could disappear, that defiance of hers now replaced with dread and something else. Fear, maybe? Regret?

Kane mutters under his breath while Mountain only watches her with an unreadable stare.

I watch as her eyes land on Kane, her breath hitching just a little. When I look at Kane, his brow is furrowed and his grip on the stick is so tight the skin of his knuckles is white as it stretches over bone. Something about her presence catches him off guard, and I make a mental note to ask him about it later.

Coach waits until we're all in front of him before he speaks again. "Kincaid's done."

The silence slams into us, and the weight of the coach's words settle around us.

"What do you mean done?" someone asks but I don't bother to see who.

Coach Barrett releases an aggravated sigh and scrubs a palm over his beard. It's bad. I can tell by the hesitation in his posture and the crow's-feet that are forming deeper around his eyes. It ages him well beyond his forty-something years.

"He won't be returning for the rest of the season. He may not return to the ice at all."

A protest erupts, a slew of profanities flying around. But all I can focus on is her. Sam flinches, tugging on her sleeves, fraying the already tattered hems even more.

She did this.

That's why she's here, right? To, what, say she's sorry for possibly fucking up our chances at nationals?

Coach doesn't let the moment breathe. "You can thank her."

His thumb jerks toward Sam, but she doesn't move or speak. She just takes it as they all start at once, spewing spiteful words and toxic energy in her direction.

"Hope you're proud of yourself!"

"You killed the fucking season!"

"Just a puck bunny doing anything to catch a mark!"

"Fucking bitch!"

Through it all, she's mute and stone-still. If anything, she shrinks back further, like she'd crawl inside her own skin if she could. Her head is down, a single curl falling from her messy bun. Their words sting, I know they do, if the subtle flinch after each accusation is any indication. She doesn't defend herself. Doesn't even try. It's nauseating, and I can't watch it anymore.

"Enough," I yell, daring anyone to challenge me. The ruckus dies down, shouts trailing off into grumbles and dirty looks.

Coach releases an exasperated breath before turning the full force of his disappointment back to us.

"You're not off the hook," he snarls, glaring at me as he does. "You knew what was at stake and still went against everything I told you."

"It's not—" Luka starts, but Coach cuts him off.

"Save it." He shakes his head in disgust. "The only acceptable response right now is 'yes, sir.'"

"Yes, sir," we all mutter in a reluctant echo.

"You boys think you're untouchable? You're not. You're sloppy. You're arrogant and apparently stupid. You're on the cusp of the best season of your lives, and you risk losing everything we've worked for."

He continues pacing, staring at each of us like he's debating who to bench next.

"You let your egos cost us Jackson. Possibly even cost us our shot. If you can't show restraint, how am I supposed to trust you'll have the discipline to bring it home?"

Another rhetorical.

"Bag skate until you puke."

Groans rippled from the group as they resentfully file out. Kane grinds his stick into the ice, his jaw ticking. Mountain lets out a slow exhale, already shifting into gear. I'm just about to fall in line, but Coach stops me in my tracks.

"Williamsburg. Stay."

I freeze, my heart sinking as the rest of the team peels off toward the center of the ice. I move toward the edge, my skates crunching over frozen ground. Now that there aren't as many eyes on her, Sam looks up, her broken eyes meeting mine.

"She's now your problem."

I frown. "What?"

"You heard me. She should be expelled, but the chancellor obviously has different plans. You're the captain, this happened at your party, so she's all yours."

Fucking thanks, Dad.

Once again, his decision affecting my life. There's been a long-standing beef between Coach and my father. They fake pleasantries in public for the sake of appearances, but beneath the veil, they hate each other. Coach can't tell my dad where to shove it, so he takes special care in taking out his disdain on me.

"She's the new equipment manager. Make sure she knows her way around so she doesn't ruin something else. If she fucks up, you're benched." He peers down at her. "You're on thin ice, so do what he says, take care of the team, and stay out of the way."

With that, Coach walks off and the rest of the team skid around us, some shooting venomous glares or snide remarks as they do.

"This is her fault," a player spits as he passes me.

Then it's just the two of us, alone for a second amid the chaos. She stares at me, bracing herself as if she expects me to deliver another blow.

I skate to the bench, not bothering to address her. I dig soakers from the box and flop down on the seat to cover my blades while taking in the scene. The boys fly back and forth across the rink during the drills, an array of cursing trailing behind them.

Shaking my head, I push off the bench and walk across the

ice, back toward Sam. She's frozen in place where I left her, head tucked into her chest, and hands shoved into the pocket of her hoodie. From this angle, I can see just how much the thing swallows her.

But she's not small. Not really.

Not with thighs like that, thick, solid, and barely contained by her jeans. It's distracting as hell, the way her body contradicts the way she carries herself—like she's trying to disappear when all she does is stand out. The sweatshirt hangs off her, but the curves underneath are undeniable. Hips made for grabbing. Lips full and parted like she's holding back a thousand words. The kind of mouth that would look good wrapped around—

I snap my gaze up before my thoughts spiral. *Jesus.*

This is the girl who ruined our season. The last person I should be looking at like that. But the more she tries to vanish, the more I notice. The rich brown skin peeking from the neckline of her hoodie, glowing under the cold fluorescents.

That's the problem. She looks too damn good in a place meant to break her.

I walk past her, not bothering to stop. "Are you coming or what?"

She shuffles behind me, flinching at every loud grunt or crash from the boys on the ice. I push open the door to the tunnel and lead her into the locker room. It's dim when we enter, quickly turning quiet when the door slams shut with an echo.

I flick on the light and watch as she blinks to adjust her eyesight. Rows of lockers and gear come into view. Still hovering by the entrance, she drags her gaze around, clearly unsure where she fits in this world.

I point to the corner stacked high with equipment. "Skates

need to be sharpened and lined up before practice. Instructions are on the side of the machine. Each player has a different cut. Get them wrong and someone can blow a knee. *Again*."

She clenches her fist at that. I push open the gear room. Sticks stacked by numbers, jerseys hung up like ghosts waiting to be worn again.

"Sticks and pucks are here. Tape is in the cabinet. Learn everyone's sizes, stick preferences, and taping styles. *Don't* touch Kane's stick unless he tells you to."

We continue farther into the space.

"Laundry room is there. Sweaters go in color-coded bins. Never mix them."

She frowns. "Sweaters?"

I huff. Of course she doesn't know shit about hockey. Why would she?

"Jerseys," I deadpan. "There's some special solution for getting the blood out. The machines are old, so you'll need to babysit them."

"God, it stinks over here." Her face twists in a snarl.

"Yeah. Welcome to hockey. We play rough, and we play hard."

I wait for her to protest, but she doesn't.

"Keep the water bottles clean and full. Durning home games, keep both locker rooms stocked with water, towels, and anything else that's needed. Don't fuck up."

I fold my arms, observing her. She reaches up to check the cabinet, her sleeve rolling back just enough to show a faint burn near her wrist. When she catches me looking, she quickly tugs the material down. My gut twists, and I don't know why.

I try to cover up the strange emotion with animosity. "No one wants you here."

For the first time since she walked into the rink, Sam stares me in the eye.

"I'm aware."

Click.

The door shuts behind me, and the air shifts. It's heavy and clinical. And as fake as the smile on the receptionist's face when she told me he was ready for me.

Being ordered to my father's office is never for a good reason. Not that much is required to set him off. Just existing irritates him. The office is spotless and sterile. He doesn't look up but immediately starts talking.

"Why must you insist on disappointing your mother and me?"

I've heard it all before. I'm an embarrassment, a disgrace.

"How do you think your failing grades make me look? Chancellor of a division one school with an idiot for a son. When are you going to learn that your behavior is a reflection on this family?"

"And here I was only thinking about myself," I huff out, my fists clenched. "If you're done, I'm late for class."

"We're done when I say we're done," he barks. "I've made arrangements with your professor to let you do makeup work and retake your exam in two months. You're going to do whatever it takes to pass, and I'll let you stay on the team."

I shift, breathing in through my nostrils.

"If you fail this exam, you're done. If you don't bring those grades up, you can kiss your Porsche, lake house, and allowance goodbye." His voice slices through me.

I stare past his head. The framed degrees behind him mock me. It's a sign of everything he is, and everything I'm not.

"You're lucky I don't pull you from the team now," he threatens.

Of course, he hasn't yet. That would mean he has to explain why the Williamsburgs are far from perfect. We're flawed beyond repair. The only real love in this family is from my mother. Otherwise, it's just cold dinners, colder silences, and a father who sees me as an extension of his image, not a son.

And when I fail—because I will—he'll act like he saw it coming. Like it was inevitable. Like I was never worth betting on in the first place.

"You better play like you give a shit. Maybe with Kincaid benched, you can actually make a contribution. You're dismissed."

Maybe I can contribute? As if I didn't help us win nationals two years in a row.

I leave before he can say anything else, my blood boiling, chest wound tight. Storming out, I run right into a warm body. And *not* the receptionist, who is nowhere to be found.

No. It's *Sam*.

I catch her falling backward before she hits the floor. Standing her back upright, she quickly shrugs me off, like she wasn't just eavesdropping while waiting in the lobby.

I pull her out into the hall and over to a secluded corner out of earshot before turning on her. "You just can't seem to stay out of places you're not wanted."

"Look, I wasn't trying to listen."

"Could have fooled me. You were right outside the door on purpose; that sounds a lot like spying to me. Trying to blackmail me?"

She frowns. "Why would I blackmail you?"

I inch closer. "Why were you listening?"

"Okay, fine. I was but not why you think. I...I can help."

I blink once. "How are you supposed to help me?"

Sam crosses her arms over her chest. "I came to this school with a 4.0 GPA. *I'm* good at this. *You* need to pass that exam and those assignments."

There's a brief silence between us as I weigh her offer.

"What do you get out of this? We've been nothing but assholes to you."

"Trust me, I don't like you any more than you like me. But I'll make sure you pass if you keep the team off my ass."

I snort. "You think helping me pass buys you a clean slate?"

"I think you're desperate enough to say yes," she says, chin lifting like she's daring me to prove her wrong.

Everything in me wants to tell her that it doesn't fix the added pressure on me because of *her* actions. But she's not wrong. And worse—she knows it. I step in closer, until there's barely any space left between us. "If I agree to this, we do it on my terms."

She nods, her brows raised, and lips pressed tight in a silent *yes*.

"We meet off campus. No one can know. Ever."

I drag my gaze over her face and the curve of her mouth. The way her jaw tightens when she's holding herself together. God, I want to ruin that composure. But Sam holds her ground.

Finally, I let out a breath. "We start before the next game."

Every part of me knows this is a mistake. But I'm going to make it anyway.

CHAPTER THIRTEEN

EVEREST (KANE)

Practice hasn't even started and I already want to punch something. The lights are too bright, and every breath tastes like blood and bile from how hard we've been working. Coach is still riding our asses, even though it's been almost three weeks since the party, since Jackson's accident, since he decided to shove Sam down our throat.

And I hate it. Having her here, being forced to see her face, constantly reminding us that she nearly kneecapped our chance at nationals.

"Hustle up," Coach yells from the sidelines, breaking my thoughts. "Finals are in three days, and losing to Baymont is not an option. You've done good the last two games without Kincaid, but win this, and it's an automatic bid into nationals. The season's riding on it."

Everything's riding on it. Which is why the second I spot Sam entering the locker room, my blood boils, that all-consuming pull of irritation biting at my skin.

"Williamsburg."

"Yes, Coach," Alex responds, fishing his way to the front.

"Warm 'em up."

Alex nods and spins on his skates. "You heard him. Let's work."

Mountain's the first to start his drills, slapping pucks off the boards like it'll quiet whatever storm's sitting behind his eyes. Alex looks like he's running on fumes—again.

I push off, immediately getting into my zone. The moment my blades touch the ice, it's as if the world ceases to exist. Nothing else matters—not the bullshit, not the pressure of working ten times harder than anyone else, and not the stack of medical bills waiting for me.

It's just me, my skates, and an inch of solid ice. This is home. Not the condo that's been empty since my mom went back into the facility, and not the room in the lake house.

I skate short bursts, stopping hard, leaving slashes in the ice. My breath sears my lungs, but it's a good burn. The kind of pain that makes you forget every fucked-up thing in your world. Time seems to stand still and before long, the guys are tapping out one by one. But I don't stop, I keep going, cutting deeper and deeper tracks across the rink. Just maybe, if I go fast enough, I'll escape the rest of this hellish life.

Alex skates up beside me, checking my speed, his eyes sharp as usual.

"Don't burn yourself out," he says between breaths.

"Don't tell me what to do."

He smirks. "Cute."

I shoot him a look and push forward, leaving him to circle back to Mountain. It's going to take everything we've got to beat Baymont, and we fucking need this win. He can act like I'm pushing too hard, but the fact is, they want this just as bad as I do.

It's evident in the way Mountain slaps pucks away from the net, all of his frustrations leaving with each block. It's in the way Alex leads the rush, practice or not. His golden boy facade is cracking under the pressure. He acts like he's got it all in check, but he's been just as on edge.

A whistle blows in the distance, bringing me out of my haze.

"Bring it in, boys. Get some rest, and be back on time tomorrow," Coach orders.

From the corner of my eye, I witness Alex glide toward the bench, tossing his stick, then unpeeling his helmet. He stands off to the side, talking to Mountain.

"Hey, Kane," Alex yells.

I skate closer, only staring at him, not bothering to respond.

"We're about to get some grub. You in?"

I wave him off and continue running, determined to go until there's nothing left. The guys disappear down the tunnel one by one until I'm alone. The way I like it.

It's another fifteen minutes before my body finally starts to quit, forcing me off the ice. As I remove my helmet, sweat drips from my hairline, blurring my vision. I walk through the tunnel, my covered blades hitting the marbled floors with a clacking sound. Pushing through the doors, I use the collar of my jersey to wipe my face.

I turn to head toward the boards and stop cold.

She's here.

She's crouched low in front of the skate sharpener like it's second nature, sleeves rolled to her elbows, a fine layer of sweat clinging to the back of her neck. My gaze runs over her, taking in the form-fitting long-sleeve tee and stretch pants that hug her body just right. But it's the tattoo peeking from above her waistband that holds my attention.

I'm not close by any means, but I can still make out the design from here. A semicolon symbol. It's small and black, inked in the dead center of her spine. The thought clouds my mind before

I can push it away, and all I can think about is when she got it and if it's the only one. If I recall, she didn't like tattoos as a kid, claiming that only bad people get them.

Does that mean she's bad? She certainly isn't innocent. Has that sweet little girl long since disappeared?

"Yo, Sam," someone calls out.

Sam sighs before he can even finish, already fed up with it all. She's only been sentenced to being our new equipment manager for three weeks now, and the fellas haven't wasted a second making her time here hell. That's what she gets. Do stupid things, win stupid prizes.

Jackson was a pain in everyone's ass. He's smug, crass, and a little sadistic, but he's a beast on the ice. So while I also wanted to punch him in the face most days, we needed him to ensure a win.

"Water bottles are empty." The voice is smug and too loud.

I shift to follow the voice. It's Ryker and one of his little minions. It's not surprising he's the first one to really go at her; just like Jackson, he's also a menace, always playing practical jokes and pushing boundaries just far enough to avoid actual trouble. But this isn't one of his usual stunts. There's something meaner in his tone today. Something *colder*.

He tosses one at her without looking. It clatters to the floor at her feet.

"Dude, give her a break. Can't you see she's busy?" His buddy snickers. "She's got skates to sniff or something."

Laughter erupts as they circle her like sharks smelling blood.

"That's what we're calling it now?" Ryker says, nodding toward the blades she's holding. "Working?"

Sam doesn't flinch. Doesn't even blink. Just tightens her grip on the skate and sets it on the sharpener with mechanical focus. She inhales slowly, her spine straight but stiff.

"I'll get to the water bottles in a minute," she says, low and even, without turning around.

"No," Ryker snaps. "You'll get to them now. Or I'll tell Coach you're slacking."

"She doesn't give a damn about the job," Issac says, sneering. "She got what she wanted, found a way to weasel her way close to the team."

"Classic puck bunny move," Ryk adds. "Start some drama. Play the victim. End up in the locker room."

Her silence only fuels them.

"You hear me?" Ryker bumps her shoulder, harder this time. "Hello?"

The skate slips, sending sparks and a loud grinding sound through the air. I flinch, but my feet don't move. Sam juts back before that could turn bad.

"Whoops." Ryker smirks then slaps Issac's arm with the back of his hand. "Got to be more careful."

"What the hell is your problem?" Sam shoots up, standing her ground, toe to toe with her bully.

"You. Whore."

Before he could dot the period in his sentence, Sam responds, her tongue just as sharp. "That's funny, I don't see your mother anywhere."

Ryker lunges forward, his hands balled into fists.

"Watch yourself. That was my brother you injured," he seethes. It's low and full of hate, but I can still hear every word.

"So being an asshole does run in the family," she bites back.

"You bit—"

"All right, that's enough," I interject, stopping things from going too far. I refuse to look at her to give her any ideas that I stepped in for her.

I didn't. *Did I?*

They stay like that for a moment, both refusing to back away. It's obvious she doesn't want to be here any more than we want her to be, but it's also clear that she isn't about to take the disrespect without a fight. And as much as I hate to admit it, her resolve is as admirable as it is infuriating.

I want her to break, but only for me, and that realization pisses me off even more. What do I even care? I shouldn't. *I don't.*

"What's your angle, huh? Where the hell did you come from?"

At Ryker's question, Sam pauses for a second. It's not long, but enough for me to catch it. Then she stands, eyes landing on me, full of disdain. I see the moment she decides not to be quiet any longer.

With a blink, she faces them, sets the skates down, and says, "Ask Kane."

Heat creeps up my neck, and my fists curl instantly. Ryker and his friend look at me, but all I'm focused on is Sam. So this is how she wants to play it? Turning the attention from her to me, potentially stirring up things I've worked hard at keeping to myself.

She's going to pay for that. If she thought being in that bathroom with me was bad, she doesn't even know the half of it.

Sam walks away, throwing an evil glance over her shoulder at me before disappearing around the lockers. Ryker and Issac stare at me for a moment before finally waving me off, cursing under their breaths as they walk away. The moment they're out of sight, I stalk in the direction Sam was heading, finding her sorting through the uniforms.

Her actually being good at this fucking job wasn't on my bingo card. In fact, I was banking on her royally screwing up so that I wouldn't have to look at her. This might be a punishment for her, but finding a good equipment manager who knows our needs isn't as easy to come by as one might think. Being good means Coach might actually start to favor her, and then I'll never be rid of her.

Sam is lost in her task, her body jerking and swaying with each aggressive shake of a garment or every toss into the respective bins.

My eyes go to her ass in those leggings before I can stop them. *Damn.*

That thin, stretchy material clings to her like a second skin, molding around every curve with zero shame. Each movement she makes sends a subtle ripple through her thighs, the muscles flexing beneath skin I suspect is smooth.

She's a nuisance. A fucking distraction. And I hate that I even look at her like that, hate myself for noticing anything other than that.

I storm forward, wrap my fingers around her arm and force her to face me. I bring my face so close to hers I can smell the Skittles she had at lunch.

"You think that was cute? I told you, Sam. Don't fucking test me."

"What's the problem? Don't want your little teammates to know you used to be friends with the girl that ruined your chances?" Sam yanks away defiantly.

"You were never my friend. Just some pathetic little girl that followed me around."

"Then why do I bother you so much?"

"You don't. I just don't want to see your face."

"Could have fooled me. You've gone out of your way to *not* be bothered."

"Don't flatter yourself. *Everyone* hates you." I snatch a jersey from her hand.

That rattles her. Sam stumbles slightly at my words but manages to pull herself together in a mere second.

"Yeah, well, I'd rather be hated than to hate myself." Sam yanks the sweater from my grip, throws it into the bin, and leaves me to sit in her resentment.

And in this moment, I realize why I hate her so much...She sees right through me.

CHAPTER FOURTEEN

BRYDEN (MOUNTAIN)

Students spill into the lecture hall, seats creaking as bodies sink into them. The sound of gum chewing mixes with a sea of voices, different tones and octaves clashing like nails on a chalkboard. It's loud, obnoxiously so, even with earbuds in.

I sit in the back today, second to last row, to put some distance between me and everyone else. Practice has been hell these last few days as we get ready for tomorrow's game. It's the finals, and everything we worked for is riding on this. Every muscle and limb are sore.

I keep my hood up and AirPods in despite no sound coming through them. People tend to stay away when they think you're not paying attention.

The usuals are here. Christina and her crew, drawing attention to themselves in the most exaggerated of manners. Short skirts, makeshift vanities set up on their desks to touch up their makeup as if it isn't only eight o'clock in the morning.

Jackson hobbles in, his crutches hitting the carpet with soft thuds.

"Out of the way," he demands to the person walking in front of him. He doesn't wait, forcing the guy to the side.

Behind him is his posse of followers, a bunch of spineless

dudes who do any and everything to stay on his good side. His family owns practically half the city and he uses that to his advantage every chance he gets. About forty-five percent of land and businesses have the Kincaid name somewhere in the fine print. Centuries of inheriting land and businesses by questionable means. Old money makes for extremely spoiled brats, and he's the biggest one of all.

He's a great player, but no one likes him. Not really. He's tolerated at best because of his talent on the ice.

He settles in next to Christina, who immediately turns her attention to him. Their relationship's a weird one—never together but off-limits to anyone else. *Maybe if they'd stuck to their usual routine, Jackson's knee would still be intact.*

He rudely plops his foot up on the back of the chair in front of him, no consideration of the person in it. The moment he and the minions are seated, he starts his usual antics, loudly joking at someone else's expense.

My eyes shift sideways, landing on Sam as she quietly enters the room, her eyes straight ahead, ignoring the glances thrown her way. She's only been a student at SKU close to three weeks and is already the most hated person on campus.

Jackson spots her, too, tapping on a teammate's shoulder and nodding in her direction.

"Bitch," he says through a fake cough, loud enough for everyone to hear, his eyes glued to the back of her head.

While everyone turns, dead set on being nosy, Sam keeps her head high. *Good girl.* Don't feed into the madness.

She takes a seat and digs her notebook from her bag. Her mechanical pencil begins scribbling across the page in her spiral notebook, the pink grip worn from use. Her face is calm in that blank way people wear when they're trying not to fall apart.

From head to toe, I watch her, locking it all to memory. The way she makes a fist with her free hand as she concentrates on what she's writing, the nervous tap of her foot against the marbled floor, and the broken strap of her book bag that's been tied in a knot one too many times.

Jackson continues but she keeps her resolve.

He's a prick who loves the attention—good or bad, he eats it up. And when he gets ignored, he eggs it on until he ultimately gets what he wants. And what he wants right now is to make her pay for what she did to him.

Her silence only fuels him more. He leans back, dropping another comment I can't fully make out. But I catch enough to know that it's something unnecessarily vulgar. Laughter flutters from the seats around him, a couple of the guys from the team joining in.

I shift in my seat, my arms folded across my chest. I don't laugh, or join in. But I don't stop it either. I just don't see the need for the bullying. Yet his knee didn't break itself, so she's far from an innocent flower.

"Quiet down," Professor Wilson says, his voice rising above the classroom noise.

Slides light up on the smartboard screen—something about case studies and comparative analysis.

As class drags on, my eyes flick back to her. My mind keeps going back to her standing against my doorjamb while I stood there, practically naked; how her eyes surveyed every inch of my frame before finally meeting my stare. She looked on like she liked what she saw, and it's something I haven't been able to get out of my head since. I ordered her to leave, pretended that it bothered me, but deep, I'm not sure I really wanted her to.

Today Sam doesn't look as scared or as lost as she did when

she arrived; still out of place, but that wide-eyed fear isn't there. It's as if she's gotten used to it all, as if being on this campus has hardened her as it has many others. If anything, she looks tired. All the time. Like she never sleeps, or when she does, it's with one eye open.

Jackson mutters again. Louder this time. Something about knees and riding sticks. Professor Wilson doesn't hear, or at the very least pretends not to.

I grit my teeth, but still stay out of it.

She did blow up the season—threw our balance off. And now Jackson is dragging his busted leg around and blaming her for it. And despite the hostility, the torture pretty much everyone on the team has put her through—sweaty jockstraps, dirty towels, late nights of sharpening blades and taping sticks—she shows up. Every day. She does the grunt work and takes the hits. She doesn't whine, doesn't crack, doesn't fold.

Not yet.

The professor changes the slide, and my ears perk up at his words. "Group project."

Groans ripple through the room at the idea of having to partner up.

"This is a semester-long assignment, due week fourteen," Professor Wilson continues.

"You'll pair up in twos, and I've taken the liberty of assigning partnerships."

With a click of a button, names flash on the screen. I scan for mine. There it is. Bryden Montour.

Paired with: Samantha Collins.

I blink, my eyes landing on her. I watch as she notices the assignment and turns. We make eye contact, and for a brief moment, everything is a blur but the two of us. There's an energy there, in our gaze, a current drawing us closer. We stare at each other for a moment, and I can't help but really take her in. Brown skin that glistens, curly hair like a halo, and eyes that are soft despite this hard world.

There's no reaction from her, and I keep my face blank. It could be worse. Could've been assigned to work with Jackson, or one of the puck chasers who doesn't know the blue line from a crease.

"It's worth half your final grade, so make it count," Professor Wilson adds. "Class dismissed."

Laptops close, a crescendo of soft clicks. People scatter, desperate to reach the exit, but I'm slower to move. I let them rush out, opting not to fight with the crowd. She moves, too, packing her stuff with that same careful energy.

"Hey." The voice is soft and delicate.

I turn to find Sam clutching her notebook like a shield.

"Where do you want to meet for the project?"

I stare a second longer than I should.

"I'll text you."

"Don't you need my number?"

"Already got it from Coach."

Her brows pinch then relax. She nods once. "Mm. O-okay."

She turns and walks the other way. I stand there a moment more, watching her disappear into the hall—still trying to understand why she pulls at my focus.

I can't help but follow slowly behind her, a far enough distance that she doesn't notice my presence. When her phone suddenly rings, she quickly clutches it to her ear, gripping it tightly like it's a weapon.

I hear her answer hurriedly. She's not yelling, but I'm just getting close enough to make out the words. Her voice is shaky and sharp around the edges.

"I want to talk to my brother."

There's a pause; whoever's on the other end must have said something she doesn't like because she halts. Shoulders hiked around her ears, tension ripping through her posture.

"No. Listen, please. J-just let me speak to him."

There's a longer pause, and she's pacing again.

"I promised him...no, Gary...don't—" She turns sharply, hoodie swaying with the motion. "Hello. Hello."

She pulls the phone away, glaring at it, checking the signal as if she hopes it's maybe just a poor connection. But I don't have to be on the line to know whoever that was ended the call.

"Hello," she rasps, the word falling apart halfway out of her mouth. Her shoulders slump, and she throws her head back, defeated...maybe even broken.

A part of me wants to comfort her, encourage her to keep that pretty head held high. And that's when it hits me: she's the distraction I'm failing to avoid. And this project might just make that even harder to do.

CHAPTER FIFTEEN

SAM

"Move," Ryker barks as he moves past me, pushing my shoulder along the way.

No surprise there.

It wouldn't be my life if a day went by without a shove here or a carefully crafted insult there. To expect anything else from him, or anyone else for that matter, would be foolish.

Today, though, it feels different. The tension is hitting before I make it through the door. It's in the way the music blares louder than usual, in how the lockers slam a little harder, how no one notices me step into the room with my crate of clean towels.

Finals is tomorrow. The moment that determines whether or not they're going all the way. Many of them have been here before since the team *has* gone to nationals four years in a row. But, while the rookies have plenty of time to showcase themselves to pro scouts, the seniors—Kane, Mountain, Alex, and a handful of others—know this is their last shot.

So it's more than a game for them.

I set the crate down, trying my damnedest not to breathe too deeply. Hell, even the air feels like it's holding its breath. But, just my luck, a stick falls over behind me, clattering against the floor. All eyes are on me in an instant.

"If we lose tomorrow, it's going to be her fucking fault," a rookie says.

"She's bad luck," another follows.

"Why don't you stop breathing around our equipment before one of us ends up benched like Jackson," a third joins in.

Well, that didn't last long now, did it?

They stand from in front of their stalls and slowly make their way toward me.

"Hey," a sharp voice cuts through the tension.

They turn to find the owner of the voice, and I follow their gaze, craning my neck to look around their large frames. Damn hockey players. Tall and massively built. Not all of them, but these three have surely been drinking GMO-filled milk since infancy.

Alex stands on the other side of the locker room, pulling his jersey over his head and yanking it into place.

"I get it. She's a bitch and we hate her, but cut it out," he orders in some half-assed attempt at keeping up his end of the bargain.

I roll my eyes. *Seriously? This jerk. What kind of defense is that?*

"We have more important shit to focus on." Alex glares around at his teammates, looking them each in the eye. "Like kicking Baymont's ass."

The room quiets as they give him their undivided attention.

"I get it. We're down a man. Jackson was . . . a good player. But so is everyone else, and we can bring this home. But not if we've got our heads up our asses."

I stare on, actually shocked. Maybe there is more to Alex Williamsburg than just hockey, obnoxious charm, and sexual prowess.

Not that I care.

But I've heard the stories. The girls talk about him like he invented orgasms. They act like he's God's gift to earth, and he eats up every second of it.

I don't get the hype. I mean...sure. He's hot. Annoyingly hot with a frame that's impossible not to notice. Broad shoulders, insanely defined arms with veins cutting down his forearms like they've got somewhere to be. The type of body that makes walls seem optional. Like he could hold you there with one hand and not break a sweat.

Hair that always looks like someone just tugged on it—just messy enough to look intentional. That stupid perfect jaw. And then his voice—smug in the worst way.

He's the kind of hot that gets girls in trouble. But I'm not one of them. I won't fall for it...I know better. He's just another spoiled, overhyped, emotionally constipated jock.

"Do you want to win?" He glances around, reaching out to slap a closed fist against Kane's chest.

Kane makes eye contact with me, his jaw set in that scowl he seems to reserve only for me. Then I look at Bryden. He doesn't notice me, too busy suiting up.

He's the only one that doesn't look at me as if he hates me, but the blankness in his eyes isn't much better. If anything, it feels worse. At least with the others, I don't have to guess at how they feel about me. Bryden...not so much.

"Huh?" Alex continues. "Do you want to win? Do you want to go to nationals?"

"Yes," they say in unison, their voices echoing through me.

It's chilling to watch. One moment they're stiff and doubtful, and just like that Alex manages to restore what little faith they had.

"Then man up, suit up, and hit the fucking ice."

Lockers slam as they quickly finish putting on their uniforms, then head to practice. One by one they stroll through the doors and down the tunnel. Slowly the volume diminishes and for a second, all I hear is the buzz from the overhead lights.

Finally, Alex glances up, and our eyes lock. There's something behind his expression—exhaustion, maybe. When he lets out a long breath, I realize what it is. It's the pressure. He's put on a front to hype up his team, to get them out of their heads, but he's feeling it, too.

"Are you going to tape up my sticks or keep staring all night?"

And the asshole returns.

My mouth presses into a line, and I fight the urge to roll my eyes again.

"Just a little shocked that your brain could form a full sentence let alone give a pep rally."

His lip twitches. It's almost a smirk—real, not fake. Almost something human.

Without another word, Alex takes off, disappearing into the tunnel behind the rest of the team.

I shake my head and put my headphones on while I walk over to the equipment room. Digging my phone out of my back pocket, I put on some music and flop down on the bench.

Tonight's priority is taping off all the sticks, including backups, and making sure the uniforms are clean and ready to go. Last night, I had to sharpen twenty-six pairs of skates, each blade a different cut.

I work fast on Alex's sticks, wrapping tape around the blades and shaft with a practiced precision.

Stretch. Press. Tear. Repeat.

I run my fingers over the fresh tape, inspecting my work before moving on to his backups. He likes his grip tight, almost suffocating. God, I hate that I know that. Hate that I cared enough to memorize their preferences.

Kane's tape job is all bark and no finesse—barely staggered grip lines and half a roll at the blade. He likes the handle thick, tape bunched where his fingers rests. He says it "feels mean."
Whatever the hell that means.

Mountain is different from them all, barely even taping his stick blade at all. Just a single strip of friction tape down the middle is how he likes it. He swears that it gives him a better feel, but I wouldn't know.

When I finish, I move on to gear check and setup. My brain works on autopilot, simmering in silent resentment. If anything is out of place, I catch it before they even notice. The last thing I want is to give them something to come at me for.

I hate this job, but I'm not expelled, which means I still have a chance at making something with this life and getting custody of my brother.

So I replace a torn glove here, a twisted chin strap there. Switch out worn laces, swap broken buckles, and cut away any snapped Velcro like my life depends on it. Because in some sick, twisted way, it does.

Next, I set out sock tape—white, black, and clear—each one unboxed and dropped at the edge of their stalls like they magically appeared. As I move on to hanging towels, my music is drowned out by the cacophony of voices coming down the tunnel.

Practice must be over.

I remove my headphones, hook them around my neck, and check my phone for the time.

It's been nearly two hours already?

The team pours in, more enthusiastic than when they went out of there. The adrenaline coursing through them is loud and alive as they talk loudly to one another, banging against cold metal.

I stop what I'm doing and step out of the locker room to give them the space to undress and shower, already prepared to be here longer than I need to be. Every practice, they take their sweet time, while I stand in this tunnel. I can't leave until all players are off the ice and out of the locker room.

The sound of the puck scraping over the ice catches my attention. Curiosity strikes and I find myself inching slowly toward the sound. The right side of the ice comes into view first; then a puck goes barreling into the net at lighting speed. A second later, so does another, each followed by an aggressive grunt.

I reach the end of the tunnel just as Alex skates across the ice, lost in a world of his own.

He doesn't stop. Another slap of the puck. Another sharp grunt. Doesn't breathe between shots, just lines them up and lets loose like something in his chest might detonate if he doesn't.

Not a single ounce of the Alex Williamsburg I've grown to hate is on that ice right now. Not the smug grin or lazy walk. Not the flirtatious banter or the too-expensive loafers.

This isn't just the guy the girls drool over. He's something else entirely.

His jersey clings to his back, drenched. The stick cracks, but he barely blinks. This isn't just practice; it's more like he's punishing himself.

Whatever he's going through, whatever he's trying to outrun, it isn't my business. So I step back before he sees me. I have uniforms to wash, towels to fold, bottles to refill, and a name to keep clean.

The locker room is empty when I reenter, so quiet you could hear a pin drop. Putting my headphones back on, I shove my phone into my back pocket and proceed to get back to work. There's no telling how long Alex is going to be on the ice tonight, so I might as well make the most of this time.

As I collect the newly discarded uniforms from the floor in front of each stall, my face scrunches up with each garment I have to touch. I'll never get used to how badly hockey equipment stinks, and today the stench is worse.

I shake my head, disgusted by the sweat-drenched jerseys.

"Eww," I mutter to no one.

Or so I thought.

When I turn the corner to enter the laundry area, I run smack-dab into a wall of muscle. The bin tips over, and jerseys spill out.

"Watch where the hell you're walking," Ryker snarls, his voice louder than my music.

I straighten fast, snatching the headphones off, and try to step around him. "Sorry. I didn't know anyone was still in here."

But Ryker doesn't let me. Instead, he steps in front of me, his eyes dark and menacing. A lump forms in my throat, and I clench my fist, prepared to defend myself.

"Alex stood up for you tonight, but don't think this means you're safe. You'd better watch your back," he threatens.

I open my mouth to dish out a snarky comment of my own, but nothing comes out. Being alone with him, up close and personal, triggers me. It takes me back to all the times I've had to shield myself from Gary's drunken wrath.

But Ryker doesn't touch me. He steps around me, his shoulder bumping into mine so hard that my headphones hit the floor. It's not until I hear the double doors swing closed that I finally let out the breath I've been holding.

CHAPTER SIXTEEN

SAM

I hate him. Hate this team. Hate Jackson for putting me here. Hate myself for going to that party.

I squeeze my eyes shut, taking in one deep inhale after the other to settle my nerves. With a shaky hand, I pick up the dirty clothes and carry them to the washing machine, leaving a trail of the items that slip from my grasp. Frantically, I shove the uniforms into the machine, my hands still trembling.

I close my eyes once more and just breathe. In through the nose. Out through the mouth.

Pushing it all to the back of my mind, I pour in the detergent and begin the wash cycle. While the clothes wash, I grab an empty bucket to carry that and bleach over to the sink to make the sanitizer solution.

I turn on the sink, testing the temperature until it's to my liking before setting the bucket inside to fill with water and bleach.

As the water runs, I quickly snatch my headphones up from the floor, where they landed after Ryker pushed me. I take them to the utility closet they gave me for breaks. There's barely space for a chair and my duffel. No windows. Just a file cabinet no one uses and floor-to-ceiling metal racks of extra equipment.

After returning to the sink, I reach in to pull out the bucket, grunting at how heavy it is. As I finally get the bucket to the brim of the sink and turn, it gets caught on the edge. Water splashes the front of my clothes and spills all over the floor, the strong scent of bleach singeing my nostrils.

"Shit."

I drop the bucket, and it clinks against the sink. I peel the fabric away from my chest, muttering curses while trying not to cry from frustration.

I sprint back to the closet, pulling out the shirt I wore here from my duffel. I reach over and tap the door closed, then pull the bleach-drenched shirt over my head and let it drop to the floor at my feet.

My eyes drop to my wet bra, and I groan before unhooking it from the front. My skin is flushed, and my nipples pebble the moment the air hits them.

It's late, and everyone should be in bed by now. No one is going to notice that I'm braless. The walk back to my dorm isn't that far.

A low, guttural groan pierces through the air. The door creaks, and I freeze, snapping my gaze forward.

Alex.

He stands in the doorway, his chest rising and falling in rapid succession. Hastily, I cover myself, using my forearms as a shield. His jersey clings to his torso, soaked. His eyes move slowly.

Then lower.

Until they catch on the curve of my breast, my very naked breast. The soft skin of my stomach. The tattoo inked across my ribs.

Neither of us speak. We only stare at each other, me with wide eyes and him...he stares like he hates me. Eyes hooded and seemingly darker than usual, lips slightly parted. He wets them, and I can't help but follow the trail of his tongue.

Alex steps in and closes the door behind him. I stumble backward over my duffel to keep the distance between us. It's futile in a space this small, even more so when heavy-duty shelves are taking up most of the footage.

I can hear his ragged breathing. It hits loud, too loud. Or maybe it just feels that way because every sense in my body is suddenly hypersensitive. I smell his scent—sweat and expensive cologne—feel him even though he hasn't touched me. Notice the vein that protrudes along his neck toward his jawline.

Then he reaches out to touch my wrist. I slap his hand away, momentarily exposing myself in the process. He tries again, and this time he succeeds. Alex grips both wrists, pinning them high above my head with my back against the shelves.

He's taller, just over six feet, but with him this close, this imposing, he feels bigger. His breath is hot, but minty, and it causes my lashes to flutter. A lump lodges in my throat, and I swallow it down.

He leans in, his mouth dangerously close to mine. I squirm to get out of his grasp, my breasts swaying and brushing against the wet knitted material of his top.

"Mmm," he moans. "You think you can just show up at my school, mess up everything, exist here like nothing matters?"

His voice is low.

I grunt, trying again to wiggle from his hold. I lift my knee to shove him, but he catches it. One hand grabs the back of my thigh, hitching my leg around his hip. He presses into me, the thick bulge forming in his pants unavoidable.

I squirm to break free, but not enough. I never permitted him to touch me like this, but I also don't say stop.

I should.

I need to.

But I *don't*.

"You make me fucking insane."

I whimper at that, my own breathing growing increasingly out of control.

"You get under my skin, and it kills me." He leans back, his eyes roaming over me as he licks his lips again. Suddenly, the pad of his thumb is on my exposed nipple, strumming it slowly. My back buckles from the contact, and a gasp slips past my lips. But it's when he leans down and suckles it into his mouth that I fall apart.

I bite back the moan, not wanting him to see how much he's affecting me. Heat slicks across my skin, my pussy throbbing like it's desperate to be touched.

He kneads my breast before flicking his tongue over my swollen bud. The sensation alone has me writhing against him. Alex switches his focus to the other breast, using the free hand to show it the same amount of attention.

His dick is hard against my stomach despite the thick uniform pants and my jeans. I find myself wanting to touch, wanting to know if the rumors are true.

When he pulls back and our eyes meet, there's something there. Something wicked and greedy.

"Tell me you don't want me to touch you."

I don't answer, I can't. I don't know why I don't stop him, why I don't use my words. He's bound my hands, locked me in place with his body, but my mouth is free. All it would take is for me to do just that. To tell him to get his filthy hands off of me.

It's that simple. Only the words never come.

Maybe it's because of the way he's looking at me, something in his gaze telling me that he needs this. Maybe I don't stop him because, deep down, I need this, too.

I need to bury myself in something that feels good to take the edge off, even when I know it's a mistake, even when I'm sure to regret it in the morning. Even though he'll have won, and I'll be just another notch on his belt.

His finger slips down my stomach until he reaches my waist. Without unbuckling my jeans, Alex dips his hand past the waistband. It's effortless how quickly he finds my clit. He strokes me through the thin material of my underwear, gently running the tips of his fingers over my bud.

He lets out a slow breath. "You're soaking these panties, Sunshine."

He moves lower, stroking my slit, the moving pressure edging me closer and closer to exploding. And when he roughly pushes my panties to the side and slips a finger inside my pussy, my head tips back with a gasp I can't swallow.

His mouth is on me, brushing my jaw, then my throat, and he moves his fingers in and out of me.

"So fucking wet. I bet your pussy would feel real good wrapped around my cock."

A strangled whimper is all I get out.

"You like this?" His voice drops lower. "Like me touching you even though you hate me."

Another moan slips out before I can stop it.

"Maybe I should ruin you," he whispers against my neck. "Fuck you against this rack until you're crying. Until you forget your name."

My body arches. I do hate him. I want to claw him open, make him pay for all the petty bullying. Take out my frustrations on him as he claims to want to do to me. Curse him for all the shit they've put me through.

But then he adds a second finger and hooks them until he finds my spot.

"Oh, fuck," I groan. "I hate you."

"Say it louder while you drip all over my hand." His mouth grazes my ear, breath hot and ragged. His fingers curl deeper, faster, knuckle grazing bone. "Do you want me to fuck you into submission, to ruin you, to break you in half until you're begging me to stop?"

"Yes!" I cry out. And I come, hard and violently, my body and breath fighting to find a rhythm. Alex doesn't stop. He keeps fingering me like it's the only thing he wants. My walls convulse, clenching around his hand in quick bursts. It's not until my breath settles and my muscles relax that he pulls his hand from my pants.

Alex steps back, fingers slick, breath ragged. Then he sucks the two middle fingers into his mouth, savoring my juices.

"Fucking sweet."

He releases my other hand, picks up my dry shirt from on top of the duffel bag, and signals for me to hold up my arms. I do as he wants, letting him put the shirt on my body. Alex puts more space between us; then he turns and leaves without a goodbye.

Not that I need one.

I stand there, my clothes too sensitive against my skin. In the distance, the shower sputters on. Alex continues with his routine, not a care in the world for what we just did... what he just did.

And me?

I'm left aroused, furious, and completely wrecked.

CHAPTER SEVENTEEN

BRYDEN (MOUNTAIN)

Before my boots even hit the pavement, I see my mother. Her arms are folded, braids perfectly tucked under her scarf, waiting with a permanent smile that nothing in this world has been able to erase.

It's my favorite thing about her. Always happy, always kind. When the planet is actively burning down around us, she's there with a hug, wisdom, and holding my favorite treat, frybread with zhiiwaagamizigan.

My father is with her, standing at her side with a hand at the small of her back. Forever the protector, always at her side, silently observing. They're so opposite, almost like night and day, but they fit so perfectly. Mom is loud and fun-loving while Dad is calm and quiet. I guess I can thank him for my *sunny* disposition.

Kai, my younger brother, notices me first, points in my direction, and speaks at a volume I can't hear from here. My mother's eyes find mine, and that smile of hers widens. They're excited, and I'm happy they're here. Knowing that my family will be in the stands keeps me grounded, keeps me focused.

"Bryden, my son," Mom calls.

She holds her arms out to me, wrapping me into a hug only

a mother could give. It's comforting, the familiarity of her perfume, the warmth in her embrace. I've missed this. The season has been stressful, the pressure mounting. But the payoff is near; all the hard work and late hours will have meant something once we win finals, then nationals—and next, get drafted.

"You look tired," she says when we break apart and runs her hands over my arms like she's checking me for injuries.

"Son." My father takes my hand firmly before pulling me into a hug.

We're similar builds, both standing a solid nine inches taller than my mother's five-foot-five-inch frame. His scowl matches mine, or so I've been told. Same features, same mannerisms.

"Dad," I say, squeezing him tight, not realizing until this very moment just how much I've needed my people.

I'm at the top of my class and my parents see to it that I don't want for anything. But even with those fortunes, I still miss being around them, miss having someone close to lean on.

I break our embrace and throw my arm around Kai to give him a noogie.

"Ouch, jerk. Stop it."

I let him go and he playfully throws up his hands. I lean forward, throwing a weak jab then effortlessly block his punch. I laugh and stand up straight, blocking another one of his hits. Then he reaches into the van and hands me a large Tupperware container.

"What's this?" I take it from him.

"Frybread with zhiiwaagamizigan," he says enthusiastically.

"Yesss," I say in a near groan, immediately cracking open the top and breaking off a piece of the frybread. I pop it into my mouth, moaning at how good it is.

"Don't let Kane eat them all," Kai orders.

We chuckle as I unzip my duffel and put the treats inside.

"Grandma made extra just for them," Mom adds.

The front window rolls down, a hand sticking out, waving me over. Grandma's there, wrapped in three shawls, and sipping tea from the dented green thermos she's had since I was a kid.

She smiles at me, her face more wrinkled than the last time I saw her, but she's beautiful. Her silver hair is hidden beneath her shawls. She raises a shaky hand, silently calling me closer. It's a weak gesture, her limbs trembling just a little.

Leaning down, I bring my face to her palm, my eyes shutting the moment she cups my face, giving my cheeks a pat.

"Grandmother."

"I've missed you, little one," she says, her tone full of warmth.

My chest swells, warmth spreading like wildflowers. It means a lot that she's here—so much honor, so much history wrapped up in her ailing body. So if she wants to call me by a pet name she's called me for as long as I can remember, so be it. Never mind the fact that I'm a six-foot, two-hundred-pound goalie who can take a hit like I'm made of steel. To Grandmother, I'll always be her little one.

I palm her hands, nuzzling my face against hers. "Thank you for being here."

She pats my face. "I wouldn't miss it. Your grandfather would be so proud of you."

I feel my mother at my side, her hand on my back.

"How are you sleeping?"

I avoid looking her in the eye. "Fine."

It's a lie. Truth is, I haven't been able to sleep in days. Maybe it's the pressure of it all; tonight, if we win, we're going to nationals. And before we know it, college will be over. If we're lucky, tonight's match puts us closer to the draft and the pro league.

She knows I'm lying, brows arched, an invisible question mark above her head. Thankfully, she doesn't push. Instead she pulls my letterman jacket closed then pats my heart.

Then my eyes drift past her across the courtyard. It's Sam, walking to the entrance, her broken backpack strap—and curvy build—an easy identifier. She's on her phone, obviously arguing with someone on the other end from what I can see.

I wonder if it's the same person from the phone call I witnessed before.

"Bryden?" Mom's voice snaps me out of my daze.

My gaze snaps back. "Yes. Sorry. What were you saying?"

"I asked if you have time this morning. Have breakfast with us."

"Can't. Meeting a class partner inside."

Mom squints at me, then nods. "Okay. We'll head to the hotel and check in. See you at the rink later."

"See you then."

We hug once more, and I savor the comfort. My dad steps closer, tapping me on the shoulder before pulling me into an embrace as well.

"Play smart tonight. Don't let anything get in your head."

"I won't."

I move to the passenger window, lean in, and kiss Grandma's cheek. She presses her thumb to mine in blessing.

"Good luck," she murmurs, then lets me go.

I step away, tapping the top of the car in silent thanks. Then I shift to reach for Kai, playfully yanking him into a hug while scuffing his hair. He laughs through a groan, batting me away yet leaning into it all the same. He wears his short, like our father, but everything else—the eyes, the jawline, the way his smile kicks up on one side—is like looking in a mirror. Ten years apart, but nearly identical. Grandma calls us niizhoopizowag—*two spirits tied together.* We're not just brothers; we're connected way deeper than that.

I glance back at my mother.

"Love you," she says.

"Gizaagi'in." *I love you.*

Dad gets into the driver's seat, Mom slides in behind him while Kai buckles in next to her. They pull off, slow and steady down the road. I watch for a beat then spin on my heel toward the school.

Sam's gone now.

I suck in a breath and move forward. It's early on a Saturday morning, so the campus is mostly empty. Only a few other students walk the grounds. As I cross paths with some of them, I keep my eyes ahead of me.

Once inside the building, I find Sam. She's just outside the library, sitting on a bench. Her hood is up, knees drawn to her chest, headset over her ears.

She doesn't seem to notice me until I'm close, standing only inches in front of her. Sam startles, wiping her face too fast.

I pretend not to notice. Pretend not to see that she's hurting. Instead, giving her space to hold on to whatever dignity she's fighting to keep.

"Ready?" I ask, making a mental note of the stiffness in the way she hugs her knees tighter.

She nods, short and automatic, more like muscle memory than anything else. Shoulders squared, her lashes flutter to keep away the tears, breaths long and audible.

I glance around, stepping closer to shield her from someone passing us by. They don't pay us any attention and yank open the library's door and step inside.

Shifting my bag on my shoulder, I peer down the hall then

back at her. Something about leaving her like this feels wrong. So I lower myself onto the bench beside her.

I unzip my bag, the sound bouncing between us. Then I remove the Tupperware container and pop the lid. Without words, I hold it in front of her, gently nudging her. Sam's eyes dart to mine, and I tip my head toward the dessert.

"What's this?" She stares at it, her brows knitted slightly.

"Try it," I encourage while opening the condiment cup. "It's frybread with zhiiwaagamizigan."

Her brows furrow as she stares at me as if she hasn't the slightest idea of what I've said. I chuckle inwardly. I don't speak my native tongue on campus normally, and when I do, I always get that look.

"It's frybread. Dip it in the maple syrup." Another nudge.

She tears off a piece and does as instructed. "You know, this is the most you've ever said to me."

I drop my chin. "Talking's not really my thing."

She huffs. "You don't say."

She inspects the dessert before popping it into her mouth. I watch her chew, somewhat excited to share a piece of my culture with someone other than Alex and Kane.

She moans almost as if she forgot where we are. It's low and throaty and definitely shooting to places it shouldn't.

Heat crawls up my nape. Clearing my throat, I look away, pretending to fix the lid on the syrup cup. Acting as if the sounds coming from her doesn't knock something loose inside me.

I shift my weight, restless, fighting the reaction the way I've learned to fight every other distraction.

"Good, huh?" I mutter, keeping my voice even,

Sam hums and nods. "Is this your way of trying to cheer me up?"

My lips press together, and I left out a breath. "Is it working?"

Sam smiles. "Thanks."

I nod. "You looked like you were about to disappear. Figured I'd keep you tethered a minute."

Her features soften, and I can tell no one's really given her that space before. The question comes before I realize that I'm speaking.

"Are you okay?"

She shakes her head. "Now would be a good time for you to resume the no talking thing."

Fair enough.

But, I can't let it go. She might not want to voice the problem or bring life to the pain she's feeling. Because that's what this is: pain. Something so bone deep that it's eating her alive.

I lift to retrieve my phone from my back pocket. Quietly, I scroll through it until I find her number. I type out a message and hit send.

> **Bryden:** Then don't talk. Type it out. Whatever you say goes into the vault and I'll delete it like it never happened.

Her phone buzzes against the bench, and she frowns as she picks it up. I watch as she recognizes my name on the screen. She peers at me, that brow now permanently pinched.

She stares at the phone, as if she's contemplating if she should respond. Or maybe she's contemplating whether she can trust me.

A deep breath escapes her, and I see the tension start to wane, if only a little. Sam types back, and instead of reading over her shoulder, I watch others enter the library. Then my phone vibrates.

Collins: It's my brother. I miss him and promised we'd talk every week, but my stepdad is a dick.

I read the message, letting it sit between us for a beat.

Bryden: Not letting you talk to him.

Collins: You guessed it. The fucker just likes to make my life hell.

Bryden: Tell me about him.

She snaps her gaze to me then back to her phone.

Collins: He's an asshole.

That brings a crooked smile to my lips.

Bryden: I mean your brother.

She hesitates.

Bryden: Mine's name is Kai. He's twelve and swears he can beat me in an arm-wrestling match. He and my parents just left. You can thank them for the treats.

She softens.

Collins: Desmond. He's the best part of my life.

Bryden: I get that.

Bryden: What about your mom? Can't she let you talk to Desmond?

All the color drains from her face, and her fingers tighten around the phone. I sense that I struck a nerve, tapped into that forbidden zone.

Bryden: Hey. Forget I asked.

Collins: She's dead.

We send simultaneously.
Sam sucks in a breath, that cold, defensive demeanor returning. She hops up, snatching her backpack up with her. Regret washes over me, and I pinch my lips.
"Ready," she huffs out.
I stand and follow her into the study hall. It smells like worn paper. It's quiet as expected, but it feels heavier than it does otherwise. Like there's a weight in the air.
We find a spot in the back near the windows. Sam immediately starts talking through the assignment. It's interesting how quickly she buries her emotions.
"I was thinking we could test kinetic and potential energy." She pulls out her notebook and textbook, turning through the pages until she finds what she's looking for.
"I'm listening."
"Something small-scale. A marble track or roller coaster model," she says while tracing invisible lines with her fingers on the table. Her voice is low, but softer, not as shattered as before. "We could measure how changes in height affect velocity. Calculate energy conservation, friction losses, stuff like that."

I like watching her think. It's attractive seeing her brain at work. The idea is solid, much better than what I conjured up. Not wanting to embarrass myself by sharing my mediocre plan, I kick my bag to the side and lean in.

"Yeah," I say finally. "We could do different surfaces. Test friction. Wood, plastic, metal."

She brightens a little. It's the type of smile that sneaks out before she can stop it.

We settle into a rhythm, working out the details. Before we know it, it's been well over an hour, but it hasn't felt nearly that long. It was comfortable and easy. Sam checks her phone.

"Shit. I'm sorry to cut this short. I need to catch the bus. Can we meet in a couple of days after the game to finish fleshing this out?"

"That works."

Sam gives me a tight smile. "Good. See you at the game?"

I nod.

She hesitates for a moment, her eyes scanning mine as if she's searching for words. But then she must change her mind because she walks away without a word.

I gather my duffel and stand to leave as well when my phone buzzes on the table. I pick it up, reading the message on the screen.

Collins: Thanks.

Collins: For not making earlier a thing.

My attention yanks to the exit just as the doors swing shut behind her. I stand there, staring at the text. Trying to figure out what to say next.

You're welcome?

No, that doesn't feel right when, frankly, there's nothing for her to thank me for. I didn't save the day or do anything grand. I just gave her space and didn't let her sit in it alone.

Why? I haven't the slightest clue. There's something about her, and whatever it is hasn't let go.

With one final exhale, I type away at the keys and hit send.

Bryden: Anytime.

CHAPTER EIGHTEEN

EVEREST (KANE)

A crash echoes through the classroom as someone knocks Sam's books off her desk and into the aisle on their way out. I'd been just about to make my own exit at the end of class when the sound stopped me.

Sam jumps to her feet, fists balled up tight, spine snapped straight, and a fire blooming in her eyes.

Fuck. I recognize that look on her face.

Before I know it, I wedge myself between Sam and the guy, my shoulder slamming into his chest. Not hard enough to drop him, but enough to warn him.

"Back off," I demand.

Glaring at him, I silently hope he gives me a reason to lose it. But he doesn't, and walks away, mumbling something under his breath.

I don't know why I do it, but I crouch to scoop up the mess of papers and textbooks. It's certainly not because I like her, or care, for that matter.

When she reaches for them, our gazes lock. There's a softness in her eyes for once, gratitude brimming in her irises. To make sure she doesn't get the wrong impression, doesn't think this means I've forgotten what she's done, I move my hand out of reach, letting them fall to her desk with a loud slap.

Her gasp cuts through the silence, but I don't care. I step around her, our bodies brushing ever so slightly. A jolt runs through me at that brief contact, all that pent-up frustration rushing to my dick.

Sam's glaring at me in disbelief as I adjust the front of my jeans and walk out of the door. My head's a mess, my hands twitch, and all I want to do is destroy something.

Maybe destroy her.

While the other girls preen for my attention, Sam couldn't care less. While the other girls would kill for a chance to be touched by me, Sam would break my fingers to keep me from touching her. And it's not like we don't know she's capable of doing just that.

She's the only one who isn't fake when she looks at me. I know exactly what I'm getting with her. She's real, unlike my facade at school and unlike everyone else who worships me because of my chance at going pro.

She hates me, plain and simple.

And, honestly, it's best that way.

Every time I sit in this chair, the air around me feels poisonous. Tainted with deep-seated, unadulterated hate. The kind that eats at you, haunts you until all that's left is hate of your own. It festers, picking at wounds—old, new, and those formed in between.

You've tried to heal them, patch up the damage, keep them from consuming you. But this hatred is too strong to bend, too rooted to erase. And what's left is the shell of a person who's fighting demons only they can see. That's been my life, and with each passing day, I grow closer to acceptance.

So I do what I always do, and that's hold my head up and keep it moving.

I let out a breath, checking the clock on the wall, mentally counting down the seconds. The chair squeaks when I shift, the leather groaning as if it despises me here just as much as he does.

He's made me wait more than ten minutes now, which is ironic considering he's the one always going on about not wasting *his* time. I guess that only applies to him. At this point, I'm convinced he does it on purpose. Simply because he can, because without him, my mother doesn't get the care she needs, bills don't get paid, and my life would look much different than it does now.

My eyes fall to the paper in my lap. It's the reason I'm here. The edges are torn from where I tugged at the corners in a mindless attempt to occupy my thoughts. It's crazy how one page that's been clutched and folded too many times to count holds so much weight. It's a violent reminder, a leash made of ink.

I suck in a breath, my shoulders sore with tension and not just because of this meeting. Everything is riding on tonight. And when we win, I'll be one step closer to putting this life behind me. I'm going pro, and this bastard won't ever have to worry about me or my mother again.

But until then, this is what I've succumbed to—begging for support from someone who would rather see me burn. I stare at the wall, my sight narrowing on the spot above the empty chair behind the large desk. Multiple degrees stare back at me, a blurred shrine to the man whose name means more to him than his blood.

None of them has my last name on them.

No, he couldn't be bothered to give me his, to include me. Not that it really mattered until now. Before my mother's mental health got worse, it never dawned on me that I didn't have a connection to my father. All my friends had theirs, and some of those relationships weren't ones to envy. And Mom made sure I didn't want for a thing, made sure his absences were unnoticeable and unfelt. She did it all.

Every milestone, every scrape and fall, school crushes and wins, she was the one who held it all together. But then, she couldn't, and we started spending more time in a mental health facility.

That's where I met Sam. We were young, barely at the age of puberty, and vulnerable beyond what we could comprehend at that time. I'd had more experience in this department than her, so when I saw her in that waiting room, tears pouring down her face, scared out of her mind, I comforted her. I kept her close, protected her, helped to explain things that her dick of a stepfather never bothered to.

And then in the blink of an eye, she was gone. Never to be seen or heard from again. I'd hoped I would; every time I checked my mom in, I secretly scanned the faces in the waiting room, wanting for one of them to be hers.

She'd left and never came back. Leaving me to wonder if her life turned out better than it had been. I was alone, but at least I had hockey and my boys. They became my family. Mom eventually got better, and things slowly returned to normal. It was great, but then something snapped, and we were right back where we started. But this time, my mother seemed to be doing much worse, and all the responsibilities fell on me. Administering her meds, making meals.

One day, while I was looking through her files for banking information, I stumbled across more than I bargained for. Documents, receipts, all evidence that showed our lives had been funded in secret, years of hush money disguised as support. As long as it never got out that I was his son, we would be set for life. That day, my world changed. I learned the truth, and every day since then, I regret ever dreaming he would accept me.

The door clicks open behind me, and my back stiffens, my fingers curling around the medical bill. His footfalls hit the carpet, slow and heavy, like he owns every inch of the air I breathe. My father comes into view—tall, his broad shoulders hiked around his ears, his light brown eyes almost a mirror to my own. They bore into me, anger etched in them. It's the only thing we have in common.

He slides the chair out and drops into it. No words. No verbal acknowledgment. Just that glare, brows cocked like my presence only annoys him.

Typical.

The clock ticks louder now, or maybe it's the blood pounding against my eardrums. I clear my throat, swallowing the lump that's formed there.

"What do you want?" is all he says. *No, hello, it's good to see you, son.*

"I've been waiting over ten minutes." I make fists against my thighs, trying to keep my nerves calm.

Papers shuffle across the desk, the scraping sound ringing louder than it is. "And your point?"

My jaw clenches. "You demand that no one waste your time. You can at the very least do the same."

I expect him to offer a rebuttal, but he doesn't.

I lean forward, tossing the crumpled-up piece of paper in front of him. And as always, he sits there uninterested.

"That's a letter from the facility. The bill is past due. And my deposit wasn't in the account this morning."

Silence answers back, and it's heavy enough to crush a man. The back of my neck burns, shame and rage racing through me. I grip the chair arms to still my temper.

"You know I can't pay without your help." The words barely make it out. I hate relying on him.

He hums, low and indifferent. "You mean without you begging."

"Begging?" I sit up, my nostrils flared. "Last I checked, you don't want your precious family to find out about your twenty-two-year-old secret."

"Watch yourself, Everest. You and your mother would be out on your asses without me." He takes his eyes off me, but his voice still rings in my ears.

I watch as he snatches open the drawer and pulls out a black leather billfold. It's the same every month. He claims to never want to see me and seems to be burdened by the fact I am a constant reminder for him. This could all be avoided, this back-and-forth, us having to speak any more than either of us wants. All it would take is him assuring that the deposit clears, and the funds are sent to the institute on time. Instead, he makes it so that I have to come to him.

He opens his suit jacket, removing a fancy pen, black with gold at the center. Twisting it open, he lowers the tip onto the blank check, scribbling away. All that's left is this—a quiet, ugly transaction.

I stare at the picture on his desk. They look so happy, father, mother, and son. Resentment builds, and I force myself to push it away. My father rips the check from the booklet, the sound traveling between us.

As he slides it toward me, the paper gliding over the polished wood with a soft whisper, I snatch it up.

I don't say thank you... never do.

"And the monthly payment?" is what I say instead. I rush to my feet, the chair scraping the carpet in the process.

He stares at me for a moment in that deliberate way that he does—smug and condescending. My stomach turns, the rage lodging under my ribs, but I don't flinch. I won't give him the satisfaction.

"I'll handle it," my father finally responds, twisting his pen closed, returning it to his pocket while sitting back in his seat.

I turn to walk away, taking one last look at that picture.

"I'm your son, too. So why do you hate me so much? Am I not good enough?" I hate the words as soon as they fall from my lips. But I'd be lying if I said I don't want the answers. The moment I learned who he was, the questions stirred. I just never had the balls to ask.

Nothing. Not a flinch, or even a twitch of muscle. Just that goddamn ticking clock mocking me. My jaw locks until my teeth grind together. My throat burns with things I can't say, things I'm not allowed to say.

"Don't mistake obligation for care. Naivety won't get you far."

My eyes fall without permission, that old reflex snapping my spine in half. The paperweight catches the light. A blend of brass and silver, a knight frozen mid-battle, twin swords crossed over its chest, bloodred pearls for eyes.

A monument to loyalty, strength, and honor.

Funny.

The man sitting behind it is none of those things. He's the worst kind of evil, the kind that hides behind his wealth, buying the silence of those he hurts. No consequences, no reckoning.

I don't need him to answer the question; the minute he decided to provide for us financially but not be in my life says it all. The shame of ever wanting more from him automatically takes hold. I hate that he gets to me. That he makes me feel like some stupid kid hoping the man who threw him away might reach back.

He never does.

And maybe that's the real curse.

Because if I'm nothing to him, then why in the hell has Richard Williamsburg been paying to keep me alive?

CHAPTER NINETEEN

SAM

As soon as I step foot inside the café, it's overwhelming. People are everywhere. In line waiting to order. Over near the napkin stations. There's even a small line starting to form outside the ladies' room.

Meeting off campus was supposed to be imperative for Alex. I can hear him now, his voice low and demanding.

Tell anyone you're tutoring me and there'll be consequences.

Fine by me, buddy. I don't exactly want anyone seeing me with him either. He's definitely no walk in the park himself, and after last night, I'm starting to second-guess this whole thing.

Offering to help was the first mistake; showing up might just be the second. I scan the room in search of him, craning to see around people, and with each passing second my nerves start to fray.

Not because I'm afraid of him. I'm not. At least that's what I keep telling myself. It's everything else that gets to me. The tension that is so clearly thickening between us, the heat still lingering beneath my skin, the ghost of his touch. And now I'm supposed to sit in front of him for the next hour and tutor him?

I can barely stand him as it is, but now that he's had his fingers inside me, every part of me feels...compromised. No one warns you that the worst part about being touched like that, despite how good said touching makes you feel, is the after. It's the act of trying to pretend everything is normal. Like you aren't hyperaware of your own body in the places where their touch still lingers. Like you don't feel it every time you shift in your seat or cross your legs or breathe too deep. Sweat slicks my palm, and suddenly there's no air left in this place.

This is Alex Williamsburg, for Christ's sake. There is absolutely no way we'll be able to just get on like nothing happened. Like I didn't fall apart in his hands, as if he didn't watch me come undone. No. Not Alex. He'll wear it like a victory and will surely find joy in rubbing my nose in it.

He had me. Not truly but close enough.

"I can't do this," I mutter, turning on my heel to head for the door.

But then reasoning starts and I stop in my tracks, hand on the knob, heart thudding as if it's arguing both sides.

Run. That would certainly be the easiest option. Only it won't solve my problem.

Remember why you're here. To make it stop—the bullying, the taunting. I just want to get through the rest of this season in one piece. Then I can put this all behind me.

With a shake of my shoulders, I pull them back and lift my chin. I'm not here because I want to be near him, but because I don't have a choice. It's a business transaction.

Pulling out my phone, I step off to the side of the café entrance, away from the swirl of latte orders and clinking mugs. My thumb hovers over our text thread, jaw clenching as I force myself to type.

Sam: I'm here. Where are you?

I hit send and stare at the screen—hoping that maybe he changed his mind. If I'm lucky, he won't show up and I won't have to see his stupid face. The message delivers, but there's no dots, or read receipts. I glance up, eyes sweeping around the crowded restaurant in search of a place to sit.

I freeze, my grip tightening around the phone.

There he is. Slouched lazily in the corner booth like the seat was carved for his body. Legs spread wide, fitted cap pulled low. He's staring at his phone, that familiar smirk tugging at his mouth. Curiosity hits, causing a million thoughts to go racing.

Which girl is he talking to now?

Did he meet her after he finished with me in the locker room?

I hate that I care, that I notice.

I move toward him, my heart in my throat, but I keep moving. One foot after the other until I'm only feet away. My phone pings and I glance at it quickly.

Asshole #1: In the back.

He looks up as I approach, all smug confidence and unbothered cool, eyes dragging over me like he's measuring the damage he caused.

Too late to run now.

Alex throws an arm over the back of the booth. "You actually showed."

"I could walk right back out," I snap back even though I'm already settled into the seat.

He shrugs, cocky and effortless. "You won't."

I suck in a breath, tuck my chin, and peer at him through my lashes. "Sure about that?"

He smiles, wetting his lips in the process. "Yeah, I am." Alex leans forward, bringing his face as close as the table will allow. "Wanna know how I'm so sure?"

I don't, but I ask anyway. "How?"

"Because I made you come the hardest you've ever come in your life."

My stomach caves in, my breath caught mid-pulse. Before I can respond, the waitress arrives.

"Looks like your friend has arrived?" the middle-aged woman says through a smile.

"We're far from friends," I seethe while glaring at him.

"She's downplaying it. She and I have been *real* close lately." Still he grins, almost as if daring me to call him out in front of this woman.

"Well, that's nice. Can I get you anything?"

I glare at him, my nostrils flared as I silently curse him. I knew this was a bad idea, the moment our eyes locked in that damn closet. I should have pushed him away—stopped him—but I didn't, and now this jerk has something to hold over my head.

Alex finally pulls his gaze from mine and picks up the small menu. "Yeah. Let me get an espresso, triple shot."

"All right. And you, sweetheart?" She turns to me, tapping her pen against her order book.

"Um. How about an iced latte? Caramel, please."

"Sure thing."

She nods and looks between us. "Would you like anything to eat?"

Alex nods in my direction. "Whatever you want. It's on me."

I wet my lips, taking another peek at the menu options. "Egg white and turkey sausage wrap."

She takes the menus and walks away to get started on our order.

"Thanks," I say, reluctant to give him any more ammunition.

I don't need him adding a ten-dollar wrap and six-dollar coffee to the list of things he's already holding over my head. But all I've had to eat today was the few bites of the frybread Mountain shared with me. So if I don't eat something, I'm going to be passed out on the floor soon.

"No problem." Alex sits up and reaches for a straw. Using his teeth, he rips the end of the wrap to remove his straw in a taunting manner. "It's the least I can do."

"You're disgusting," I bite out, picking up the glass of water on the table.

Alex laughs and it only pisses me off. He sticks the straw in the glass, balls up the paper, and tosses it on the table.

"You weren't complaining last night." He leans in further. "In fact, you seemed—"

My spine stiffens. I want to throw something, maybe even punch him in the face.

"Enough," I blurt, shifting my gaze around. "Keep your voice down."

He holds up his hands in mock surrender. "Okay. I'll chill."

"And just so you know. Last night will never happen again."

I wait for one of his smart-alecky retorts, but he only smiles.

"Now, even though you didn't hold up your end of the bargain. Let's get started. I'd like to not waste any more of my time on you than I have to."

"Ouch." He flicks his wrist, feigning hurt. "And what are you talking about? I told them to back off."

Pulling my textbook from my bag, I let it fall on the table with a soft slap. "And you were a complete asshole about it. *'I know she's a bitch but lay off'*? You call that helping? How do you expect them to listen when you can't stop being a dick toward me yourself?"

"Okay. Maybe the bitch line was uncalled for." Alex holds his hands palms up with a tilt of his head. "I apologize. But, I did tell them to stop."

"And they didn't listen," I quip. "I mean I came to you because you're the captain, but if you can't even get your team to listen to you, then this was useless."

Alex frowns, and for a moment he seems really confused. "What do you mean?"

"While you were taking out your frustrations on the pucks, one of your guys cornered me in the locker room."

"After I told them to back off?"

I nod, short and clipped.

Something flickers across his face. Pure anger. And something closer to...regret. He sits up straighter, dropping his phone on the tabletop. "Who? Did he hurt you?"

"Ryker. No, he just wanted to intimidate me."

His jaw ticks. "I'll handle it."

For some strange reason, I believe him. I don't know why, but I do, even though everything in me tells me not to.

"Good." I pause, contemplating my next thought. "Because now, I want something else."

His brow twitches, that grin forming again. "I'll be happy to."

"Eww. Not that, asshole. Information."

He doesn't blink, only leans forward, curiosity etched into his features. "You're going to have to narrow that down."

I take a breath, bracing myself. "I need to know why I'm here."

He shifts. "What do you mean? You're tutoring me."

I shake my head. "At this school. Why I was denied a scholarship and acceptance, then suddenly handed one a year later with everything magically covered—meals, housing, tuition. Why your father swept my incident under the rug."

Alex's silence is louder than the café's espresso machine.

I lean in. "I'm grateful for the scholarship, I am. But it feels like there is something more to it, and everyone I've asked in administration brushes it off. You don't find that suspicious?"

His jaw works, like he's chewing glass. "You shouldn't question my father."

I sit back. "Yeah, well, I shouldn't be your guys' personal punching bag either, but here we are."

He shrugs again, playing with the wrapping of a straw. "I'm sure you're just overthinking it. The school has lots of programs to help those who qualify. Just take advantage of it."

I watch him. That answer is too polished, rehearsed.

"Right," I murmur.

He grabs his notebook, flips it open, ready to move on. "Come on. Let's get this over with. We've got pregame in two hours."

I want to push, force him to tell me what he knows, make him promise to help. But it's the dreaded look at the mention of his father that makes me think twice about it. There's something there, something I've seen before. He hates that man. I know because it's the same reaction I've had myself. So instead, I put my focus on the textbook, hesitantly accepting that I'm going to have to do this on my own.

Eventually, the hour winds down, and once we're done, I pack up fast. The café isn't as busy now as it was when I first arrived, so the noise has dissipated some. As I shove the rest of my things into my bag, I make eye contact with Alex.

He stands, reaching for his backpack and unzipping it. I try not to watch as he reaches inside for something.

"I'm thinking our next session should be Wednesday. I only have one class, so I'll be pretty wide open that day." The moment I finish that statement I regret it. I snap straight, staring at him with wide eyes.

Alex tips his head to look at me, a smirk tugging at the corners of his lips.

"Shut up," I quip before he can get a word out.

"I didn't even say anything." He pulls something from his bag and tosses it in my direction.

I catch it. "You were thinking it."

"Damn, a guy can't even have thoughts." He smiles while licking his lips.

"About me. No." I unfold the fabric. "What's this?"

"Don't worry about the ruined team shirt from last night. You have to wear a jersey anyway." He rezips his bag then flings it over his shoulder. "And I'll see about getting you some extra ones, so Coach won't be on your ass."

I stare at the jersey, confusion pulling at my features. "But does it have to be your jersey?"

He shrugs. "It's regulation, but—" He yanks it back. "If you want to go out there in that bleached shirt, be my gu—"

"Fine." I snatch it back.

Alex chuckles. "Come on, I'll give you a ride back to campus."

He steps around me, deliberately brushing against me. I hesitate for a moment, not sure if I should decline or follow behind him. Quickly, I check the time. The next bus isn't for another twenty minutes, and the ride is double that considering all the stops.

I choose the latter.

"I'm coming."

Alex spins and walks backward, the cocky grin back on his mug. "You did last—"

"Shut up!"

He holds the door open for me and I try not to meet his eyes.

God, he's infuriating. We step out into the cool air, and I stop to take in a breath.

He walks around me and straight to the expensive car parked directly in front of the café.

"Who even drives a Porsche in college?" I let it slip without thinking.

"Someone who can afford to make people forget his grades suck."

CHAPTER TWENTY

SAM

It's finals night and the entire campus is buzzing. Everywhere I went today there was someone chanting or yelling, fist in the air, aggression already seeping to the surface.

Go Knights.

I'll never understand the hivemind of sports fans. They're loud and territorial. With the painted faces, the ceremonial portrayal of stripping off shirts, getting so angry they'll shatter the TV. And the screams that are so loud you can barely hear yourself think. God forbid the team loses. A fight would be guaranteed to break out.

It's fascinating, but also a little scary. I shake my head at the thought and continue working my way through my checklist at the rink and get to work. During practice, I only have the main locker room to worry about, but during home games, I handle the visiting team's locker needs as well.

It's not nearly as much work as what I do for my boys, but it's still quite a bit to get through. I start with the water bottles first, filling each to the brim. Then the med kit and towels.

When I'm done, I check my clipboard for the fourth time tonight. Not that the boys would be pissed if I screwed something up; they hate Baymont. One of the guys on my team even tried to bribe me into slipping laxatives in their bottles. He said it was a joke, but something tells me it wasn't.

Voices spill in behind me as the other team comes pouring in, loud, cocky, and full of that out-of-town swagger. More like cross-town confidence. I may not like or know much about the sport, but I've lived in this town my entire life. If the headlines tell me anything, it's that Baymont is damn good this year, with a new captain who's as hungry as anyone on this team.

And if the game footage the Knights have been reviewing in preparation for tonight is any indication, Baymont is about to give them a run for the title. *Good.* They deserve a good ass whooping. Maybe a little humbling will do them some good.

I glance behind them, taking in the multiracial team. They don't seem to notice me, all in their own world. The game's about to start, so I make quick work of my final task.

I'm stacking the last of the Gatorade bottles when I hear it.

"Damn. Who's that?"

I glance up. One of Baymont's players leans against the lockers, his eyes glued to my ass. He's tall and built—which is par for the course—with floppy hair and a porn stache.

"You're the chick that took out Kincaid, right?" He points at me, then brings his fist to his mouth to hide his laughter. "You are. My homeboy said they made you the towel girl as like punishment or something."

I turn, attempting to ignore him. Seriously? They said school gossip spread fast around here, but for it to make it all the way across town, to another university, is crazy. Besides, what am I going to say? Yes, that was me, the knee shatterer here. No, that'll only stir up more drama. Jackson has already made things hell for me, spending every chance he gets to chastise me. Sending his brother to do his dirty work. I don't need to add anything else on top of that.

"Shit. Maybe I should be thanking you for taking out the competition."

His teammates laugh as he daps up the person closest to him.

"I'm Aaron." He moves closer, holding out a hand for me to take.

"I don't care," I mutter instead, picking up my crate and turning.

"Williamsburg?" he questions like he's disappointed.

The jersey. That sneaky bastard. He didn't give this shirt to me to help me out. He did it to mark his territory in front of the other team. Jerk. And because wearing the school's gear is mandatory, there's nothing I can do about his name on my back. Like a brand.

Fucking perfect.

"You'd look better with my name on your back."

I blink, unsure if I should laugh or be disturbed. They're all the same, douchey, arrogant dickheads that need to be taken down a notch. I turn to face him. "That line ever work on anyone who isn't brain-dead?"

He laughs. "Guess I'll have to find out."

"Keep dreaming." I storm away, catching a glimpse of his eyes falling to my backside. I don't look back, but my skin itches the whole way out.

Back in the main hallway, the crowd's pouring in. Drums, chants, and shrieks fill the rink. Girls line up in the first row, all eager to get a peek at the players. Nothing surprising, really. They're at every practice, oohing and aahing like these boys are God's gift.

I scan the seats, craning around to focus.

"Gracie should be here by now," I mutter and pull out my phone.

Sam: Where are you? The game is about to start, and you promised.

I hit send and head down the tunnel. My phone buzzes, and I pause to read the message.

Roomie 😎**:** I'm here.

Roomie 😎**:** Regretfully.

Sam: Thank you, roomie.

Roomie 😎**:** Yeah. Yeah. I hope your team loses.

Sam: That makes two of us. But, after the run-in I just had with one of the Baymont players, I kinda want the Knights to win.

Sam: It's like some universal asshole trait among the hockey players.

Roomie 😎**:** Oh God. What happened?

Sam: Nothing I can't handle.

I tuck my phone away and search the rink again. Finally I spot her sitting at the center of her section. She's not close to the bench, but with where she's sitting, I can at least make eye contact with her throughout the night.

Getting her to agree to this was like pulling teeth. I don't know what her beef is with the team, but every time I talk about them, she gets a little weird. Like now. She's here but doesn't seem to really be present. She's wearing a hoodie that's pulled tight. Her arms are locked and her eyes flick around the stadium.

It's different from her usually bubbly self. When we're alone in our dorm or in the cafeteria, she's the life of the party, always making me laugh. But as soon as I let off my late-night, I-hate-them rant, or we cross paths with one of them, her entire demeanor shifts. It's like she becomes a different person.

It was the same when I cursed the chancellor for making me do this. Gracie flinched, but quickly pulled herself together. It was subtle, barely there, but I caught it.

I push the thoughts from my mind. No sense in dwelling. If she doesn't want to talk about it, I can't force it. I mean, who am I to demand that of her when I've been keeping things bottled up, too. I guess we have more in common than I thought.

The bench tunnel looms ahead. The only thing left on my list is setting up the hydration station. I stroll forward, more on reflex, as I watch players move to the ice. The sound of blades echoes off the concrete walls. When I put my attention back in front of me, I freeze, barely keeping myself from running into him.

Jackson. He hops by, his crutches thudding against the cement flooring. He's flanked by a few guys, some I recognize from class and others I don't. Every single one of them stares. Hard. Their eyes sharp with accusation, disgust etched deep in their brows. If looks could kill, I'd be face down in a pool of my own blood.

A chill licks up my spine, and the only thing colder is the pit forming in my stomach. They don't speak. Hell, they don't need to. The hatred is clear—pure vitriol. I try to ignore them and keep on my way, but before my feet can move, I see Christina.

Her squad of all glossy hair and perfectly rehearsed laughter saunters by, and I'm met with the same energy. It oozes from them—tight smiles and eye rolls. They don't even know why they don't like me. Just that their precious leader told them to.

It shouldn't come as a surprise. It just sucks that it took me nearly being assaulted to finally see the validity in Gracie's warning.

Christina is a mean girl, through and through.

She played the ally. Pretended to be friendly, inclusive, supportive. Until I injured her precious Jackson.

The moment that incident happened with Jackson, she showed her true colors. She joined in on the antics, getting just as big a laugh as anyone else when Jackson and his crew taunted me.

They move on, taking seats directly behind the bench tunnel, forcing the girls who were sitting there to move. I shake my head and suck in a breath, deciding not to let them get in my head. There are more important things for me to worry about.

"Waiting on me?" I hear a voice behind me and turn to see who it belongs to.

Aaron.

Uggh, I groan. "Don't flatter yourself."

I turn to walk away, but he jumps around me, blocking my path, his smirk stretching wider now. "Look. Some of us are having a party tonight. You should come hang out. Bring that mouth. I like the attitude."

My grip tightens around my crate, the plastic digging into my fingers. Before I can respond, a hand clamps down on my arm. Confused, I glance to my left.

Alex.

He steps between us, his jaw clenched. The rival hockey captain doesn't move, but the shift in the air is sharp enough to cut through bone.

"She's not going anywhere with you," Alex seethes.

Aaron shrugs. "Didn't know she was claimed. I mean I saw your name on her back but I didn't think that was for real."

Alex leans in, low and lethal. "Now you do."

The guy finally backs off, holding his hands up in surrender. Alex turns to me, eyes still dark. He grips my wrist, pulling me away from the tunnel.

"Stay away from him."

I yank away. "Let go of me."

Alex doesn't protest. Instead, he stalks away, opens the gate, and hits the ice.

At the edge of the tunnel, I look back at the bleachers. Gracie's watching, sitting on the edge of her seat with a frown imprinted in place.

My phone buzzes again.

Roomie 😎: What the hell was that?

CHAPTER TWENTY-ONE

ALEX

The crowd is going crazy.

Tonight isn't just for us—it's for them. This game *has* been the most anticipated game of the season. The tension runs deep with Baymont. For years they've been our rival, and every year we've whooped their asses.

Of course, then we had Jackson. And now that he's out, everyone is damn near betting against us. It's bullshit. Every player on this team is the reason we're at the top of our sport, one of the best in the country. Not just Kincaid.

I know that. We know that.

But the lack of faith seeps deep, so deep that the team has been on edge for weeks. Tonight's not just about getting to nationals. It's about proving that I'm a damn good captain and can lead a badass team, with or without Jackson. It's about finally getting my father to see me. Not the player, not a commodity—but his son.

"Let's go, Knights," someone shouts from the stands, and the cheering commences. As the seconds tick on, more fans join in until they're so loud I can barely register the words.

Across the rink, the opposing team's faces twist into smirks and sneers. They don't look rattled. If anything, they look amused. Like we're just background noise in their highlight reel.

My sights land on Aaron. He slaps the backs of his hands against his teammate's shoulders, jutting his chin in our direction and saying something that makes him laugh.

My jaw ticks, the pressure building until my teeth ache. Aaron Walton has been—no, *is*—the biggest bane of my existence. Ever since we were kids, he and Jackson have found numerous ways to get us all in trouble.

Once upon a time, he *was* a Knight. Until he fucked that up and nearly ruined our entire track two seasons ago. He's smug. Reckless. And an asshole with a superiority complex. Acted like he was bigger than the program. Like rules didn't apply to him. Like he belonged on a pedestal.

I know I'm bad, but he was worse. Much worse.

And with a penchant for dirty plays, Coach had no choice but to bench him. Hits from behind. Cheap shots. Late checks. Shit that could've ended careers. Aaron didn't take the benching quietly, and neither did his father. The Walton name carries weight in this town, and they made sure to use it. They took to social media with a full-blown smear campaign against the school. Accusations. Edited footage.

"Blackballed for being too aggressive," they'd claimed.

It almost worked. Almost.

It cost my father and the school thousands to clean it up before it could morph into a scandal. But even after we buried it, the stain stuck. His name was ruined. No team would touch him. He was a loose cannon, and a liability.

Except Baymont. They were desperate and needed a captain. Rumor is, Daddy Walton cut them a fat check to make it happen. Coach says not to engage. Says to focus on the fact that we know Aaron's every move. His tricks. His tells. His weaknesses. Says to play the game but leave it on the ice.

But then this dick winks at me from across the rink, taunting me. And then he flirted with *her*.

Sam isn't just wearing a jersey tonight. She's wearing *mine*. I picked it. Handed it to her without saying why. Could've grabbed any number, but I didn't. I wanted her in my name. Wanted it loud, visible, and branded on her back like a warning.

He saw that.

And he still had the balls to make a move on her in my rink, in my house. It was for me, the flirting and cocky glances, the dirty way he let his eyes drag over her.

He doesn't want her.

He wants *me* rattled.

And it's working. *Why is it fucking working?* I shouldn't care, but I do. More than I want to admit. This jersey was just a way to claim her, show the other team who she belongs to. Nothing more. Yet seeing Aaron talking to her lit something ablaze inside me. A fire I can't fucking put out.

I was supposed to meet up with Kenzie last night, something easy with no strings. A sure thing to take the edge off. But she quickly became an afterthought when I walked in and saw Sam. Half-dressed, her perfect tits just there for me to devour. Then my fingers were inside her, her moans stuck under my skin, her scent clinging to me. I can still feel the heat of her thighs tightening around my wrist. Still hear the way she gasped like it wasn't supposed to happen, but she *needed* it anyway.

And now I can't fucking shake it. And this asshole just threw gasoline on the entire goddamn thing. He saw my name and knew that circling her like a damn vulture would get under my skin.

So sorry, Coach. Going up against him tonight is going to be bittersweet. And when I make him my bitch on that ice, it's probably going to be better than sex.

I shift on the bench, unfisting my gloved hands and unlocking my elbows. Kane is next to me, rolling his shoulders as if he's already skating laps in his head. Mountain cracks his neck loud enough to make a freshman flinch. Everyone's hungry.

The buzzer sounds, and the ref skates out.

Kane taps his stick twice against the boards. "Let's go."

I'm the last to stand, and when I do, I slap my helmet on and strap it into place.

We hit the ice. The crowd explodes around us, shaking the boards. Every stomp reverberates through my chest. Lights cut across the rink, cameras flash.

I lower my head and skate fast, slicing through the ice, the cold stinging my cheeks. My blades bite hard, carving lines into the fresh sheet as we circle the center. I glance into the stands, my eyes locking on my father's. He's sitting there, all snarl and stillness, arms folded across his chest, his jaw locked. No clapping like the rest. No standing in excitement. He just watches with that same look he always gives me—measured and unimpressed.

Dad doesn't nod nor blink. Doesn't acknowledge me at all. It's like I'm a ghost in his arena. My stomach twists, but determination bites at my flesh. This is my last chance to step up and make him see me. Tonight, winning is the only option.

The whistle blows, and I snap my head back to center ice. Aaron skates close, huddling beside me.

"Sure you can focus tonight?" He smirks.

I ignore him. My fist tightens around my stick.

"With an ass like that, I know I wouldn't be able to," he continues, his gaze shifting past me to the bench.

Inadvertently, I follow his line of sight. Sam's there, her back to us, as she places a stack of clean towels on the bench.

"And that mouthpiece on her. Feisty. I like her. Better keep her close."

Still, I don't bite back. I won't give him the satisfaction. *Keep in it on the ice* is all that replays in my head.

"Bet she likes to be choked, too. You ever try it? You should. She looks like she'd love being pinned down."

Blood rushes to my ears. Hot and violent. He skates backward now, smirking as he eases into face-off position across from Kane.

"Think about it," he continues loud enough for the others to hear, then smirks.

Kane gives me a quick side glance, and I know it's his way of checking if I need to be reeled in. I don't move. Instead, I lock in.

Game on, motherfucker.

The puck drops and we're in it. Kane wins the face-off and drops it to me. I grab it, cut left, and drive it down the boards. Baymont's right wing collides with me at the blue line. Hard. Shoulder to shoulder.

Good. I need the hit, need the pain to shake the fury loose, to exorcise the weight of expectation and let go of the pressure.

My body rocks, and my skates scrape as my breath punches out of me. The puck skips ahead, just out of reach. I recover fast, pivoting off the boards and hooking around their defender. My stick taps the puck, drags it back in before it crosses the line.

I swing wide behind the net and scan the ice. Kane's battling at the top of the crease, and another teammate's crashing down on the right side. I fake the pass, force the defenseman to shift with me, then cut inside.

Another defender charges. I drop my shoulder, slip the check, toe-drag left, and fire. Wide. The glass rings as the puck slams off it right next to the net. Groans swell from the crowd like a punch to the ribs. I circle hard, my lips tight while chewing on the rubber mouth guard.

That should have been in.

Baymont grabs possession, pushing the rush. I skate hard, chasing back, pumping my legs, lungs burning with cold rage. One of their wings tries to thread a pass through the slot, clean and confident. But Kane reads it early. He cuts it off, redirects it to Ryker, who hammers it down the boards for a clear shot.

Until the whistle blows.

I skate toward the bench, adrenaline pumping through my veins. My focus is ironclad but is momentarily swayed when Aaron skates up beside me.

"Whole lot of effort just to hit the glass, Williamsburg," he taunts.

I shoulder-check him, fighting to keep my composure. Things are already bad enough; going off on him early into the game would only make shit worse. Aaron laughs.

"Hope she wasn't watching that—kinda ruins the fantasy, don't you think?" He bumps my shoulder as we cross paths. "Don't worry, there's still time to *try* and impress her."

I slide through the gate and drop down on the bench without a word. I keep my helmet on, but my ears are burning as I clutch my stick so hard it might snap clean in half. Across the rink, Aaron tosses a look over his shoulder, winking in Sam's direction.

Mountain leans close. "Let it go, man. Keep your head in the game."

I don't respond. Instead, I bite down on the mouthguard and stare ahead as the next shift takes the ice.

Let it go? Not a chance. I'm wired too tight.

The next shift starts, and I jump the boards before Coach

even finishes the call. I hit the ice, my knees low, my chest buzzing. The puck moves quickly, kicked around in the neutral zone. I scan the area until I track Aaron down, my focus locking tight. He circles, reading his play while waiting for the perfect break.

The second the puck crosses into our zone, I press forward. The pass is sloppy at best, too soft and too slow. Aaron pounces, cuts left, catches it clean, and drives down the wing.

Got you, bitch.

Closing the gap, I match his stride. My stick digs into the ice, blade tight against his hip as I pin him to the boards. The hit lands. It's not dirty, but it's not light either. He elbows back—quick and sharp—buried in my ribs. I flinch, the pain blooming through my side, but I absorb it and skate through it.

The ref doesn't call it, barely even sees it. One thing about Aaron, he's always been good at riding the edge. Cheap shots, sneaky hits that are always legal enough to stay on the ice. But just dirty enough to get under your skin.

We battle for control in the corner. Skates tangling. Shoulders shoving. I keep my head down and jaw locked. He tries to spin out again, but I cut him off. He resets near the circle, slow and smug, like he's just biding time.

Then he crosses the line.

"Ain't your daddy watching?" he sneers, skating into my space like he owns it. "Bet he's real proud that his son hasn't scored."

"Fuck off." I shove him. Not hard. Just enough. Enough to remind him that this rink isn't his. It's mine.

Aaron doesn't move back. He only grins wider, leaning in like he wants me to lose it. Coach's voice flashes through my head again. *Play the game. Keep your head. He's going to bait all of you. Don't let him.*

So, I skate. I stay on him, shoulder to shoulder, as he gets the puck again. He tries to pivot, but I read it. I drop my shoulder, time it clean, then cut him off and slam him as he releases the puck.

It fumbles free.

Kane snags it and clears. He drives it to the net, weaving around our opponents, dodging hits and...

Score.

The fans jump up, hooting and hollering. Aaron chuckles breathlessly and wipes his glove across his mouth.

"You skating tonight?" he goads. "Or are you going to keep playing like a little bitch?"

My grip tightens on the stick, jaw pulsing as I bite the inside of my cheek so hard I taste the blood. Coppery and metallic.

But I don't swing; instead, I keep skating, swallowing back every curse that wants to claw its way from my throat. Because Coach is watching. And so is my father. And I refuse to give either of them another thing to be disappointed about.

Mountain's barking from the crease, his gloved hand slapping the post, eyes narrowed in as Baymont resets at the blue line.

"Back check! Watch the left!" he shouts.

I shift on instinct and drop into coverage. Kane intercepts a lazy pass and flips it high off the glass. The puck bounces off a stanchion and ricochets right to me at center ice. I catch it off the blade.

The zone's open, just me and two defenders. I fake left, push right, dip my shoulder, and slide between them. I barely miss a poke check as I keep the puck tight to my stick. One of them clips the back of my skate. I stumble, recover, and keep going.

The crowd shouts, their voices crescendoing off the ceiling. Adrenaline roars in my ears as I shift my weight, wind up, and snap the shot.

Top shelf.

Bar down.

It clangs off the crossbar and drops behind the goalie. *Goal.*

The boys explode on the bench, slamming the boards, screaming. I'm already skating back to center. I don't need the celebration. I just need the next face-off.

Aaron is already there, waiting with sweat beading along his chin, but he's still smirking. I skate up, square off across the circle from him. He leans on his stick, his voice low, just for me.

"Looks like your girl's impressed." He tips his head.

I follow his gaze to find Sam standing at the edge of the tunnel, her eyes trained on me. She's invested, but that doesn't mean she's invested in me. Hockey is a different beast live; even a person like her who hates the sport is bound to appreciate it up close.

"You gave her your number, but maybe when I wipe the floor with you punks, I'll give her mine. Bet she'll look real good in nothing but my sweater."

It happens before I can stop it. Everything snaps. The noise, the ice, the air. All I see is his face and the sound of my gloves hitting the ice. I lunge, my fist connecting with his cheek. His head jerks to the side, but he recovers fast and swings wildly. I duck, slam my shoulder into his chest, and drive him to the ice.

"Stay the fuck away from her," I seethe.

We hit the ground hard, him beneath me as he grabs the front of my jersey. I hammer him again—his jaw, ribs, whatever I can reach. The crowd loses it as the refs race toward us. Hands grab at my shoulder, my arms, and neck, but I don't stop. It's as if I see red, and it takes them pulling me by the collar to finally snap me out of it.

My fist aches, but it's the look on his face that makes it worth it. Aaron takes the beating in stride, running the tip of his glove over his lip to check for blood. It's split, and there's a decent-sized gash above his eye. But he's still grinning as if he's the one who won.

"All that rage and you fight like you fuck. *Weak*." He shrugs from the ref's grip, his eyes boring into me.

I snap at him again, but someone grabs me.

"Penalty box, now," the ref barks.

I cross the ice, still seething. Sam makes eye contact with me, concern etched in hers. A part of me hates that she saw that, hates that she's seen me lose it. But the other half of me is glad she saw it. Not because I want her scared or anything close to that. Because I want her to *know*.

She's not just wearing my jersey.

She's wearing *me*.

And anyone who thinks they can mess with that? They'll bleed.

I drop down on the bench, not daring to glance up at my father. I don't need to. I can feel his eyes glaring into me. I've once again embarrassed his name, and he's going to make sure I know it.

Shift after shift, I stay glued to the bench, eyes fixed on the ice. Anything to avoid facing Coach's rage. I should have been back on the ice by now. The average penalty for misconduct is ten minutes, but he's punishing me. He gave me an order, and I did the opposite. Aaron's back out by the fifth shift. He's been taped up, but still smirking, and I only hope his lips re-split every time he grins. I hope it fucking burns.

Baymont scores on a lucky bounce that skips past Mountain's blocker side. Our second line answers quickly. Kane crashes the net and hammers the rebound home. Four–five our way.

Baymont gets another breakaway. Mountain sprawls and

makes the glove save of the night. He pops up with a snarl that whips the crowd into a frenzy. He bangs his stick against the post and points at the scoreboard like it owes him something. People whisper behind me, shocked by his outburst. I get it. Mountain is usually the quiet one, but when it comes to this game, he becomes someone else entirely.

Both teams go back and forth until Baymont finally clears another shot. Then the whistle blows.

Third period. Five–five. Tied.

Whatever tension I had before is at an all-time high now. Coach finally taps my shoulder. I glance up at him, and he tips his head toward the ice. I nod and hop the boards. The weight hits me the second my skates touch the sheet. Every eye in the house, every whisper, every click of a camera feels especially daunting. They're all watching. All counting on me to help bring it home.

I roll my neck, mentally preparing myself, pushing all of the negative thoughts from my mind. I home in until there is nothing but me, the referee, and the puck in his hand. Tonight's win will be mine. My father will finally see that I'm more than what he's damned me to be, and Aaron will eat shit.

The puck drops, and we control possession. Blood rushes to my ears, and I pump hard, cutting across and dodging a check. My boys watch me closely, blocking anyone in my path. I get the puck, run it home, the sound of guys being knocked to the side behind me as my backdrop.

This is it. The winning shot. It's clear, and wide open. I suck in a breath, raise my stick, and shoot.

Too high.

It slams into the glass with a hollow thud.

Shit. Shit. Shit.

I wheel back, ready to chase the puck, but Kane snags it, turns, and rifles it into the top corner. The goal light flares, the horn screams, and the bench erupts.

We won.

Bodies fly onto the ice, swarming Kane, helmets and gloves thrown to the floor, sticks lifted. As I peel toward my friend, my mouth is instantly dry. We won; that's a good thing, right? Then why does it feel like a failure?

When I reach Kane, his eyes drift to the private area where my father and the sponsors sit to watch the games. I follow his line of sight, expecting to see my father's angry mug. But the section is empty. No suit, no snarl, no Richard Williamsburg. Didn't even bother to stay for the win.

Why would he? I'd already lost the puck several times and spent the bulk of the game on the bench. I know what to expect from my father, but his coldness and the dismissal don't hurt any less.

I push off the ice and down the tunnel, the noise from the arena fading with each stride. My gear feels heavy, my chest even more so.

Sam's standing at the end, a clipboard in hand, one foot propped against the cinderblock wall. Her gaze flicks up as I approach. She stands, and a playful smile starts to form on her lips.

"You're not terrible," she says, tone light and easy. "Kind of hoped you were garbage for all the shit y'all have put me through. But it turns out... you're actually good."

While her words heal some wound inside, I don't smile. My lips and fist still sting from the fight, and all the rage from my father's rejection starts to boil inside me again.

"You want information?" I ask, no warning and no warm-up.

She straightens, slightly surprised if the knitted brows are any indication.

"Meet me tonight." I walk past her, the heat in my body coiling tighter with each step. The adrenaline is still humming. The shame is pooling behind my ribs. Or maybe it's something else—something hotter, darker. Then it hits me.

It's not shame at all. *It's control.*

And I don't have it, but I'm going to take it back.

Starting with her.

CHAPTER TWENTY-TWO

SAM

What the hell was he thinking? Better yet, what the hell was I thinking?

And now that I'm sneaking around after dark like a two-dollar hooker, I'm questioning my own intellect. Why would I expect anything decent from him? Of course, aligning myself to him couldn't possibly result in anything good.

It seems he has a knack for off-the-wall things that seem to usually land him in trouble. And now, it's literal breaking and entering. *Into the administration office.*

Maybe Aaron knocked him upside his head a little too hard in that fight. Because there is no way he thought this through. Right?

When I said I wanted his help getting information, I was thinking more along the lines of maybe *accidentally* stumbling across his dad's emails. Or, I don't know, maybe just ask questions. Not committing a freaking felony.

He just went from zero to a hundred, passed go, and did not collect two hundred dollars.

And I get it. His father practically owns this school, and he's like a god around here. But, if we get caught, it won't be a slap on the wrist for me. It'll mean getting expelled.

Yeah, this is a bad, bad idea.

"Alex." I crouch low to the redbrick wall like a bandit in the night while throwing my gaze around to make sure no one sees us. "We can't do this."

But he keeps moving, ignoring me as he peeks around the corner.

"Alex," I whisper-shout, my fingers tingling as numbness pricks at my skin.

"Come on, the guard just walked down the hall," Alex announces over his shoulder with a wave of his hand and the tilt of his head.

Before I can protest, he's on the move, staying close to the building, occasionally shifting his gaze across the courtyard. My chest tightens, and every step feels like a countdown.

I should leave. Right now. Thank him for his consideration and get the hell out of Dodge.

I move, but not in the opposite direction. I find myself closer to Alex.

Walking away would be the right thing, the non-criminal thing. But then, I'll never get my answers, and the suspicion around my scholarship will drive me insane.

I pause, flaying tentatively, battling between turning around and trekking forward. And then out of nowhere, shouts erupt in the distance.

I flinch, and my throat drops into the pit of my stomach. I snap around, my nerves now a fragile mess. Across the quad, there's a group of students, six of them, all in a world of their own. They're swaying and laughing among one another, clearly having had a little too much to drink.

The sound of a lock clicks, and I turn to Alex slowly inching the door open and scanning the area. He doesn't need words to tell me to follow him.

I hesitate for a beat, knowing that the moment I step into this building, there's no turning back. And even though he hasn't asked for anything in return, it would be foolish to think this could just be labeled as a good deed.

No. Allowing him to do this for me gives him leverage. He'll own me. There will be no escaping him. I'll be bound to him despite how much we dislike each other.

But the alternative is never getting answers, never knowing the truth. So I throw caution to the wind and step in behind him.

I'm careful not to touch the door, using the sleeve of my shirt to keep from leaving fingerprints behind. But not him. He just raw-dogs the door, his prints all over it. *Amateur.* Not leaving proof is Burglary 101. Not that I would know.

The lights are out, save for the neon red signs above all the exits, and the lights flooding in from outside. The lobby is hollow, the soft pads of our footfalls bouncing off the walls.

"Stay close," Alex whispers while turning his head from one direction to the other.

I huddle in behind him, grabbing the tail of his shirt to keep from losing him in the darkness. My eyes have yet to adjust, and I end up running into his back.

He grunts. "I said stay close, not run me over. But if you wanted to be that close to me all you had to do is ask, Sunshine."

"Shut up. I couldn't see."

Alex chuckles and I just know he's got that stupid, crooked smile plastered to his face. *God, he makes me sick.*

He takes out his phone, fumbling around with it before the flashlight beams onto the wall. I feel small under the scrutiny of the decades of academic scholars whose portraits hang on the walls. I feel their eyes following us—judging us.

"If we get caught, Alex, I'm going to kill you," I announce.

"Do you want the information or not?" he says as we approach the registrar's office door.

"Y-yes," I stutter. "I do."

"Okay then." He peers at me for a beat, one hand on the knob. "We won't get caught. Besides, it's only breaking in when you don't have a key."

Alex holds it up, the dull gold gleaming under the flashlight.

"And you just *happened* to have one?" I narrow my eyes at him.

"I cloned a copy from my father's key ring years ago," he admits and inserts it into the lock. It clicks and he pushes the door open.

"Of course you did."

Alex steps aside, one arm sweeping out like he's welcoming me into a five-star hotel. "After you."

"Just a regular rule breaker," I mutter as I walk through the door.

"What's that supposed to mean?" Alex follows me in, shutting the door behind us with a soft click.

The air inside is stale. It's laced with that old institutional smell—dust, toner, and floor wax.

"You're always doing something you shouldn't." I peer around to gather my bearings. "Like that fight earlier. What was that about?"

"He's a dick. And was asking for it," he replies flatly, his delivery cold and indifferent.

I continue on. "So, you just go around punching people you deem a dick?"

"That's gold coming from you." His voice cuts through the stale air like a blade. "Do you just go around breaking the kneecaps of anyone who pisses you off? What's that about?"

I suck in a breath. *I walked right into that one, didn't I?*

I groan, regretting that I said anything at all.

"Never mind." I move around the front desk, checking for unlocked drawers.

"Not buying it. What could have possibly been a good enough reason to assault Jackson?"

I wince at that. There's that word again, and like before it's being directed at the wrong person.

"What difference does it make?" I shrug, moving on to the next drawer. "It's not like anyone will believe what I have to say anyway."

Alex stands in the center of the room, his silhouette looming. "Try me."

"There's nothing to tell. I broke his knee, plain and simple." What's the point in telling him? It was so easy for them all to believe that bullshit ass story Jackson gave.

"He tried something, didn't he?"

I freeze, my eyes snapping to him. Thank God he can't look into mine right now. I wouldn't be able to hide the truth.

"All of these drawers are locked," I say instead, then rush to the closest door. *Nothing.*

He huffs again, and I know it's because I just changed the subject.

"The hard copies of records should be in that room straight ahead. And here." He tosses the key, and to both our surprise, I catch it. "I'll keep watch."

My boots make the softest squeak on the linoleum as I move past the front desk and into the dark corridor. Every shadow feels like it could swallow us whole.

I dig out my phone from my back pocket and turn on my flash as well. Sweat forms on my palms, forcing me to wipe them on the front of my jeans, but I'm thankful to be putting distance between us, even if it's only a brief reprieve.

Being careful to use my sleeve to avoid touching things, I insert the key and push inside. It clicks shut behind me, and I hold my phone up to see what's in front of me.

A wall of cabinets looms ahead, their drawers tucked beneath rows of labels. Finally, my eyes adjust to the lighting, and I inch toward the cabinets. I read the labels, stopping when I find the first drawer labeled C, and pull it open. The metal creaks like it's protesting, and it's loud as hell in the silence.

I wince, listening to be sure it didn't alert the guard. But nothing. Alex never calls out to me, and when I glance behind me through the threshold, he's still in place.

I refocus, my fingers working fast as I flip through names. But my file isn't in this one. *Damn*. Just how many students do they have with a last name that starts with a C? I move to the next drawer, scanning through those until I finally see it. My name jumps out in sharp print.

COLLINS, SAMANTHA.

My stomach knots. For weeks questions have swirled around in my mind. So why am I so scared to find out the truth?

I inhale deeply and reach for the file, setting it on top of the others to thumb through it. Anticipation builds and I brace myself. Best case scenario, it's fine and I've made a big deal out of nothing. And maybe good things really do happen to people.

The sound of the pages turning fill the dead air. There's nothing out of the ordinary here. Just standard stuff—name, date of birth, home address.

I flip to another. *The original rejection letter.*

And the next. *The acceptance letter.*

I read them both carefully, something deep down not allowing me to move on. It's a generic template; with the exception of my name and the SKU logo, it's your run-of-the-mill text.

Nothing special on these pages. But then I get to the signature line and the frown forms before I fully register it.

The name on the rejection letter is not the same as on the acceptance. I hadn't realized that before. I received them a year apart and trashed the first one.

I scan to the bottom of the acceptance letter.

Richard Williamsburg, School Chancellor.

I rifle back to the rejection.

Alice Drumming, Dean of Admissions.

Confused and curious, I dig out another student's record. I aggressively flip through the pages until I land on their offer.

Alice Drumming, Dean of Admissions.

I shake my head, trying to come up with a reasonable explanation. Quickly I grab another folder, and it's the same.

Alice Drumming, Dean of Admissions.

My fingers shake. Once is weird. Twice is a pattern. Three times is a brick through a glass window.

Why would the chancellor sign off on my acceptance?

I turn back to my file, flipping fast. The syllabi, course schedule, personal records, everything starting to blur, just blobs of black ink on the page.

There's no award letter.

No scholarship breakdown.

But then I find something else instead. A single-page document, tucked behind a transfer credit audit. The heading makes my stomach pitch.

COST OF ATTENDANCE SUMMARY | SPRING SOPHOMORE YEAR – SENIOR YEAR

Tuition (5 semesters): $137,000

Room & Board: $49,750

Student Fees: $9,000
Books & Supplies: $4,800
Total Charges: $200,500
Amount Paid: $200,500
Payment Method: Internal Transfer—Office of the Chancellor
Balance: $0.00

I blink twice, trying and failing to wrap my mind around this. But no matter how long I stare at the page, the numbers don't change. There's no mention of a scholarship. No foundation, no donor, no award title—nothing. Just cold numbers and a mystery payment.

"Internal Transfer—Office of the Chancellor"?

I grip the paper tighter, shaking my head. This wasn't a scholarship. It wasn't based on merit, need, or on anything that I earned. It was paid for.

My heart hammers so hard, I'm afraid someone will hear it thumping. My vision tilts, the file wobbling in my hands as the world narrows into a single thought. I wasn't accepted at all. I was placed in this school. But why?

"Sam," Alex whispers, his voice rough and full of urgency. "Hurry up."

I jerk like I've been yanked, my hands fumbling as I shove papers back into the folder. They crumple at the edges and nothing wants to slide in right. It's as if my fingers no longer belong to me, doing the opposite of what my brain wants them to.

I shove the two students' records back in place, then reopen my own. Quickly I snap photos of the letters and the cost summary. The flash is off and the angles are sure to be shit, but that doesn't matter, I just need the proof.

Finally, I tuck the manila folder back in its place, taking extra care that I didn't mess up the alphabetical order. And just as I'm about to close the drawer, my eyes catch something—a name.

COLLINS, MIRANDA.

My body locks up, every limb wired tight. A noise scratches at my throat, but nothing comes out.

"Mom?" The word comes out broken, that single syllable crushing me.

Everything goes blank, and my knees wobble. I grip the drawer to keep myself from crashing to the floor. Her name stares back at me, and my whole world shatters. And suddenly I'm that little girl that found her face down on her bed with an empty pill bottle in her hand.

I hesitate to pull her folder out but manage to get it together long enough to do so. The pages have turned a dull yellow, the print slightly faded. My eyes narrow in on the graduation date—nineteen years ago. She would have been about twenty-one at the time.

"She was a student here? Why didn't she ever tell me?" I whisper. This is all too much, too suffocating.

"Sam," Alex hisses again, snapping me out of it. "We need to go now."

I force the file back in place but then think better of it. I need to know more. So I snatch up the contents but leave the empty folder behind. That way, if someone were to look, they wouldn't know at first glance that her actual file is missing.

Lifting my shirt, I tuck the pages into my waistband and hurriedly cover them. The drawer slams shut behind me as I rush out of the office. Suddenly, I remember the door was locked and make quick work of reengaging it. The moment I make it to the front, a light flashes through the glass and I step back, pressing my back into the nearest wall like I want to melt into it.

Alex brings a finger to his lips and tucks himself into the dark corner by the entrance. The shadow of a man reflects on the floor, and I hold a hand over my mouth to still my breaths.

My heart thumps against my ribs as he walks nearer before pausing. It feels like forever before he turns and leaves. I finally exhale shakily.

Alex holds up a hand, silently telling me to stay put. He inches toward the door, his back to the wall as he checks the lobby. After a beat, he grabs the knob and slowly peeks his head out. Without looking back, he waves me forward and I race to him, staying close.

He locks the door from the inside, and we bolt, jetting for the exit, only to hear the footsteps of the security office coming down the left hallway. Alex grabs my hand, tugging me behind a pillar, shielding me between his back and the wall. I grab hold of his shirt, squeezing for dear life.

The man moves past us, and Alex, who's still holding my hand, guides me away. "It's clear. Let's go."

How is he so calm? We nearly got caught.

We walk to the exit, and when he pushes the door, it creaks loudly. We freeze.

"Hey! Who's there?"

Alex yanks me through the threshold. His arm wraps around my waist, spinning me toward the door so fast the files crush between my spine and the door as he uses my body to close it. Then he's on me, and I barely gasp before his mouth crashes onto mine.

There's no warning. Just heat, teeth, and an unexpected possession. The moan escapes me, and his tongue drags against mine like he's searching for something. Like he's trying to shove himself inside me. I don't have time to think, and my body reacts all on its own. My head tilts, and lips part. I lean into him, his hands anchoring my hips, his body pressing me harder into the glass.

Then his mouth is on my neck, teeth and tongue taking turns devouring my flesh. He sucks and my knees almost buckle, but it's the sharp nip of teeth that does me in. Alex groans against my throat, almost as if he can feel that I'm melting against him.

It's not until the tap on the window that I remember where we are. The security officer forces the door open, and Alex moves me from in front of it. The guard flashes his light between us to get a good look at our faces.

"What are you two doing out here?" His voice comes out annoyed.

Still close to my jaw, still sounding like lust and defiance, Alex says, "Sorry, man. We got a little carried away."

I can barely breathe. My lips feel swollen, and my heart is going haywire.

The security officer makes a noise somewhere between irritation and disinterest. "Well, do it somewhere else." The man grunts, closing the door and locking it.

Alex steps back like nothing happened, then holds his phone light up to my neck. I swear the flicker of a smirk forms, but it falters as quickly as it appeared.

"You can take off my sweater." He leans in again, his voice right at my ear. "But try covering up that mark."

And just like that, he walks off. I don't move right away, my mind busy trying to decipher everything that's happened tonight. My body's still shaking, both from nearly getting caught and—whether I want to admit it or not—that kiss.

CHAPTER TWENTY-THREE

SAM

It's been two days since Alex and I broke into the admissions office, and I still haven't caught my breath. The pages with my mother's name on them are fanned out on my bed. I stare at them, hoping that the answers to the millions of questions racing through my mind will somehow materialize. Hoping that there is any sort of explanation. But they don't, and there isn't. And I'd know because I've been staring at them for hours, rereading things that aren't new to me.

Name: Collins, Miranda
DOB: May 25, 1984
Address: 713 Bell Ave

We haven't lived there since before Momma met Gary, but the memories are vivid. Life was good back then. Just me, her, and my grandparents before they passed away. She smiled all the time then, and was the light in every room she walked into. We'd stay up all night with her braiding my hair and telling me about all the wonderful things waiting for me in life.

But she never told me this. Sovereign King's University is not just the best school in the county. Kids come from all over the country to attend. Getting accepted into this school was the goal. Of course, now that I've been here and have almost been assaulted and bullied damn near every day, I know that to be a farce.

It's hell on this campus, but their track record for producing solid careers for their students is almost unmatched.

They have one of the highest ratings in the country, graduating ninety-five percent of each class. Students go on to become doctors, lawyers, politicians, business owners, and successful athletes. The connections you make can be priceless. Yet she never told me that she was a student.

But then it leaves another question. If SKU is so great at producing success in their students, what about her? She had a decent job, but worked long, excruciating hours to do it. She didn't get the life they promised. She was rich with family, with love, with me and Desmond, but clearly not rich enough.

I reach out for one of the pages, her transcript. She was smart, damn near a straight A student. There's no surprise there; I have to get my brains from someone. A smile spreads across my face. It feels good to share similarities to her. When she was alive, I got told every day how much I looked like her, so much so that folks in the old neighborhood referred to me as *Lil Miranda*, instead of Samantha.

"Lil Miranda, come here and let me look at you."

"Lil Miranda, take this to your granny for me."

A tear falls and I swiftly wipe it away. "God, I miss you, Ma."

The bathroom door flies open, and Gracie exits wearing a towel. I don't bother to look up, my focus glued to the pages, but from the corner of my eye, I see her moving about. She's at her dresser, pulling items from the drawer.

"What's all that?" she asks.

I shake away the emotions, letting my eyes meet hers.

Gracie turns forward again, her towel wrapped around her waist as she slips a sports bra over her head. When I don't respond right away, she glances back at me.

"Earth to Sam." She slips on her panties before removing the towel and tossing it into the hamper near her closet. "You've been staring at those papers like they're possessed or something."

"Sorry." I take a deep breath. "It's nothing."

Gracie continues to dress, throwing on leggings, a T-shirt, and crew socks. "Bullshit."

She lets her sock snap into place, the sound of the elastic hitting her leg sounding off through the room. She turns on her heel and saunters in my direction.

"You come in here every other day ranting about the boys. Stayed out later than usual last night. Skipped class today, which is hella sus considering you're probably the only person I know that actually enjoys learning. And don't think I forgot about Alex getting between you and Aaron minutes before decking him in the jaw."

I open my mouth to respond, but the words never come.

"You've been staring at those pages all day, and please don't think you're hiding that massive hickey on your neck." Gracie points at the spot where Alex marked me.

Nervously, I lift my shoulder and pull my collar up as if it will actually hide the damn thing. Gracie sits at the edge of my bed, one leg folded under her. Tilting her head, she reads one of the pages.

"Who's Miranda?"

My shoulders slump, and something in me caves.

"My mom."

Gracie snaps her gaze to me, but she doesn't say anything

right away. She only looks at me in that patient way that she does when she knows I'm trying not to spiral.

I pick at the corner of the page, nails catching on the edge like I'm trying to peel away the truth. "Apparently, she was a student here," I murmur. "I didn't know. All the years we talked about college, and how much fun it can be, and she never mentioned that she went here."

Gracie shifts slightly but still doesn't interrupt.

"There was no diploma lying around, no photos from her time here, nothing. But then I found this last night and nothing makes sense." I huff, toss the transcript down, and pull one leg close. To anchor myself, to keep from feeling like I'm living in the matrix, I scratch my nails over my ankle hard enough to feel but not enough to break skin.

"Where did you get this?" she finally asks while picking up one of the pages.

I pause, then exhale slowly, debating whether or not to share. Not because I don't trust her. She's probably the only person at this school that I feel safe enough to open up to. It's just that so much has happened since stepping foot on this campus. Things that bring more questions than I am able to answer, not without pissing some people off.

But if I keep it bottled in, it'll fester and eat me from the inside out. It'll drive me crazy, until I don't know where the truth ends and the lie begins. I can trust Gracie. Right? I read her for a moment, taking in her features. They're soft as always, concern evident in the worry lines above her brow.

"You have to promise not to freak out."

Gracie cocks a brow, jutting her head back just a little. "That's never a good sign."

I lean back against the wooden headboard, bringing my knees to my chest. "Alex and I..."

"Fucked," she blurts.

I frown and shake my head. "Eww, no—well, not exactly. He did give me this hickey but that's beside the point."

"Okay," she drags out while repositioning herself so that she is fully seated, crisscross applesauce, at the foot of my bed.

"We broke into the admin building."

Her head jerks back. "You *what?*"

"You're freaking out," I hiss.

Her eyes are wide now, but there's more curiosity than judgment. "No. I'm just shocked. But I'm listening."

I release a breath. "My acceptance here is suspicious. Nothing was making sense, and I needed answers."

"What do you mean?" Gracie swallows hard, the bob of her throat visible as she shifts uncomfortably, much like she does wherever Christina or the guys are concerned.

"I was previously rejected. Which was fine. People get denied their dream school all the time. But then a year later, I received an out-of-the-blue acceptance and a scholarship."

Gracie shrugs. "I'm not following. Why is that bad?"

"It's not, although strange. But then, they aren't just covering my tuition." I snatch up my phone, unlock it, and scroll to the photos from last night. "My dorm, meals, supplies—everything is fully covered. They put me in the junior/senior dorm instead of the lowerclassmen building. And let me off for breaking that asshole's knee with just community service, when it was very clear Mr. Kincaid wanted to press charges."

Gracie's eyes slide away at that as she rubs her arms nervously.

"You okay?"

"Yeah, sorry. Had a chill." She pauses and rubs her palms over her arms. "So, what do you think?"

I frown at her changing the topic but decide not to push it. I'm the last person to get on someone for keeping things to themselves.

"I don't know. But it doesn't add up, and whenever I ask the staff to give me details of this *scholarship*, they get cagey or dismissive. So, I went to Alex."

"Before or after you *didn't really screw* and he left that love bite," she teases.

"It's not a love bite. But after the not really screwing part."

"But before he sucked your neck like a Popsicle."

I huff. "Can I finish?"

She holds up her hands. "My bad."

"I asked him to help me find out information. His father runs the school and if anyone could get access to stuff, I figured it would be him."

I click on the picture of the cost summary and turn the phone for her to see.

"This is what we found. The chancellor signed my offer letter instead of the dean of admissions. And not only is there not a scholarship, someone paid over two hundred grand to make sure I got in."

Gracie takes the phone and sits up straight, flipping through the images as if she'd be able to make sense of any of it.

"While I was looking for my file," I say, my voice thinning, "I saw my mom's."

Gracie's lips part and her shoulders go rigid.

"I think it has something to do with the fact that she was a student here, too," I admit, the only thing that makes sense to me.

She shakes her head. "Wow. This is...a lot, Sam. How can you be sure?"

I inhale, my shoulders pinned by my ears. "I can't. But something deep down won't let it rest. My mother was a student and, nineteen years later, some anonymous benefactor covers two and a half years of my education. What aren't they telling me?"

I sigh.

"I thought getting my records would shed light on things, but it's only left me with more questions."

"Have you tried the library archives? They keep everything. Yearbooks, old club records, alumni information, school paper articles. If she was a student here, she's in there somewhere."

"You really think so?"

Gracie hops off the bed, the mattress shifting from the change in weight. "I think if my mom kept something this big from me, I'd want to find out why. Maybe finding stuff on her can help shed some light on all the other questions."

She walks over to her closet and retrieves a pair of sneakers. Then she picks up mine from by the foot of my bed and holds them out to me.

"Come on. We're not going to find the answers sitting here staring at papers."

The library is nearly empty with the exception of a handful of students. The library assistant is restocking books as she listens to something through her headphones. Class finals aren't close enough yet to bring in the caffeine-fueled panic, so we get a computer right away. Gracie pulls out the chair, the legs scraping over the carpet.

I take a seat and cue up the log-in screen. After typing in my student information, the desktop view loads. Gracie points to an icon—a stack of books. My chest pulses at the single word beneath it. Archives.

I click on the app, and it takes a second for the muted blue background to morph into a bright white with **Sovereign King's Archives** above an empty search bar. I type in my mother's name, hesitating for a beat before clicking the magnifying glass beside the bar.

Gracie points at a listing in the middle of the screen. "There."

Miranda Collins...student records...2001-2005.

I click the hyperlink, my nerves already getting the best of me. My fingers go numb, and what little breath I have left leaves as information populates.

"Wow." I blink.

I stare at the details, completely caught off guard by some of the things listed. She was on the yearbook committee, and in a few different clubs: Future Economists of SKU, Student Justice Coalition, and Poetry Club.

There's even a list of awards she won.

Poetry awards. Yearbook committee recognitions. A campus leadership medal with her name etched in a bold serif font. She was brilliant. And she never told me. My throat goes tight, and I press a fist to my mouth to keep steady.

All these years, I thought she was just floating through life, just surviving parenthood, bills, her mental demons...and Gary. And this whole time, she was someone else, too. Someone with a voice and dreams. Someone who once had a life here.

Beneath the text and awards is a grid of photos, and my heart stops. There she is, smiling and alive in a way I've never seen her. In one of the images, her hair is longer, a little wild around the edges as if the wind was too much that day. In an another, she's eating soft-serve ice cream, strands of her perfectly laid sew-in tucked behind her ear. There's one of her with some girl whose arm is around my mom's shoulders, and they're laughing, both bent over and unable to keep it together.

It's been years since I've seen her like this. And I don't know what's worse—that she had this whole life that I never knew about, or that something must have happened to make her bury it. I don't know this version of her, but I want to. And while this doesn't bring her back, it heals a part of me.

"Damn, Sam. You look so much like her. You could be her twin," Gracie says, pulling me from my thoughts.

My eyes sting, but I blink away the tears. "Yeah," is all I say, my voice catching.

Gracie leans closer, quieter now. She rubs my shoulder, but I can tell she's not sure how to comfort me. Why would she? Her mom is alive and well; they speak every other day and seem to be the best of friends. I love that for her.

Pulling myself together, I survey the other images, each one making me more emotional than the last. But the final one stands out to me the most.

I freeze, tension spreading through my body. Gracie sits up, just as curious as I.

"What?" I whisper.

"That's my mom," Gracie blurts and points to the woman on my mother's left. They're similar, she and Gracie. The same warm brown complexion, big doe eyes, and long curly brown hair.

And Kane's mom.

She's to my mother's right, and looks exactly how I remember her, but younger and brighter. Healthier, mentally and physically. Her skin is a deep sepia brown that shines from the sunlight. The sharp lines of her pixie cut frame her face perfectly, and her red lips are bold, loud, and full of life. I don't point out her identity to Gracie because I'd have to explain how I knew her.

My chest tightens once more, and my head starts to spin. Not only did my mother attend here, but so did Kane's. And they were friends. All this time, I thought they met at the facility, but—

"Who is this?" I ask, pointing to the taller blond woman, with long wavy hair and the greenest eyes I've ever seen.

I read the names as if somehow it'll change the faces staring back at me.

Ladies of Aurelian Circle: La'Kia Kane, Miranda Collins, Desiree Del Rosario, Amber Whitney, and Lynn Hansely.

"Amber is Alex's mom." Gracie points to the taller of the two, and then the other. "And Lynn is Christina's."

No fucking way. But she's right. I see the resemblance, her eyes the same shade of green as his. He looks like his father, but he definitely has his mother's hair and eyes.

"What's the Aurelian Circle?" I ask.

When I got my acceptance, I studied every extracurricular this school had to offer, and I don't recall seeing this listed anywhere.

She shrugs. "Never heard of it. See if it'll let you click on it."

I do as she suggests and another page loads.

The Aurelian Circle, an invitation only social club for high-performing Sovereign King's University students with a desire to make a change in the world through charity and philanthropic efforts.

Gracie points to a line on the screen. "Looks like it was defuncted, in the spring of '05."

My expression knits, and I scowl without meaning to. "That's the year my mother graduated."

"Does it say why they shut it down? My mom never said anything about being in this club." Gracie reaches over me to take the mouse and control the search. "That's it?"

She goes to the top and types the club name into the search bar, but the only thing that pulls up is the same description. That's weird. Everything else we've searched had loads of results but this stops here. The more I look into things, the deeper the hole gets, and I'm no closer to finding out the truth.

Before I can say anything else, a voice cuts through the quiet behind us.

"Look, girls. If it isn't the rejects."

Christina.

They laugh as I hop to my feet and spin to face them. Christina walks closer with two girls at her side, both in matching sneers.

"What did you just say?" I step forward, my fist already balled tight.

My nerves and emotions have been dragged through the mud more times than I'd like in the last forty-eight hours. The last thing I have time for is this bitch and her band of flunkies.

"You heard me," she snaps back.

Gracie stands, and I don't miss the way her entire posture changes. Her spine snaps straight, eyes blinking rapidly, breaths uneven.

"Hey, Gracie Poo." Christina waves, her tone antagonizing.

"Fuck off," Gracie bites back.

She cackles. "That's the best you can do?" She peers at her friends, who join in on the laughter. "Oooh, I'm scared."

"I don't know what your problem is with me or Gracie, but this little mean girl act of yours is getting real old."

"I told you Jackson was off-limits. But you had to go throw

yourself at him like some desperate puck bunny. But why am I surprised? Sluts flock together, right? First Gracie, then you."

From the corner of my eye, I notice the color drain from Gracie's face as her body starts to shake.

"The only desperate one around here is you. Hung up on a boy who's clearly not that fucking into you. Maybe your focus should be on your self-esteem and not who does or doesn't want your sloppy seconds. And fighting over a piece of shit like that... Girl, are you good?"

"Watch yourself," she seethes.

"I've played it cool, let all the little slick comments and jabs slide, but I'm warning you. Back the hell off."

"Ladies," a stern voices cuts through the tension. "Do I need to call security?"

Neither Christina nor I break eye contact, but I can feel the librarian looming near us.

"Let it, go, Christina," one of her friends advises while grabbing her wrist and pulling her toward the exit.

Christina walks away, her shoulders rising and falling in rapid succession. She's not used to people standing up to her—girls like that never are. They expect people to just roll over and take whatever they dish out. Think they can do what they want, consequences be damned.

I've kept my cool, stopped myself from fighting back because all it would take is for one more thing to get back to Chancellor Williamsburg, and he'll make good on his threat. But not tonight. All the pent-up emotions, all the years of anger and resentment, came boiling to the surface, and I can't just let this go. Not this time.

Christina throws a glance back at us. "Bitch."

"Your momma," I snap back before she makes it out of the library.

CHAPTER TWENTY-FOUR

BRYDEN (MOUNTAIN)

I've been up for the last hour but haven't moved. The blinds are cracked just enough to let the gray light bleed through. It paints thin bars across the ceiling, broken up by the slow sweep of shadows from swaying branches. My phone buzzes on the nightstand, but I don't reach for it right away.

I should be up. Mondays are light for me with no classes scheduled, so I generally take that time getting in more practice. By now, I'd already be dressed, taped, and halfway through drills before the rest of the campus opens their eyes. But not today.

Today, I'm trying something new.

Resting... or having a slow morning, as the girls call it. It's a rarity for me, or a miracle depending on who you ask. My mother would say *"about time."* Alex and Kane would think I'd been abducted by aliens. And that's exactly why I haven't gone into the kitchen to make my morning protein shake. They'll never let it go, making a bigger deal out of it than it is.

You don't become the best by lying around. No, you do that with discipline and routine.

When I finally sit up, the sheets fall heavily off my chest. I rub a hand over my face and reach for the phone. There're several notifications—a string from the team chat, one from the group chat I share with Alex and Kane, spam texts, and an email. The most recent of them is a text from Kai.

Lil Bro: Game Request. Basketball.

My lips twitch. Not a smile, not really, more like muscle memory than anything else.

Bryden: Good morning to you too, lil bro.

Another buzz hits before I can even lock the screen.

Lil Bro: First to 20. Loser owes Steambucks.

This kid wakes up like he's been shot out of a cannon after downing a gallon of energy drinks.
And of course, the prize is only something he would want, but I know he looks forward to these games. It's how we stay connected with me being away at college. The reservation isn't too far away, but it was much easier for me to move in here with the boys instead of commuting in every day. And much cheaper than room and board on campus.

Bryden: You're going down.

Lil Bro: In your dreams, big head. 😈🏀💨😏🔥

What does that even mean? I smirk.

Lil Bro: 🐐

Wow. At least that one, I get. He's GOATed.

I tap the link, and the game loads. It's our favorite. You get thirty seconds to get as many shots as possible. I swipe the screen, sinking the first shot. Then four. Then twelve. And with ten seconds left on the clock, I move at a snail's pace, making only one in that time. And then the round is over.

A minute later, Kai texts again.

Lil Bro: You can't see me. 💥

Lil Bro: (Breakdancing gif)

He claimed twenty shots to my *seventeen*.

Bryden: Dang. You got me.

Lil Bro: 😜 😜 😜

I stare at the screen for a second, lips twitching again. The dancing gif is still looping at the top of the thread. I click on the pay icon beneath the message thread, and key in twenty-five with no hesitation and send it. The transaction sends, the total staring back at me boldly.

I can already see his reaction. And it's not lost on me that he'll probably blow through this before I set my phone down. No reply ever comes, but I don't expect it to. I toss the device on the pillow next to me and grab my laptop from the spot beneath it.

There're a few weeks before nationals roll around, and since I'm not doing anything else, I decide to review the opposing team's game footage. We've played Westover before and they were easy wins, but you can never be too careful. They're going to pull out their best stops to take nationals home, so I want to be prepared. If there's a weakness, I need to know it. A strength, I need to be ready for it.

My phone rings again, and I turn my gaze to read it. I set the computer across my lap and reach for it.

Collins: You're not resting, are you?

My lip twitches again as I sit back against the headboard.

Bryden: Actually, I'm still in bed.

The dots appear right away.

Collins: 🐨

I huff. It's not a laugh, not quite, but it's the closest I've come in months.

I gloss over our previous conversation, the thread stretching longer than I remember. We've texted pretty regularly since that first meeting in the library, and slowly it's becoming our thing. Usually the conversations are clinical, task-oriented, and focus entirely on the physics project.

But every so often, something normal slips in—something personal. Not nearly as personal as that first thread about her stepfather. They're more lighthearted, friendlier. I discarded the original conversation as I promised, but everything else, I've kept. And somewhere between winning finals, graphs, and formula theories, the banter started.

Or more like teasing. The other day for example.

Collins: Do you ever smile? Like, ever?

Bryden: Not really. Never felt the need to.

Collins: I'm pretty sure there's a study that says people who don't smile are serial killers.

Bryden: Really? Where are these studies?

Collins: The internet. 🤷

Bryden: Hm. 🤔

Collins: See. I can feel the lack of smiling through the text.

Collins: I bet you don't even know how to rest. Probably have a whole routine you're a stickler for.

Bryden: What's wrong with routine?

Bryden: And I can rest.

Collins: Prove it. When don't you have class?

Bryden: Monday.

Collins: Sleep in. Take a slow morning.

Bryden: A slow morning?

Collins: I bet you won't, but since you said that you know rest, I dare you to.

Bryden: $5 says you're wrong.

Collins: Bet. But I'll need proof. Send a pic or it didn't happen.

I shake my head, her next response bringing me back to the present.

Collins: You know. I didn't think you had it in you. Guess you gotta pay up.

I adjust myself in bed, position the laptop so that the screen is in the shot, then run a hand over my chest, lift my phone, and snap the photo before I can second-guess it. It's me, still in bed, game footage paused in the background, light barely filtering in through the blinds.
I send it and wait.
Her reply is instant.

Collins: The Mountain is still in bed, and shirtless no less. I guess I've been bested.

My lips pull again, and this time I don't try to stop it. Even if I don't realize it until after it happens.

Collins: Though I'm inclined to say it doesn't count since you're reviewing Westover footage. That's technically working.

Bryden: I disagree. I'd say it's closer to a study session.
And I'm impressed that you knew who was on the screen.

Collins: It's kind of hard not to when you guys have damn near drilled all things hockey into my brain.

Collins: I even dream about blade measurements now.

Collins: 😫

I smile harder. Sam's been working with us for over a month now and I can't say that I'm surprised at all. She's smart, probably too smart. And the way her brain works, how she's always thinking ahead, is intriguing. She's disciplined, taking everything she does seriously. We're alike in that way, eyes on the prize and not letting up until we achieve it. I sense that about her, just from watching her master her tasks as our equipment manager.

Collins: Still on for the supply run for our project? I just finished at the library with Gracie, and I could use the distraction.

Instantly, I'm curious.

Bryden: Yeah. I'll drive.

She sends back a thumbs-up emoji, then a meme of a little boy resting his chin on his palm while tapping his other hand on the table—waiting. It's one of those black-and-white shots from an old-timey show. I don't laugh out loud, but my mouth pulls at the corners.

I send one back, the one of Forrest Gump running. Sam hearts it, and I find myself sitting there with my hand on my chest before climbing out of bed, quickly brushing my teeth, and then getting dressed.

The boys are gone now. I heard their cars pull out of the graveled drive just a few minutes ago. Which is good because that means I get to avoid explaining why I'm in civilian clothes and not my practice gear or toting my backpack. I also wouldn't even begin to know how to explain that I'm going to pick up the girl they both hate.

It's simple enough. We're physics partners, and I have no choice.

Only that no longer feels entirely true. I've started to look forward to our messages, to seeing her at practice. There's still so much I don't know about her, but the more time we spend together, the more I realize how refreshing she is.

Sam couldn't care less about status, about the game, or about us. She does her time and moves on.

I like that about her.

By the time we pull away from the school, she's already scrolling through a Pinterest board on her phone. I know because every time she adds something, I get an alert from the app she made me download.

I smile inwardly, appreciating how thorough she is. It's funny really. She teases me about being so anal, so particular about things, but doesn't even realize she's the same way.

It's so subtle that if you aren't paying attention, you'll miss it.

The Pinterest board, notebook full of ideas, the iCloud photo album she shared with me the other day, even down to the process she's created for the team. Checking everything four times before calling it done, memorizing all of our preferences and setting up a system to keep it all organized.

I keep my eyes on the road, not because I have to, but because it's better than staring too long.

"I think we should hit up the art supply store first. We should be able to get most of what we need there," Sam says while still scrolling on her phone.

I brave a quick glance, letting my eyes fall over her face, lingering a little longer than intended on her mouth.

"Sounds good," I add, forcing myself to look forward again, but not before reaching over and turning on the radio.

A sound plays through the speaker system, and she immediately starts to bob her head to the rhythm. I cock a lopsided smile, and adjust in my seat, one hand on the wheel and the other resting along my chin.

The drive to the nearest shopping center isn't a long one. We pull into the parking lot, just as a car shoots out in front of us. I slam on the brakes, my arm instinctively flying out to brace her.

Sam pushes up onto the seat, leaning forward to scream at the driver. "Why are you speeding through a parking lot, asshole?"

Okay, that's another knowledge point unlocked. *She has road rage.*

I try to focus on the car that flew past us, but her body presses against my forearm, and my brain nearly short-circuits. My eyes fall to the space where we connect, my breath hitching for a beat. Electricity zips up my arm, settling somewhere in my gut.

"Some people shouldn't be given driver's licenses," she huffs with a flick of her wrist. Sam settles back into her seat, effectively and disappointingly breaking that connection.

Putting both hands on the steering wheel, I check both ways

before pressing my foot on the gas. We pull up in front of the craft store, and I whip the car into park. I kill the engine, run my palms over the front of my jeans, then reach for my wallet out of the cupholder. While Sam looks for something in her bag, I hop out of the car, letting my door slam shut.

I round the back of the car until I'm standing on the passenger side. I reach for the handle and pull the door open for her. Sam's eyes dart to mine, almost as if she's shocked.

"Thanks." She takes my hand, allowing me to help her out of the car.

"Mm-hmm," I mutter and hit the lock button on the handle.

Sam walks ahead of me, and I follow closely behind her, fighting to keep my eyes above her waist. We reach the entrance, and I reach around her to open it.

"Thank you again." She enters the store, the threshold sensor dinging.

"Mm-hmm," I respond.

Sam glances around the store then turns to face me. "What we need are going to be in different parts of the store. I'll take the first half and you take the last."

I nod and she pulls out her phone to share her list with me. Of course, she organized the list by what aisle they're in in the store.

And she calls me a stickler.

"All right. See you in a bit." Sam waves awkwardly and is off without another word.

I watch her grab a basket, then walk to the farthest aisle, realizing that she's going to work her way back to the front. That way she's closer to the register once she's finished shopping. I shake my head, grab a basket of my own, and walk to my side of the store.

Following her lead, I start at the last aisle. There's a woman with a cart full of supplies. She smiles at me, and I tip my head in response, caving into myself to move past her. A second later, my phone buzzes and I glance down to a message from Sam.

Collins: Did you know that acrylic paint wasn't a thing until the 40s, and because of how fast they dry, it became the go-to for modern artists?

I frown, now curious.

Bryden: No????

Collins: Neither did I until the guy next to me wouldn't stop talking to me about it. Send help.

I smirk and inadvertently glance up at the woman in the aisle with me. My face twists, my nose scrunching in disgust.

Bryden: I'll trade you. The lady in my aisle just dug out a massive booger and wiped it on her pants.

Collins: 🤢

Quickly, I speed-walk to the next row. After a few more minutes, we meet at the checkout line. Sam is walking toward me, huddling close as she tries to hold back a laugh. She tilts her head, signaling for me to come closer. I lean into her, immediately wrapped into the scent of her perfume. It smells sweet like vanilla, and, boy, is it intoxicating.

"That's the guy." She points behind her then steps around me to let out a laugh.

The guy makes brief eye contact with me, before turning his attention to one of the endcap items. I face forward and saunter up behind Sam as we wait for our turn. She stands just under my chin, and I don't think I noticed how short she was before now.

The line moves, and she sways just a bit as her feet start to move. My front grazes her back and every muscle in my core clenches, but I suck in a breath to compose myself.

"Register four is open," the clerk blurts out, raising her hand high for us to see.

Sam strolls to the counter with me hot on her heels. We set both baskets on the surface.

"Good evening," Sam greets.

But the clerk barely acknowledges us. Doesn't say hello, doesn't look up. She just starts ringing up items with the aggressiveness of a person who hates their job. I notice the smile on Sam's face falter, and she looks at me as if to mentally see if I saw that, too.

The woman lets out a deep breath and pretty much throws the items in the bag.

"Total's sixty-nine fifty-seven."

Annoyed by the woman's actions, Sam peers at her while digging into her back pocket and holds out a twenty-dollar bill. "Sorry, this is all I have."

"I've got it." I wedge myself in front of the card reader and pull my card out of my wallet to pay.

"Thanks," she says and returns her money to her pocket and grabs the bag from the lady.

Sam walks away before I can take the receipt, and I have to take long strides to catch up with her outside.

"That type of stuff really bothers me," she says.

Tucking my wallet into my back pocket, I reach down to take the bags from her.

When we reach the car, I unlock the passenger side, waiting for Sam to climb inside.

"That doesn't get under your skin?"

"Some stuff just isn't worth the energy. She could have been having a bad day." I hand her the bags then close her in. The moment I'm seated behind the wheel, Sam turns to me.

"How are you always just so ... calm? It's like nothing bothers you. Just Mr. Perfect, all the time." Her eyes narrow on me. "Do you even curse? Like ever?"

"No."

"You're infuriatingly impossible." She faces forward, a soft laugh escaping her.

"Cursing is just a crutch for people who can't express themselves properly."

"Okay. I'll bite." She crosses her arms and turns to me again. "What does that mean?"

I tip my head. "It's a lack of self-control and is, oftentimes, not very effective."

"Did you just call me emotionally immature?" she asks sarcastically.

I fight the urge to laugh. "I'm saying that I don't need to curse anyone out to make my point."

"Yeah. It still sounds like you're clowning me."

The chuckle wins. "I'm not. All I'm saying is, the lady might have been having a bad day, and we should give her a break."

Sam stares at me for a moment, a playful gleam behind her eyes, but if I didn't know any better, I'd say there was something else there, too.

"Fine. You win. But if you're going to be all kumbaya this whole project, I don't think I'll survive."

"I believe in you," I deadpan, meeting her gaze.

We stay like this for a beat, staring at each other without a word between us. Suddenly the moment feels charged, like there's so much we want to say but haven't quite built the courage to. I glance to her mouth, locking the shape to memory, and find myself wanting to know what she tastes like. Then she smiles at me, and my heart skips a beat. There's something about this girl, something about the unfamiliar feelings I get whenever I'm in her presence. And if I don't reel this in, if I cross that line, I'm not sure either of us will be able to come back from that.

"We should go," I say but don't pull my eyes away from her mouth.

As if to purposely taunt me, Sam licks her lips. I groan at that, my hands fisting the steering wheel to keep me grounded.

"That's probably for the best," she says, pinning me with a look that's so close to getting us both in trouble.

I start the engine, stealing one final glance before pulling off to our next destination.

CHAPTER TWENTY-FIVE

ALEX

"You think you're hot shit, don't you?" Coach snaps, slapping a thick manila folder down on his desk. Pages scatter from the folder, and I catch a glimpse of my file...grades, warning slips, and whatever else fits inside.

"I've never cared to measure the temp of my shit, but yeah, let's say it's hot."

I can see the moment he goes from mad to livid. It shouldn't be funny but watching his anger *literally load* is definitely comical, his ivory-colored flesh slowly turning red from the neck up.

"Does this look like a fucking joke to you?" he barks.

I don't respond, only sit here, jaw clenched so tight it aches.

"Huh? You're Mr. Fucking Untouchable, right? I have very few rules, Williamsburg."

Lies. His rules, they run longer than the Nile.

"And you've managed to break every one of them. But do you want to explain this?" He opens the folder and pushes the report of my grades in front of me. "Fucking failing, Alex. Seriously?"

I open my mouth to speak but he continues before I can get out a word.

"We're heading to nationals, and you're risking *everything*.

All we've worked for. Kincaid is out *because* of your party and instead of leading by example, you constantly fuck up."

I flinch at that.

"I'm this close to benching you for the conference." He holds up two fingers, barely pinching them together.

My vision tunnels, and a tightness forms in my chest. "You can't do that."

He tilts his head back, thrown off by my response. "Hell if I can't. You know the rules. Maintain a C average to stay on the ice. You're barely scraping together a D. And your fight on the ice just made the decision a lot easier."

I get it. I screwed up, lost my cool when everything was riding on that game. And if it weren't for Kane coming in with the save at the very end, we'd be fucked. But Walton tested me.

"You don't understand. Walton—"

"I don't care," he snaps. "I told you to keep your head in the game but like always, you do what you want. You want to throw away your shot? Fine. But you won't mess it up for the rest of the team."

"Coach—" I breathe.

"You're dismissed," he says coolly.

"What about the game?" I force out the words, my throat burning, my voice singed as if I swallowed a gallon of acid. "Are you benching me?"

Silence stretches between us, and it feels as if suddenly all the oxygen in the room has evaporated. Coach doesn't glance away; he doesn't even blink. He just stares at me with steady disappointment. And somehow that cuts more than if he had just continued yelling at me.

"I earned my spot on that ice," I whisper more to myself than him. "You know that."

"You should have thought about that before you turned the rink into a UFC match. You can go. I'll let you know what I decide."

I stand up too fast, the weight of his words weighing down on me. Storming out without another word, I slam the door shut behind me hard enough to make the office window rattle. My pulse jackhammers in my chest, a blind rage burning deep as I head straight for the locker room. I shove through the double doors. Practice is over and everyone has left for the night.

"Shit," I grunt out, knocking over the nearest laundry bin. It clatters to the floor with a thud as the items inside spill across the floor.

When I finally let my gaze settle, I realize Sam is still here—in the threshold of the utility closet. It's the very place where she came on my hand. My chest tightens at the memory, my eyes roaming over her from head to toe. Sam cocks a brow and awkwardly rolls her shoulders. Her eyes lock on mine and I notice a slight change in her breath as her hand lifts to the reddish hickey on her neck. My cock twitches at the sight of it, knowing my mark is on her and the team is none the wiser.

I remember the way she melted into me even though every fiber of her being wanted to push me away. Remember the warm vanilla that seemed to be soaked into her flesh. It carries, even in the distance. I don't have to see her in a room to know she's present; I smell her. And it pisses me off. If she were any other girl, I would have moved on by now, but instead, she's deep in my head.

Bullying her started off as just a way to make her pay. For what exactly? I'm not sure. I told myself it's because she benched Kincaid.

Truth is, I do it because she's always seen through the facade.

Saw me at my lowest and, wildly enough, never judged me for it. Can't say I'm used to that, or people knowing things that they don't rub in your face later. She offered to help, albeit for a favor, but she doesn't hold it over my head. So now, with each passing day, I want less and less to have anything to do with *making her suffer*.

"Take a picture, it'll last longer," she taunts, that wicked smirk tugging at the corners of her mouth.

God, she's infuriating. And fuck if she isn't sexy as hell when she's being a menace. And then she's bending ever so slightly to pick up the laundry I knocked over.

"You're going to help or keep staring like a weirdo?" She sets the bin upright and frustratingly tosses a garment inside.

Stepping closer, I continue watching as Sam yanks up a handful of sweaters and stuffs them in the bin along with the rest. Then she's on the move, dragging the heavy gray container behind her. I glance around once more before following her into the laundry room.

Sam grunts as she flings the basket in front of the washing machines. She doesn't notice I'm behind her, so I stand there for a moment, just watching her.

"You finally want to tell me what you were looking for in the admin office?"

Sam startles, spinning to face me, but the moment her eyes settle on mine she relaxes some. I don't know if I should be pissed or flattered that my presence no longer rattles her. The latter would mean this dynamic between us has definitely shifted.

It's not all in my head. She came to me when she needed help, let me touch her even though she claims to be disgusted by me. It means that kiss interrupted her spirit just as much as it did mine.

"Excuse me." She frowns and returns to stuffing uniforms into the machines.

"The other night. What were you looking for?"

She peers back at me, a crease forming above her brows. The hesitation is evident, and I can see the wheels turning behind her eyes. She sucks in a breath, fidgeting from one foot to the other.

Looking her over again, I step closer. "I committed a crime for you. Risked expulsion. The least you can do is tell me what you were looking for."

She snaps her head to me, lips pressed tight as if something I said was crazy.

"You and I both know you weren't getting expelled. And the crime was your idea."

"Doesn't erase the fact that I did it for you."

"It's an even exchange. You helped me and I tutor you." She continues working.

I'm close now, barely half a foot between us now. She feels me there, I can tell from the way her shoulders tense and her spine straightens. Just like the night in the utility closet the moment she felt me near. She can tell herself she doesn't like me all she wants, but her body definitely has a mind of its own.

"I'd hardly call breaking and entering even with a couple of study sessions. What were you looking for?"

Sam faces me, searching my face, but doesn't answer me.

"So, you just used me?" I tip my head. "Cool."

"I wasn't trying to use you." Her eyes soften.

"Then tell me."

Sam sucks in a breath, staring at me a minute longer. "I told you I had questions about my scholarship."

I stare at her collarbone and bring my thumb up to stroke the place where I left my mark.

"And you thought my father might have something to do with it."

A shiver runs through her at my touch, and my cock jumps knowing I affect her. Still touching her soft flesh, I meet her eyes again.

Why is she so fucking tempting?

"Well? What did you find out?"

She swallows. "There never was a scholarship. Someone paid for me to be here."

I freeze but never break contact. "Who?"

"I don't know. But your father might. His name was on the acceptance letter and the financial statement."

I frown. "Why?"

She shrugs. "That's what I have to figure out. But I wasn't just using you."

I stare at her for a beat, watching her chest rise and fall. Her breathing is steady, but her shoulders have tensed again.

"What if I wanted you to?" The words are out before I realize what I'm saying.

"What?"

"We'll have multiple study sessions." I pause, waiting for her to interject but she never does. I inch dangerously close now, her signature scent filling my lungs. "I'll keep helping you."

She peers up at me with a hitch in her breath. "Though you felt like I was using you?"

I shrug and slowly bring my lips closer to her ear.

"We can use each other," I whisper. "Let me touch you again. Let me make you come."

A moan escapes me. I expect her to push me away, tell me to go to hell, but she never does. Instead, she stares at me, mouth agape, eyes searching mine for seriousness.

"Just let me taste you." It comes out desperate now, my voice raw and guttural like I've been starving and she's the only one who can feed me.

It's the truth. I haven't so much as looked at another girl since touching her.

Her lips part, but no words come out. She just breathes one shaky, shallow breath after the other. Her pupils dilate, her eyes flicking from my eyes to my mouth and back up again.

I bring my mouth closer to hers, all while continuing to stare into her eyes. If the way she presses into me is any indication, she wants this just as much as I do. My eyes fall to her neck and I nuzzle my nose against that hickey, my cock already straining against my pants.

"Alex," she mutters against my ear.

I groan at the sound of her voice saying my name and have to grip the machine behind her to keep from losing myself. My breath quickens, pulse racing. Sam palms my throat, her small hand applying just enough pressure to force my eyes to hers. Then suddenly she pushes me away.

"You'll beg before I ever let you touch me again." There's annoyance in her tone now. "I don't fuck for favors."

Then she shoulders past me, bumping me hard enough to send me stumbling backward. She shoots daggers at me, and she stomps over to the supply closet for detergent.

"Fuck," I utter under my breath. Trying to reach out for her only to miss her by a hair. "That's not what I—"

"Save it, Alex. Please take your shower so I can get the hell out of here."

I drop my hand at my side, staring at her back a little longer. When she turns in my direction again, I try to read her expression, try to get her to look at me, but it's useless. Her features are stone now, eyes glued ahead of her as if I don't even exist.

"Sam," I try again, only to go ignored as she unscrews the cap and pours laundry soap into the slot.

She doesn't respond, her walls already up. I pivot and exit the laundry room back into the main portion of the locker room. Stripping the rest of my gear along the way, I turn the corner and step into the shower stalls. The showers are empty, but the air is still damp.

Snatching a towel from the clean rack, I hang it on the nearest hook and step into the first stall. The sound of the shower rings scrapes across the metal bar when I yank the curtain closed. I smack the knob upward and the water sputters to life.

Dipping under the stream, I let the hot droplets beat down on me. Thank God for great water pressure. It seems this is the only tension release I'll be getting. It wasn't my intention to offend her, and I clearly misread the moment.

Fuck. Now she probably hates my guts more than she already does. She's probably filed me away in the category of *audacious asshole*. Yet another thing I screwed up.

My father was right. Coach was right. *I am a fuck-up*.

Maybe it's time to stop fighting that label and embrace it. It'll sure as hell make shit easier. I'd no longer need to force myself into the mold my father created for me. I've been so busy trying to find a version that doesn't exist instead of just being me... every disgruntled fiber.

As I contemplate the idea of letting go of all of it, Sam grunts in the distance, distracting me. My gaze drifts toward the partially open curtain. The slit is small but large enough for me to see her without having to squint. She picks up abandoned gear, rolling her eyes, and is completely unaware that I'm watching her. And for some sick twisted reason, I like knowing I can see her, but she can't see me. She moves about, following her checklist meticulously.

Always with that fucking list.

I pump soap into my palm and lather it over my body. When I get to my dick, Sam bends over again, that pretty ass of hers spreading just right.

"Shit," I groan low in my throat.

The ache, the sudden need to release is full-body, and pricks like static beneath my skin. It's all-consuming, goading me past all logic, all sense of reasoning. Because the last thing I need is for her to catch me like this, cock in hand, jacking off to her. After that ultimate fail of a proposition, this will sure get me labeled a creep. But I can't stop touching myself. Can't stop picturing Sam's hand in place of mine.

My fist closes around my soap-slicked length and I work it. My grip is rough, hands calloused, my strokes careless and brute, but the only thing on my mind is coming. I know it's been far too long because white-hot passion blurs my vision.

All I can think about is her.

Does she like it rough? Or is she a gentle lover? Does she like to be talked through it? I already know she's not a silent lover, but now I wonder just how loud she can get. Can she contain herself? Or will everyone in a twenty-foot radius know my name?

My cock throbs at the thought, veins pulsing as I squeeze tighter, pumping up and down my shaft with measured, angry pulls. Pre-cum mixes in with the water, milking from my tip and hitting the shower floor.

What if she walked in here right now and caught me?

Tipping my head, a tingling sensation shoots up my spine, and I let my mind fill in the blanks. And it's a vivid image. The thought alone is enough to nearly send me over the edge before I even get started.

She pulls the curtain back, eyes growing wide as she realizes what I'm doing. But I don't stop. I can't. Instead, my gaze locks on hers, then trails the length of her body. She doesn't say a word, but she doesn't have to. Her nipples harden to tight little peaks staring at me through my sweater, my number etched on her front, the hemline falling just above her bare thighs.

Sam's eyes fall to my dick, and it's hard as steel in my grasp. I follow her gaze, periodically flicking my sights between her and my hand moving along my shaft. Her eyes grow wide, lips slightly parted just before she licks them. There's hunger in her eyes as she drinks me in. Sam's hand bunches the jersey, revealing more of those thighs. I want to touch them, feel them wrapped around my waist. Slowly she inches the fabric higher, teasing me, but those sexy as fuck brown orbs never break from me. And I don't know what's sexier, fisting my cock with her in front of me, or her watching me like this is the only thing that matters.

My grip tightens and my hips piston to meet my strokes. I pull on my cock, tight quick pumps, then slow and measured pulls. The water still beats down on me, the soap now an afterthought.

"You just going to stand there and watch, Sunshine?" I let out. I want her to touch me, but I might come the moment she does.

Sam doesn't answer me, not with words at least. Instead, she hitches my jersey around her waist, her pretty bare pussy glistening. I watch her slip a finger between her slit, her breath hitching and back bucking a bit the moment she presses against her clit.

"Spread it," I say in a near whisper, jutting my chin in her direction.

And she does, using that same hand to spread her lips between her fingers.

"Fuck," I groan, and wet my lips.

Glaring back at me is the prettiest clit I've ever seen. I can't see past the obscene blur of movement, her brown skin and pink seam. It's swollen, preening, and screaming to be touched.

"Pet it for me." My vision tunnels and I focus on the movement of that middle finger, and I'm suddenly envious that it isn't my finger.

"Come here. Now," I demand.

She sucks in a breath and takes a step forward, all the while still touching her pussy. I continue fucking my hand, the grunts coming out of me more animalistic the closer she gets. With my free hand, I reach out and yank her flush to me. Neither of us stop what we're doing. Every taut motion on her clit clashes with me fucking my palm, increasing the friction.

Sam leans in, taking my mouth with hers, and bringing us even closer than what's humanly possible. We stare at each other, breaths now erratic, and when I feel her soft hands on my dick, I lose it. Head falling back, eyes shut, mouth agape. Something guttural escapes me and my brain empties.

The only thing I can think about are those small, greedy hands working my cock. The smooth wetness of her palm gliding over my angry, dripping tip.

It's fucking perfect. Better than perfect. Her grip, the low moans slipping past her lips, the unwavering furrow in her brow...her.

Lightning shoots through my spine and straight to my skull. She focuses on the head again and I choke out a shiver. It's like she's been stroking me for years, hitting the right pressure, the right rhythm, and I can't help the way my hips flex into her palm.

Suddenly, she walks me backward, pushing until my back catches the cold tile. She cages me there, still stroking me.

"This is what you wanted, right?" she whispers, her mouth dangerously close to mine. "Want me to use you?"

I nod feverishly, chasing her lips as she pulls away before I can taste them.

"Why are you so fucking hard for me?" she growls, like she hates herself for even asking. "You hate me, remember?"

"Because you're a fucking menace," I manage, my voice breaking.

A sinister smile forms at the corner of her mouth right before she drops to her knees. My back buckles, my cock throbbing in anticipation. I adjust myself, pushing toward her full lips. Her tongue flicks out to tease the crown, droplets of water pouring down the sides of her face.

"Damn," I mutter and reach out to touch her, toying with her now drenched curls.

Sam licks the tip, it's quick at first but enough to make my toes curl. I watch as she savors my pre-cum then takes me whole. The way her lips purse around the head, her tongue swirling lazily. She works me slowly, taking me deeper, inch by inch, just to torment me further.

She's not gentle, not really. She has a kind of calculated mischief that makes my knees weak. I hit the back of her throat, expecting her to gag, but it never comes, and she doesn't let up.

I cup her chin, tilting her head back, and she follows the command without even being told. She lets me take control, my hand now fisting the hair at her nape. I hold her in place, my grip tight as I move my hips. Slow at first, picking up speed with each thrust until I'm pounding. And she lets me.

She doesn't push away when it gets to be too much, doesn't flinch when my fingers dig into her neck, doesn't choke when I cram myself as far as I can go.

Suddenly, the sound of her moving around in the locker room snaps me out of my head. I peer at her through the opening, still stroking my cock while she remains oblivious to what she's doing to me. Pressure builds and it's unbearable now. My breathing quickens into a ragged pant. I bite down so hard my molars ache from me fighting back a howl.

My vision blurs, fireworks of white-hot relief detonating up my spine. And when my orgasm hits, it's like a goddamn freight train. Over and over, long ropes of cum shoot to the floor. My breathing finally settles, and my eyesight clears.

Completely spent, I stare at her a little while longer. I've pleasured myself plenty of times, but it was never like that. It probably doesn't help that her hand around my throat is etched into my memory. And when she told me to beg, I almost dropped to my knees then and there.

But I don't beg.

Girls come to me, and that's not about to change just because I can't seem to get *this* girl out of my mind.

CHAPTER TWENTY-SIX

BRYDEN (MOUNTAIN)

I lean back in my seat, one ankle balanced on the opposite knee. My attention should be at the front of the class. I might not need the credits but I'm here.

Instead, I'm half-listening and throwing my gaze around the room while Professor Wilson drones on about something. It's probably important, final grade worthy, I bet. But it seems people watching is more interesting today.

It's been like that a lot lately, especially after winning the finals. It's the only thing that matters. You'd think that being in this position before, I'd rest easy about the looming Nationals Conference, but it never gets easier. In fact, the stress feels worse. Mainly due to the fact this is the end of our collegiate run.

That's where my head is at these days. On the ice. On the game. Even when it feels as if I'm the only one with my eye on the prize. The whole team is up in arms, running ourselves to the brink of exhaustion. So much so that we played terribly in that last match. Yes, Kane took the winning shot, but it was a close game when it should have been a cake walk.

Kane's usual disposition is heavier lately, more jaded. And I don't even know what's up with Alex. He's moodier this season for sure. The pressure of being captain getting to him, perhaps even the tension from the team because of Sam. She wouldn't be working for us if it weren't for *his* father.

I find Sam two rows up, jotting down notes from the lecture. She's quiet as usual, only speaking when called on. I realize it's more of a tactic. The quieter she stays, the more invisible she remains. It makes sense why she chooses solitude over attention. It's safer that way.

We're alike in that regard. She's more outgoing than me, more outspoken when called for. Smart, and resourceful, and even though it's only been a few weeks of knowing her, I see her resilience.

I also see that she sees me. All my life people have had preconceived notions based on my stature. When you're over six feet tall and a hundred eighty pounds by middle school, you're bound to get attention. I hate it.

Except on the ice, then no one else exists. I'm a man of few words, and she gets that and doesn't judge me for it. Sure, she jokes about my demeanor and teases me about being so straitlaced, but it's different with her. It feels like she's showing me just how much she sees Bryden, the man. Not just the Mountain.

I clear my throat when she answers a question from the professor.

"Good job, Ms. Collins. You walked us through that perfectly. Impressive. I look forward to your and Mr. Montour's presentation." Professor Wilson points at Sam before continuing.

A smile threatens to pull at my lips, but I bite it back. That's another thing about her. I've never been much of a smiler, but wherever she's concerned one always tries to sneak through.

Sam nods, then subtly glances back at me. Her eyes are bright, somewhat mischievous, and I can picture the arrogance running through her mind from here. We spent last night debating about this very theory.

Picking up my phone, I scroll to our text thread.

Bryden: Teacher's pet.

Bryden: GIF of Matilda, in church, sticking her tongue out.

I watch as she glances at her phone, the corners of her lips tilting up. Sam's typing something in response, if the slight movement of her shoulders mean anything.

Collins: Are you being a hater, Mr. Montour? 😛

I lick my lips to keep from grinning.

Bryden: I've never hated on anyone in my life.

Collins: That's not what it looks like from here.

I tip my head and key in my next reply.

Bryden: Maybe it's time for some glasses, onzaamiziinsiwi.

Collins: Care to translate that, big guy?

Bryden: It means scrappy or fierce little one.

Collins: I don't know if I should be offended you called me scrappy or flattered you think I'm fierce.

Bryden: Tough decision.

Collins: Admit it.

Bryden: What?

Collins: You're obsessed with me.

My heart tugs at that.
I might be. But there's no way I'm telling her that.

Bryden: I think you should focus on the lecture. You might miss something important.

Sam reads the message, a soft breath escaping her. She doesn't look back, doesn't acknowledge that I completely changed the subject. And that's what I mean about her seeing me. She doesn't make it awkward and always keeps things playful. Though sometimes I can't tell if it's her being my friend or something more.

For the next few minutes, I fight to follow my own advice and pay attention to the lecture. But no matter how hard I try, my eyes find their way back to Sam. One moment she's twirling her pen between her fingers, and the next she's chewing on the cap. But the next time I glance up, I don't look away. It's Jackson I'm focused on now. He's slouched low in his seat, his good foot pressed into the back of Sam's chair.

She rolls her neck but doesn't give him the satisfaction of looking back. That clearly sets him off because he pushes the sole of his boot harder into the chair, causing Sam to jerk forward. Her mouth is moving, and if I had to guess, she's cursing him.

I shift in my seat, jaw ticking, heat flaring in my chest.

Everyone around us is oblivious to his bullying, or at the very least pretending to be. She sits there, shoulders tensing with each deliberate movement from Jackson. A comment here, a hit to the back of her chair there. They're small reactions, tiny flinches that are so subtle they're barely even there.

But I see them. Her discomfort, the petrified silence, it's the loudest thing in the room. She's afraid, and I don't need context to see that.

In the beginning, I understood why Jackson—why everyone—was upset. In the matter of one night, everything he'd worked for had been snatched right from under him. No finals. No nationals. Any chance he has of going pro is now entirely dependent on how well he recovers—if he recovers.

So he's angry, fine. But this is getting to be ridiculous. No one deserves this, especially Sam. And maybe I'm biased. These last few weeks of getting to know her, I've seen the light she brings to a room.

She's not the aggressively loud, problematic person they claim her to be. She's the opposite, and as I sit here, watching as Jackson continues to act like a middle school bully, I can't help but sense that there's more to the story.

My foot drops to the floor before my brain catches up. Eyes follow me as I stand, snatch up my duffel and phone, then step into the aisle. But I pay them no mind, my vision tunneled on Sam. Everyone at the front of the room continues on without a care in the world, while those closest to me whisper among themselves.

I don't rush or make a sound, just take one step after the other, one row, then another.

Jackson leans back in his seat, lifting his hand to flick his pen cap at her back. It lodges in her curls, and she isn't even aware. I'm close enough to hear his and Christina's group now, the snickers and the amusement they get out of giving someone else a hard time.

"What's she going to do about it?" I hear Christina say, not even trying to be subtle.

From the corner of my eye, I notice one of them gesturing in my direction at the same time someone whispers my name.

"Mountain." He says it like a warning, like I'm about to make a scene. But that's not my style. I don't need volume to be heard, don't need to inflict misery to get my point across. Besides, they're not worth the energy. My only concern is Sam.

I close in, but she doesn't notice me. Instead, Sam shifts like she wants to disappear, her chin tucked, hands fisting in her lap, breath hitched. Pivoting, I stop at her aisle, letting my eyes settle on her. She finally glances up, a flick of her eyes as if she felt me before she saw me. I nod once, just so she knows she's not alone. Then I lower into the seat next to her, the metal chair squeaking under my weight. My bag falls to the floor between our feet, but it doesn't stop the closeness I feel the moment my thigh brushes against hers.

I reach around Sam and push Jackson's foot off her chair. We make eye contact for a moment before she drops her gaze to my bicep. I see the questions swirling, but surprisingly, they never come. We stay like that for a beat, so much being said between us without words. Her gaze is one of thanks for the solidarity, and mine is a silent *don't mention it*.

Removing the pen cap, I peer behind me and flick it back at Jackson. Not bothering to look at him, I turn around and settle in. And the moment my back hits the seat, it goes quiet behind me. It's classic behavior. They treat the small person like trash but tighten up in the presence of someone they can't push over. Someone mutters something but I can't make out what.

"Chill," Jackson orders. It's hushed and reeks of annoyance.

"Hey," I say to Sam. "You good?"

Sam blinks, then gives the smallest smile, her eyes and shoulders softening just a little, almost as if she now feels safe.

She nods, quick and clipped. "Yeah."

I don't believe it. But I know that if I push it, so close for them to hear, she'll shut down.

So I take out my phone and do the only thing I know to do. Holding it low beneath the desk, I type:

Bryden: Be real with me.

Bryden: This is getting out of control. Tell me what's up?

I watch her phone light up and her head slowly turn toward it. She stares at my name, then back at me, confusion creasing her brow. She opens the text, reading each line painfully slowly.

Sam looks at me, her eyes pleading.

Bryden: Did something happen that night? Why is he being so mean to you?

Collins: Why does anyone do anything? Because they can.
Just leave it alone.

"Look at me," I say, more sternly than I intend to.

She does, and that's when I see it. The pain. The fear. Something snaps in my chest, something deep in my subconscious telling me that whatever she's holding is enough to break her if she lets it.

Bryden: What. Happened.

I stare at the phone, even though she's next to me, my pulse racing, fingers tingling. The silence starts to mount, and pressure builds behind my eyes. I'm usually a patient person. Things don't bother me, don't set my nerves on fire. I don't get involved in things that don't pertain to me, but something about Sam's stillness feels eerie. Feels haunting.

Collins: Haven't you heard? I raged out and broke his knee.

Bryden: Sam.

She holds the device, her grasp tightening like it's her lifeline. Then she takes a breath, her shoulders shaking. With a sway of her head, Sam punches into the keypad.

I glance at her, catching a glimpse of something playing on her features. But it's the uneasy, now awkward shifting from Jackson that I catch from the corner of my eye.

Collins: Vault.

I breathe.

Bryden: Done.

She braves another peek at me before focusing on her phone again. Her fingers trembling slightly as she types.

Collins: You have to promise not to get upset. I don't want to make a big deal out of it.

My heart stops.

Bryden: I promise.

I send, though I'm not sure it's one I can keep.

Collins: He attacked me.

Those three little words stare back at me, and I stop breathing.

Collins: That night at your party, he offered me a drink. I said no, but he insisted.

The next line tightens something inside me until there's no slack left.

Collins: So I took it but I didn't drink it.

Collins: Then he asked me to follow him outside to smoke. I went but drugs aren't my thing.

My jaw locks, my pulse slamming through my neck. I don't want her to continue, can't stomach knowing what's next, but I need to know.

Bryden: Did he hurt you?

Sucking in a breath, I brace myself.

Collins: No.

The exhale that escapes me is a heavy one, a grateful one. But my spirit tells me there's more. And it's right.

Collins: But, when I wouldn't drink, he got upset. That's when I saw that he'd slipped something in my cup. He got defensive before I even called him on it, then he snapped. Got aggressive, started cursing me, grabbing me.

My hand jolts out, white-knuckling the desk to ground me. Reading this sends my mind racing and I think back to last term, to the party that got shut down. Someone claimed to have been raped. They never shared who made the accusation, or who did it. And then it was labeled a lie, swept away like it never happened. No charges ever came about, only a curfew to reprimand us for daring to break the rules.

Collins: And when he tried to choke me, I blanked. I wasn't trying to hurt him. I swear. But I just saw darkness and I wasn't about to let him hurt me.

Bryden: I believe you. And I hate myself for not asking the truth sooner.

She smiles gingerly.

Collins: What would you have done? Fought him?

Bryden: We need to report him.

Collins: You don't think I tried? I did. But of course, he lied, and they believed him. And now I'm sentenced to work with the team until the end of the season as punishment.

Bryden: What do you mean they believed him?

Collins: He's rich, Bryden. And I'm a nobody next to him. Who do you think they'll believe? Not some poor girl from the "wrong" side of town. It's a boys' club and women are just collateral damage.

I want to tear this desk in half. I want to put my fist through his face. No, I want to shove that smirk he wears down his throat.

Bryden: Then I'll handle it.

Collins: And get caught up in something that could mess up everything you and your family's worked for? No. I know they love you around here, being the best goalie and all, but please don't.

My nerves get the best of me, and my leg bounces under the desk, the metal bracket digging into my thigh. The pressure's the only thing keeping me grounded and from losing my mind.

I could kill him.

He touched her, tried to hurt her. He intended to rape her. And she's had to just exist in his orbit, pretending that he didn't violate her.

Jackson laughs at something behind us, and something inside me fractures. Red lines my vision, my skin growing hotter by the second. I shift, legs tense, body halfway rising from my chair when Sam's hand rests on my wrist. Her touch is warm, her hand small against my forearm, but it anchors me.

"Don't," she whispers.

I look at her, my blood still boiling, and she squeezes before pulling away to send another text.

Collins: Please leave it alone.

My teeth grind as I reply.

Bryden: He deserves to rot in jail.

Collins: But he won't. I already tried to tell, and they have made my life hell in retaliation. It'll only make it worse. Forget I told you.

Bryden: I can't promise that.

Collins: I'm fine, Bryden. I swear. He wasn't successful and I got away. I just need to get through the season, and it'll all be over.

Fine? She keeps saying it as if to convince herself more than me. But it doesn't erase the truth.

Bryden: And he gets off unscathed. You should have broken more than a knee.

Then there's a pause, a long and heavy one.

Collins: Please. Let it go. As my friend.

Collins: You promised.

No. Don't say it. Don't—

Collins: Vault, remember.

My grip firms, knuckles bleaching white as the screen protector cracks against the pressure. A war rages in my chest—rage against control.

I hate that she knows I won't break her trust. That's why it exists, right? To give us both the space to speak freely, no judgment, no interrogation.

Bryden: Vault.

I shut my eyes, breathing deep and slow, because if I don't, I'll explode. So, instead, I sit back, shoving the pieces of my temper down my throat. It kills me, but I won't be the reason her world burns faster than it already is.

But if he so much as looks at her wrong again, I'll crush him.

Vault or not.

Sam sets her eyes back on Professor Wilson, but I leave mine on her. She's probably the strongest person I know, and from this moment on, she'll never have to go it alone again.

Typing into my phone, I send her another message.

Bryden: It's the latter.

Collins: Huh?

Bryden: You are fierce.

CHAPTER TWENTY-SEVEN

EVEREST (KANE)

RW: My office. One hour.

That's it. Not even a goddamn hello. Just another one of his orders like I'm supposed to drop everything and come running because the Grand High Asshole of SKU wants a meeting.

It takes everything in me not to tell him to eat shit. My fingers even hover over the reply button, but what comes out is the complete opposite.

Kane: All right.

Nearly an hour later, I enter the reception area, letting the door swing shut behind me. I slow in front of the office door and reach for the knob as it's instantly yanked open. I'm nearly run over by someone. She freezes, eyes wide, skin drained of life, with something between panic and shame tightening her whole frame.

"Excuse me." She pushes past me, her eyes downcast as she sprints away.

Gracie?

I watch as she races for the exit. She's a mess, eyes red,

shoulders curled inward like she's trying to disappear into herself.

What the hell?

I glance toward my father's door. If he's not being an asshole to everyone he comes in contact with, then the world is sure as shit coming to an end. But it is strange that he's meeting students so late in the night.

I hear his voice through the cracked opening. It's low and sharp as steel.

"I don't know what she was looking for, but I don't care. Make sure there's nothing to be found."

He ends the call as I step into the room. We make eye contact, and for the first time that permanent snarl of his isn't meant for me but for whoever is on the other end of the line.

"Have a seat." He gestures to the leather covered chair, but I'm already settling into it before he can finish the statement.

"What's this about?"

His eyes fall to the laptop on his desk, and his jaw ticks as he sucks in a breath.

I frown at that, a subtle tick in my face as I wonder what's gotten him so worked up. Whatever he's looking at has his grip strangling the mouse and his teeth grinding like he's holding something back.

"Samantha Collins," he deadpans.

I wince at the mention of her name. Why on earth is he asking me about her?

"What about her?"

With the flick of his wrist, he spins the laptop around. My brows pull tight as I try to register what I'm seeing. Security footage of Sam outside the admin building at night.

But that's not what perplexes me the most. She's not alone, and she's doing a lot more than sneaking around. Alex is with her, his body pressed into hers, and her mouth on his, back arched, eyes closed like she's savoring every second of it. He has one hand on her hip, the other laced at the nape of her neck, while mine curls into a fist against my lap. I feel the frown lines cementing in place, disdain bubbling at the back of my throat.

It shouldn't surprise me. This is Alex we're talking about—golden boy, campus charmer, always gets what he wants. I just didn't think Sam would be on that wish list.

And that shouldn't get to me. I don't care about Sam, what she does, or who she does it with. But maybe that's another lie I've told myself, right along with the one about not caring about anything. It was working. People looked at me and saw exactly what I wanted them to—the bitter asshole too checked out to feel anything about anyone, someone cold enough to be untouchable.

But no matter how hard I try to keep her at bay, try to ignore her existence, she's there. She's everywhere, incessantly getting under my skin, plaguing me at practice, at games, and in my head.

Hell, I can't even escape her during a meeting with my father. Richard studies me, almost as if he's waiting for me to react. As if showing me this solves the question of why I'm here. Or answers why seeing them together angers me so much.

"What's this have to do with me?" I shift in my seat, working overtime to steel my emotions, refusing to let him see that he's rattled me.

"I know her mother was a patient at the same facility as yours ten years ago. Know that you were friendly with her."

I flinch, every nerve tingling as numbness rushes through my veins. *He's been watching. All this time.* I've known for two years that he's been aware of me, but he wasn't a parent, never truly gave a damn aside from financially providing for us. Like I'm some experiment left to rot in the corner while he poured all his attention into the golden boy Alex—my brother.

For years he denied us that relationship, kept us so far removed from each other, but close enough to be nothing more than friends. He's never asked about my mother's episodes, never called after the emergency admissions. Never visited, not that I really expected that since she was clearly his mistress. But somehow, he knows the year that my life crossed paths with Sam's.

Is that why she's here? Was this some meticulous dossier he's been curating from afar?

What stings the most isn't the kiss, or that my father only cares right now because it pertains to Alex. But because Alex already has everything. The name, the praise. The acceptance.

Sam was mine. She hates me and I her, but that relationship was mine. Our history—our connection—is twisted, toxic, and half-drowned in silence, but it belonged to me. It was something unfiltered, the one thing I had that no one else did.

But now, it seems Alex has that, too.

"Why am I here?" I bite out. "What does my past with Sam have to do with you?"

"I don't know where your little relationship with her stands, but I need you to watch her." He leans back in his chair, his elbows resting on the armrest, his fingers intertwined.

I frown, I'm more curious now than when I came in here.

"Watch her?" My voice cuts through the room.

What could she possibly have done to put her on his watch list?

Is it because of what happened to Jackson? Or something else entirely?

I frown, more curious now than I was when I walked in here. "You're serious."

"She's digging," he says. "Into things that don't concern her. And dragging Alex into it."

"I'm not doing this," I snap and push up from my seat. "If you think I'm going to clean up your mess—"

"Son."

I dart my gaze to him, completely caught off guard. *Son?* How fucking dare he? In all this time, he's never addressed me as such, but now that he needs something from me, now that Alex has got himself caught up with Sam, I'm his son.

I lean in, my voice dropping to a growl.

"Don't call me your son just because you've run out of ways to control Alex. You want him away from Sam? Figure that shit out yourself. But whatever you do, keep me out of it."

I turn to exit, still seething at the audacity.

"Your mother's care is expensive. I'd hate to see anything interfere with that," he says, staring as if he just handed me a deal and not a threat.

My vision goes red, and I lunge forward, my fist cocked and ready to send it straight through his smug face.

"Don't be stupid, Everest." He shoots up, standing his ground. "You want the money? Do this and your mother's treatment will be covered in full by tomorrow."

He knows the exact strings to pull to keep me in check. Bastard. As much as I want to walk out right now, and tell him where he can shove it, I don't.

"What do I need to do?" I snarl.

"Watch the harlot and keep her away from your brother. Find out what she's after, and dead it."

"How do you even know that she's been looking for something? What if you're—"

"I have eyes all over this campus."

I stare at him, trying to process all that's he's said. What is Sam involved in?

"How am I supposed to do that when you won't tell me what I'm supposed to be looking for? She and I aren't exactly friends."

"You're smart." He shrugs. "Handsome. I'm sure you can find ways to convince her."

"Trying to pimp me out?"

"Whatever it takes." He breathes out. "She's already made a mess with Kincaid, and I've protected her. But if she starts digging in the wrong places, it won't end well for her."

Before I can respond or demand answers he'll never give, his cell buzzes against his desk. His wife's picture flashes on the screen. He picks up the cell and adjusts the sleeve of his blazer.

"You can go," he orders before answering and bringing it to his ear.

Whatever Sam's *digging* into—whatever *this* is—it's bigger than some kiss outside an admin building. Bigger than him pitting me against my brother.

This isn't about protecting Alex. It's about control. And if he thinks I'm going to play the loyal son now, he's got another think coming. I don't know what Sam's gotten herself into, but I'm going to find out.

And when I do, he won't be the only one pulling strings.

I should leave.

But I can't turn away.

I try. I mentally will myself to move my feet back in the other direction. My brain must have other plans because instead I remain cemented in place. A part of me needs to know why my father's interested in her and how she's involved with Alex. I meant it when I told Richard that who Alex fucks is none of my business.

Only this feels like my business. *She* feels like my business, and that irritates me. Whether I want to admit it out loud or not.

My knuckles rap against the door, and I wait. When no one comes, I knock once more, this time harder. Then it opens, and Sam's face appears. Even in the shit glow of the hallway, I can see the panic spread on her face.

Without a word, I push against the door and step inside. No greeting or introduction needed. She looks at me like I crawled out of hell. And maybe I did. Sam's frozen state lasts only a moment before she snatches up the throw blanket on her bed and haphazardly throws it over her laptop and papers there.

"What are you doing here?" Sam asks, the frown forming before she finishes the question, her eyes falling to the bottle of whiskey still in my hand.

Her eyes barely meet mine as she moves over to the desk on the left side of the room, skittishly crossing her arms in front of her.

"Why are you here, Kane? What do you want?"

I rake a hand through my tight curls, feeling the sting in my scalp from the pull, and laugh under my breath. It's bitter and hollow.

"I don't know."

"You're drunk." Her lips press into a thin line. "What's wrong with you?"

"Hmph," I huff. "What's wrong with me?"

I pace in front of her, bring the bottle to my lips and toss it back. My reflection catches in the full-length mirror on the bathroom door, and I despise what I'm looking at.

"What's not wrong?" I mutter more to myself than Sam

before turning back to her. "You. You're what the fuck's wrong with me."

A wrinkle deepens between her brows. "What?"

I step closer, looming over her.

"I said you're the problem," I grind out, dragging a hand down my face, hoping to calm the riot under my skin. "Everywhere I go, you're there. Always breathing my air, taking up space in my head."

Her jaw clenches. "Then stay away from me."

"I've tried." I sneer, jabbing a finger against my temple. "But I can't get you out my goddamn head."

We're so close now, the warmth of her body meeting mine, and I was right. Frustratingly so. The scent of vanilla cocoons me.

"Like you're some walk in the damn park." Sam inches forward, causing me to take one step back. "You think I like having to see *you*? Think I spend my days thinking about *you*?"

Cute. Using my own shit against me.

"News flash, jerk. I don't." She jabs a finger in my chest, eyes blazing. "Being here hasn't been easy, and I damn sure don't want to be y'all's locker room flunky, but it is what it is."

"Then leave SKU. Whatever you're doing here, whatever you're up to... forget it. Go away and don't look back."

Her eyes flick to the bed, and I follow her gaze to the mountain of stuff beneath that blanket. Then she shifts, subtle but stupid, like moving an inch to the left will block it from view.

And just like that, the truth clicks. My father wasn't bluffing. That smug bastard said she was digging, poking around in shit that didn't concern her. And I wanted so badly for it to be one of his manipulative power plays.

But it isn't. She's hiding something.

"What were you doing?" I tilt my chin toward the bed.

"Don't worry about it."

I take another swig. "You need to tell me, now."

Her face contorts, and she snaps her head back as if that's the craziest thing she's ever heard. "Or what?"

I let out a breath, raising a hand in frustration before lunging closer. "Damn it, Sam, I'm—"

"Full of yourself."

She pauses, and all I can do is stare.

"You don't like me, fine. Get in line. You know, I've kept to myself. Haven't pushed the fact that once upon a time you were kind to me—*were my friend*. Something clearly changed you into this angry bulldog, but trust me, the bit is getting old. I might have to do what you guys say in the rink, but outside of it, you don't control me. And I have as much right to be here as the next person."

"You don't belong here," I grit out.

"And you do? You seem to fit in real nice around here," she says, her tone almost mocking me.

The words hit harder than I expect them to.

Silence hangs thick between us, and I drop my gaze for a second, letting her words sink in. They cut deep.

"You don't get it," I mutter.

"I'm just trying to survive this place. You're the one showing up uninvited, drunk, and barking orders like I'm supposed to jump."

"Still so fucking stubborn," I snap.

"Ditto." She folds her arms over her chest.

I huff. "Just stop digging."

Her eyes widen and her breath quickens.

"And stay away from Alex."

"Alex? What does he have to do with this?" She frowns, confusion written all over her face. Her perfectly pouty, gorgeous face.

I don't respond, only bring the bottle to my lips again, but

Sam interferes, snatching it from me. I attempt to grab it back, but she jerks away.

"What does Alex have to do with anything?"

"I know you kissed him."

She staggers backward, caught off guard. "You spied on me?"

"I wasn't spying."

"So then you're jealous? That's why you've come storming in here wasted?"

I smirk, bitter and hard. "You think I give a shit who you let touch you?"

Her jaw clenches. She doesn't believe me, and neither do I.

I saw the video. Saw the way her mouth moved against his, the way she leaned in. That fucking hickey on her neck, the proof that she let him close.

"Alex put that there." I point.

She covers it without answering, but there's no use. I've already memorized the shape of it. Before I realize it, I'm inching closer. Sam shuffles back, that tough girl facade waning just a little. And something about that makes me feel like I won.

"Did you like him kissing you?" I seethe, eyes fixed on her.

"Yes."

"Did you fuck him?" My voice bounces off the close-set cinderblock, and Sam blanches.

The second it slips, I want to rip it back. But I can't. And maybe I don't really want to. It's clawing at the inside of my chest, demanding an answer.

She stares at me in disbelief, probably wondering where I get the audacity. I've been nothing but rude to her since she showed, made her feel unwanted and unremembered, but have the balls to ask her something like that. For a second, I expect her to swing at me, a right hook to the chin to put me in my place. Instead, brown eyes bore into me.

The silence stretches, and something about her not responding makes it worse, gives too much room for my imagination to run wild. To replay that kiss in my head—her mouth on his, the way she melted into him like it meant something.

A laugh almost slips out, hollow and crooked. I'm unraveling and she sees it.

"Everest," she says quietly, reaching out to touch me. "What's going on with you?"

The sound of my name on her tongue snaps something in me. She doesn't call me Kane, not the asshole she's learned to hate, but Everest. A name that no longer belongs to me. I lunge forward, fast enough to make her flinch. My forehead presses against hers, my breath short, fist clenched at my sides to keep from grabbing her outright.

"I told you not to call me that."

"Tell me something else." She breathes. "Why do you hate me so much?"

"To protect you," is all I offer.

She swallows. "From what?"

I pause. "Just stay away from Alex."

"This isn't really about Alex. Is it?" She pauses, and when I don't respond, she continues. "This is about you not wanting anyone else to touch me."

I shake my head.

"Because seeing me with Alex got under your skin. You wanted it to be you."

I suck in a breath, my eyes darting across her features. "Don't flatter yourself."

"I'm right."

"No," I bite.

"Kiss me."

The air punches out of my lungs, and I stand frozen, trapped between the desire to do exactly what she's asked of me and walking the hell out of here. If she were any other girl, the decision would be easy: fuck her and leave.

But, God, standing here with her feels easier. It's anger and passion, raw beyond restraints, but still the simplest thing in my life. My eyes fall to her mouth, slightly parted with full lips, gloss covering every inch.

When I peer back at her eyes, I find them watching my mouth, and for the first time I notice that her breathing has changed, low and labored now.

"What's it going to be?" she asks. "Kiss me." Her chest rises with a deep inhale. "Or get the fuck out."

It doesn't come out sweet or shy. She throws it at me. Doesn't ask but dares. Bracing myself, I walk forward until I back her against the edge of the bed. I can feel her chest lifting and easing against mine. Feel this moment turning into something else.

Then her scent hits me and I break.

Without much thought or effort, I fist the material of her shorts, letting all four fingers graze the crease between her thigh and hip. I trace my eyes over her collarbone, over the curve of her cleavage and back up.

She's beautiful. Infuriatingly so.

I despise that she's letting me stand this close. That she's not shoving me away. That I want to kiss her. Then my sight drags across her neck and there it is again.

It's dull, merely a faded bruise just under her jaw. But I see it, and it reminds me that it's Alex's mark. It snaps something loose in me. My jaw locks, heat pulsing behind my eyes.

She let him kiss her, let him touch her, and I hate that, too. We've shared before, he and I, sometimes at the same time, but the idea of him having her... I groan deep in my throat.

What is she doing to me? Why is she making me feel anything at all?

And I realize that I won't be able to shake this feeling—not until I get her out of my system. Otherwise, I'll spend the remainder of the year torturing us both. *Just once.* That's all I need to rid her from my subconscious.

"Just once," I whisper more to myself than her and crash our mouths together, every ounce of restraint dying on my tongue.

Sam slips her hands around my neck, and my body jerks in response. The second her mouth opens for me, I lose my fucking mind.

She digs her nails into my shoulder as if to peel me open and I grip her waist like I want to brand her into me. Her moan rips up my spine, and I bite her bottom lip in return.

Sam yanks me closer, even though there's no more room between us. She moans again, loud enough to make my dick twitch in my jeans. Cupping her face, palm over jaw, I tilt her head so I can slide my tongue deeper. Sam stands on her toes in an attempt to meet my height.

It's like she wants to crawl inside me, the way she's kissing me, giving it back just as aggressively. Sam moves to the corner of my mouth, then my chin, slowly licking her way down to my neck. It feels amazing, too good if the unexpected tingle down my spine is any indication.

My eyes close of their own accord and I tilt my head to give her better access. Then they flicker open, and I see it again, Alex's hickey staring back at me. My stomach knots, rage coiling deep. I tear my mouth from hers, angrily and desperately kissing the spot where he once did. I suck and nibble until I know it'll bloom red. Until it's my mark on her skin.

She hisses through clenched teeth, her fingers twisting tighter in my shirt. When I finally pull back, breath ragged and lips tingling, I stare at the bruised patch of skin like it's proof. Then she grips my shirt and pulls me to her height to bite my jaw. The roughness of it floors me and I'm not ready for the way my skin prickles, or how my body surges forward.

The need to taste, to devour her, takes over, and I travel down her body, kissing through the thin fabric of her tank until I'm kneeling in front of her. I hook a finger under the hem of her tiny slip shorts and move them to the side and freeze.

No panties.

"Fuck," I mutter lowly.

I grip her thigh with my free hand to ground myself as I drag my gaze upward. She's watching me, mouth open, brows knitted, and eyes glued to where my knuckles are so close to her cleanly shaved pussy.

Without breaking the stare, I release her thigh and run the pad of my middle finger between her slit.

Damn it, she's so wet, so slippery. My finger's coated in her arousal, and I bring it to my mouth and lick it off. Sam gasps, and I feel her leg muscles flutter. The taste of her is all sweet and heat.

"Mm," she groans, pushing her pelvis closer to my face. I smirk. *Greedy little slut.*

With her shorts still gripped to the side, I use both thumbs to part her lips. As soon as her bud is exposed to me, already flushed, swollen, and preening, I growl deep in my chest. I lean in, and the moment the tip of my tongue connects with her clit, Sam shudders, another whimper escaping her.

I drag my tongue up, pausing to breathe her in, and her knees buckle, damn near taking me down with her. So I grip her left leg and toss it over my shoulder to help her keep her balance. Sam claws at my hair, her fingers fisting so tight it fucking hurts, but I don't care. If that means she comes in my mouth, then so be it.

Parting her again, I flick her bud with the pad of my thumb, then rub slow tight circles before diving back in. I suck her into my mouth, massaging her clit with my tongue, all while running a finger through her juices. Once they're nice and coated, I slip one inside her heat. I angle the inside of my wrist upward and pump in and out of her tight little hole while continuing to devour her clit.

Her back arches, nearly bowing off the edge of the mattress, but I hold her down, refusing to let up, not until she falls apart and gives it all to me. The moans, the shivers, and her cum. I slip in a second finger, and Sam grinds, fucking my hand and humping my face. I push deeper, curl my fingers against that soft, spongy spot that makes her cry out. I don't let up, my mouth greedy and coated, her release running along my chin. She tries to squirm away, but I pin her in place until she shatters, one hand tangled in my hair.

"Fuuuuck, Kane," she breathes, barely above a whisper.

My muscles tense at my name on her lips, her moans wrapped around it. I pull out of her and hook around her thigh, gripping her tightly as a jolt of satisfaction, pure and raw, rushes through my veins. But that name also hits a nerve at the same time. I don't like it.

Kane is the one who breaks things, the cynic that hurts first to avoid getting hurt himself.

But Everest...

Everest is who she remembers, who's making her body scream. That's the name she should be muttering.

Her eyes are blinking slowly, nearly under a fog of sleep. I reach for the throw blanket to cover her up. Sam's still out, her back rising and falling with each intake of breath. But the moment I uncover her things, it's like the sex haze is lifted and she hurries to yank it back.

My eyes land on one of the printouts, and everything in me goes cold. I reach over her, snatching it up, dodging Sam's attempt to keep me from it.

My mother's face stares back at me, and next to her are Sam's and Alex's moms along with two other women.

"What the fuck is this?"

CHAPTER TWENTY-EIGHT

SAM

"Whatever you're up to," Kane seethes, his fist balled tight around the photo of our mothers, "it ends now. You don't know what you're getting yourself into." With that, he slams the door without so much as a *fuck you*.

One moment, we're coming off a sex-induced high, and the next all that hatred returns as if he didn't just have my pussy in his mouth. It figures. Kane's picture has to be listed under *asshole* in the dictionary.

Before he showed up out of the blue, I'd spent the last three hours combing through articles and other resources to piece together any details about my mother and the Aurelian Circle.

But nothing.

It's like it never existed—all traces of the club completely wiped from the school archives. We weren't supposed to find that photo. Whoever deleted the records probably never realized that they missed it. But it's quickly become my Roman Empire.

And now Kane knows it exists, too.

"Uggh," I groan, opening my laptop again.

No sooner than the sound leaves my throat, the door to my dorm flies open and Gracie enters. It's late, and I mentally note that she's been doing that a lot recently. Coming home well into the night, always appearing more tired than when she left.

I never ask what that's about since it's not my business. My world is spiraling enough on its own to keep tabs on anyone else. Besides, I know that her kinesiology class has been kicking her butt.

"Uh-oh," she says. "What's that face for?"

I peer up at her, letting out an aggravated breath. "It's—" I toss my hand in defeat, knowing I can't tell her about my recent interaction with Kane. "I've been looking into the club, the one mentioned in that picture we found of our moms."

Gracie hangs her keys on the hook near the door, and they rattle softly against the wall. "Yeah. Find anything?"

I shake my head. "No."

She removes her jacket, tossing it on the back of her desk chair.

"I've searched every possible source on the school's website but there's nothing."

Gracie removes her shoes and throws her socks in the hamper before slipping on her fuzzy slippers and sauntering toward me.

Gracie pushes my throw blanket to the side and settles in cross-legged at the foot of my bed. "Let me see."

I hand her the laptop, then fall back against the cubby that serves as a headboard. Gracie studies the screen, her fingers moving along the trackpad.

"I'm telling you, Gracie." I scooch farther into my bed, my hand finding its way to my hair, raking it out of my face. "Somebody's gone through a lot to make sure there isn't anything tangible."

I pause as Gracie keeps her focus on her search.

"How can it be there one day, and gone with barely a trace the next?" I ramble, shaking my head while trying to make sense of it all.

Gracie stills, her brows furrowing, but I'm too busy ranting to truly notice.

"Wait," she blurts, hovering closer to the computer.

I lean in as she shifts on the bed and turns the laptop so that we can both see it.

"I think I've found something." She points, her eyes following as I pick up the device to get a closer look.

A web page stares back at me. It doesn't belong to the school, but instead to the local newspaper. My brows pinch tight almost instantly, the curiosity mounting now. I skim the page until one headline stands out from the rest. The letters aren't bolded, there're no graphic details—only a subtle caption buried at the bottom of the page.

Student-led society disbands following a psych ward admittance.

I click the hyperlink, and the article loads painfully slowly. When it finally loads, we huddle together. The language is vague, almost sterile. But then there's a string of specific sentences that cause us to pause.

A student suffered a psychotic break.

Another student died.

A tragic episode of mental instability.

Silence sweeps over us, the kind that's bone-deep and can drown out even the loudest of noises.

"Does it say what happened?" I whisper.

Gracie's shoulders brush against mine as she points again. "Right there."

I scroll and highlight the block of text, as Gracie reads it aloud.

"'Sources confirm that during an off-campus event for members of Sovereign King's Aurelian Circle social club, a female student, age twenty-two, attacked another student in what officials are calling a "disassociated episode." Witnesses described the student as "vacant" and "not herself" in the moments leading up to the incident. She allegedly came to only after the other student had succumbed to injuries sustained during the attack. The motive remains unclear, and no substances were reported in her system at the time of the incident.'"

My eyes skate over the next line, and something clenches in my chest.

The student was admitted to the Wyndmoor Psychiatric Facility.

"Wyndmoor," I mutter, grabbing Gracie's attention. "My mom was a patient there before she killed herself."

Gracie gasps, and it dawns on me that I said that last part out loud. Not that it was some kind of secret. I've shared with her that I lost my mom years ago, but how I lost her isn't something I willingly divulge. People get weird when they know the full story, that sympathy turning into what feels more like pity.

"O-oh," she stammers. "Sam, I'm so sorry."

"It's fine," I say, hoping to shift the conversation.

"It's not. And finding out all of this right now, all the questions it's stirred up... that can't be easy."

Tears prick the back of my eyes, but I blink them away and adjust myself so that I'm sitting upright. "Yeah, well, there's not much I can do about that. She's gone, and I miss her, but it is what it is."

"Sam."

"Gracie. Seriously. Thank you, but I don't want to talk about that."

"All right." Reluctantly she nods, and sucks air into her lungs. "Do you think your mom was the student?"

All I can do is blink, my thoughts spinning on overdrive. Truth is, I don't know what I think anymore. Nothing makes sense, and with each new piece of information, something bigger is uncovered. Just bits and pieces, a blanket of words, and occasional images that somehow say everything and nothing all at once.

"I don't know," I mutter.

"We'll keep looking," she adds with a soft smile.

Gracie continues reading.

"'Authorities do not believe she poses an ongoing threat to the community. However, due to the sensitive nature of the occurrence, the student-led society involved is being disbanded immediately while investigators complete their case.'"

I snap my gaze to hers. "Did you ask your mom about the picture? What did she say? Does she remember my mom?"

"Not much." She shakes her head. "Just that she knew of her. They had a few classes together. Some of the same extracurriculars. That she was nice." Gracie lets out a breath, a flicker of sadness brimming behind her eyes, almost as if she hates that there isn't more she can tell me.

I huff. *Yeah, me too.*

"Said she wouldn't call her a friend, though. Just a kind acquaintance."

I frown. "Really?"

She nods.

"That picture of them looked a lot like they were more than acquaintances."

My eyes flick to the pages I stole from my mother's file, and I realize the photo is gone. *He took it.*

Before we left the library, I quickly printed it out. I'm not sure why, maybe some part of me just wanted to have a keepsake of a time when she seemed happy. Although Kane stole it, I can still remember it clearly. Our mothers, shoulder to shoulder, laughing and familiar. That's not just some casual interaction. There's history in the way their bodies relax together.

But I don't say that out loud; instead, I say, "Did she mention anything about the club, about a student dying?"

"No," she says regretfully.

Maybe that's a good thing. If the student who attacked the other was my mother, surely Gracie mentioning her to her mom would have triggered something. *Right?*

"It's weird because I've never heard any stories about a death on campus before. Both of my parents attended this school, and I can't recall them talking about it," Gracie continues.

"Yeah." I release a breath, my shoulders rattling. "I never heard my mom mention it before either. But of course, I didn't know she went here." I grunt. "Why is everything so much of a fucking secret around here? And what does any of this have to do with my scholarship?"

Gracie takes the computer. "Let me see. You know my father's a state senator, so I've learned a trick or two about digging up stuff over the years." She types away, her focus narrowing in on whatever she finds. "Here. I did a search of deaths around the date of that article. Found this obituary."

"It's her," I say, pointing to the line with school's name in it. "Emily Croswell, twenty-one, was an honor student at SKU, daughter of prominent businessman Edward Croswell."

"She was pretty," Gracie mutters.

She was, and was so young, and just like that her life was over.

Gracie types on the keyboard again, and I watch closely as she cross-references and reverse searches Emily's name and death date. And then she freezes, her eyes going wide.

I follow her gaze. It's another article, buried on the tenth page of the search engine. My chest pulls tight before I even finish reading the words, my heart racing with every line I take in.

> **Emily Croswell, 21-year-old student, pushed during an altercation where she slipped, fell, and hit her head on a boulder. The student who pushed her was said to not know what they were doing, authorities report. The student blacked out, had some sort of mental break and has been admitted to Wyndmoor. The case has been labeled manslaughter, and due to the psychiatric and physical state of the suspect, the student will not spend time in prison, but will receive the help she needs at Wyndmoor.**

"Physical state?" I question as if Gracie knows the answer.

"It says she was pregnant."

My heart lurches. "Emily?"

She shakes her head. "The other student."

"It wasn't my mom," I blurt, a weight immediately lifting off my shoulders with the realization.

"How do you know?"

"According to this, Emily died the winter of 2005. I wasn't born until 2006, which means my mother wouldn't have been pregnant with me at that time."

Unless that's something else she's lied to me about. Could I have had another sibling?

"Okay. That's good. Now we know it wasn't her. But why hasn't anyone talked about this? They just pretend it didn't happen?"

Something feels off about all the secrets and hidden facts. Deep down, something tells me it's all connected. Me being brought to this school, my mom, and theirs...Emily. It's all a part of some web I can't even begin to untangle.

There's a brief pause while Gracie continues reading, and then she snaps her eyes back to me.

"There's a name," she says, barely above a whisper.

My stomach flips, because even after what I've just said, the truth is, I don't really know. *Please don't be my mom.* She was a member at that time and clearly suffered mentally.

Gracie turns the laptop toward me. Every muscle locks as my gaze fixes on the text, and my mouth goes dry.

La'Kia Kane.

"Kane's mother," we say in unison.

We stare at the screen, the room spinning a little slower. I never questioned what put Kane's mom in the facility. I was too busy learning how to keep mine from jumping out of a window. But now, it's clear that they didn't meet by chance. They've all known one another—Alex's mom, Christina's, and even Gracie's.

And for two girls from the same elite circle to land in the same locked ward, it's not a coincidence—it's a pattern.

And as I try to wrap my mind around that, my phone vibrates in my hoodie pocket. I peel my eyes away from Gracie's long enough to retrieve the device and stare down at the screen. What's staring back sucks all the air from my lungs.

Unknown Number: Watch your back bitch.

CHAPTER TWENTY-NINE

EVEREST (KANE)

My head is pounding. That's what happens when you throw back half a bottle of whiskey like you need it for hydration.

Most of last night is a blur, bits and pieces flashing through my mind. Showing up at my father's office. The liquor store. Banging down Sam's door, drunk off my ass. Tasting Sam.

Marking her.

It's all there, playing like the movie trailer for a night that went every way but right.

I had hoped I dreamed it. Prayed it was merely a figment of my imagination. There's absolutely no way I allowed my emotions to get me so far into my head that I sought comfort in the one person I told myself to stay away from.

I went there for answers, only to leave with more questions. The photo I found in her room, the one now resting in my passenger seat, clawed at me all night. My mom's face next to theirs, all lined up like they're close friends, taunts me. And Sam didn't help, tensing up the moment I saw it.

She's up to something, and whatever it is has to do with my mother.

But what?

Could this picture be what has my father so riled up?

I need answers, and there is only one person I can trust to give them to me.

My tires screech as I whip into the parking space in front of the psychiatric facility. The car jolts, still in motion when I throw the door open and jump out. My shoes hit the pavement, and I'm on the move, not bothering to lock it. The air feels more stilted now, heavier and thicker than when I left the house. It's as if the clouds are closing in around me.

Wyndmoor looms ahead. Even from the outside, it's clinical and emotionless. Ironic given this is the very place one comes when emotions have begun to be too much.

Climbing the stairs, I fold the printed image and shove it into my back pocket before entering the building, cool air immediately hitting me. Approaching the front desk, I make eye contact with the nurse. She knows me by name at this point, so she doesn't ask for my ID, and passes me the clipboard where I scribble my signature.

She takes it back from me. "She's in the rec room today."

I nod then round the corner and push through a set of doors. Voices bleed together, mixing with the clatter of board game pieces to my left, and the low hum of a daytime talk show on the right. The room is bright as if it'll mask the gloom of this place.

A man in a checkered robe paces near the window, mouthing words I can't hear, his fingers twitching. A woman rocks gently in the corner with her eyes fixed on something behind me. On the other end, two younger patients laugh over a game of Connect Four. Someone coughs in the distance, another hums, while someone else stares into space. They don't acknowledge me as I pass. They never do. Always in a world of their own, and oftentimes I envy that.

I continue on until finally I spot her. She's nestled at a table in the center of the room, a game of solitaire splayed out before her, and from the looks of it, she's winning. It takes a second before she notices me. Then she lifts her gaze and pins me with a smile. Mine forms without effort, much like it always does when I see her.

Her smile is contagious, and it always has been. Even with everything going on with her mental state, a bad day would hate to see her coming. The building could be on fire, and she'd find a way to calm those around her.

"Everest," she says, her eyes softening.

Her voice is clearer today, more grounded and alive.

"Hey, Ma."

She stands to meet my height. Half of Richard's DNA may be running through my veins, but I'm definitely my mother's child. We have nearly matching heights and identical features—the same cheekbones, strong nose, and even the shape of our eyes. Though where mine are slightly lighter, hers are a deep shade of brown. She's wearing her signature red lipstick, and her hair is longer than it was last week.

My mother wraps me into a hug, and I plant a kiss on her cheek.

"What are you doing here?" she asks while searching my eyes. "How was your game?"

I grin. "I took the winning shot."

She playfully smacks my arm. "Get out. You did?"

"Yeah. It was a close game, but we won."

She shakes her head, her smile now reaching her eyes. "I'm so proud of you. You boys off to nationals yet again."

"Thanks."

"Come. Sit with me." She gestures to the chair beside her. "How's Alex and Bryden?"

"Good. Actually, I wanted to see if you wanted to get some fresh air and walk with me."

"Yes. Let me clean up my cards."

Patiently, I wait for her to scoop up the cards and stuff them into the box before we head over to the nurses' station to check her out for a walk outside.

My mother slips her hand into the crook of my elbow and pats my bicep as we go through the double doors. "Good thing I have on my thick sweater, I know it's chilly out there."

I remove my hockey jacket. "Here. This should help keep you warm."

"Nonsense. Then you'll be cold."

"I work out six days a week, with less than ten percent body fat. I'll be fine."

She shakes her head and smirks. "You athletes."

"As if you weren't one," I counter.

Back in the day, she was a beast on the track. She had record-breaking stats, and a full-ride offer, her name in bold on the SKU bulletin boards. Hell, she's the reason I wanted to go to Sovereign King's. She was a star; everyone knew La'Kia Kane—the sprinter, jumper, and champion. She used to joke that the only thing faster than her legs was her mouth. Which was an understatement because the woman could talk a mile a minute.

I guess I get the competitive gene honestly. Because I damn sure didn't get it from Richard; neither did Alex, for that matter.

I watch her, remembering the stories she shared, remembering the medals she had hanging on her bedroom wall. Even remember the photo of her midair during a hurdle framed on my grandparents' wall, thinking that's what strength looked like. What resilience looked like.

Richard gave me hatred; she gave me everything else.

We descend from the deck, and my mother waves to others as we step into the yard.

I step into the grass first, holding out a hand to help her down the small flight of stairs. Flowers and neatly trimmed bushes line the property. There are benches scattered throughout along with some oversize outdoor games to entertain everyone.

I match her pace, and she wraps her arms around mine. We approach the fountain, and she gazes at it for a moment too long.

"You never told me how the boys are?" She breaks the silence.

I suck in a breath. This isn't what I want to talk about, but until I muster the courage, I go with it.

"They're good. Mrs. Montour sent us some snacks not too long ago."

"That's nice of her." We continue walking. "And Alex. How's he?"

I freeze at that. Her concern for Alex isn't anything new. We've been friends our whole lives, so it makes sense that she'd check on him. Only the question hits different ever since I found out the truth. I haven't shared that I know he's my brother for fear of triggering her. She's kept this from me all this time, and something tells me that's because she can't face it.

Having spent the last two years dealing with Richard, I get why she hid it. He didn't want me, and she kept that from me to protect me.

"He's good."

She nods and stops to pluck a rose from the bush. We move again as she leisurely plucks petals and lets them float in the wind.

"And your grades?"

"Three-point eight GPA," I say matter-of-factly.

"You've always been so smart."

I don't respond; instead I contemplate all the ways to bring up my questions.

"You get that from your grandmother." She plucks another petal. "She was a genius."

I smile. "She was."

"So are there any girls that caught your eye?"

I sigh.

"I've just been focused on the game." *If only that were the truth.*

"I know. But please tell me you're having fun, too. College should be all about the experiences."

Again, I say nothing.

"Ma?" I kick at a dandelion. "Do you remember Samantha?"

She frowns. "Samantha." She repeats as if it'll refresh her memory. "No."

"Collins? Her mother was a patient here with you about eight to ten years ago."

There's a subtle shift in her shoulders, but she recovers instantly. I frown and decide not to push it.

"Oh. Yeah. What about her?"

"She's a student at SKU now."

My mother doesn't look at me, her shoulders tensing just a bit.

"You don't say." She stares straight ahead. "How's her mother?"

"I'm not sure." Now's my chance. I slide the folded page from my back pocket and hand it to her. "But I had always thought the first time you met was here."

My mother opens it, and her face goes still, then it breaks. First, there's a twitch of her lips; then her hands start to shake. "Where... where did you get this?"

"From Sam. She found it in the school archives. Says you were in a club together. You never told me you knew her mom from school."

Her breathing turns shallow. I move to steady her, but she

jerks away like my touch burns. Her eyes dart around the courtyard. She drops the page, and it floats to the ground.

"They said it was over," she whispers, her voice cracking. "They promised..."

"Who?" I press, searching her eyes. "What's over?"

But she's gone. Just like that, her eyes glaze over, panic rolling off her in waves.

"Mom. Why didn't you tell me you all knew each other?"

She lets out a broken sob, hands clamping over her ears.

"I didn't mean to," she rambles. "They can't know. They can't know we remember."

"Ma. Look at me." I cup her face. "Remember what?"

Then she screams, her cries coming out ragged and as if something feral just ripped out of her chest. Her entire body jerks, her knees buckling as if the memories are physically dragging her under.

"Ma. I'm sorry. Forget I asked."

She collapses against me. Before I can make sense of anything, two nurses rush over. I back off as they swoop in, soothing her, checking her pulse, and guiding her away.

"She's overstimulated," one of them says. "You'll need to leave now."

"I'm sorry," I whisper, still standing there, rooted to the grass, my fist curling tight as my nails bite into my palms.

This encounter, her reaction to that picture, only leaves me with more questions and no goddamn answers.

They disappear with my mother through the doors. After a while, I snatch up the photo and I finally head back toward the building.

What the hell happened back then? And why the hell is Sam looking into it?

I inch through the halls, my mind racing to put the pieces of the puzzle together. And as I turn the corner and step into the lobby, my name cuts through the chaos in my head.

"Kane."

I glance up. Sam stands from the bench in front of the reception desk, her arms wrapped around herself as if she's bracing for something. My jaw clenches, and I lunge forward. Her eyes widen as I close the distance and grip her arm to pull her through the front door and down the steps.

"You're hurting me."

I'm blinded by the rage building in my gut but still loosen my hold. People stare, but I don't give a shit. I reach into my pocket for my fob to pop the lock on my Audi then yank the passenger door open the moment we reach it.

"Get in," I demand.

Sam stares for a beat but doesn't challenge me. She gets in, and I slam the door shut before rounding the front and climbing behind the wheel. I power on the car and peel away from the curb, my foot heavy on the gas.

"Kane. Slow down," she pleads while fumbling to put on her seat belt.

I ignore her and tighten my grip on the wheel. The engine growls as if it knows I need to outrun these emotions, but I don't know where I'm going. All I know is that I need to be far away from that place, away from my mother's screams.

I cut a hard right, tires screeching as we duck down a side street behind a diner, past the train station and the school district offices. The entrance of an alleyway comes into view beside an abandoned convenience store, and I yank the wheel, barely missing the brick wall. I slam into park, sending gravel spinning beneath my tires. Sam breathes hard, her chest heaving as she clutches her seat belt.

"What is wrong with you?"

I don't answer her; I can't. My lungs constrict and my knees bounce as I twitch with unspent anger. I stare ahead, my teeth grinding so hard it hurts.

"I didn't know," she says.

I hate the sincerity in her voice. Hate that she's seeing right through me, that she's showing concern.

"Has she been in there all this time?" she whispers.

"Start talking...now. I showed my mom that picture and she fucking lost it."

"Oh. I'm sor—"

"Why were you there?"

Sam drops her gaze. "I was hoping to speak to someone about my mom and saw your car out front."

"What the fuck is going on?" My voice shatters the air between us. "What was that picture? Why are our parents in it? Why did it trigger her?" My last question comes out choked.

"I don't know."

"You know something," I snap.

"Gracie and I were just investigating," she blurts.

My ears perk up at that. "What?"

Her eyes flick to mine. "I wasn't looking for it. I just found it."

"Then what were you looking for?"

"Why I'm here. I had questions about my scholarship, but every person I asked was cagey about it. So I asked Alex—"

"Alex? What's he know about this?"

"Nothing. I'm just as lost as you. But something wasn't adding up, so I asked Alex to help me look into it. His father seemed to be hiding something about how I got in this school, and I knew he could help me."

She had questions and went to him?

"Help you with what?"

"Information. We snuck into the administration building and while I was looking for my records, I learned that my mother was a student here."

"Well, what did your mother say?"

She stays silent, and a lone tear trails her cheek.

"She can't say anything from the grave."

My heart pulses. "Shit. I didn't know."

"How could you when you've been treating me like the enemy instead of a friend?"

Fuck. She's right. I've spent so much time trying to keep her from knowing the truth about my mom that I didn't care to inquire about hers.

"Sorry."

She peers at me, and without thinking, I reach out and wipe her tears away with the pad of my thumb. Sam palms my hand, locking eyes with me.

"Me too," she mutters.

I want to break the connection, put distance between us again, but I can't. Last night should have gotten her out of my system, but it's only made it worse. I believe her. She's just as lost in all of this as I am, and whatever it is has something to do with not just my mom and hers, but all of ours.

"Tell me everything. What have you found?"

CHAPTER THIRTY

SAM

Agreeing to meet Mountain at the house he shares with Alex and Kane is probably a bad idea. Because being in the same house, *alone*, with the three guys I clearly have complicated relationships with can't lead to anything good.

Right? Surely, this will all blow up in my face, a recipe for disaster if I've ever seen one.

It's even more awkward considering I haven't spoken to Alex or Kane in a few days. After Alex called himself propositioning me and running into Kane while investigating at Wyndmoor, I needed space to clear my mind.

And then there's whatever this is with Mountain. He's so different from the others, and with everything that's been going on lately, I can use his brand of simple. He's peace and stability packed into a burly six-foot, two-hundred-something frame. It's easy with him, and that's something I haven't had in a long time. He settles my nervous system, while the others have done nothing but wreak havoc on it.

So here I am, in his room, staring at pictures from his childhood and taking in just how methodical his space is. Everything in its place, and there's not a speck of dust in sight. Shoes are perfectly shelved on the wall. Hockey gear is stacked neatly in the corner behind the door. His bed is made to perfection, the corners tucked and pillows fluffed.

I stroll over to the books arranged by trim size on his bookshelf. It's an array of topics from textbooks to sports magazines and a handful of fiction titles.

The bathroom door flies open, and Mountain steps into the room. I peer at him as his eyes roam over my frame. There's a softness in his gaze that I haven't seen him give anyone else.

Lately, the air seems to still when he looks at me. At first, it caught me off guard, made me feel vulnerable. Now I welcome his attention. I'm sure it has a lot to do with the fact that with him, I never feel judged or mocked. When the world is so busy *telling* me who I am, Bryden sees me for me, every broken inch.

Yes, I've crossed a line I can't come back from with both Alex and Kane, but Mountain? He's the one I'm not sure about. He's always kind, always respectful. But he never makes a move, never slips, and never relents.

"Come on. Let's knock out this project." He crosses the space while his eyes remain fixed on me, and for a moment I freeze. He towers close, peering down at me as I stand there like a deer in headlights. I lean in, our chests only a hair apart. When I breathe deep, so does he.

"Sam," he utters my name. It's low, and if I didn't know better, it's sensual.

"Yes?" I whisper.

"I need you to move so I can get into the closet."

"Oh. Yeah. Sorry," I stammer and move to the side and suck in a breath.

The sound of the closet door fills the space, followed by the ruffling of a plastic bag.

He closes the door and gestures for me to follow him over to the desk. After setting the bag of supplies down, Mountain walks over to the left corner of the room to grab another chair, holding it out for me to sit. We briefly make eye contact again as I settle into the chair and allow him to push me closer to the desk. Mountain claims his spot, his leg brushing against mine, and I squirm.

As he settles and removes things from the bag, his legs spread ever so slightly. I can't help but take in his thickness. Ever since walking in on him that night, it's hard not to let my mind wander. And right now, in his room alone with him, my eyes find their way to that bulge, and I have to force myself to look away.

He lays everything out in front of us. I should be paying attention, mentally preparing myself to work on the project. Instead, I'm busy watching the veins in his forearm every single time he reaches in front of me.

For the next hour, we work through our notes and piece our structure together. Working alongside Mountain is easy. He listens intently, never tries to control the narrative, and truly values my input. He's always on time and actually puts in as much effort as me.

Mountain puts the final screw into place then sits back, his hands out at his side as if it'll come crashing down if he moves too quickly.

"Done," he says proudly.

"Oh we're definitely getting an A."

Mountain looks at me. "I'm glad you think so."

"And you don't? The calculations are solid, we've tested and proved our theory, and it's sturdy. We've got this in the bag."

"I love your confidence."

I smile at that, throwing my gaze around to mask the heat I feel rushing to my cheeks. He moves to clean up the leftover supplies, tossing scraps into the plastic bag.

I stand and go back to browsing his books.

He glances at me between each piece he picks up. "What?"

Holding up one, a popular graphic novel about a superhero kid, I smirk, my brow cocked.

He scratches his nape. "Yeah. I've been doing a buddy read with my little brother."

"So?" Smiling, I return it to its place next to the others.

When I turn to face him again, Mountain is already at my side, not so subtly fixing the pile to his liking. He's not rude about it, and if I had to bet, he doesn't even realize he's doing it.

"So what?" He quizzes, awkwardly turning toward me.

"What did you think?"

Mountain stares at me, confusion written across his handsome features.

"The book." I nod to the red cover on his desk. "I read it with my little brother, too."

"Oh." He scratches his head again. "It was good."

"I liked the villain," I admit while picking up his hockey stick.

"Really?" Mountain narrows his eyes at me, amusement beaming in them.

"Yeah. I personally feel like he's misunderstood. Besides, I usually go for the villain of the story anyway."

"Why the villain?"

I avert my gaze and put the stick back where I got it. "They have the most to gain, and most of the time, they were antagonized themselves. Not to mention, villains are more fun."

"And more dangerous."

"You say that like it's a bad thing."

"So that's your thing? The bad boy?"

"Let's just say walking red flags are hot when they're fictional."

"It's fiction. Where are you seeing this *hotness*?"

I snap my gaze to him. "We're judging now?"

Mountain smirks, the hint of a smile attempting to show, but he holds it in. He always does. One of these days, I'll get through to him, get him to cave.

"No. No. I just never get how you ladies get over book characters."

"I don't know if I should be offended."

He laughs, and I can't help but do the same. There it is—a smile. It's barely there, the smallest of tugs, but I see it.

He holds up his hands in mock surrender. "You know what, I believe in letting people love what they love. And if that's super-villains for you, then love away."

I smirk. "I'm definitely feeling judged."

We laugh.

"I may be surprised by some of the books on your shelf, but what isn't a surprise to me is your room. I've actually pictured that it would look something like this."

His brows pull tight in confusion. "You pictured it? But you've seen my room before... the night of the party."

"I mean, yeah, but I was looking for the bathroom, and there you were damn near naked. Remembering what your room actually looked like was the last thing on my mind."

Mountain meets my eyes at that, another slight smile fighting to peek through. "Fair enough. Expand on that then."

"You can tell a lot about what a person's space might look like based on how they carry themselves."

He glances around. "I'll bite."

He leans back, crossing his arms over his chest, the thin fabric of his T-shirt stretching over his muscles. And he's not even flexing.

"This is technically your first time in my room."

First? Will there be a second? I utter inwardly.

"Does my personality accurately represent my room?"

I wet my lips, more out of habit than anything else. "Yeah."

I pause and return to my seat next to his, taking another look around. "It's very military-like. Everything has its place. There's nothing personal left out in the open aside from the family pictures on your mirror. Your bed is made with tight corners and the surfaces are spotless."

He raises a brow, and I can tell he's waiting for the punchline.

"You like order and have scary good control over every aspect of your life. You don't get upset, don't curse, always on time, constantly watching. Even down to only communicating through texts. It allows you to control what emotions you show. You can tell me everything is fine, while falling apart on the inside."

His face gives nothing away, but he's listening.

"Predictability makes you feel safe. You don't hoard, and from what I can tell you don't collect either. You are ritualistic about the game. Your locker is bare save for the essentials, and I'd bet if I walked into your private bathroom right now, there are just the staples."

I tilt my head, meeting his stare.

"You're disciplined. Because if things are airtight, then nothing can fall apart. Right?"

"You say that like it's a bad thing," he finally speaks, throwing my words back at me.

"Not bad, per se. But it can't be all good either." I peer at him. "Having that kind of control, it's fine—safe. But then you're not really living. And trust me, I've had my fair share of wanting to give up living because God knows life fucking sucks. But I'm living and feeling."

For a moment, he doesn't move or breathe, and then just barely his jaw flexes. *Bull's-eye.*

"Sorry if that came off as offensive."

"No." His features soften as he shifts. "I'm actually just impressed really. No one's ever really noticed *me* before. So it's just a little strange to hear. I'm not ashamed of who I am, so hearing how you view me doesn't offend me."

My muscles soothe at that. "I like who you are. It drives me crazy how perfectly intact you are emotionally, but I like it."

A smile almost forms on his lips, but he bites it away. "Okay. So you think there's some benefit in being imperfectly intact?"

"I mean yeah. It kind of adds a little razzle-dazzle to life."

He smirks. "Razzle-dazzle. Nice. So how do you propose I spice mine up?"

My eyes go wide. "What?"

"You basically said I have a stick up my butt."

"Ass. You have a stick up your *ass*." I giggle. "Okay. Start there."

He frowns. "Where?"

"I dare you to curse. Just once. Say ass."

He looks away, hiding another grin. "No. I don't need to curse. Dare something else."

Something stirs in my chest, slow and low, as my smile fades. My gaze drops to Mountain's mouth. Full lips that are always pressed into a tight, unreadable line.

"I dare you to let go and do something you've held yourself back from."

His gaze snaps back to mine, that hidden grin dying almost instantly.

"What would that be?"

"You tell me." I stare at his lips and back to his eyes.

Charged silence crackles between us, and it's thick and deafening. I should say that I'm kidding. Should laugh it off and let him off the hook. But I don't. Lately I can't seem to stop doing things I shouldn't.

He doesn't move save for the rapid rise and fall of his chest and that same unreadable look. I think he's going to tell me to chill out, or worse, get the hell out. Then suddenly, his hand shoots out and grabs the leg of my chair. Mountain drags me toward him in one fluid motion, the legs scraping against the hardwood flooring.

My stomach jolts as a whimper slips out of me before I can stop it. His legs bracket mine now, the heat of him pressing into every edge of my composure. He doesn't touch me, instead keeps one hand fisting the leg of the chair and the other curled against his right thigh.

Finally, he unballs that fist on his lap and lifts his hand painstakingly slowly. I track the movement, my eyes and head following its path. His fingers hover, a slight twitch evident now. My chin tucks against my collarbone, not intentionally but because I can't seem to peel my sight away from his traveling hand.

Then he cups the back of my neck, his palm spreading wide along my nape. His skin is warm and rough from years of stick handling and gloves, but his touch—it's unexpectedly gentle. Gentle but firm and dare I say possessive even. He kneads into the base of my skull, coaxing, no, more like subtly demanding me to look at him.

I force my stare back up, trembling under the intensity of his gaze. Mountain searches my face, studying every stutter in my breath, almost as if he's checking for all the ways I might pull back.

My body leans into him with a mind of its own. Blood racing, pulse stuttering, and thighs clenching. My eyes drop to his lips where he licks them slowly. I can't breathe, and honestly, I'm not even sure I remember how to. And when he finally looks down at my mouth, staring at it as if it's the only thing in this godforsaken room, I nearly pass out.

He hasn't even kissed me yet and I'm already about to lose my shit. Why is he having this effect on me? I mean I quite literally asked for this, but I guess I never expected him to do anything about it.

"You sure?" His voice is a growl when it comes out.

I nod.

And then his mouth crushes into mine. All of his gentleness, that composure of steel breaks. His kiss isn't soft; it's not even careful. It's all heat and need, like he's been starving for this all along. His other hand moves from the chair, joining the other around my neck as he pulls me into him, one thigh between mine anchoring me in place. His lips part mine, tongue licking deep and rough. He's claiming me in the moment, finally giving himself permission to let go. I can feel it in the way his fingers bite into my neck like he's trying to claw his way into my skin.

It stings but feels good at the same time. Too good that the sounds come out of me before either of us can make sense of the moment.

"Mmmm," I moan, sharp and breathy.

Mountain groans, swallowing it like a challenge. I grip his shirt, my fingers twisting in the fabric as I hold on for dear life. With each stroke of his tongue against mine, he tugs me closer until I'm practically straddling his thigh. Every shift of his mouth is a contradiction. It's chaotic and controlled. Practiced precision and desperation all in one. It's as if he's still trying to stay composed but also rip that control to shreds.

And it's the hottest shit ever. To know that I'm the reason he's teetering that edge sends shock waves through every nerve in my body. The need to touch him takes over and I cup his face.

"Fu—" he starts but it's drowned out by his heavy breaths. "Mmm," he mutters instead.

I stroke his cheek, needing to hear him moan again, wanting

to finally break through that wall. Mountain moves his touch to the small of my back, his massive hand nearly covering it entirely. I'm not tiny by any means, but next to him, I'm dainty. He wraps his arms around me until we're chest to chest, his strong arms caging me in. I'm planted firmly in his grasp, and it feels amazing, the kind of calming weight that soothes nervous systems.

Wanting to feel closer to him, I finger the hem of his T-shirt until I feel the warmth of his skin. It's hot and taut, and ridged to perfection.

"S-Sam," he whispers against my lips, shaking his head slowly, but not once does he pull away.

"Bryden," I utter back.

The kiss deepens; then he sucks my tongue into his mouth.

"We should stop," he breathes out.

"Mm-hmm," I agree but don't move and neither does he.

We stay like this. Lips swollen, breaths tangled, bodies pressed so close it's hard to tell where I end and he begins.

A sharp throat clears, slicing through the room, snapping us out of our haze. We jolt, and stare at the door simultaneously.

"Look what we have here." Alex leans against the doorjamb, arms crossed. Mouth curved into that frustrating smirk of his. He looks amused, but he also looks pissed.

Beside him, Kane stands stiff as stone, his eyes narrowed like two blades. He doesn't say anything, but he doesn't have to; the glare in his eyes says it all.

Bryden doesn't release me; instead he holds me tighter and I swear I hear him mutter the word *mine*.

"Shit," I whisper.

No one moves. No one speaks.

But something deep down tells me that I just bit off more than I can chew.

CHAPTER THIRTY-ONE

ALEX

I've barely spoken to Sam since my idiotic move after practice. But now, I'm standing outside her dorm waiting for her to open up.

The door swings open just as I raise my fist to knock one more time.

"Alex." Gracie frowns at me. "What are you doing here?"

I shove the rolled-up pages in my left hand into my pocket. "Sam. Is she here?"

A second later, Sam exits their bathroom. She isn't looking up, her attention focused on the bracelet she's attempting to slap into place.

"Gracie. I need to run off campus for a few—" Sam pauses the moment she looks up and her eyes land on me. "Alex?"

With her brows knitted tight, she glances from me to Gracie.

"What are you doing here?"

Gracie watches us, a suggestive grin slowly forming on her lips. "I'm going to give you two a minute."

Gracie and I turn and slip past each other, trading places at the threshold. I catch a glimpse of Gracie pinning Sam with a very animated questioning look before she walks off. When I look back at Sam, she's still holding on to the unclasped bracelet.

I step farther into the room, closing the door behind me without taking my eyes off her. As we stare at each other, I step forward. Every instinct in my body tells me that being in her space is the kind of intimacy that'll only get me in trouble.

The last time I got too close, the last time I breathed in her scent, I ended up with a constant hard-on for a girl who's made it very clear she'd never let me touch her again unless I begged. The same girl I caught practically riding my very shy, very brutish best friend's thigh. *In my house, mind you.*

Seeing that affected me more than I care to admit. Sam is the only girl who has ever gotten in my head, the first girl to truly reject me. And I don't mean the kind of denial where you play hard to get to not seem so easy. She genuinely seems to despise me. But she likes Bryden, though?

Honestly, I'm not even all that mad, because I get it. She gets to you, and once you've let her in, involuntarily or not, that's it. She's a fucking siren. Didn't care to have it right in my face under my own roof, but I get it.

Kane didn't seem too keen on it either. He didn't say anything, but with how tight his jaw was, I'd say she's gotten to him, too. But before Mountain told us to get out, I noticed the way Kane looked at her. He stared like he wanted to bite her and fuck her at the same time.

Get in line, bro.

I step closer, no words between us as I reach out and take her wrist into my hands. Sam keeps her eyes trained on me while I work to fasten the hook for her.

"I thought I was meeting you in the parking lot?" she asks, forcing me out of my daze.

Pulling the scroll from my pocket, I hold it out to her. Sam stares at it, confusion forming. "I figured it's better that I talk about this here rather than out in public. You said you couldn't find out why my dad's name was on your scholarship stuff, so I looked into it."

"You didn't have to do this."

I smile. "I know. But I wanted to, and it's the least I can do."

"Alex—" she starts, but I hold up a hand to stop her.

"Sam. I was a dick before, and you didn't deserve that."

The lines around her eyes seem to soften with that, a silent appreciation. She focuses back on the page, and hers grow wide.

"You were right." I pause and Sam paces. "My dad definitely had something to do with it. Scholarships, award letters, anything that pertains to that, come from the financial department, but not yours. There wasn't much that I could find, not on his work computer. I'd have to sneak into his home office. Check his personal computer."

"Absolutely not, Alex. I can't let you do that."

"It's the only way to get the truth."

She pauses for a beat, reading me before speaking again. "Why do you care so much?"

I stare at her, the answer dying on my tongue. The truth is, this is more for me than it is for her. That man has made my life hell, and I guess knowing there is information out there that I could use as leverage entices me the most.

"My father doesn't do anything out of the kindness of his heart," I answer. "There might not have been much, but I did find a name on the transfer and traced it back to an offshore account in the Cayman Islands."

She snaps her gaze to mine.

"It's at the bottom of the second page. There wasn't much I could find on the company. They don't seem to have much of an internet presence. Just a name and a barely there trail to the account."

"What's the name?" Sam turns the page to read the last line.

At the same time, I answer her. "Aurelian Ltd."

She stands there, eyes wide like she's seen a ghost. Then she's on the move, heading straight for the nightstand next to the bed. Her phone rings, but Sam ignores it. I watch as the screen goes black then focus back on the folder that Sam pulls out of her drawer. She flops it on the mattress and aggressively flips through it until she lands on the page she's looking for.

From here, I can see that it's a photo, printed on regular computer paper. From the looks of it, it's seen better days. Wrinkles riddle the page, and it crumples under her touch. She holds it out and stalks back toward me.

"Have you seen this picture before?"

I take in the image. It's my turn to be confused.

It's a picture of our moms—mine, Kane's, Gracie's, Christina's, and, from the striking resemblance, Sam's. They're young, probably about our age now. They're on campus, which makes sense given that my mother, Gracie's, and Christina's are alumni. But I never knew Kane's mom was, too. He never told us much about her.

"No, I haven't."

Sam hovers close to me, damn near too close. Her signature scent envelops me, and I have to force myself to think straight. The phone goes off again, and again she ignores it. But this time there's a twitch in her jaw. Her eyes flicker toward the phone, and her fingers curl slightly against the photo.

"Look at the name of the club." Sam points to the fine print beneath our mothers' faces.

"The Aurelian Circle," I mutter. "Wait. You don't think this is the same Aurelian as the offshore account?"

Sam shakes her head before throwing her hands up in defeat.

"I don't know what to think. But it's a hell of a coincidence, right?" She shrugs. "It's the only thing that makes sense. Because, believe me, I've been searching for days and nothing adds up."

I take the photo from her and stare at it some more. It's crazy staring at a younger version of my mother. The years hadn't caught up with her, no grays, no crow's-feet. I look at the date. I would have been born a year after this.

"Where did you get this?"

"The library archives. Gracie and I were trying to find out what we could about my scholarship and my mom, and we stumbled across it."

"You had to search up your mom? Why not just talk to her?"

Sam drops her head. "I would if she was alive."

My heart pits in my stomach. "Shit. I'm sorry. I didn't know."

She shakes her head. "It's fine. But she never mentioned being a student here. And now you find the club's name on banking information. I...I'm so fucking confused." She flails her arms around. "I'm supposed to be making something of myself so that I can fight for custody of my brother, but instead, I ended up in this never-ending rabbit hole. And—"

She's spiraling, her breathing now erratic, and tears form in her eyes. That damn phone buzzes again.

I step forward, grabbing her by the shoulders to ground her. "Breathe, Sunshine."

She swallows then slowly drags her eyes to mine.

"Just breathe. We'll figure it out. I'll ask my mom, and maybe we can ask Kane—"

"He doesn't know anything."

"Kane knows about this?"

Sam nods but before she can open her mouth to say anything, that incessant phone goes off one more time.

"Please, answer the phone. Whoever that is is desperate to reach you."

Sam clenches her teeth together, and her shoulders draw up tight. There it is again. That look, like she's bracing for impact. And the phone keeps ringing. Her whole body hums with tension, locked so tight I can feel it vibrating through my palms.

I might not be the sharpest tack in the box, but anyone can see she's scared and dodging whoever the hell that is. Without much thought, I drop my hands at my sides and stomp over to her bed in three long strides. Snatching up the phone, I stare at the caller ID. Unknown Caller.

"Who's calling you?"

She shakes her head. "No one."

"Sam." I search her face, that curiosity quickly turning into concern. "Is someone harassing you?"

The screen lights up as I let it ring for a beat, waiting for Sam to answer me. But she doesn't have to; it's written all over her face. Heat creeps up my nape and my free hand curls at my side. I answer the call but put it on speaker and don't say a word.

"I'm going to gut you, you fucking cunt." The deep voice is full of malice.

Click.

My gaze darts to Sam, my brows pulled together so tight it hurts, and I instantly see red.

I know that voice all too well.

"Why the fuck is Jackson threatening you?"

CHAPTER THIRTY-TWO

SAM

The locker room is the loudest it's ever been, but I'm not sure if it's the actual volume or if my senses are just that heightened. Then there is also the fact that sleeping last night was out of the question. Alex was so pissed about the call from Jackson that we never got around to making it to that study session.

I mean how could we? He single-handedly dropped a massive bomb on me with his discovery about the offshore account. And after all of that, I am no closer to finding out what the hell is going on.

But there's one thing that's starting to come together. Whatever's going on, whatever happened back when our mothers were students here, it all has something to do with that damn club.

The Aurelian Circle.

And from the sound of things, I was right, Chancellor Williamsburg is wrapped up in it. And maybe the Kincaids, too. It's the only thing that explains why Mr. Kincaid and the chancellor stepped out of the office that day and let me off the hook.

I scan the space, my eyes landing on Mountain, who's standing on the other side of the room with his back against the wall. He's wearing his usual disposition, permanently furrowed brows, lips pressed thin, arms folded over his broad chest. And while his posture hasn't changed, his eyes have more expression in them as he stares at me.

We haven't spoken since that kiss.

Kane moves closer to Mountain. He's shirtless, his skin glistening even under the fluorescent lighting. He's taller than the others, not by a lot but it's noticeable. He, too, is wearing that permanent scowl. I didn't get what he was so angry about before. But now I understand.

In that alley he filled me in on how his mom has spent more time in that facility over the years than she did at home. And when I asked if the guys knew, he never answered, but his eyes said it all. He was alone in this.

Finally, Kane looks at me, his gaze darkening as a chill runs the length of my spine. I'm sure it's because of seeing me with Alex and Mountain. He's jealous, and oddly enough, I like it. Knowing that I make him like that does something to me.

I blink to clear my head, try to look away, but neither he nor Mountain breaks their stare. It doesn't matter that there's a locker room full of guys, or that all it would take is for one person to catch the glances between us and find a way to use it against me. Many of them already think I injured Jackson. I can hear the rumor mill now: *Slutty Sam, Puck Bunny of the Year.*

I shake my head and try to focus on my task. But then the hairs on my neck rise. I snap my head just in time to watch Alex walk into view, his green eyes locked onto mine. His usually arrogant grin is replaced with a clenched jaw. Alex peers at Kane and Mountain before bringing his attention back to me. His shoulders tense, and it feels like he's questioning me.

Me? Or them? I can hear loud and clear even though he never opens his mouth.

There's a tightness around my lungs, and I have to force myself to breathe. Alex inches forward, one foot after the other, in my direction. But he never breaks eye contact, even when I shuffle nervously in place or drop my chin to my chest. From my peripheral vision, I notice Kane and Mountain shift in place but neither of them move.

"What are you doing, Sam?" I mutter to myself. "They're friends, for Christ's sake."

Alex is in front of me now, looming over me, his voice low and pointed. "You okay?"

He's concerned about me.

With a wavering gaze, I nod. "If you're asking if he called back, no."

Alex steps forward, closing what little distance is between us. A shudder rolls through me, his manly scent damn near overwhelming me. He's pinned me between the concrete pillar and his hard chest. Then he touches me, his fingers wrapping around mine so innocently. Heat slicks across my skin, and I swallow down a lump.

"I'm going to take care of him."

I shake my head but before the words can leave my lips, a voice breaks out behind us.

"You bitches miss me?" Jackson blurts out.

And I go still as I peer around Alex to see Jackson limping in. He's no longer on crutches but instead he wears a hard cast. It's like someone lit a fuse the way the team's excitement explodes. Several of the players rush toward him, their voices blurring together.

"Took your sweet-ass time to come see us," someone jokes.

"Had to make an entrance." Jackson shrugs.

"Think you'll be cleared in time for nationals?" goes a different person.

As soon as the words leave his lips, Jackson glares at me from across the room. And then everything from that second on moves at breakneck speed. Anger flickers in Alex's eyes, and he's off before I can stop him. I claw at his arm, but he jerks away, fist curled at his side.

"Alex. Let it go," I plead but it's useless.

Simultaneously, Mountain pushes off the wall, stoically stalking over to me. He doesn't acknowledge Jackson, his only focus being me. *My quiet protector.* Kane watches us, his brows furrowing as he braces himself, and when he reads the emotions coming off of Alex, he weaves through the crowd to reach him.

"Kincaid," Alex barks. There's venom in his tone, sharp and icy. "Why the fuck have you been threatening her?"

Like a true psychopath, Jackson smiles, completely unfazed. The way his shoulders pull back, the pride in his stance tells me he knows exactly what Alex is referring to.

"What's gotten into you, Williamsburg?" Jackson smirks. "Let me guess—" His eyes trail around Alex to me. The sick bastard is enjoying this. Feeding off it.

Alex lunges forward.

Kane steps in fast, shoving a hand against Alex's chest. "We don't need another fight."

Alex is seething, unsuccessfully moving Kane out of the way.

"You fucking pussy," Alex spits. "You think that shit's cool."

A screeching silence sweeps across the room, as everyone stares on in confusion.

"Going after a girl," Alex continues.

"I don't know what you're talking about," Jackson lies.

"You know exactly what the fuck you did." Alex points over Kane's shoulder.

"Alex. What the fuck is going on?" Kane demands to know, craning his neck to keep Alex's eyes on him.

"Whatever that bitch told you is a lie," Jackson snaps, that cold demeanor shattering just a bit.

"Watch your—"

Mountain is in front of me now, using his large frame like a barrier. "Eyes on me."

I nod, inhaling deeply, but it does nothing to settle the raging emotions.

"Boys," a deep voice slices through the air.

Every head turns to the sound of it. Chancellor Williamsburg strolls into the locker room with Coach Barrett only a few feet behind him. He walks like he owns the place. The effect is immediate—an invisible leash that tightens around every throat.

Alex stiffens beside Kane, and for the first time, I see it—that barely perceptible shift. A crack in the composure they wore like armor. Both of them straighten.

"Our focus needs to be on being ready to take home another championship." The chancellor peers around the room into the faces of everyone here.

Everyone but me. No, he treats me as if I'm invisible. Typical.

"Understand?"

"Yes, sir," the team responds in unison. Except for my guys. They can't... won't make that promise.

"Make the school proud. As you know, we host a celebratory dinner in honor of your efforts each year. I've come to formally invite you all to our estate this Saturday at seven-thirty. There will be some very important benefactors in attendance, so make sure you're presentable." He turns his gaze to Alex. "And on your best behavior."

Alex clenches his fist but manages to keep his composure.

"That's it. You boys have a good practice. Coach Barrett, can I have a word in your office?" He glances back at the coach, whose only response is a nod.

The two men leave the room, and the tension thickens again. But thankfully, Ryker steps in front of his brother and escorts him out of the locker room. Others grab their gear and begin to file out. The moment we're alone, Kane and Alex stomp toward Mountain and me.

"Want to tell me what that was all about?" Kane glances between the three of us.

Mountain looks at me, using his eyes to ask permission. I nod.

"Jackson tried to drug Sam the night of the party, but she fought him off."

Kane snaps his head in my direction. Anger builds behind his irises.

"And he's been harassing her, calling and sending threatening messages," Alex adds.

Mountain's whole body goes stiff.

Kane aggressively peers at me. "Why'd you keep this from me?"

"Because none of you would've picked *me* over him."

"I don't know how I can do this anymore," I tell Evan as I hold the phone up to see his face, my desperate strides taking me away from the rink.

Practice is nowhere near over, and once Coach realizes I've abandoned post, he's going to be pissed. But there was no way I was waiting for Jackson to sneak back into the locker room while I was alone.

It's early, and because of that there aren't many other students out in the quad. The first thing I did after getting out of the locker room was FaceTime Evan. He's the only one who can calm me down right now.

"Wait. Slow down. What are you talking about? Can't do what?" Evan questions, his voice still groggy from sleep.

"Everything. This school, the people... I can't do it. I want to come home."

Evan sighs and sits up in bed. "Okay. Relax, Sam. You didn't get into that school just to throw it all away before the end of the semester. What's going on?"

I can't tell him everything, not when I barely know what's happening myself. All I know is, I'm not going to survive this school. Too much has happened, and every day it's looking more and more like none of it is worth it. And if he knew what I've been through, if he knew about Jackson, Evan would burn the world for me, even if that meant burning himself, too. That can't happen, so I tell him the only thing I can tell him.

"I miss you. I miss my brother and just want to be with him."

Evan rubs his eyes. "We miss you, too. But something tells me it's more than that. Did something happen? The team still giving you a hard time?"

The one thing I did share with Evan was how much I hated working for the hockey team. Which was funny to him because he knows how much I hate sports.

I shake my head. "I just don't want Des to be alone."

"He's not. And you know that. Me and Grandma Harris are looking out for him. There was a reason you left, stick to the plan. Whatever it is, you've got this. Nothing can kill you—"

"As long as I don't let it," I mutter, finishing his statement. It's something he's said to me many times throughout our friendship.

"Exactly. You've accomplished a lot of things, and you'll get through this, too."

"You promise?" I stare at him, knowing he'd never be able to. No one can. Life is going to do what it does, with or without your permission.

"I do. You're the strongest person I know."

I don't know if I believe that anymore, but I don't tell him that; instead, I say, "Love you."

"Me too. Now, I'm going to go back to sleep, I don't have class for a few more hours."

We say our goodbyes and hang up just as I near a wooded part of the campus. Less than a minute later, the hair on my arms stands at attention, goose bumps dancing across my skin. Eeriness washes over me and my senses are tingling, and I can't shake the feeling that someone is watching me. Leaves rustle in the distance, drawing my gaze to the trees. I fixate on my surroundings but there's no one there. Throwing one more look around, I step off the curb to cross the parking lot toward my dorm.

And that's when I see it. A blacked-out van idling at the end of the street, windows tinted, engine quiet. I may not be able to see who's behind that wheel, but something tells me whoever it is has their sights set on me.

I move faster, rushing across the road, glancing back every so often. They stay there for a moment, but as soon as my soles hit the grass, they roll forward.

Suddenly, my mind starts to race.

Could that be Jackson? It can't be. He wouldn't have had time to limp to an unmarked van and follow me without me noticing.

Which means, it's someone else entirely.

Blood starts to pump in my ears, the adrenaline spiking. Keeping my eyes ahead of me, I move deeper into the yard so that if they get out to grab me, I'd have a head start at getting away. The window starts to inch down, and my heart hammers in my chest.

"Sam," a deep voice belts out, and that's all it takes for me to book it.

I take off in a full sprint, weaving across the lawn and straight for the glass double doors of my dorm. The sound of tires screeching and someone racing behind me lights a fire under me. I yank the door open and run into the stairwell, taking them two at a time, determined not to stop until I reach the top. My lungs are on fire, legs aching with every forward motion.

By the time I make it to the second level, the door opens on the first and I peer down just long enough to see a man's hand grip the railing just seconds before the pads of his shoes hit the threading.

"Fuck. Fuck. Fuck." I go faster now, pulling myself up by the railing.

Thinking quickly, I yank open the second-floor door and let it slam then snatch my sneakers off to stifle my footfalls as I make a dash up the final flight of stairs, being careful to stay against the wall to avoid being seen. Thankfully, the stairwell is well lit, so my position won't be given away by the light shining in from my floor.

I close the door softly and bolt down the hall to my room, fumbling to pull my keys from my hoodie along the way. I finally make it to my door and get the key into the lock just as I hear the door burst open at the end of the hall. Panicked and out of breath, I get the lock free and storm inside, frantically locking it again.

Needing to know if my theory is correct, I look down at my phone and frantically swipe through the messages from the unknown caller. It was easy to assume it was Jackson harassing me; he does hate me after all. That *was* his voice on the other end of the line last night, right? But this... it can't be him.

I reread the messages, my back nearly buckling when I really take in the words:

Unknown Number: I'm going to get you bitch.

Unknown Number: Whatever you're looking for, end it.

Unknown Number: Nearly 1,000 girls go missing every day. Don't end up as one of them.

Just then, my phone buzzes, and another text loads in the thread.

Unknown Number: I'm sure Miranda can't wait to be reunited with her precious daughter. But then what would happen to poor little Desmond?

"O-oh God," I stammer, my hand instantly going to my mouth to silence the scream building in my throat. My hands are shaking, and there is no holding back the emotions now. My vision blurs as the tears fall, heavy droplets trailing my face then through my fingers.

Suddenly there's a bang at my door—loud and aggressive. The phone falls to the floor, muffled by the old carpet. The scream is right there, but I squeeze my mouth so tight, my lips twist together as pain shoots through my face.

"Sam. Open up, it's me, Kane."

And just like that, everything stills, my limbs go numb, and my legs give in.

"Sam," Kane calls out again, this time his voice softer than before.

It takes a beat for me to pull myself up and step toward the door before hesitantly opening it. His eyes trail my body from my feet up and once his eyes land on mine, the dam breaks. I collapse into him, and he catches me in his big strong arms.

"I got you," he whispers and walks me back into the room, closing the door and securing us inside.

The sobs are audible now, and Kane moves us over to my bed where he guides me to sit next to him. I sniffle, my vision still obstructed from the tears.

"What happened?" he asks after giving me a bit to calm down. "Sam. Please. Talk to me."

It sounds like a plea, like he's begging me to confide in him. The look in his eyes when we realized that I'd told Mountain and Alex about Jackson but not him almost crushed me.

"It's not Jackson," I hitch out.

Kane frowns. "What do you mean?"

I swallow hard and point to my phone in the middle of the floor.

Kane follows my finger, glancing between me and the device before he gets up to get it. He stares at the screen, jaw increasingly tensing as he reads the messages.

"That's not Jackson who was texting me."

He stares at me, perplexed. "Alex said he called last night."

I nod. "He did. Well, I think he did. Alex says it was his voice. But those text messages, it can't be him, Kane. They know my mother's name, my brother's. Jackson wouldn't know that. Told me to stop digging. He wouldn't know that either."

"Then who?"

I shrug, my entire body shaking. "I don't know. The person who was just following me."

He frowns again. "Sam. I was just following you."

"No. There was a black van." I breathe out. "Outside the dorms. Chasing me, yelling my name, and then they sent that message."

Kane shakes his head. "I left practice as soon as I saw you leave. Was behind you the entire time. No one but me was following you. I don't think the van was there for you. You're upset and I—"

"No." I shake my head, refusing to believe otherwise. "I know what I saw, Kane."

"Look at me." Kane cups my face, lowering himself so that he is eye level with me. "No one is going to touch you."

I look at him, my bottom lip trembling. "I'm scared. It can be anyone. I just—" I stop short and reach into my drawer for the files I've stashed there. Frantically, snatch up the picture of our mothers and tear it in half.

"Wait. Sam, what are—"

"Just get rid of it. It's not worth it."

"Sam. Stop." Kane grabs my wrists, shaking me enough to force my attention to him.

My lip trembles, and my eyes sting. "Des. I can't leave him alone in this world."

Kane stares at me for the briefest of moments, a heavy sigh slipping from his lungs. I can see the care in his eyes, and it's rare coming from him.

"You won't," is all he says, but he never lets me go. "Nothing is going to happen to you. I'll die before I let that happen."

My breath hitches and I search his features. He drops his gaze, but his hands squeeze me just a little tighter as the words settle around us. He's serious.

"I... *we* won't let anything get to you. Or Desmond. We'll get to the bottom of this."

CHAPTER THIRTY-THREE

KANE

Kane: We need to talk.

I type the message, sending it to the group chat I have with Alex and Mountain.

Spinning on my heel, I face Sam. She's pacing, still staring at her phone as if she'll see something different on it. Every inch of her frame is rigid. Seeing her like this, afraid and lost, rocks me to my core.

I was so busy taking out my pain on her, she only trusted Alex and Mountain enough to share what had happened to her. Sure, she shared about the photo of our moms and how she found it. But she left a hell of a lot of things out. And I have to live with that.

"You should sit," I suggest as my phone vibrates in my grasp. I glance back to Sam and wave a hand toward the bed before clicking on the text alert.

Alex: Where'd you go?

Mountain: Have you seen Sam?

Alex: Coach is pissed.

Kane: Tell him I had an emergency.

Kane: Sam's with me, meet us at the crib after practice.

Mountain: Is she okay?

I glance at her and release a sigh. Regret swells in my chest; the resentment for my father is heavier now than it's ever been. This is his doing, I know it. And that call I walked in on was the moment he ordered all of this to start.

Kane: I don't think so.

I shove my phone into my pocket and quickly gather the papers to stuff them back into the folder. Sam stops moving, turning to me with confusion written all over her face. At least the pacing stopped—that means she's present again. And if she's present, then she's not losing it, and we can fix this.

"What are you doing?" she asks.

"Get your keys. We're going to the lake house."

"Why?"

I hold the pages at my side. "The guys are going to meet us there after practice. We should probably talk about all of this." I hold up the folder with the pages sloppily shoved inside it. "Away from here. They threatened you because your looking is digging up something they obviously want to stay buried. Which means staying here isn't an option."

"I can't just—"

"Pack a bag. Enough for a couple of days until we figure this out. Where's Gracie?"

"She works out every morning before class."

I nod. "Tell her to meet us at my place."

"Okay... but—"

"Pack. Now," I blurt out louder than I intend to.

Sam flinches at my tone, but she doesn't fight back. She rushes to her closet for a beat-up book bag and then rushes over to her dresser and stuffs as much of her essentials as she can inside it.

When she's done, she stands in the middle of the floor, nervously waiting for my next instruction. I snatch up the backpack and drape it over my shoulder as I walk toward her.

I nod at the door, silently telling her that it's time to go.

Sam jumps when the door slams shut behind us.

"Sorry," I say when she makes eye contact with me. Setting my bag against the wall, I gesture for Sam to head farther into the house. I step around her to avoid bumping into her as we both enter the living room. She peers around awkwardly as if she hasn't been here before.

"It'll be a few hours before practice is over and the guys get here."

"That's fine." Sam awkwardly waves her phone. "I texted Gracie, she probably won't come till later, too."

I nod, fidgeting in place. "Are you hungry?"

Sam turns her head in my direction and nods gingerly.

"I'll order food. We probably only have protein and supplements in there."

That makes her laugh. It's a barely there chuckle, her lips hardly tilting up, but her eyes soften.

"Can you order me a breakfast sandwich, anything really, and orange juice?"

"Yeah." Pulling out my phone, I quickly open the delivery app and order food for both of us. "I'm going to change out of my practice gear right quick."

Sam nods. "Okay."

I race off to undress, returning just as Sam's phone lights up in her grasp. Her muscles tense, fear rearing its ugly head again. Concerned, I move toward her, nervous and already on edge, but when her features soften, my heart rate settles.

"That was my best friend, Evan. I texted him to make sure my brother was okay, and he just texted back a picture of him with a milk mustache."

I breathe out a sigh of relief. "Does he know what's going on...Evan?"

She shakes her head. "No. I don't want him mixed up in any of this. Honestly, if I had known it was this deep, I never would have pushed it or involved any of you."

I reach out to touch her hand without registering what I'm doing. We stare at the connection for a beat, as if neither of us expected it. Yeah, we might have crossed a line already, but that was hate-filled and spur-of-the-moment. It was also supposed to be just once.

Besides, she has Alex and Mountain and neither of them have the complicated history with her that I have. But touching her now—even just the back of her hand—is electrifying.

"This isn't your fault."

She huffs. "It sure isn't anyone else's." She looks away. "And I've gotten you all wrapped up in this."

"That picture had all our moms in it. We were already wrapped up in whatever this is long before we were born. But when the boys and Gracie get here, we're going to figure this out."

"I don't want anything to—"

"Nothing is going to happen."

"You can't be sure of that. It's hard to defend yourself against something when you don't know who's coming after you. I think it's the chancellor, but without solid proof—or even a clear crime—it means nothing. I don't want to risk leaving Des alone."

Her voice lowers. "He's already been through so much, he can't lose me, too."

"He won't," I promise. "What happened with your mom... after she left the facility?"

Sam sighs. "She was in and out of Wyndmoor during those last years. And she seemed to be doing better, taking her meds and using all the coping skills they taught her. But, one day she just—" Sam chokes on her words. "Life just became too much, I guess."

I open my mouth to speak but the words die on my tongue. There's no right thing, no magic phrase that'll make this wound less raw.

Sam starts to pace, but before she can walk away, I catch her wrist. She doesn't pull away like I expect her to; instead she peers up at me and for the first time I see everything she's been holding back. It's all there, the pain, the anger, the vulnerability.

I pull her in slowly enough to give her an out, but she doesn't take it. We're only inches apart, sharing the same air. Her eyes dart between mine, and I feel the shift in her breathing. It's slow and labored, almost deliberate, like she does it to ground herself. I can't help it when my gaze falls to her lips, where I watch her mouth part.

She feels good in my arms, soft and delicate. The last time I got to touch her, it was rough and heated, but this time, it's gentle. Then Sam rises on the tips of her toes and brings her mouth to mine. The kiss is tentative at first, and all the noise of the day melts away. A low moan rumbles in my throat as Sam throws her arms around my neck to pull me close. The moment her front presses against me, my entire body twitches.

It remembers her. Her warmth. Her taste. And I want her again. It was foolish to think I'd be able to have her only once, and it's been hell trying to pretend I didn't want to rip her clothes off every time I saw her.

Reluctantly, I break away and lean back to look at her. Sam stares at me, want and confusion hanging from her now swollen lips.

"What about Alex and Mountain?" I ask, hating how nervous I am for the answer. I would never have thought I would be here, caring as much as I do about anyone other than myself. I don't get attached to girls, don't care who they spend their time with. But I do with her.

Sam searches my face, her eyes softening. When she cups my cheek, my eyes close involuntarily, my heart skipping a beat. And when I open them again, I see the sincerity in her eyes.

"Right now. I only want you."

The moment the words slip past her lips, I yank her close and crash my mouth down on hers again. I bunch the hem of her hoodie in my grasp and pull it over her head in one smooth motion. She's wearing a vintage tee that's fitted to perfection, and jeans that look like they've been painted on. I fumble with the tail of her shirt until I finally meet her skin.

She abruptly pulls away, then pushes me back into the couch. I fall with a thud and Sam doesn't miss a beat. Before I can make sense of anything, Sam climbs into my lap like she's claiming her territory. And when she grinds against me, there's no stopping the groan that pours from me.

She grips my shirt and yanks it over my head, tossing it to the side. Then I slide my hands under her shirt. I feel the lines of a tattoo in the center of her spine and let my fingers linger there a moment longer before finally reaching up to unclasp her bra. Sam removes it along with her shirt, tossing it next to mine.

She runs her hands over my chest, and down my stomach, then hooks her fingers into the waistband of my pants. Sam lifts just enough to slip her tiny hand inside and wrap those delicate fingers around my length. She kisses me again, slowly stroking my dick and squeezing just a bit. Without breaking our connection, I reach between us and unfasten her jeans.

"Lie down," I whisper and tilt my head toward the empty seat.

She climbs off me and settles against the cushions. I turn to finish working on her jeans, pulling them down around her ass, and off one leg at a time. I drop them on the floor then stand with my hands gripping my pants.

Slowly, I yank them down, my dick springing free, already hard and desperate for her. With only her lace panties remaining, Sam peers up at me, and it's the sexiest shit I've ever seen. I want her so bad, I can't fucking stand it. Pre-cum beads at the tip.

I shake my head, stroking myself. "You're so fucking beautiful."

Still jerking myself, I lower on my knees between her thighs. She has one leg bent against the back of the couch and the other hanging over the edge as her eyes move from my face to my dick. She licks her lips, and something akin to hunger flashes across her features.

"Shit," I groan and reach down to run the pad of my finger over her pussy through the fabric of her underwear.

Sam's hips jut forward, greedily searching for friction. And I give her just that when I swipe firmly back down from her clit to her slit. As I settle on my knees facing her, the couch dips from my weight. I hook my hands around her thighs and yank her closer so that her sex is lined up perfectly with my dick. I press the head against her clit, leaving the material as a barrier between us.

Sam moans and I exhale deeply, mentally telling myself to calm down. I want to take my time with her. I want her to remember me even when I'm not there, need to be imprinted so deep she can never forget me. I inch her underwear to the side and stare down at her pretty pussy. Her clit pulses, begging for my attention. I slap my dick against it, and she bucks.

Her hands are everywhere. On my shoulders, my face, my neck. And when she pulls me on top of her, she bites my earlobe, then licks the sweat off my collarbone. I can't get enough of her. I want to be inside her, to feel her squeeze around me and never let go.

"Fuck me," she whispers.

Eager to oblige, I line myself up with her center, but I don't enter her just yet. Instead, I hover over her to steal one more kiss. Gripping my shaft, I slowly press inside.

She gasps.

At the same time, I mutter, "Shit, you're so tight."

Not just tight, she's perfectly warm and wet and I have to close my eyes to keep from losing it too soon. I move in and out of her, eyes still shut to savor the feeling. Besides, the moment I look at her taking my dick, I'll fucking explode.

Sam clearly has other plans because she fucks me back. I open my eyes to her hips rocking with a ferocity I never expected, slamming herself against me over and over, using me to find her own relief. I love it. As much as I wanted to pace this, I want her to take everything she needs. So I lean back on my palms and meet her thrust for fucking thrust. The sound of our skin slapping and the scent of our sex fill the air and it's intoxicating.

But the sight of her working my dick like she owns it, her

pussy swallowing and releasing me is pure heaven. Every sense is heightened, and every nerve in my body is on fire when I touch her. There's absolutely no way one time will ever be enough.

I'll need her again and again. And if I have to share her, I may be willing.

"Damn, baby," I mutter. "You look so fucking perfect taking my dick."

I reach for her clit, rubbing tight circles around it and watch as her eyes flutter to the back of her head. With a groan, I keep feeding her dick and playing with her bud. She tightens around me, her walls hugging me close.

Bringing my chest to hers, I whisper in her ear, "That's right, baby. Take what you need. Take all of it."

She claws at my back, her nails sharp enough to leave marks. Then I reach down to grip her thigh to open her wider for me, hooking it in place with my forearm. I dive deep, bottoming out.

The couch creaks under us, but I don't care. Her pace gets frantic, then erratic, and I can tell she's close. Sam buries her face into my neck, breathing hard, making little whimpers that turn me inside out. I buck into her, matching her rhythm, the feeling building until I can't hold it any longer.

I lose it and quickly pull out, coming all over her stomach.

Sam clings to me as our bodies ride out the tremors together. I search her face, not quite sure what I'm looking for. She really is beautiful, and I hate that it took me this long to truly see her.

Sam is it for me, and I know it's crazy considering we were just at each other's throats. But I think deep down, that's why I pushed her way. I knew that the moment I let her in, I'd be done for.

Then I remember that I'm not the only one who feels this way.

If today told me anything, it's that Mountain and Alex care for her, too. And now I need to know.

Sitting up, I rub my temple. "Not to kill the mood, but I need to ask."

She lifts up on her elbows.

"Where do we all fit in in this? Me?" I swallow. "And the guys? Who do you choose?"

Her shoulders slump; then she shrugs. "I...I...what if I can't choose?"

CHAPTER THIRTY-FOUR

SAM

My life has never been more complicated than it is right now.

I'm sitting in the living room across from Kane, Alex, Mountain, and Gracie, as they collectively wait for me to start the conversation. It would fall on me, right? I mean, I am the reason we're all here.

Mountain sits next to me, his large frame expectantly comforting. Alex is across from us, leaning against the dining room table with a beer in his hand. Kane is settled next to Gracie on the larger couch, and I have to force myself to not make eye contact with him. Not only did we just have sex right where Gracie is sitting, that question still looms between us: What if I can't choose?

"So does someone want to tell me why I'm here?" Gracie asks, staring between the four of us, but no one answers. "What's this all about?"

"It's about what we found. The questionable details of my scholarship, the pictures we found, the articles. Someone knows, and they're threatening me."

Gracie's eyes grow wide, nearly bulging out of their sockets.

"What?" She scoots to the edge of her seat, shoulders tensing, posture going rigid.

"I haven't told you, but shortly after we found that article, I started getting very disturbing text messages. At first, it didn't register that it had anything to do with what we'd found. It could have come from anyone. The whole team practically hated me. Jackson. Christina. So I just ignored it and stopped reading them."

The boys shift awkwardly at that, regret written all over their faces. Even Bryden's, when he was the only one who didn't treat me poorly.

"I'm confused." Gracie holds up a hand. "Why would we think these texts were from Christina or Jackson?"

I glance at the boys, taking a moment to find the right words. "Jackson tried to drug me and when I reported it, the chancellor and coach protected him. Threatened to expel me unless I dropped the accusation and worked for the team for the rest of the season. And Christina? Well, why does she do anything she does? My guess is she is fully aware of what Jackson tried to do to me, and because she and him have that weird relationship, she chose to join in on the hatred."

Gracie's spine snaps straight, her eyes shifting awkwardly. "I'm sorry. I didn't know."

"I'm fine, and I should've told you." I fidget with my fingers. "Last night, when Alex stopped by, it was because he had found information that tied my scholarship to the social club our parents were in. And while he was there, Jackson called. We only know it was him because Alex recognized his voice. But I don't know if he was just trying to mess with me or if he's the one that's been calling all along. The calls are always blocked, so I never could figure that out. Then he showed up at practice today and everything got out of control, so I left and I swear someone was following me. There was a black van, completely blacked out, and unmarked."

"Sam says they were tailing her until I showed up, must have scared them off," Kane adds.

"Oh my God, Sam," Gracie says, her voice full of sincerity. "That's scary. So, we were right?" Gracie peers back to me. "The chancellor is involved, and something definitely went down with that club?"

"We think so."

Alex nods, scratches his head before crossing his arms over his chest. "Yeah. Sam told me about my father's name being in her file, so I snuck into his work computer. It wasn't much there, but I found a wire transfer from the bank."

"I don't understand. What club?" Mountain, who'd been observing quietly, finally asks.

I catch Mountain up, filling in all the gaps.

"When we were looking up info on Sam's mom, we found a photo of all of our moms. Which was a shock because she didn't know her mother was a student at SKU," Gracie interjects.

"Your moms?"

"Yeah. Sam's, mine, Kane's, Alex's, and Christina's. They were part of some club called the Aurelian Circle. But everything we looked up about it is either nonexistent or vague. It was shut down in '05 after a student killed another student."

"Wait. Killed. Who?"

My gaze darts to Kane's. To tell Mountain anything more would be sharing something that isn't mine to tell. Gracie knows, but only because she was there when I found out. And when I told Kane what we found, filled him in on his mother being named in Emily's death, he didn't take it too well.

And I get it. Everyone has a version of the people they love that they want to cherish, and in a matter of minutes, that viewpoint was altered. It leaves more questions that he'll probably never get the answer to.

"A girl named Emily Croswell, and apparently the person who killed her was my mother," Kane answers.

Alex shoots up, perplexed, but he doesn't speak. The room quiets as we give Kane the space to work through whatever he's feeling around that confession. After a beat, he opens up, sharing about his mother's mental health struggles, and how hard it's been.

And like the good friends that they are, neither of them questions him. Instead, Alex walks over to Kane and pulls him into a hug. I watch the tension leave his body as relief enters it.

"Sorry to hear that, bro," Mountain says. "I can only imagine what that's like, but know that we have your back. Always."

Alex releases him, but we remain silent, none of us knowing what to say next. So much information has been shared and we're still no closer to understanding it all.

"So what are we going to do? Clearly someone's trying to scare her, and I'm convinced my father has something to do with it," Alex says while taking a seat on the arm of the sofa.

"He does," Kane blurts.

We turn our attention to him.

"Your dad is involved." Kane stares at me, something akin to remorse steeped into the lines above his brow. Then he looks away, his shoulders slumped, fingers curling into fist. "A little while ago, he called me to his office. It was late and he wanted to talk."

Alex frowns. "About what?"

"He had a video of you and Sam outside the admin building."

"That's how you knew about Alex kissing me?" I say in a whisper, but not low enough. All eyes point to me, and I feel the moment Mountain grows a little uncomfortable.

"Shit. Security cameras," Alex mutters. "But what did he call you for?"

"He asked me to keep Sam away from you. Said that she was digging into some stuff that could get her hurt and he didn't want you to get caught up with her. Asked me to watch her."

As soon as he starts to explain, memories of the night he showed up at my dorm drunk off his ass rush to the front of my mind. Now it makes sense. I couldn't put it together that night how he knew or why he was acting the way he was. My blood boils, the anger starting to fester. He played me and I fell for it.

"So all this time he knew we broke in. But why did he ask you? Why not just come to me? Or go to Sam?"

Kane shrugs. "He knew about Sam's and my history, about our mothers both being patients at Wyndmoor around the same time. Figured because I knew her before, I could convince her to stay away from you."

"All this time, you knew I was in danger and said nothing?"

I can't believe him. All that talk about having me, about keeping me safe, and the whole time he's known. I don't know if it's the lie that hurts or that I fell for it. I jump to my feet and move toward the kitchen, needing to put some much-needed distance between Kane and me.

"Sam. It's not like that." Kane stands and reaches for me, but I jerk away. "I didn't tell him anything and I was never going to. I don't even think I fully believed him. But I got a weird vibe and told Sam to stay away."

"We all keep secrets, Sam," Gracie chimes in, stopping me in my tracks. "I get this came out of left field, but you can't really blame him when you've done the same. The look on Mountain's face tells me he didn't know about any of this until this very moment."

"It's not the same."

"It's not much different. You didn't share because you didn't have all the information. He was doing the same thing. And while I get it, I think none of us knows what we're dealing with and we're just trying to piece it all together."

"He knew that Chancellor Richardson was watching me and said nothing."

"He's telling us now. Give him the benefit of the doubt. Just like they're all giving you."

I sigh. She's right. It doesn't feel like it at the moment, but she has a point. This isn't mine or Kane's fault. It's much bigger than us.

"All right."

Kane and I stare at each other, knowing we'll need to talk after this.

"We need to break into my father's personal computer."

We all turn toward Alex in disbelief.

His gaze bounces between us. "The way he keeps his home office locked down, we'll find what we're looking for in there. I know it."

"What?"

"We can't."

"How are we supposed to do that?"

Our questions and statements fly out in rapid succession.

"The party at my house."

Groans of protest erupt through the room.

"Listen. I know it's crazy, but it's the perfect time to do it. He's going to be distracted with the guests."

"Okay, say we do this. What's your plan?" Kane asks.

"While the party is going, we sneak into his office. We'll have to be there, including you, Sam, since you're technically a member of the team. We can get in and out without anyone noticing."

Seriously, what is with this guy and his love for breaking and entering?

"If he's as uptight about his office as you say, how are we supposed to get in?" Kane inquires.

"I know the passcode."

I roll my eyes, throwing my hands up. "Of course you do."

"Look. If we want to figure this out, that's the only time we'll be able to. If he's already aware of the break-in and the files you took, then he's probably got people watching. But he doesn't know that we know, and he won't suspect we'd be bold enough to do this. The house would be packed, and with people all over the place, he'll never notice that we're missing."

"I don't know, Alex," I say, shaking my head. "This is crazy."

"Do you want answers or not?" he deadpans.

"Why do *you* want to do this?" Mountain interjects.

Alex looks at him for a beat. "That bastard has made my life a living hell, so sue me for wanting to get back at him."

Kane winces at that, and shifts awkwardly, peering around as if to make sure no one notices. But I do.

"It'll only work if we're all there." Alex points his gaze at each of us.

"Well. Good luck with that," Gracie adds as she nervously runs her hands over the front of her jeans.

"All of us, Gracie. You're as much a part of this as the rest of us. We need a lookout and distraction. And it's not like you haven't been to these before," Alex continues.

"Well, that was then and this is now. We can get caught. Get expelled."

"We won't." Alex pauses. "Not if we all work together and do our part."

"He's right," I finally join in. "I don't necessarily like it, but how else are we supposed to find out what's going on. All of our moms were in that photo, which means this involves each of us.

Something happened all those years ago and they are working really hard to keep it hidden."

She shakes her head again.

"Please. You're one of the few people I trust here, Gracie. Don't make me do this without you," I beg.

She sighs, staring at each of us before finally nodding. "Fine. But, we better not get caught."

Alex perks up, bouncing on his toes with excitement. "All right. So this is how we have to do it."

CHAPTER THIRTY-FIVE

ALEX

Sunlight wakes me up out of my sleep. I sit up, staring around the living room. I don't know what time we finally called it a night, but what I do know is the sun is an asshole this morning. Its rays poke between the blinds directly into my eyes like it's demanding I get up and start my day.

"All right. You win," I mutter and rub the sleep from my eyes. As if it'll answer me back.

It's quiet in that special way that only happens after a night full of unresolved shit. But then I hear the shower turn on upstairs, the pipes moaning through the walls. There's a kink in my neck, and I move it around in an attempt to release it. It's useless, though. That's what happens when you give up your bed in the name of being a gentleman.

But then again, this is Sam we're talking about. And after everything, making sure she's good is the only thing on my mind. So, if that means crashing on a sofa that is too small and has seen more ass than a little bit, so be it.

Besides, if my mother knew I didn't give my room up to a woman, she'd rip me a new one. And as sweet as Amber Williamsburg is, you don't want to get on her bad side.

There is absolutely no way I'm spending another night on this sofa, though. Today's a free day for me, so I'll certainly be picking up an air mattress later.

Kane was smart to insist Sam crash here until it all blows over. Staying with us is the best and safest option.

It's probably the most complicated option given this little situation between us, not quite a triangle, more of a square than anything else—the romantic and sexual tension that's so thick we can cut through it. The fact that we all seem to want Sam and vice versa. It's wild and convoluted, and no one on the outside looking in would understand, but it feels right.

Kane and Mountain are already off for the day. There's no practice, and I don't have any classes, so that means it'll just be me and Sam. With everything we know now, Sam will be staying with us while Gracie stays with her parents until it all blows over.

After fixing two cups of coffee in the kitchen, I climb the stairs and approach my bedroom door. The shower has stopped, but I knock just to be sure.

"Come in," Sam's voice reaches past the threshold.

Juggling the mugs, I manage to get the door open and use my foot to push it wide. Sam is fully dressed, pulling at the hem of her shirt.

"Morning." She smiles at me.

"Morning. How was your sleep?"

She's gorgeous in the morning, eyes not fully open, voice low and raspy, hair in a bun on top of her head. I stare at her for beat, admiring how natural her beauty is.

"It was fine." Sam's eyes fall to the mugs. "Is one of those for me?"

"Yeah." I nervously hold it out for her. "Sorry."

"Thanks." Sam brings it to her lips, blowing on it before sipping.

"Since I'm free today, I plan on going to the store for groceries and an air mattress. Wanna come with?"

Sam swallows her drink and nods. "That'd be cool. But I'm happy to take the couch the rest of the time."

"I'm happy to let you sleep in my bed."

"Alex, no. I will not put you out of your room. I'm sleeping on the couch."

Something tells me she isn't going to let up, so instead of pushing, I let the conversation be. She might insist, but so do I.

"Are you ready for the party? Do you have a dress? It's a black-tie thing since my father's obsessed with appearances."

"I'll just borrow something from Gracie. I don't really have the money for a new dress that I'm probably never going to wear again."

"Okay." I pause and shift in place. "Well, I'm going to shower really quick, then we can go to the store."

"All right." Sam grabs her phone from my nightstand. "I'll give you some privacy and wait out in the living room."

She slips past me, eyes trained on mine as she exits. All I can do is shake my head and wonder what we've gotten ourselves into.

As we turn into the lot of the luxury strip mall, Sam snaps her eyes to me. "I thought we were going to the grocery store?"

I roll into park and kill the engine. "We are. But we need to stop here first."

I exit first, rounding the front of the vehicle. Sam opens her door just as I reach her side of the car to hold out my hand. She stares at it for a second before accepting the gesture and wrapping her small fingers around mine. Letting the door close, I pull

Sam toward one of the boutiques. It's my mother's favorite place to shop, and having come here with her plenty of times over the years, I'm certain they'll have something that'll be perfect on Sam.

Sam plants her feet and pulls against me. "Alex, no. This place is expensive."

Looks like she put two and two together. "You need a dress and, from what my mother tells me, they're the best in town."

"I'll borrow something from Gracie."

I turn to face her but never let go of her hand. "You deserve something of your own. Let me do this for you."

She huffs, and cranes around me to stare at all the dresses in the window. She doesn't take well to people doing things for her, that much is clear. I don't know if she's just not used to it or maybe she feels as if she'll owe me.

"I want to do this." I shift to make her look back at me. "Okay. No strings, no catches."

This time she allows me to lead her all the way. The bell above the door chimes as Sam enters first.

"Welcome. I'm Clarissa, how can I help you?" the store clerk asks the moment we step past the threshold. She's a young Black girl with long braids. She smiles at Sam before turning her attention to me.

"We're here to look for a dress for a black-tie event," I answer.

"Absolutely. Do we have a price range we're trying to stick to, sir?"

"We're probably the same age, so you don't have to call me sir. And no limit, whatever she likes."

The girl smiles again, her brows rising. "All right then. Follow me."

Sam steps off first with me directly behind her.

We approach the dressing area, which is nothing more than a row of stalls with curtains and bench seating in front. It's early so there aren't many other shoppers around. I step around the bench, flopping down on the white leather seat. Clarissa pulls back the curtains on the center stall and waves for Sam to enter.

"I'm going to place you here and will be right back with some styles that I think you'll look good in."

Sam nods.

Clarissa gives her a once-over then saunters off, leaving us alone. We're quiet for a moment, the silence settling around us awkwardly. When she glances in my direction, I pretend not to stare, act as if I'm not locking everything about her to memory.

"When I was a little girl, I promised my mother that I would grow up and buy us a dress out of here one day," Sam says, but there isn't sadness in her voice. She's smiling as she takes in her surroundings.

I don't respond. Something tells me that was wasn't for me to speak to but a happy memory only for her.

"Thanks for doing this, Alex. I appreciate it."

"You don't have to keep thanking me."

Clarissa returns with a rack full of clothes in an array of styles. "I also brought a few pairs of shoes for you to try just in case you needed to see what the whole look would be."

"That's great." Sam stands, shoving her cell into the pocket of her jeans.

"If something doesn't fit or you want to see something else, just ring that bell." She points to the button in the center of the coffee table. "And I'll be right over."

"Okay."

Sam turns to stroll over to the dresses and take a few into the stall with her. A moment later, I hear her unzip her jeans and shuffle in my seat. And when each garment falls at her feet, my breath catches. Just the thought of her being naked on the other side of that curtain shoots right to my cock.

Moments later, Sam exits the stall wearing a loose-fitting number. It looks nice, long and flowy, the color nice on her skin, but it isn't it. Doesn't suit her.

"What do you think?" She stares at herself in the mirror.

At the same time, we both shake our heads. Sam reenters and reemerges in a copper-colored dress with thin straps. And again, nice, but not the one. But she doesn't ask my opinion on this one, silently making the decision herself with her nose scrunched up. We go on like this for a few more dresses, and none of them worked for her.

Just then, Clarissa returns with a different dress, holding it out to Sam. "One more. I think you'll like this one." Sam takes it from her then retreats into the stall. Meanwhile, I take out my phone to scroll through social media while I wait. Not long after, Sam steps out of the dressing room, and I nearly forget how to fucking breathe.

It's black, simple at first glance, but then she moves directly in front of me, spinning with the biggest grin on her gorgeous face.

"Think I should try it with heels?" she asks but doesn't wait for me to answer her.

Not that I have words anyway. She tiptoes over to the rack and picks out a pair from the choices Clarissa left for her. Then she bends just enough for me to get a peek at her thighs. Sam slips her feet into the stilettos and struts over to me. I squirm in my seat, swallowing down a lump as she closes in. Sam puts her foot on the sliver of bench that peeks out between my legs, and I swallow again. Without instruction, I get to work fastening the straps around her ankles, letting my finger brush against her soft flesh.

She makes eye contact with me as I finish with the last latch, completely unaware of what that one little gesture does to me. This isn't like me, smitten beyond my own comprehension, taking a girl shopping, wanting to do whatever she wants if it means seeing the smile she's sporting right now. Sam backs away to look at herself in the mirror.

The fabric molds to her like it was made just for her. The neckline is high, and her shoulders are completely bare. The silhouette is elegant enough to be the safest choice. But on her, it's not safe at all. It's lethal. And I won't be the only person at the party who won't be able to keep my eyes off her.

She turns slightly to look at herself, and I see the way her eyes light up. It's as if she's not used to seeing herself like this, and that does something to me. It's better than any drug.

She looks good, and she fucking knows it.

I shift in my seat, casually adjusting the leg of my joggers more for survival than comfort. My fingers flex on my knee, my jaw locked so tight it hurts.

Clarissa approaches. "That's the one. And the strappy heels are perfect with it. Don't you think?" She directs that question at me.

All I can do is nod in rapid succession.

"Do you have any gold accessories?" Sam asks.

"I do and it'll be perfect. One sec." Clarissa races off, only to return a few seconds later. "It's one of our matching sets. Comes with gold leaf earrings, a black and gold clutch, and solid gold cuff."

Sam looks at everything, her eyes sparkling in excitement.

"We'll take it. Shoes too," I finally manage to get out.

"You've got a good man." Clarissa beams. "I'll take these to the register and meet you up there. Take your time."

With that, Sam makes eye contact with me, her gaze shifting tentatively. She didn't correct Clarissa when she called me her man, and I won't correct her either. Because it feels right.

"I'm going to change out of this one."

I nod as my phone buzzes in my hand. An email alert dances across the top of my screen, and I sit up, my nerves getting the best of me.

```
Subject: Williamsburg, Alexander Makeup Exam
Score
```

My entire future is riding on the results in this email. If I don't pass and bring my grade up to at least a C, I can forget convincing Coach to let me play during the conference.

The email loads, and I hold my breath.

```
Congrats, Mr. Williamsburg. You've successfully
passed the makeup exam with a solid ninety-two.
If you can turn in even a portion of the extra
credit work, I'll make sure to get your grades
updated in time for the game, as promised. I'll
see you in tomorrow's class.

Professor Lewis
```

The sigh of relief is massive, and the tightening in my chest disappears.

"Yes," I say louder than I realize.

"What?" Sam asks from behind the curtain.

I lean back, raking a hand through my hair, unable to contain my smile. "Just got my results from the exam."

"Don't leave me hanging. What's the verdict?"

I exhale. "Ninety-two."

"That's amazing, Alex." She pokes her head out. "But I'm not surprised. I knew you could do it."

"Thanks," I say, my heart full.

"For what? I didn't take the exam. That was all you. You should be proud." She ducks back behind the makeshift door to finish undressing.

All I can do is watch the curtain close. She's being humble. We both know I wouldn't have been able to pass without her help. But it feels good knowing someone believes in me.

"Alex."

"Yeah."

"I'm kind of stuck. Need you to unzip me."

I flick my gaze at the subtle sway of the curtain, my nerves suddenly out of whack. After wiping my hands along the front of my pants, I rise off the bench and inch closer. My fingers wrap around the thick fabric, the rings scraping along the metal rod. Sam meets my eyes through the mirror and all the blood in my body rushes to my toes.

"Didn't want to risk forcing it and ruining it. Do you mind?" She presents her back to me.

I nod shakily.

I slip inside. The space is small, barely any room for her let alone the two of us. Her back is to me, the little black dress halfway down her shoulders, the zipper stuck at the middle of her spine. The angle exposes more skin than I am even remotely equipped to handle right now, but I focus on that zipper anyway.

My knuckles brush against her back, and her body jolts. Her skin is warm and soft, and suddenly the whole room feels ten degrees hotter. The zipper finally moves, and I peel it the rest of the way down, this time allowing the back of my hand to feel her.

I run my gaze across her back, and over her shoulder blades. She's braless under this thing, and I want so badly to kiss where her bra straps would normally sit. I'm so focused that it takes a minute before I realize that she's watching me through the mirror.

I huff. "Caught in four-k?"

Sam chuckles but it's so low that it might as well just be a breath of air. "Thank you."

She looks at the floor again then back at my reflection. Something takes me over and before I know it, before I can stop it, I'm stepping all the way into the stall. Sam turns to face me, still holding the dress to her chest to keep from revealing too much.

Letting the pad of my thumb stroke her cheek, I watch her lips and note the rhythm of her breaths. When she doesn't pull away, I lower my mouth down on hers. I kiss her softly at first, a low groan rumbling in my throat when she rises on her toes to kiss me back. Her tongue dances with mine, needy and hungry. I cup her face, holding her close, tilting her head so that I may deepen our embrace. Kneading her nape, I trail my lips from her mouth, over her chin, and down to her neck.

She moans softly, her throat vibrating against my tongue. My cock twitches, slowly tenting my pants. She feels it, if the grind of her pelvis against me is any indication. Then I pull back, one hand still in her hair and the other softly around her throat. I force her to meet my eyes, holding her head still to keep her from breaking the gaze.

"I know you have feelings for Kane," I admit, and study her reaction. "And Mountain."

Sam grabs my wrist, and the soft touch of her palm on me is enough to send me into a frenzy.

"Alex—"

"And I don't care."

She frowns, unable to look away even if she wanted to.

"I have eyes. See the way they look at you, the way they are around you. Just like I know they see how I feel, too. And see the way *you* look at us."

I pause, the air now heavy between us.

"And. I. Don't. Care." Lowering myself so that I'm dangerously close to tasting her lips again. "Just don't leave me out."

"I won't... what are you doing?" As she finally speaks, I drop to my knees in front of her.

I grip the back of her knees and peer up at her. "You said I'd have to beg you to touch me again." I tighten my hold. "This is me begging."

Sam stares at me a moment longer than I know what to do with. Defeat is just about to seep in when she cups my chin and guides me back to my feet. Then her mouth is on mine, teeth and tongue colliding as she melds our bodies together. Her hands tangle in my hair, gripping tight as if she's afraid I'd disappear. I wrap one arm around her waist while closing the curtain behind us with the other. Then I back her against the wall. The tension grows between us and before we can come to our senses, her dress is bunched up around her waist.

Sam shivers as I cup her pussy and find her clit through her panties.

"Can you stay quiet for me?"

Sam swallows and nods.

I grip her shoulders and spin her around abruptly until her back is flush against me and her face is pressed against the mirror.

I free my cock, the head engorged and preening, arousal

already leaking from the tip. I grit my teeth and mutter, "Fuck. You're so perfect."

Sliding her panties to the side, I run my cock through her already dripping folds. I lean in to kiss her back, then grip her chin with one hand while choking my shaft with the other. I force her head back and kiss her hard. Her neck is craned, the top of her head pushed directly in my chest, but she doesn't seem to mind.

As I shove my tongue in her mouth, I press my cock into her, feeding her with both parts of me.

"Ffff," she groans, her body trembling as I move in and out of her.

"Sh–shit," I breath. "So, fucking tight. Ah... and all mine."

"Alex," she moans my name, and I thrust into her.

Over and over, I pump into her pussy, keeping her ass glued to my front to avoid alerting anyone to what we're doing.

"Fuck, Sam," I whisper in her ear, while tightening my grip on her neck. "You don't know how long I've dreamt of this. Of fucking you."

I thrust hard.

"Of making you come on my cock."

Thrust twice.

"Of stretching this sweet little pussy until I've drained your body of everything it has."

She fights to breathe, and I release my hold, taking her by the wrist and placing them behind her back for balance. Sam lets me twist her body, fucking her to my heart's content. She tries to fuck me back, throwing her ass against me, but I know if she does that, I won't be able to keep quiet. Once I see her perfect ass bouncing on my dick, I wouldn't give a damn that we're in public. So, I hold her still and do all the work myself.

Sam finds my wrist and she squeezes, letting me know that she's close to breaking. Her nails dig into me, encouraging me to pump harder. I'm buried to the hilt, and I reach around her a find her clit.

"So fucking beautiful," I whisper while continuing to fuck, flick, and pinch her. "Look at yourself. Look how pretty you look taking this cock."

She groans, unable to hold it in. Without skipping a beat, I let go of her wrist and cover her mouth.

"You're going to come for me?"

"Yes." She tries to speak but it's muffled by my palm.

"That's my girl." I moan in her ear. "That's. My. Fucking. Girl."

And when I pinch her clit, that's all it takes to shatter the levee. Sam thrashes against me, and her pussy convulses, milking me. A soft cry escapes her just as her body falls limp. But I manage to hold her up, still fucking her at the same time. But I don't stop stroking, and I don't stop petting until she's damn near crying for me to give her a break.

She looks so good like this, wholly sated, completely spent but still in position for me. My grip tightens on her hips, nails digging into her skin as the pressure builds in my gut, and white explodes across my vision. But it's the moment she does a Kegel with me buried deep inside that does me in. Quickly, I pull out only seconds before thick ropes of cum cover the back of her thighs.

"Shit," I breathe out and plant a kiss to the side of her head. "That was fucking amazing."

Sam doesn't speak; only a nod tells me she agrees.

Once I'm sure she can stand on her own, I let her go and bring my soaked fingers to my mouth and lick her juices off them.

"Mm. You even taste like Sunshine."

CHAPTER THIRTY-SIX

BRYDEN (MOUNTAIN)

We've been here over an hour, the party nearly at capacity now. It's been a few days since I let them convince me to go along with this asinine plan.

Breaking into the chancellor's office? I've never broken into anything in my life. Haven't even been grounded before, always following the rules. But here am, stepping completely outside of myself because there's no way I could sit this out.

All I know is that if Sam is in any kind of danger, I'll do whatever it takes to keep her safe. Including risking expulsion. Because that's absolutely what's going to happen if we get caught.

But if all goes as planned, Alex will sneak in, clone the files, and get out before anyone notices we're gone. Gracie's supposed to keep an eye on the party and signal to Kane if the chancellor or anyone else for that matter comes that way, while Alex, Sam, and I search the office.

Speaking of Sam, I throw my gaze around, checking to see if she's finally arrived. She and Gracie sent us ahead of them so they could take their time getting ready. Besides, people would be suspicious if all five of us arrived at the same time, perhaps a dead giveaway.

She's nowhere in sight, though. Removing my phone from the inside pocket of my red and black blazer, I check to see if she texted. She hasn't.

Bryden: Are you here?

I hit send and glance around. It's crowded, the faces of everyone but who I want to see line my vision. Jackson's here. My jaw clenches at the sight of him.

It's been hard not confronting him, but I made Sam a promise, and I don't break my word. Beside him are his brother and their group of flunkies. Christina and her friends are a few feet away at the open bar.

My phone vibrates and I peer down at it.

Collins: Gracie and I just parked out front. I'll come find you.

I stuff the phone back in my pocket as someone taps me on the shoulder. It's one of the senators. He comes to every party and never misses a game.

"Congratulations. Can't wait to see you boys crush the conference."

"Yes, sir," is all I give, accompanied with a grateful nod.

He moves, turning his attention to a local businessman. They shake hands, moving on as if there isn't anyone else around them. People sway around me while my eyes find Alex across the way.

Clearly, he's being forced into a conversation with his dad and one of the donors, if the snarl on his mug is saying anything. He brings a tumbler to his lip, stopping mid-sip as he stares off in the distance, obviously distracted by something.

I follow his gaze, and the moment I see what he sees, the whole world stops. The room quiets—at least it does for me. Sam stands in the foyer with Gracie at her side. She's peering around, nervous but also the most beautiful woman in here.

And that dress—God, that dress. It's black, and simple, but perfect for her. It hugs her waist like it was stitched together on her body, then flares out at her hips with subtle ruffles. It's effortless, stopping just above her knee, showing off surprisingly toned legs. And the heels she's wearing look like sin. The kind of sin I'll never recover from.

My jaw ticks and I tell myself to look away, but I can't.

It should be a crime to want someone as bad as I want her. I've tried to ignore the feeling, tried to pretend we were nothing more than friends. But that ship sailed the first time she smiled at me.

Finally, she finds me in the crowd, the smile spreading across her face bringing one to mine. She nudges Gracie and points in my direction. Gracie nods as Sam steps farther into the house, weaving through the sea of people. From the corner of my eye, I notice Kane and Alex watching, their muscles tensing at the sight of her. Then I catch Jackson tipping his head in her direction, while Christina and her friends stare in disbelief. It's obvious they didn't expect to see her here, and they probably hate that she looks more like she belongs here than they do.

It's funny how heavy she stays on their minds, while she couldn't care less that they exist. She glides gracefully toward me, that smile of hers getting wider.

"Well, well. Someone cleans up nice?" she says once she's within earshot. "I love the outfit."

Heat creeps up my neck, and I bite back a grin.

"Thanks," I respond and lick my lips. "You look stunning."

She stares down at her dress then back at me. "I tried."

I don't respond and just fully take her in.

"Where are the others?" she asks.

I point to Alex. "Alex is talking to his father."

Sam follows my finger, her eyes lighting up when she spots him. He raises his glass, tipping his head in acknowledgment.

"Kane's over there, talking with one of our sponsors."

She finds him standing all the way on the other side of the floor. We're separated by an oversize fixture in the center of the foyer. It never ceases to amaze me how massive Alex's childhood home is. The living room area is one open floor plan that spans the width of the house, two enclaves of space on both ends. It's like it was made for hosting.

I get why Alex despises this life; it's flashy and fake. Always having to perform for a bunch of people you couldn't care less about has to be exhausting.

Sam's spine straightens when Kane peers back at her. I suck in a breath, watching her interaction with the guys who are like brothers to me. I roll my shoulder and tug on my collar. She focuses on me again, slipping her arm through mine. A tingle races up my spine, but I push it down to play it cool.

She doesn't even realize what she's doing to us. She's turned us into a bunch of guys who can't breathe properly in her presence. Heartbeats race; words get jumbled in our minds.

"Hey," someone says behind us.

We glance back to Gracie, and Sam scoots over to make space for her. I instantly miss the closeness.

"When are we going to do this?" Gracie asks quietly.

"After his speech. He'll be expecting to see our faces—Alex and all the players. And, given the circumstances, maybe even Sam's."

"Okay." Gracie shimmies. "I'm nervous."

"Me too," Sam admits.

We throw our gazes around, observing our surroundings. When Gracie stares ahead, she tenses—her posture shifting from squirmy to iron rod straight. Sam notices, following her line of sight.

"Who's that?" she asks.

Gracie swallows. "My dad."

Senator Martinez crosses the floor, heading in our direction. Gracie exhales deeply, almost like she's bracing herself.

"Gracie?" he says with his hands in his pockets.

"Hi, Father."

The moment is awkward.

Sam frowns, and we discreetly peer at one another.

"Mr. Montour. You're going to help bring us another championship home?" He holds out a hand for me to shake.

"I'm going to do my best, sir."

He nods and smiles. "I don't doubt it. You're one of the best goalies on the ice this season. Hell, who am I kidding? Every season."

"I appreciate that."

Then he turns his attention to Sam, his eyes brightening as he takes her in. Not in a weird way, more familiar than anything.

"And you must be Samantha?" He gestures to shake her hand as well.

"Yes." Sam perks up and shakes his hand. "It's so nice to meet you, Mr. Martinez...Senator...Sorry."

He waves her off. "Mr. is fine. Gracie tells me a lot about you." Senator Martinez glances to his daughter, who is visibly upset by his presence.

"All good I hope," Sam jokes.

"Of course. I hope you're enjoying your time at Sovereign King's. It'll bring you a lot of opportunity for success."

Sam swallows down whatever truth she has to share. "That's what I'm hoping for."

"All right. Well, I'll leave you kids be. There's someone I need to speak with."

"Nice meeting you," Sam says.

"Gracie. I guess I'll be seeing you at home, seeing how your mother told me you'll be staying with us for a few days."

She gives him a curt nod. The senator doesn't acknowledge her behavior but instead places an awkward kiss on her forehead before finally walking away.

"Everything okay?" Sam asks Gracie the moment he's out of earshot.

"Yeah." She sighs. "I need a drink," Gracie blurts and takes off before either of us can say anything.

"That was weird." Sam glances at me.

"Seems there is a lot of hostility between families tonight."

"Tell me about it. Look, I'm going to find the restroom. Be right back."

"I'll walk you."

"I'm fine. I think I can manage it on my own. But I have my phone. I'll text you if I get lost."

I don't like it, but I agree anyway. Sam pats my shoulder then takes off in search of the restroom. Immediately I look over where I saw Jackson earlier, but he's long gone. I'm uncomfortable with that, but before I can really think about it, Chancellor Williamsburg is at the front of the room—mic in one hand and a drink in the other.

Alex stands reluctantly on his left while Mrs. Williamsburg beams like the doting wife and mother that she is. They're vastly different, the two of them, and it's fascinating how Alex has a little of them both in him. He can be charming like his mother in one breath, and just as cold as his father in the next.

On cue, the chancellor begins his speech, directing kind words to his son as if he really means it. Alex forces a smile at the crowd as they hang on every word. This goes on for several minutes with him doing exactly as Alex said he would: making our victories this season about him.

Suddenly, I realize Sam hasn't returned. It's been only ten minutes, but something doesn't sit right with me.

Bryden: Find the bathroom?

I stare at the screen for her reply but those three little dots never appear.

Bryden: Sam?

Still nothing.

Excusing myself, I sway through the sea of people and head down the long hall that leads deeper into the estate. It's quiet save for the chancellor's voice blaring through the halls. But the farther I walk, the more muffled his speech becomes. When I reach the end, I glance both ways, but it's empty. So I move over to the bathroom, and tap on the door. Putting my ear to it, I listen for Sam.

Nothing.

Hesitantly, I knock once more for safe measure and grip the knob to check it. It's unlocked. When I open it, I find that it's empty, no sign of Sam anywhere in sight. But I hear the faint sound of voices around the corner.

"Don't touch me, asshole."

Sam?

I rush forward, glancing over my shoulder to be sure I'm not being followed before focusing on her voice.

"You're going to learn to keep my name out your mouth, bitch."

That's Jackson's voice.

Red blurs my vision as I close the distance in three long strides. I turn the corner to find Sam stuck between a wall and Jackson.

"I've already broken one knee; don't make me break the other," she bites out.

"And you're going to pay for that. Maybe I'll finally do to you what I did to that bitch Gracie. Only you'll have to be awake through it when I fuck you." He reaches for her, and I snap.

I storm forward, my hand palming the back of his head as I shove him from in front of her. Relief flashes in Sam's eyes. Positioning myself between the two of them, I take him by the throat and force him to look at me.

At the same time, he blurts out, "What the fuck?"

When he realizes it's me, his face goes slack. Without words or warnings, I drive my fist into his face. He stumbles backward, falling to the floor and attempting to crawl-walk away with a bleeding nose. But I'm on him immediately, throwing blow after blow to his body. Then I yank him by the collar, drawing my hand back in an attempt to knock his head off his shoulders.

A small hand wraps around my bicep, stopping me.

"Bryden. Stop. Stop." Sam's voice breaks with emotion. "He's not worth it."

Jackson groans beneath me, holding his ribs with one hand and blocking me with the other. I tug him close, and glare at him.

"If you come near her again, I won't stop. I'll be sure to break a lot more than a knee."

"Bryden. Let's go." Sam pulls me up and I allow her to.

Jackson moans on the floor as Sam drags me away, searching around before pulling me into a room at the end of the hall. Alex's family library is covered wall to wall in books.

I step inside the darkness while she closes the door behind us. I hear the lock click. Staring at the large, uncovered windows, I try to gather myself. I hate that she's seen me like that, but I don't regret it.

Then she's behind me, a gentle hand on my shoulder to ground me. I face her, and Sam's eyes fall to my bruised hand.

"Your hand." She takes it in hers to examine me.

I pull away. "It's fine."

She sets her clutch down on the nearest surface and snatches my hand back. "It's not. It's bruised. The game. You could have broken it."

"I didn't."

"He isn't worth you risking the game. You shouldn't have let him make you lose control."

It feels good that she recognizes how important my hand is, how important these games are to me. But I straighten my spine and bring myself to eye level with her so that she knows how serious I am.

"I'll lose every ounce of control when it comes to you."

Silence slams down on us and all we can do is stare at each other. She searches my face like she's trying to determine if I mean it. And I'm reading her to make sure she understands exactly where I stand.

"I'll hurt anyone who tries to harm you. Do you get that?"

Light from the floodlights outside the window beam on us. Her eyes dart between mine, her breath catching.

"I can't worry about hockey if I'm worried about you," I seethe, breathing in the smell of old books and Sam.

It happens all at once.

She erases what little distance is between us and kisses me. It's nothing sweet about it, not like the first time. Then, I wanted to make it perfect, wanted to show her how she makes me feel. But now, all want to do is show her what she does to me.

I kiss back hard and rough, and her hands come to my face as I try to drink her in. I want to bury myself beneath her skin, needing to be close to her, needing to feel her. We're wild and hungry, our bodies flailing around as we fight for dominance. And when we crash against one of the bookshelves, books fall to the marble floor.

Neither of us stops, our focus only on each other.

Her breath is all over my lips, her hands lacing in my hair then over the slope of my shoulders. Sam pulls back, and I watch breathlessly as she takes my injured hand in hers. She brings it close to her mouth while staring deep into my soul.

"Thank you for always protecting me." Then she goes and drive me wild. Her soft, wet lips move across every battered knuckle as she kisses each one.

If I wasn't hard before, I'm rock hard now. I groan and scoop her into my arms. Her legs wrap around me as I carry her to the large library desk, pushing her purse out of the way when I lower her on to it.

Hovering over her, I cup her face, burying my tongue so deep we might as well become one. Sam's dress rises, and I settle between her thighs. So close that I feel my erection pressing against her. It's impossible to ignore, hard even through two layers of fabric. She scrapes her heel up the back of my leg, drawing me closer. She's almost eye level with my dick and it almost makes me cream my pants. My body shakes, but whether it's from adrenaline or restraint, I have no idea.

When she reaches between us and rubs me through my slacks, I jolt from the sensation. Then she shocks me by shoving me backward, hopping off the table, and guiding me to the chair. I allow her to control the moment.

She straddles me, grinding her heat into me. "I want you."

Every muscle jumps in anticipation. "I want you, too."

"But before we go any further, I have to be honest with you." When I don't respond, she continues. "I care about you and never want to do anything to hurt you."

I nod.

"I like you. A lot. But I also care about—"

"I know you have feelings for Alex and Kane. It's okay."

"If this is too much for you, I'll stop right now, and we can go back to friendly text messages and banter."

I grip her tight. "I don't want to be just your friend. I'm too far gone for that."

She exhales, strokes my face, then crashes her mouth on mine again. Sam rolls her hips against my lap, shredding what little resistance I have left. I clutch her hips, kneading her butt and dragging her across my lap. The friction is all consuming.

Sam moans and feverishly reaches between us to fight with my zipper. Finally, she yanks it down and reaches inside. Her delicate fingers find my shaft and pull me out.

Greedily, I hike her dress up, letting my palms roam over her soft skin until I find the seam of her panties and drag the thin material to the side. Sam strokes me, her eyes glued to my expression. She rises on her toes and positions me right at her center.

The moment she sinks down on me, my eyes roll to the back of my head, and I bite back a curse. The first push is almost too much for her. I can tell by the way she shifts a little and digs her nails into my shoulders.

"Shit, you're so big," she protests.

I rub her cheeks, kneading them both to spread her a little wider. "It'll fit."

I press into her, her tight opening giving way just a bit.

"Just breathe through it."

And she does, letting out an exhale with each inch that I feed her. Finally, I'm in to the hilt.

"There you go. You can take it. Ff...Mm," I moan.

Then she starts to move, her hips stuttering at first but then we find a rhythm. I'm not gentle, and I piston into her. Her head falls back, and I watch the rise and fall of her breasts.

We find a brutal pace, and every time I bottom out inside her, I dig my fingers into her hips like an anchor. She leans into me, taking everything I have to give and more. The sound of her slapping against my lap is muffled but still loud enough to echo through the room.

But I don't care.

Sam places her palm on my chest for balance as she bounces on me, her walls hugging me on the way down and milking me on the way up. Her movements get sloppier, more desperate as she uses me to find her release, and it's the hottest thing I've ever seen.

"Shit, Bryden, I'm so close." She wraps an arm around me and moans in my ear.

"Me too."

I splay my hands under her, holding her in place while I thrust into her, fast and hard. White dots flash in my eyes, and all the blood rushes to my balls.

"I'm coming. I'm coming. I'm coming." Her cries fuel my fire.

Choking out a growl, I lift her off just in time for my cum to shoot out in thick, messy spurts all over her thighs.

"Fuuuck," I roar, my back bucking.

Sam kisses me again, this one more tender. But then she cracks a smile.

"What?" I breathe out.

"You cursed."

I laugh, though it's hard to get it out with how out of breath I am. "I guess I'm done being *perfectly intact*."

CHAPTER THIRTY-SEVEN

ALEX

It's time.

Kane tips his head, signaling to me. I nod and force my attention back to the crowd. Rolling my shoulders, I lock my hands in front of me and wait for Dear Ole Dad to finally come to the end of his speech. It's been well over twenty minutes, and a new record. It doesn't surprise me; he loves to hear himself talk.

"As always, we're proud of all our teams, more specifically, our hockey players."

Gee, I wonder why?

"Every season they prove why SKU is the best in the nation, and I can't be more elated that my *only* son—"

And there it is. He doesn't care about this team. Only the extension of his image.

I dart my eyes to Kane, giving him a tight-lipped pointed stare. He knows just like I do that this is all an act. Kane squares his shoulders, his jaw visibly clenched. My father places a hand on my shoulder, forcing me to look in his direction. He smiles, patting my back with more care than I've ever received from him.

"Alexander Williamsburg—he's named after my great-great-great-grandfather in case you didn't know," he says jokingly and the crowd laughs. "He was a pioneer of a man that paved the way for the Sovereign King's University that we have today. He was an idol and we"—he glances to my mother, taking her hand in his free one—"couldn't be more honored to have named this kid after him. Son, you've made your mother and me proud. You've led this team to victories many times over, following in your ancestor's footsteps in a way that would make him proud."

Ancestor? I huff. You mean the angry old bastard that hated everyone. Yeah, I'm *so* grateful to share a name with that asshole.

"I think everyone in the room would agree that we will be rooting for you as you make your transition into the NHL."

The room erupts in applause, and I give a curt nod, lips pressed into a thin line. I wave, but it's stiff and fake, just like this father-son dynamic he's trying to paint.

As soon as the moment passes, I climb down from the makeshift stage. I maneuver through the crowd, being stopped along the way.

"Alex," Mr. Sheffield, one of my father's business partners, says, taking my hand in his. "You know your father's right. You've been a damn good captain."

I squeeze his hand, giving him a firm shake. "Appreciate the recognition."

"Of course. Any idea who you think will draft you?"

I shake my head. "I'll just be honored to continue to play."

It's the truth. Anywhere I can do exactly what my mother wants for me. I can make a name for myself and finally get out from under my father's shadow.

"It was nice seeing you. I'm going to go speak with some of my teammates." No sooner than the words leave my mouth, I'm off in Kane's direction. He's holding two tumblers of brown liquor, and I take one as soon as I'm within arm's reach.

"Figured you'd need it after suffering through that."

I huff. "Yeah. He's fake as shit." I bring the tumbler to my lips and down the shot.

Kane does the same. When I look back at him, I finally take him in, somewhat surprised.

"Hmph," I mutter and set my empty glass on the tray of a passing server.

"Why are you looking at me like that?"

"No. Nothing. Just you look good, bro."

Kane scoffs. "Fuck off."

"No, seriously. The turtleneck looks good," I tease. "It really *hugs* your muscles. The chain's a nice touch, too."

Kane laughs. "Whatever, jerk. Could you have found a tighter button-up?"

For the first time tonight, I let out a smirk. "Where's everyone?"

We glance around.

"Gracie's right—" Kane points to our left, but we don't see Gracie. "She was right over there."

"Mm? Mountain and Sam?"

"Haven't seen them."

I frown at that and pull my phone from my inside vest pocket. Unlocking my phone with face recognition, I scroll to our group chat and key in a message.

Alex: We need to do this now while my father is making his rounds.

Shoving the phone into my back pocket, I tap Kane's shoulder with the back of my hand. "Come on."

With a quick peek over my shoulder, I walk around Kane and

toward the hall. Kane looks around then follows behind me. Quickly, we move down the hall, nerves rattling through us. If things don't go according to plan, we're fucked.

Nothing is going to happen to me, but if my father catches on, he won't spare them. He'll know that I know he's a fraud, and he'll make them pay for daring to challenge him. But something tells me that it's Sam he'll go after the most. She's the common denominator in all of this—the reason we even know that he's got some shady dealings.

Plus, he'd focus on her just because she means something to me.

When we reach the end of the hall, we make a left away from the guest bathrooms and library. Taking the winding staircase two at a time, we climb to the second floor. The noise from the party fades out to nothing more than a low hum.

No one's allowed past the ground floor except staff, so we should be fine. As long as we can get what we need before my father realizes we're missing, we'll get away with it.

Taking out my phone again, I check for a reply.

Nothing.

"Where the fuck are they?" I say aggravatedly.

Punching in a text, I mash send.

Alex: We're on the second floor. Third room at the left.

"Fuck. If we don't want to get caught, we need to do this now."

Just then, Sam and Mountain come rushing up the stairs, breathless.

"We're here," Sam whispers.

"There you go. Where the hell have y'all been?" Kane quizzes.

My gaze narrows to them, taking in their very disheveled

appearances. Sam's lips are bare, despite being painted red when she arrived, and swollen like she's just been kissed. Mountain's hair is slightly ruffled, opposed to how meticulously combed it was earlier. Mountain catches me looking.

I huff and shake my head. We're on a time crunch and these two found time to bang. *Rich*.

"Where's Gracie?" Sam asks when she doesn't see her roommate.

Kane shrugs. "Don't know. Hopefully she's in position at the party to let me know when anyone leaves. Y'all go ahead, I'll keep watch here." He keys something in his phone, probably typing in the safe word just so he doesn't have to waste time trying to type a message if we're going to get caught.

We nod and take off with me leading the charge. Sam is on my heels with Mountain only feet behind her. Approaching my father's office, I punch in the code to disengage the lock: the date my great-great-great-grandfather migrated to this country. His obsession with legacy should be studied. The lock releases and I push inside. We immediately turn on our flashlights and close the door behind us.

Mountain stays close to the door, peeking out every so often to ensure no one is nearby.

"Sam, check those cabinets over there. Look for anything that looks like it matches the name of the club, initials, names. Anything."

Setting her clutch on the desk, Sam rushes to the cabinet and crouches down to eye level. "It needs a code."

I let out a breath and jog over to her. After inputting the code, it opens. I smirk. For a man with several masters and a doctorate, he isn't very smart. But I've also been breaking into his shit since I was a kid.

"Thanks," Sam whispers and reaches for the drawer.

I place my hand on top of hers, drawing her eyes to mine. "I hope he made you cum."

Sam's eyes go wide, and I can't stop the grin from forming. She's cute when she's flustered. I point my eyes to the wet spot on the front of Mountain's slacks.

Sam's cheeks grow flushed as she hides her face in her palm. "Oh my God."

I smirk then stand and return to my father's desk.

Sam searches through the files, taking pictures of anything she finds, while I work on getting into his computer. At least he was smart enough to use a different password this time, but I eventually figure it out—a combination of my and my mother's birthdates.

The screen loads up, and an image of our family as the wallpaper stares back at me. I was about eight here, standing in front of an NHL arena. That was my first game, and the day I decided I wanted to play hockey.

I shake away the thoughts and click through his folders. Everything is systematically labeled, from business files, pictures, and other important stuff like his will and life insurance policies. All standard things, and nothing suspicious. Until I move the cursor over the screen and an icon lights up.

At first glance there's nothing there, but with the mouse directly on it, I can see the folder. It's hidden, damn near invisible. The sneaky bastard used the section of the background photo as the icon image so that it blends in perfectly. Only he would know that it's there. It isn't labeled, just a discreet little square that fits like a puzzle piece. *Smart.*

I click on it. **Encrypted.**

I stare at the screen, something telling me that this password wouldn't be like the others. It would be something no one but him would ever guess. My eyes fall on different parts of the room in search of anything of significance. Then my gaze falls to the framed photo on his desk. It's him and members of his graduating class, Mr. Kincaid, Senator Martinez, Mr. Sheffield, and several others.

I type in the year he graduated. **Incorrect.**

Then I try the day and month he graduated, and file after file floods the screen, sending a flash of light through the room.

"Bingo." I flop down in the chair and scan the screen for anything that stands out.

There are more neatly categorized folders, seemingly organized by class year. When I find 2005 among the list, I hesitate for a beat, then open it. More folders glare at me, this time with names instead of dates. In the first row, a name stands out.

Collins, Miranda.

"Got it," I beam.

"Good because I'm not finding much over here," Sam says, still crouching low.

"Shh," Mountain orders and gently closes the door, leaving it cracked just enough for him to peek out. "Okay, false alarm."

We turn our lights back on and I remove the thumb drive I stuffed in the pocket of my slacks. I insert the device into the USB port and wait for it to register. As it does that, I click back out of that folder and skim over the others. Deciding to search for keywords instead of scrolling through every item, I key in the name and wait to see what pulls up.

Aurelian.

Files began to isolate, several documents labeled only by two letters and a date.

Initials.

I find one with SC and click the first one I see.

SC01252025.

A bank statement loads, and it matches the date and amount of what I found on his work computer. We definitely got it. Satisfied, I copy the folder and am about to exit it when another pair of initials catches my attention.

EK.

Several of them. All one month apart dating back years. I open the first one dated last week. The transaction details stare me in the face.

ACH Withdrawal Everest Kane....................-$10,000

A numbness pricks at my skin, and suddenly it's hot in here. I open another.

EK03032025—ACH Withdrawal Everest Kane....................-$10,000

And another...

EK02032025—ACH Withdrawal Everest Kane...................-$10,000

On the third of every month like clockwork, there's a bank transfer in Kane's name.

"What the actual fuck?" I murmur.

CHAPTER THIRTY-EIGHT

KANE

"Amber," a voice calls out near the bottom of the stairs.

Quietly, I peek over the railing just in time to see Mrs. Williamsburg pause with her hand against the banister. She turns to face someone, her brows raised in curiosity.

"Oh, Lynn. I didn't see you out there," Mrs. Williamsburg says, her tone full of fake enthusiasm.

I smirk at that.

"I was mingling. I must say, you've outdone yourself as always. Everything is immaculate."

Mrs. Williamsburg huffs and shrugs. "Thank you, but you know Richard. All of this is his idea."

"You're being modest. We both know those husbands of ours don't have a coordinated bone in their bodies."

Alex's mom laughs at that. "You're not wrong."

"Anyway. I was hoping to chat with you about the fundraiser. I have ideas that I think would work great."

"Oh. Of course. I was just on my way to clean up this unfortunate wine stain from my blouse. How about I come find you when I'm done?"

"Sure," Mrs. Lindsey says, then turns to walk away.

Mrs. Williamsburg resumes climbing the stairs, and I quickly move across the landing and tuck myself behind the obnoxiously large vase. She reaches the top step, then turns to walk down the hall where Alex and the others are.

My thumb hovers over my phone, ready to send the warning text but I never have to. She walks right past the office and turns at the end of the hall toward her and Richard's bedroom.

I let out a breath, my shoulders relaxing. Lowering the phone, I stay put because at some point she's going to return. If Alex is right, we've got about five more minutes before Richard finishes his rounds and notices we're not in the room. They've already been in the office longer than we planned.

With my nerves on edge, I decide to send a text.

Kane: Hurry up.

Those three dots appear on the screen, and at the same time I hear voices coming from downstairs. Familiar voices, a man and woman. I creep back to the stairs and peer over the banister. They're standing just out of view, their faces hidden by the shadow of the stairwell. Curious, I descend a few steps, being sure not to give myself away.

"You lied to me," the girl says angrily.

"You're in no position to speak to me that way." The man glances around to be sure no one is around.

From this angle, I still can't see either of their faces, only their silhouettes. So I move farther down, my body locking once I finally see their profiles.

Gracie?

Richard?

Gracie tenses and grits her teeth. "You promised that you would make sure he never hurt anyone else. But you lied. He attacked Sam, and you—"

"Enough," he barks. "Jackson is being handled. Now, what do you know? What is your little friend looking for?"

"What the fuck?" I whisper.

"Nothing," Gracie responds.

"Don't lie to me."

"I'm not. She'd just found out that her mother was a student here and wants to know about her."

"Why?"

"Because she's grieving."

Richard stands there for a minute, contemplating whether or not to believe her. And I guess he does because his tone softens.

"Fair enough." He fastens his blazer. "Remember our deal. If I find out you're lying... let's just say I'd hate to see your father's reputation ruined." Without another word, he turns on his heel, leaving her standing alone.

With a deep breath, Gracie removes her phone from her clutch and checks it.

"Shit," she mutters.

"This whole time you've been working with him?" I blurt while stalking down the stairs until I'm directly in front of her.

Gracie startles, her eyes snapping to mine, wide and full of regret. "Kane."

"When I caught you coming out of his office, it wasn't school related. You were spying on Sam."

"No," she stammers.

"You're lying. I just heard it all."

"I swear, it's not what it looks like."

My nostrils flare. "Then how is it?"

Gracie stares at me for a moment. I can see the wheels turning for her.

She exhales deeply. "I was the one that reported Jackson last term for raping me."

Shock drops my jaw. "Gracie, I'm so sor—"

"It's fine. It's over now. But when I reported him, instead of them holding him accountable, they protected him. Just like they're doing with Sam. If I didn't drop the charges, didn't pretend it never happened, Richard would use information he has to ruin my father's reputation. And, as much as our relationship isn't great, I can't let that happen to my family. But Richard didn't stop there, and now he's been blackmailing me into telling him information about Sam. But I promise, I never told him anything important, and I never would. I'm just stuck, Kane, and when I learned Jackson tried to hurt her, too, I—"

"You're not stuck."

"You don't get it." She pauses. "I don't think we know the half of what we're up against. The things he has on my father... something tells me it's nothing compared to the chancellor."

I tense at that, my mind racing a mile a minute. I don't know what I expected us to find, but it wasn't this. Wasn't this dark, this dangerous. If he'll go to these lengths, exploitation, coercion, threats—Gracie might just be right.

"But, Kane." She sighs and sniffles again. "There's something else."

Just then, Sam, Alex, and Mountain come briskly down the stairs.

"We got it, let's go," Sam orders.

Gracie stands, silently pleading with me not to say anything. I nod, not because I want to keep another secret, but because I wouldn't know where to start. Besides, this isn't really my story to tell.

Once Sam reaches the bottom, she throws her arm around Gracie's neck and squeezes her tight. No words, only comfort as if she knows that something isn't right. Gracie peers at me over Sam's shoulder, and I shrug.

Then I look over at Alex. He's the last to descend the stairs, and his eyes are piercing me like daggers.

CHAPTER THIRTY-NINE

SAM

We rejoin the crowd, blending in as if we aren't pumped full of adrenaline.

Gracie and I settle toward the back of the room, neither of us feeling quite like we fit in here.

A second later, Jackson comes into view, touching his lips and checking for blood. Thankfully he doesn't notice us and angrily hobbles toward the exit. I notice Gracie's body lock up, her breath changing drastically. Then I remember him cornering me in the hallway, admitting everything.

Maybe I'll finally do to you what I did to that bitch Gracie. Only you'll have to be awake through it when I fuck you.

I reach for her, realizing that she's shaking. It all makes sense now. Her warning me when we first met, the literal unease that riddled her body when I practically made her attend the game, her reluctantly agreeing to do this tonight, her questioning what happened when I broke his knee.

Gracie peers at me, her eyes brimming with tears. There's a pit in my stomach seeing her like this, hating that I can never take away her pain. Gripping her hand, I pull her away, not stopping until we're back in the hall and far away from everyone. As soon as we're out of sight, I wrap my arms around her neck and squeeze her tight.

"I'm so sorry, Gracie. I didn't know he did that to you," I choke out.

She stares at me, speechless.

"You could have told me what he'd done. I would have been there for you. I hate that you've been dealing with this alone."

The tears are heavier now, but no sound escapes her. It's as if for the first time she's truly allowing herself to feel her own pain.

"I couldn't tell you." Her words come out choppy, diluted behind her cries. "And I've hated myself because you never would have gone to that party if I had."

"Hey. Look at me, Gracie." I cup her cheek. "That's not your fault, and I got away. Okay? I'm fine. And we won't let him break us. He'll pay. I promise."

She sniffles and shakes her head. "No, he won't. None of them will."

I frown at that. "None of who?"

She opens her clutch and removes a tissue to wipe her eyes. "I reported him. And they protected him. What's worse is that they never even opened an investigation. Instead, they cornered me in that office, by myself, with a bunch of men who clearly didn't mean me well."

She drops her chin to her chest, fiddling with the clasps on her bag.

"I was iced out of my own friend group. Kids I've known my entire life sided with him. They didn't realize it, but none of them questioned why I'd been so isolated, so different. They just hang out with the guy who violated me, and I have to watch it every day. He told Christina that I came on to him, and she believed him. We were best friends, and she took his word over mine."

And now I know the issue between the two of them. Sadly, it doesn't surprise me because she did the same with me. Although I didn't have a relationship with her to feel the level of betrayal Gracie does.

"The reason I didn't want to come here tonight is because whatever you guys find on that drive isn't going to be good. There's going to be stuff about my father that changes everything. Bad things, Sam. Things I only know an ounce about because Mr. Kincaid and Chancellor Williamsburg threatened to expose secrets that could ruin my father's life. Pursue these rape allegations, and they'll leak what they have to the press. Or, choose to protect my father's legacy, and they'll ensure Jackson never hurts anyone else."

"Oh my God, Gracie."

"And I'm supposed to be spying on you, too."

I frown.

"But I didn't. I wouldn't. You have to know that."

I don't know how to explain it, but I do. From the day we met, I've sensed her genuineness toward me.

"I believe you."

She nods while fighting back tears. "My dad's been a good man my whole life. But the things the chancellor claims he was a part of... I can't reconcile that with the dad I know. So, I've been avoiding it, trying not to hate him."

So that's why their conversation seemed so awkward earlier.

I pull her in for another hug, whispering over and over that it'll be okay. But the truth is, I'm not sure I believe it. I've had my suspicions that Chancellor Williamsburg had something to hide, for him to go to the lengths he has to scare me. It's got to be bad.

But we deserve the truth, because whatever it is, all of our moms were involved.

"Listen to me. We've got the files, and we'll figure it out together. And I promise you. Jackson will never hurt anyone else again. Want to know how I know?"

Gracie doesn't respond; she only looks at me.

Pulling my phone out of my purse, I unlock the screen and pull up my camera roll. I switch down the volume just to be safe, press play, and hand her the phone. Her eyes grow wider as she watches the poorly angled video. He's not fully in the frame, but enough of his profile is visible and I made sure to say his name loud and clear. At first, I just pressed record for myself, because if he attacked me again, they wouldn't be able to argue irrefutable proof. What I didn't know at the time was that what I was getting was a confession.

"This is your proof, so you can finally make him pay for what he did to you."

Her breath catches as she fights to keep her composure. With each hitch, she nods, the weight visibly lifting off her shoulders.

"Thank you," she whispers and hugs me again.

"Do you want to go?"

She nods.

"Let's do that. I'll tell the boys that we're leaving, and I'll meet them back at the lake house."

We take a moment for her to get herself together and then head back to the party. Along the way, I text our group chat.

Sam: Gracie and I are going to head out. I'll meet you all back at your place.

A second later, my phone buzzes.

Kane—Asshole #2: Drive safe and share your location. Text us when you get there.

After Gracie dropped me off a few hours ago, the first thing I did was take a shower. It's been a long few days but an even longer night. I still can't believe we pulled it off. While this has been the closest to finding answers, I have to admit I'm a little scared of what we'll see on that drive.

Gracie said that the chancellor has some damning things on her father, so what if it's something we can't handle? They've gone to extreme lengths to keep this hidden; are we opening up an even larger can of worms?

I guess we'll find out when the boys get home.

As soon as the thought registers in my mind, the front door flies open. Mountain steps into the living room, a smile tilting his lips. The closer he gets, the more my excitement grows, chest fluttering just a bit.

"Hey." I smile.

Mountain wraps his arms around me, lowering himself to meet my height. "Hi."

He kisses me, and I melt against him.

"What was that for?" I ask through a grin.

He stares for a minute, raking his eyes over my face. "I guess I just missed you."

I exhale, letting his confession sink in. It's not lost on me that he's consistently come out of his shell. It makes me feel good that I make him comfortable enough to do that.

"Missed you, too."

"I'm going to change." He walks around me, his hand grazing over the sliver of flesh above my shorts' waistband.

Kane enters next.

His eyes are tired like he's struggling to keep them open. When he finally looks at me, he tips his head, signaling for me to come to him. One foot after the other, I move forward until his cologne floods my senses.

Kane strokes my cheek then twirls a damp curl around his finger. He doesn't speak, though, only admires me.

"You look like you're ready for bed."

He nods, his brows hiked into his hairline. "I am. Ready for a shower. You were gorgeous tonight."

I smile. "So were you. I like the tight sweater look on you," I tease.

He smirks, glancing away while rubbing a palm over his face.

"I do. It shows off the muscle."

He huffs. "Sure. I'ma get out of this tight sweater." He tugs me close. "Join me tonight?"

"Maybe."

Kane pats my ass then turns toward his room, which is just past the kitchen. Once he's no longer blocking my view, I see Alex standing in the threshold watching Kane with a strange look.

"Hey," I mutter.

He doesn't answer. Instead, he steps into the living room, his face contorted.

"Something's been bothering me all night," he blurts.

Kane turns to see who he's speaking to. But it's obvious to me that he's not talking to me, not when he's shooting daggers into his bestie's back.

"All the stuff the other night about why my father asked you to spy on Sam." Alex inches closer to Kane, who's now giving him his full attention.

Mountain comes back downstairs, clearly not making it to his room to change yet.

"I couldn't quite understand it, but you're my bro." He shrugs, his hands flailing about. "Never had a reason to doubt you." Alex goes to step forward but stumbles instead, grabbing the back of the couch to catch his balance.

"What? You're drunk," Kane adds, visibly confused.

"But then I found your name in the file. Which isn't that alarming considering all of our names were in that file. But yours was—"

"Man, it's late. You've been drinking and not making much sense," Kane cuts in.

Alex points, shaking his finger. "No. What doesn't make sense is why my father would be sending you ten thousand dollars on the third of every month. For years."

I gasp then glance over at Mountain, who's now standing directly beside me. He and I stare between the two of them.

"What?" we say in unison.

Kane's shoulders slump and I know right then that this isn't some drunken misunderstanding.

Dropping his chin to his chest, Kane says, "I didn't want you to find out like this."

Alex stalks forward, sizing Kane up and staring him down. "Find out what? That you're a fucking liar? Hm? Why don't you spell it the fuck out?"

Mountain moves quickly, planting himself between the two

of them. "Come on, Alex. Calm down and let him speak. Everyone's tired, am sure there's a reasonable—"

Alex yanks free from his grasp. "Don't tell me to calm down."

"You're drunk and coming at your friend like he's the enemy. So, yeah, you need to calm down."

"Richard is my father," Kane deadpans.

Silence. It's heavy, dark, and full of disbelief, emotions, and everything in between.

Alex stumbles back, not quite wrapping his mind around what Kane just said. Quite frankly, neither can I. The chancellor is his dad?

Kane releases a breath. Pain brims in his eyes but there's something else—relief maybe?

"We're brothers. Your father got my mother pregnant a month before your mom got pregnant with you."

CHAPTER FORTY

ALEX

Sleep was the last thing on my mind last night.

After Kane dropped that bomb, I didn't know what to do with that information. My best friend since second grade just told me that he is my half-brother. That my father—*our father*—cheated on my mother and all but abandoned him.

All these years, he let us know each other while lying to our faces. The number of times Kane stayed over or spent time at my house after practice. My mother nurtured him and his did the same the few times I've seen her. But now knowing about her mental struggles, I know why Kane preferred that we always stayed at my house.

He didn't want any of us to know, but I can't help but feel that was my father's doing as well. He certainly couldn't send me to his mistress's house. No, he needed to control the narrative, and he can only do that in a space he governs.

It's beyond fucked up the lengths that man goes to break the people around him. Because that's all it's ever about for him. Certified God complex.

And while I realize that this is tough for Kane, I can't get over the lies.

Clearly, he knew, and not once did he tell me. Why? We're

bros. Loved each other like brothers. Or at least I thought. Maybe it was never that deep for him; maybe being my brother wasn't something he wanted. That fucking hurts.

"Good morning," Sam's soft voice calls out behind me, followed by the sound of the screen door sliding open.

I've been standing on the back deck staring into space for the last hour. My mind's so gone, the chill in the air doesn't even faze me.

Glancing over my shoulder, I take her in from head to toe. Her thighs are completely exposed, but she's wearing that infamous hoodie. Her hair is covered in a leopard print bonnet, and her glasses are nowhere in sight. In her hands, she carries two coffee mugs, the steam swirling in the air. A smile tugs at my lips as I turn to face her.

Out of all the fucked-up shit that's happened in the last few months, she's the only good thing. Which is a crazy concept for me. I've never been the relationship type. Then she shows up and turns my entire world on its axis. Literally, because if she would have never shown up to SKU, I would have never gotten the courage to go up against my dad, never would have believed I can be anything other than what I am right now. We wouldn't have broken into his office, and Kane would have taken that secret to the grave.

"Hey," is all I say.

She holds out a mug and I take it.

"How are you?" she asks and stands beside me.

I continue to face the house while Sam looks out into the distance.

I shrug. "I'm confused. Conflicted."

She nods and places a hand over my chest. "I get that."

We hear voices from inside the house, both glancing back to

see Kane enter the kitchen. He's watching us through the sliding door, and for what it's worth, it looks like he didn't sleep a wink either.

"You should talk to him." Sam tips her head in Kane's direction.

I face forward again, taking a long sip of the piping hot drink. "I don't have anything to say."

"Alex," she groans. "You have plenty to say. You guys have been friends forever; you have to talk this out."

"And say what, huh? Geez, thanks for finally telling me we're blood brothers, let's create a new secret handshake."

"You're hurt." She nods. "Understandably so but—"

"No. I'm beyond hurt. I'm pissed. He lied to me for God knows how long"—I point toward the house but keep my sights fixed on Sam—"and had it not been for me finding his name in that file, he never would have said anything."

"It's complicated. I seriously doubt he wanted to keep that from you."

"I treated him like a brother, Sam. What was mine was his. Never held anything back, trust him with my life." Now I'm pointing at myself, my finger sharp against my chest. "But he didn't trust me." I huff. "What am I supposed to do with that?"

"Talk to him. I get that this fucked your world up. But try to imagine what he's feeling in all this. There's a reason he didn't tell, and I'm sure that's been hard for him. He feels alone, Alex. Kept everything he's been dealing with to himself, and the only other family he has, he's *had* to lie to. He's a victim in this, too. The person you should be angry with is your father."

All I can do is stare at her. I know she's right, this isn't his fault, but he was supposed to trust me. We could have maneuvered this together.

"Think about it. Okay? You're going to need each other." She pats my chest then lets her touch linger along my biceps. Rising on her toes, she places a kiss to the side of my mouth and retreats back into the house.

Taking a large sip from the coffee, I turn on my heel to follow behind her. The moment I open the patio door, their voices fill the space. I close it behind me, set the empty mug on the counter, then enter the living room. The three of them are sitting around the living room—Kane's on the loveseat, Mountain is positioned on the larger sofa, and Sam settles opposite him.

"I was up all night going through the drive and found a lot of disturbing stuff," Mountain says without looking at either of us. "It's a lot, so I focused on your moms, given that all this started because you found that picture."

"What does it say?" Sam questions and tucks both legs beneath her before covering herself with the blanket.

Mountain scoffs. "What doesn't it say?" He shakes his head. "From what I can tell, your father"—he looks between Kane and me—"isn't the only person involved. And it goes back years. Though it seems to have stopped or slowed down in 2005."

"When Emily died?" Sam interjects.

Mountain shrugs. "I don't know."

"My father—our father wasn't the only one involved in what?" I ask.

"Some very, very disgusting things. That club Sam and Gracie found out about? Turns out it was a front."

"Front for what?" Kane asks, adjusting in his seat.

"Some sort of secret society. I mean, I guess it wasn't so secret considering the name you found, the Aurelian Circle, is public information, but it went beyond being a social club. At face value, it was an official school program but not an open one. I mean they have school activities, and fundraisers, and all the usual stuff. But membership was extremely exclusive, and invitation only. All the male members were the elite, sons of mayors, senators, etc. And the women varied from wealthy families and poorer families."

Snagging a chair from the dining room table, I drag it into the living room and flop into it.

"And they documented everything. When I say everything, I mean *everything*. Age, sex, degree program, background information, anything there was to know about someone, they have it."

"Okay, so they were extremely organized," I interject. "What does that have to do with our moms?"

Mountain pauses for a moment, dread washing over his features. It's the kind of look you give just before saying something you'll never be able to take back. Like it physically hurts him to bring this into the open.

"Just say it, man," Kane blurts.

"It was some kind of sex cult, and the girls were...recruited."

"For sex?" Sam asks, though it's more of a reiteration than a question. "Like they were trafficked."

"No. Not in the sense we think. But handpicked. Each male member picked a girl or multiple to recruit. Promised status, money, whatever they were looking for. And once they got in, they were claimed. Marked by the guy that recruited them."

I feel my stomach twist.

"Like I said, they kept files on everyone, recorded meetings, calls. You name it. It seems they would get these women to agree to participate, and once a month they would go on these 'field trips.' On the surface, the club was off doing something related to what the school's bylaws say, but in actuality, they were at some undisclosed location where they would drink and have sex with each other."

"So, they were freaked out?" I shrug.

"It gets worse. Sick. They would drug the women without consent and once they were incapacitated, they'd have their way with them. Vile and deplorable things. Rape. And the sick bastards recorded it."

We sit up, and I feel like I'm going to vomit.

"See for yourself." Mountain passes the computer to Sam.

Kane and I rush over to watch over Sam's shoulder. She takes the laptop, placing it on her lap, reluctantly pressing play on the video Mountain left on the screen. It's innocent at first, a bunch of college-age kids, partying and making out. It appears they're somewhere far from civilization, up in the mountains surrounded by trees and boulders.

The camera pans around, documenting the experience. It feels likes one of those end-of-year videos where the kids interview their friends before they go off and join the real world. Everyone's laughing or dancing. No different from the parties I've thrown over the years. My mother comes into view, and my nerves tingle. She's young here, sitting next to a girl. They're laughing and drinking.

"That's Emily. The girl—" Sam starts.

"The girl my mother killed," Kane cuts her short.

Sam reaches behind her to take his hand in hers. I peer at him, wanting to offer comfort but not quite sure where to begin. So I keep watching. We all do.

The shot moves on to another group of students, our dad, Mr. Kincaid, Senator Martinez, and a few of the other prominent figures in our town. Then we see Kane's mom, and next to her is Sam's mother.

Sam gasps, squeezing Kane's hand so tight he winces, but he doesn't stop her. Reaching over, I speed up the clip, stopping when something strange appears. Based on the time stamp, it's at night, but the women are unconscious and completely nude. And the things that are being done to them, no one should ever have to see.

Sam's shaking now and forces her eyes away before abruptly shutting the video off. "That's horrible."

"Fuck," I let out. When we started this, I wasn't expecting that.

Kane takes the laptop, determined to keep looking. He closes that video and scrolls the folder until he finds his mother's name. Loads of files pull up, medical records, payments, but then he pulls up a voice note, his entire body going rigid when he hears his mother's voice. She's rambling on, her words incoherent. The only thing we can make out is one saying over and over.

"What did they give me? What did they give me?"

Another voice tries to calm her down. "La'Kia. You're panicking, just sit down. Here have some water."

"No. No. No," she continues ranting. "Don't touch me. Don't touch me."

And then it sounds like skin hitting skin, followed by a grunt and then a scream. And then nothing. Screams break out, the sound of people running closer to the recording.

"Oh my God, what did you do?"

"What did they give me? What did they give me?"

"Kia, look at me," a soft, pleading voice says.

Sam gasps again, her hands going to her mouth. "That's my mom's voice."

"Kia, let's have a seat," Miranda continues.

"Don't touch me. Don't touch me."

"She's dead," a deep baritone voice cuts through the chaos.

"Fuck. This isn't good. How much did you give her?" another male voice asks.

"It doesn't matter. We just need to make sure this is covered up."

And then it just ends.

Kane tosses the computer onto the sofa and storms off toward his room, slamming the door so hard a painting falls off the wall. Sam is crying full force now, her body rocking as she continues to cover her mouth. I glance at Mountain, who reaches for her while signaling for me to go after my brother.

I take off at a sprint, not bothering to knock. The moment I open the door, Kane swipes his arm across his desk, knocking everything to the floor. I rush to him, wrapping my arms around him to calm him down. It's a struggle, but I don't let go.

"Get the fuck off me," he barks, fighting to get free.

Still, I hold him, grounding him, letting him feel everything. After a moment, once he's exhausted, his legs give way, but I manage to keep him upright long enough to get him to the bed.

"They did this to her." The tears pour down his face. "Whatever they gave her, what they were doing, they're the reason she snapped. And they covered it up, leaving her to suffer through this all alone."

"They'll pay. You hear me. We have all the evidence. We'll make sure of it." Tears prick my eyes, but somehow, I hold it together for him.

Kane looks at me and hugs me. All his pain, years of doing this alone, I can feel it. Here I am upset that he's kept a secret when he's had to endure so much hurt alone. Disposed of and hidden in plain sight.

"I'm sorry," he says barely above a whisper. "I wanted to tell you. I found out two years ago. My mother had another episode that landed her back in Wyndmoor. She's been in and out of there my whole life, but I never really understood why. But this time, her doctor decided she needed long-term care, which meant I was left paying the bills and for her treatment. That's when I found all this documentation, my birth certificate, receipts of payments from your father dating back to the moment I was born. We only met because he put in a word to get me transferred to your school and has had a hand in making sure my education and our lives were funded. But only if she never tells me that he is my father. I confronted him about it and laid it all out. He spent the last two years holding it over my head, threatening to cancel my mom's treatment. If I even dreamt of telling you the truth, he would take it all away. And I just—" His voice cracks.

"It's okay. We're good. We didn't need his permission to be brothers. We've been that from the moment we met."

My father has treated me like shit my entire life, but I can't imagine what this has done to Kane. I don't know how we're going to handle this going forward, but I do know he'll never be alone again.

CHAPTER FORTY-ONE

BRYDEN (MOUNTAIN)

I hate that she's hurting. Hate that she had to see, read, and hear those things. She's been searching for answers, trying to put the pieces of the puzzle together since her mother passed, and I just made it worse. I want to tell her everything that I found in those clips was just the tip of the iceberg. But she can't handle that right now.

So I just hold her close, giving her the space she needs to feel. We're way past vault status, beyond burying the hard feelings in the depths of my phone's deleted folder. This is too big, too heavy to just erase once it's over. It's going to live with them for years to come. Alex, Kane, Sam, Gracie... even Christina, Jackson, and so many of our other peers. They're all unknowingly wrapped up in this. And given their ages in relation to when some of that footage was taken, it's looking more and more to me like some breeding cult. Except Sam, having been born a year after the club shut down.

But what I don't get the most is if that's what they were doing, breeding these women, why raise some of the children themselves but not others? Clearly they've at the very least still provided for them, considering what we now know about Kane's monthly payments.

Why do any of this at all?

Sam settles into me, her cries piercing me to the core. How do you comfort an invisible pain? Sure, I can hold her like I am, kiss her and prove that I'm here, but it won't stop this from festering. She'll move on, seem well for a while, and then something will trigger these memories, and she'll hurt all over again.

So, no, right now, I won't tell her about everything else I saw. Instead, I'll share the one thing that I know will give her hope.

Sam sniffles and dries her eyes. When she pulls away, her face is puffy, eyes now beaming red. Each breath she takes is shallow, as if getting enough oxygen is the hardest thing for her to do. And maybe it is.

"Why would they do something like this?"

"I think we'll never understand the minds of people who do bad things. And while these women willingly joined that club, there's enough evidence that proves nonconsent. We can only hope they get their justice, and maybe then the world will be just a little safer."

"I didn't expect this." She shakes her head. "I just wanted to know about my damn scholarship."

"Look at me," I demand.

She does and wipes her nose in the process.

"I know today was hard. Seeing that wasn't easy for any of us. But I found something else that might make you feel better."

Sam stares at me, confused, but she doesn't ask me to elaborate. Picking up the laptop, I open a transaction document. As the page pulls up, Kane and Alex rejoin us. Whatever animosity was brewing between them has seemingly faded away. Good. Because the tension I saw coming from them last night and this morning wasn't like them. And I get it, secrets were held in, but they were brothers long before last night.

Sam points her attention to them, her expression twisting into concern. She tosses the covers from over her legs and stands. Her eyes are trained on Kane, and I watch the way his body relaxes under her gaze. Like her presence soothes the turmoil inside of him. It makes sense given they've been bonded since they were kids. She knows his pain because she's lived it.

Alex moves out of the way, making room for her to get to Kane. She throws her arms around his neck, and he wraps his around her waist, pulling her so close they might as well be one. Neither of them says a thing. They only stay like that, holding each other until Alex speaks, drawing everyone's attention.

"What's going on?" he asks, his eyes taking in the items on the screen.

I glance at him, then down to the laptop.

"He said he found something that I needed to see," Sam interjects as she finally releases her hold on Kane and retakes her seat.

Resting my arm on her thigh, I take in a breath. "While I was digging around, I concentrated on finding out more about Sam's 'scholarship,'" I add with air quotes. "Every transaction is labeled with initials and a transmission date. Which we learned last night." I point to the $200,500 payment.

Sam follows my finger.

"What I found might be the answer to Sam being able to get custody of her brother."

It's not something we've talked about much. Family is a touchy subject for Sam, and I get that. Losing her mom so young, having to watch her struggle through years of abuse, living a life filled with toxicity at the hands of the very person who did the abusing. From what Sam's told me, her stepfather wasn't home when it happened and was visibly broken when they found her. But he wasn't innocent, and how could he have been when he's spent years contributing to breaking her down mentally and physically?

As we got to know each other, she shared her story, her reason for coming to SKU in the first place. And that was for her brother, so that she may one day make enough money to convince a judge to grant her custody. But she's only nineteen and in no way financially capable.

Today that might change.

"Okay." The skepticism in her voice is glaring, but she trusts me anyway.

"Kane isn't the only person receiving monthly payments from the club," I say matter-of-factly.

Sam watches my every move, her attention fully on the screen as I click out of the document to pull up the folder with a full list of payment transfers. Kane sits on the arm of the chair directly behind Sam while Alex observes from the center of the room. When I type her initials into the search bar, her eyes grow as over seventy transactions load.

"This one—" I point. "The fourth one. That's your scholarship payment."

"All right. So, what are the other ones?" she quizzes.

I release a breath. "Monthly payments."

"To who?"

"You." I pause.

"Me?"

I nod. "And they go back a little over six years, give or take a couple of months."

Her spine snaps straight, and I see the moment she registers what I'm insinuating.

"When my mom died." Her voice is merely a whisper, the tremble she had just a bit ago slowly creeping its way back.

Kane rubs her shoulder, kneading it to comfort her.

"Remembering the bits you've shared about your mom, I decided to search for her initials. And given that Kane has been receiving payments, first to his mom and then two years ago, it switched to him, figured maybe it was the same for you."

I type in the initials MC and an entire new list populates.

"So, I searched for your mother. There were nearly a hundred seventy payments wired to Miranda Collins before the same amounts started being transferred to an account in your name."

Sam's forehead creases, and she exhales deeply while hanging on every word.

"And there're so many like this. I check the initials and names on the statements against the different folders and it all matches."

"So, these women join for money?" Alex asks.

"I don't think so. There are some of these names without payments. Like your mom. And Gracie's mom. Even Christina's."

"The wives?" Kane interjects.

"So, what, they marry some and not the others?" Sam scratches her head.

"I think it's deeper than that. I think them and any of the women without payments were girlfriends of some of the members. At least that's true for Alex's and Gracie's moms. Their folders clearly state that they were in relationships with your father and Senator Martinez."

"So they partied normally with their girlfriends, but did worse things to the girls they drugged?" Sam tilts her head, blowing out a heavy sigh.

I nod.

"It's the only thing that makes sense. Your mom and Ms. Kane knew each other from school and this club before you met at Wyndmoor. And based on the audio and the article you and Gracie found,

Ms. Kane clearly had some type of psychiatric break. What are the odds that two of their members end up in a mental institution?"

"Whatever they were doing to them triggered something and drove them insane," she speculates. She shuffles in place, goose bumps pebbling on her legs against my forearm. "They were paying them off. Funding their lives to keep them from talking."

"That's what I'm thinking. The payments started when the club closed in 2005."

"Before we were born," Kane adds.

"Some received lump sums, others residuals. But they all signed NDAs. Including your mom, Alex. It's all in the files, every detailed documented from the women joining and who they were *assigned* to. The things they did to them. Even personal information, medical history, everything. They even paid for your moms' mental health treatments," I continue.

"So, they just pay these women for emotional damages as if it makes up for what they've done? For how long? The rest of their lives?"

"Unless they have children," Alex deadpans.

"That would it explain the payments switching to me when my mom was readmitted," Kane says.

"And why your mom's payments were canceled and moved to an account in your name, Sam."

"They did god knows what to these women and use this one account to pay them all?" she asks.

"That way no one can ever trace it back to them," Kane utters.

"And my guess is my father has all of this for leverage," Alex assumes.

"Or they all have copies. Everyone's name is in there, right?" Sam stares between us, the question rhetorical. "Why would they give one person that kind of power?"

"Because there isn't leverage," I concur.

"This was some sick twisted game for them. They control everything. The women have been paid. Most probably want to forget what happened," Sam says, sitting with the weight of that.

"If they remember," Kane deadpans. "When I showed my mother that picture, she kept saying, 'They can't know we remember.'"

"And I bet your mothers aren't the only women who've suffered some mental struggles after that." Alex rakes a hand over his head.

"This is so fucked," Sam groans out. "Those poor women."

"You said this would help Sam get custody of her brother?" Kane asks.

"Yeah. She needs money, and according to this, she has it. Probably a lot of it at this point."

"And you didn't know about that?" Alex directs his question to Sam.

"You think I would have continued living with my asshole of a stepfather if I had?"

"Then he's getting the payments and just never told you," Alex assumes.

"No. This says that they have been sending upwards of ten thousand dollars a month to me. If Gary was getting those checks, I would have noticed. No one can have access to that type of money and show no signs."

"True."

"So then where is the money?" Alex crosses one hand over his chest, the other out at his side. "If he doesn't have it, where is it?"

"I don't know. But if we can at least find a name of the bank in the files, maybe we can get her access to it," I suggest.

"I'll have the means to get custody of Desmond."

I rub her leg, kneading her knee as I watch tears pool in her eyes.

"What are we going to do?" Kane asks.

The three of us look at Alex. These files were found on his father's—their father's—computer, and while this incriminates so many others, this is about the chancellor. If anyone should make the decision, it should be Alex.

"We report it. Give them what we found. They don't deserve to get off freely while the women they harmed still suffer the consequences." He crosses his arms over his chest. "So, we go to the police. Today."

CHAPTER FORTY-TWO

SAM

The car ride back to the lake house is so silent I wonder at what point the life left our bodies. Was it after leaving the police station? Or before?

At this point, it all feels like a fever dream I can't wait to wake up from. Now we're headed *home*. That's what they've said to me more than once now. For the first time in a long time, that word doesn't disrupt my nervous system. In fact, a sense of safety washed over me the moment we hit the mountainous road.

We pull into the driveway, the gravel crunching beneath the tires. Kane rolls the car into park and kills the engine. No one moves for a long time. And when we do, Kane is the first to exit, the car shifting with his weight. I watch through the window as he stares into space, his mind clearly occupied as he instinctively opens the back door for me. I step out, searching his face in the process. The others exit at the same time and still we don't speak.

I enter the house before them, heading straight to the kitchen for water bottles, immediately opening mine and downing half of it in one go. When I return to the living room, the boys are waiting for me. I hand them each a water bottle, and we each move to our own corner. Alex plops down in the center of the sofa, Kane stands in the middle of the room, and Mountain stands next to me as I sit on the arm of the loveseat.

After a beat, Kane turns and glances at me, holding my gaze for what feels like an eternity.

"What are we doing?"

Confused, I frown. "What do you mean? We just have to wait to hear what the invest—"

He shakes his head. "That's not what I'm asking."

Mountain's spine straightens, and Alex sits up. We stare at Kane, each impatiently waiting for him to continue.

"This." He pauses. "Us. What are we doing? It's clear that we all have feelings for you. Clear that we all want you."

My shoulders slump, that dreadful question brimming just beneath the surface.

"But who do you want, Sam? Who do you choose?"

I stand up, frozen in place, my emotions fighting against my thoughts, everything I know and want colliding like a tidal wave. Suddenly it's hard to breathe, and I have to squeeze my eyes shut. Maybe if I will it away, if I pray hard enough, that question would fade into oblivion. Only I know it won't. Deep down I've known all along. The moment I realized that things with them were shifting, I knew I was in over my head. With each passing day, every study session, every coded argument, every text, I found myself falling off the deep end, and now I'm drowning in them.

I should put them out of their misery and finally make a decision. One by one, I take them in, locking the way they're watching me into memory. Alex already told me where he stands and, in a way, so has Mountain. I expect one of them to come to my aid, but they don't. And I realize it's an answer they want to know as well. Kane's just the only one willing to ask out loud.

"Me? Alex? Or Bry?"

I sigh, squeezing my eyes shut one more time, but it doesn't stop my skin from prickling under their scrutiny. Then I look at him.

"I choose you all." I stare between them. "I didn't expect to fall for any of you, didn't expect to care. But I did. And I do. So I'm sorry, but I can't think of being with one of you and not the others. And it's not fair. I know that." I exhale. "It's crazy and people will talk, but that doesn't matter. It's all noise that gets drowned out the moment I look into your eyes."

Turning to Alex, I continue. "Or when you make me laugh or bring me into one of your impulsive moods."

Then I peer up at Mountain. "Or when you just give me space to feel safe around you."

"What are you saying?" Alex interjects.

I shrug helplessly. "I guess I'm saying that if I have to pick one of you, then I can't pick at all." I stare at each of them. "It'll hurt too much, and if that's not something any of you want, I'll respect that. The last thing I want is to hurt any of you. For me, it's all or nothing. But this is your lives, too, so you're going to have to make your decision."

The room is quiet for a moment. This time heavier, more like gravity than tension. And we sit, our gazes passing around the room like we need someone else to break the ice. Alex does the honor, reaching out for my hand, and brings me close, letting his fingers brush against my thigh. His touch is subtle, stifled by the fabric of my jeans, but it stills sends a chill through my body.

"I've already told you where I stand," he says, his voice low yet full of conviction. "I want you."

Mountain inches closer, his hand at the small of my back as he hooks a finger under my chin to bring my gaze to his. "I'd rather share you than not have you."

We turn our heads to Kane.

"How is this even supposed to work?" Kane says after a long moment.

I shake my head. "I don't know how any of this works. I've never had an actual boyfriend, let alone three. We'll be figuring it out together. But it shouldn't be hard as long as we love each other. Right?"

"You love us?"

I look at them, my heart fuller than it's ever been. Never in a million years did I think I would be in such a position, and maybe it's a trauma bond and I'll soon learn that it's a mistake. But it's one I'm willing to make.

"Yes. I love you, Kane. And if I'm being honest, I probably have since we were kids."

He blinks, a smile beginning to tug at his lips, but he manages to keep it from forming.

"And as much as you got under my skin"—I grip Alex's jaw, and he nestles his face against my palm—"I love you, too."

Turning my head to Mountain, I smile before laying my other hand on his chest.

"And falling in love with you has been the easiest thing of my life."

"So, you'll be with all of us?" Kane asks.

"Yes."

He nods coolly. "Together? At the same time?"

"I mean, she does have three holes," Alex interjects sarcastically.

"Pause," I quip. "This is my first quartet—"

"Is that what it's called?" Mountain chimes in.

I shrug. "Four-way? I don't know. Either way...we should hold off on the butt stuff for a while."

Alex chuckles.

"But I'd love to be with you together," I continue.

Kane swallows, his sight shifting between us. "Four might be a crowd."

"Crowds can be fun," I whisper, my breathing now labored.

Mountain groans beside me, his fingers twitching at the small of my back while Alex claws at my denim-clad thigh. Without another word, Alex stands to his full height.

"We've shared before, but never with someone who mattered. Imagine how good it'll be with someone we care about." And with that, Alex reaches across me, cups my cheek, and forces me to look at him. Towering over me, he strokes my cheek and lowers his mouth to mine. "Thank you for not counting me out."

And then his mouth is on mine, hot and heavy. His tongue slips past my lips, and I grip his sweater to pull him close. I moan against him, feeling the heat of his body radiating through me. Alex's hands find their way into my hair, and he gently tugs like he wants to keep me from moving.

When our foreheads touch, and his nose brushes against mine, I feel his brows pinch and open my eyes the same time he does.

"I fucking love you," he admits low enough for only me to hear. We're in the center of the room with his best friend and brother watching, yet this moment still feels so personal.

Reluctantly, I break our kiss but keep our closeness and turn to face Mountain. Mountain inches close, his strong arm wrapping around my body as he tugs me to him. Like always, it's safety and warmth, but there's also aggression. Like he's claiming me right here and right now.

Our chests collide, and a rush of air escapes me. Then his palm touches my skin, and he strokes my cheek, his eyes falling to my mouth and back to my eyes before finally kissing me.

He smells good, his scent heady and intoxicating. Our tongues dance, a battle for dominance that I lose the moment he sucks mine into his mouth.

Their tastes mix together, and I realize I'll never get enough. This is indeed it for me. They are it for me. Breathless, I lean back just long enough to look back at Alex and call him to us. He closes the distance, his hard body pressing into my back as Mountain's even harder frame encapsulates my front. I'm bracketed by them, and I feel so alive that I want to crawl out of my skin.

Alex slips a finger beneath my hoodie, and skates it over the bare skin of my hip. Then he slides both hands up and, in a single motion, he removes it and tosses it off to the side. Mountain's big hands settle on my hips, his thumb tracing lazy circles, and I bring his mouth back to mine. I fumble between us, gripping the hem of my shirt and yank it over my head, relinquishing it to Alex without a thought. He tosses that, too, the sound of it falling softly against the couch the only thing I hear.

Alex is behind me again, sandwiching me between an immovable Mountain and his own eager heat. Mountain's hand threads into my hair, pulling my mouth back to his. Alex's lips find the hollow of my neck, then my ear, his teeth scraping a path that makes my knees weak. Suddenly, we're a triptych of hands and hungry mouths.

I give in to them, the world narrowing to the feel of our bodies, the sound of their breaths, and the shuddering in my own chest. Every nerve in my body is on fire, every sense acutely aware of their touch, their scent, their need.

Hungrily, I pull back, struggling to get Mountain out of his jacket. He helps me, and it falls to the floor by his feet. Then his shirt goes next. I watch his body flex and twist as he drags the fabric up his body. Blood rushes to my core, my pussy pulsing from the anticipation. The thought of being stretched so deliciously by them is enough to send me into a frenzy.

I feel Alex remove his shirt, his flesh against mine. He reaches around me, cupping my breasts through the fabric of my bra where he slowly focuses on my nipples, rubbing tight circles until they've budded. My eyes flutter closed, and I settle against his chest. He continues to touch me like that, teasing me as Mountain watches through hooded eyes.

"Mm," I moan, my breaths now long and deep.

Alex tucks his face into the crook of my neck and runs his tongue along my shoulder blade before taking my earlobe into his mouth. He growls and I shudder.

"You can't wait for us to fuck you, can you?" Alex whispers between licks and nibbles.

I nod, the words strangled by a throaty moan that rips out of me.

"Say it," he demands, slow and sultry. "Tell him you want us to fuck you." Alex pivots us so that I can see Kane's face.

Kane doesn't say a word. He just watches us, his stare both yearning and restrained. As if he's trying to decide if giving in to this will be worth any fallout.

Alex slips his left hand behind me and undoes my bra in one smooth motion. I watch Kane's gaze darken, see the way he rolls his neck in an attempt to keep his composure. I want him to break. Want him to touch me and help them take me over the edge. Alex pinches both nipples, forcing my eyes shut yet again. Then he moves his right hand down my stomach and works the button of my jeans. And when he reaches inside, he glides past my panties and cups my pussy. The pads of his fingers part me and roughly find my clit.

"Tell him, Sunshine." He plays with my clit, rubbing up and down, and with each pass he gets a little lower. "Say it."

"I want you to fuck me," I manage to get out, each word clipped and breathless.

Kane bites his lip but still doesn't move. I keep my eyes on him and lose myself in the moment. So focused on the feeling coursing through me, I don't even realize Alex is removing my jeans until I feel the soft bite marks along my bare leg. As soon as I glance down, he peers up at me while patting my calf, signaling me to step out of my pants.

When he stands again, his hard dick brushes along my ass. I reach behind to touch him, finding his tip through the denim and attempt to tease him as he has me. His body shudders against my back, and I fight back a smile. Glancing to my left, I make eye contact with Mountain. Sensing my needs, Alex turns my body for Mountain to see me fully exposed, and Alex finally slips a finger inside me.

"She looks so pretty like this, doesn't she?" Alex asks. "You should feel how wet she is."

Mountain's jaw ticks as he briefly makes eye contact with Alex then drags his sights back to me. He wets his lips, watching the rise and fall of my chest, all in tune with the rhythm of Alex fingering me. Mountain inches forward, cupping my chin, smashing my breasts between his chest and Alex's hand.

My muscles clench, and I groan low as Mountain kisses me. It's slow at first, like he needs to take his time, but the aggression grows. Then he pulls back and lowers himself until he's eye level with my tits. Alex releases the left one, giving Mountain the space to claim them both, kneading and squeezing them together. Mountain's mouth closes over my nipples one at a time, his tongue massaging and licking as if it's his favorite thing. Alex moves inside me again, this time adding a finger. The sensation of Mountain sucking my breast while Alex finger-fucks me is so sharp I cry.

"F-fuck," I moan, only for it to be swallowed up by Alex forcing my head back and kissing me, urgent and greedy. I reach behind me, rake my hands in his hair, and pull him close while Mountain devours my breast.

Alex moves in and out of me, the sound of my wetness echoing between us. Pleasure builds in my gut, spreading across every limb. Blood rushes to the places they touch me, and it takes every ounce of willpower not to crumble to the floor. Not that I could with the grip they have on me. I arch into Mountain just as he takes his mouth off of me with a wet suction sound.

His hand moves down my stomach, his fingers crawling beneath Alex's wrist. Once he finds my clit, he rubs it in a quick burst, his actions aligning with Alex's, and I swear I see stars. My vision blurs, and the muscles in my legs start to give way, but they hold me in place, all while still working my sex.

"I want to feel you cum on my hand, Sunshine," Alex mutters against my lips. "You like him touching your clit while I stroke your pussy from the inside?"

"Yes," I moan.

"Tell us how much you like it." Alex's voice is rougher now, and he quickens the pump of his wrist, hitting that spot just right.

"O-ohhh. So much. So fucking much," I cry out, each syllable exaggerated.

"We know you do," he boasts. "And you're ready to come, aren't you?"

I nod.

"How many times are you going to come for us? Hm? Once

on each of our dicks?" Alex thrusts his fingers, his effort to bring down my climax relentless.

Mountain continues to match his energy, torturing my clit until it's pulsing and sensitive.

"Mmmm, shit."

"You're gonna be good for us, right. Gonna let Mountain stretch this pretty pussy?"

I nod again.

"Let me fuck this throat?"

"Yeah."

"Gonna let my brother use you up?"

Another nod as white-hot passion explodes across my vision. Tremors wreck through my body, and my toes curl.

"Yeah, you will. 'Cause you're ours. All. Fucking. Ours."

And I come. My orgasm comes sharp and fast, ecstasy crashing over me so hard I nearly black out. I scream, probably louder than I mean to, but none of them seem to mind. Not even Kane. They hold me in place, letting me ride it out before moving me to the sofa. Mountain helps me into a seated position, his hands roaming over my naked frame. I thrash from his touch, my body still on fire.

"Lie back," Mountain says as he drops to his knees, grips my thighs, and tugs me toward him until my ass is at the edge of the couch.

He rises above me, one hand gripping the back of the couch for balance, and kisses me softly.

"You're mine."

When I search his face, he smiles.

I nod. "I am."

He kisses me again, then my neck, my breast, and my stomach, but he lingers at the spot beneath my belly button, blowing on my flesh. I shiver and reach down to touch his hair. He looks up at me, a smile on his lips, and it's the sexiest shit ever. His smile, the one he's hidden from the world for so long.

Alex moves closer into view, watching me watch Mountain. And when Bryden finally kisses my pussy, I look at Alex. His mouth is parted, eyes glued to me, dick out, gorged and red at the tip. Pre-cum beads smear all over as he strokes himself. My mouth waters, and all I can think about is doing exactly what he asked of me, letting him fuck my throat.

But then my attention is pulled between my thighs as Mountains swipes from my clit down to my entrance and slips two fingers in me.

"Spread those legs for him," Alex orders.

I don't know what's hotter, Alex talking us through this, or Mountain's willingness to please while another man directs me. I do as I'm told, opening my legs wide.

Deep and guttural groans ripple off the walls, but it's Kane's moan that draws my focus. He's sitting now, his eyes fixed on the scene in front of him. He adjusts his crotch as the people he cares about most do things to my body in front of him. He wants this, whether he's ready to admit it out loud or not.

I try to keep looking at him so he knows that I want him just as much as I want them, but that lasts all of three seconds before I feel Mountain's mouth on my clit. Peering down at him, my brows pinched tight, I bite my bottom lip. Mountain laps at my pussy.

Alex kneels on the couch to kiss me, then brings his cock close to my mouth. With his hand on the back of my head, he angles me in place, running his tip over my bottom lip.

"Open that mouth."

I do.

"Tongue out."

I obey.

Alex slaps his cock on my tongue. When I attempt to seal my lips around him, he pulls back.

"Keep it open," he insists, then glides the underside of his dick over my tongue. "Fuck. Look at you." He tips his head. "Okay. Suck."

Lifting on my elbows for balance, I wrap my fingers around his thick dick, and take him into my mouth, sucking him deep and watching as his eyes roll to the back of his head. Alex feeds his dick to me, squeezing my face with each thrust forward. Mountain continues to eat my pussy, making it hard to keep focus. My eyes flutter between the two of them. All I want to do is please them and let them use me until we're all sated.

Suddenly Mountain breaks away, and Alex does, too. They stand before me, each removing the remainder of their clothing until I'm not the only one naked. Alex is touching himself, his hand moving steadily over his shaft. Then I focus on Mountain, his huge dick preening and at full staff. Maybe I am getting in over my head.

Mountain takes my hands and helps me up. I wrap my arms around his neck, reveling in the feel of his naked body against mine. The first time we were together, we didn't bother to undress, so finally being able to see and feel all of him is perfect. Alex, too, considering there was no way we could get completely nude in that dressing room. Mountain positions me ass up over the arm of the couch, guiding my legs until I'm arched to his liking.

As he saddles up behind me, Alex rounds the arm of the sofa, his cock staring me in the face. He leans down to kiss me, then lines his dick up with my mouth. I'm not given a moment to brace myself before they enter me at the same time. Just like before, Mountain barely fits, only this time, my whine is stifled by Alex's dick. My body winces, but Mountain rubs my back, gently deepening my arch and keeping his hand in place.

"Just breathe. It fit before, and it'll fit again," he says behind me.

I gush at that, my core pulsing with need. I've already come once tonight, but I can do it again with one of them buried inside me. They take their time with me, slowly fucking me from both ends, goading me until I have no choice but to believe I can take all of them. Over and over Mountain fucks my dripping pussy while Alex has his way with my face.

"Hhm," Alex grunts. "So fucking perfect taking us both."

Mountain's hand comes down on my ass, and I whimper around Alex's shaft. Propping a leg directly behind mine, Mountain grips my waist and digs deeper until he bottoms out inside me.

"Fuck, Sam," Mountain roars, and it sends me over the edge again.

My walls contract around him, milking him. My vision blurs again, the telltale sign that I'm just on the brink of my second orgasm for the night.

"You're coming. I feel you," Mountain announces, his grip tightening.

"Shit," Alex mutters. "I'm right there, too."

Alex holds my head, while Mountain continues to guide my hips. I meet them halfway, throwing my ass back on Mountain and cupping Alex's sac, sucking him like my life depends on it. Then the floodgates open. Blood rushes to my ears, and my body turns molten. Every nerve ending lights up, overwhelmed and electric.

Mountain groans behind me as he slams deeper and harder. My thighs tremble, slick with sweat and shaky. Alex curses and fists my curls, barely keeping still while I take him to the base.

"Fuck, it's coming," Alex grits out, his voice ragged. He pulls back just enough for me to continue sucking the tip while he jerks the base with rapid succession.

Anchoring me in place, Mountain grinds slow, devastating strokes, stretching and owning me. And when my climax slams down on me, it's violent and life changing. I'm a shuddering mess, crying out around Alex's length as he shoots his seed down my throat.

Alex moans.

I feel Mountain tense behind us, feel the shift in his stroke enough to know he's teetering right behind us. Then he quickly pulls out, finishing and coating my back in his essence.

"Sam," he groans before collapsing on me, wrecked and panting. Once he finally catches his breath, he kisses my shoulder. "You okay?"

Alex strokes my hair, voice hoarse. "Too much?"

I shake my head. "That was perfect. But now—"

We turn to Kane, and I can't believe what I'm looking at. He hasn't moved an inch, but the slow movement of his hand in his pants gives away his desire. He didn't just watch them wring me dry, he touched himself to the sight of it.

Mountain helps me up, not letting go until he's sure I can manage. I saunter forward, feeling like the sexiest woman in the world with the way he's watching me, eyes glued to my swollen, freshly fucked mouth and tight nipples, before he finally focuses on the space between my legs. The closer I get to Kane, the deeper he sinks into the dining room chair, his legs opening wide for me.

I reach to cup his face, searching his gaze for any sign that he doesn't want this. My stomach churns at the thought of him not choosing me.

"Your turn?" I whisper, though it's more of a question.

Then he takes my hand, and I release a breath. My shoulders relax as emotions swell in my chest. Kane pulls me into his lap. There's nothing gentle about it. There aren't any pretenses, and he doesn't hold back. I straddle him, my bare skin brushing denim, and let him look at me.

He touches my face, his thumb rough against my cheek. He brings our foreheads together, and for a second, neither of us breathes. Then his mouth is on mine. It's not a kiss as much as it is survival, like if he lets go for even a second, we'll both disappear. He bites my lip hard enough to sting and I moan, leaning in, subconsciously daring him to do it again. And he does, this time like a brand. I arch into him, grinding down. Kane shudders, his hands finding my hips.

"Do you want this?" I ask, somewhat afraid for the answer. "Do you want me?"

He breathes for a moment, then looks me in the eye. "No."

My heart stops, devastation blooming inside me.

"I need this. Need you." His eyes flick across my face.

My breath hitches, and a single tear falls.

"I'm in this." He nods. "You're ours."

I kiss him and eagerly peel his shirt over his head. He helps me, then lifts enough to free his dick. Kane lines himself up and thrusts into me in one brutal stroke. He glides in, deep, the pressure shocking. I gasp, and he groans while bucking up into me. We find a rhythm that's savage and unrestrained. He fucks me like he's punishing us both, and I meet every thrust with equal force, loving the way he fills me.

We barely notice the others, but I know they're there, watching. And it's almost overwhelming. We're doing this. It's unconventional, but it's ours. Throwing my head back, I ride the wave, giving myself to him fully. It doesn't take long for my body to chase another release.

I'm close, so close, and he senses it. Kane slows down, rolling his hips, changing the angle until I see stars. He brushes my hair out of my face, holds my chin so that I have no choice but to look at him. I watch his face twist in pleasure, feel his grip tightening.

Then he kisses, deep and slow, while keeping pace. I fall apart on him, sobbing his name. Having come three times back-to-back, Kane has to wrap an arm around me to keep me from falling into a puddle around him. After a few more thrusts, he quickly lifts me up and finishes on my stomach.

Breathless, he kisses me before tucking his face against my ear. "I love you, too."

An hour later, a knock at the door jars our attention. We stare at each other, equally confused.

"Who's that?" Kane asks as he stands.

"Don't ask me, this is your house," I answer and glance at Alex.

Mountain fixes his eyes on the door. "One of you expecting someone?"

Alex peers out the window, his brows creasing. "It's Gracie."

Moving toward the door, Alex unlocks it and pulls it open.

"Hey," Gracie mutters, and there's sadness in her tone.

The moment Gracie sees me her entire body shudders. Sad eyes stare back at me, and I immediately sense she is not okay.

"What's wrong?" I reach out to hug her.

Gracie's shoulders shake before the sound of her cries fills the air. Guiding her farther into the house, I continue to hold her. Alex closes the door, then joins my side. Thinking fast, he rushes into the kitchen and returns a second later with paper towels. I take them from him, and without breaking my hold on Gracie, I slowly walk us over to the loveseat.

"Did something happen? Are you okay?"

Finally, I pull away and allow her to sit. Her eyes are bloodshot red, far redder than they should be for this to be the first time she's cried today. Whatever it is, it's eating at her. I can see the worry in her gaze, the fear, the regret. She takes the paper towel when I hand it to her, using it to dry her eyes.

"What's wrong, Gracie?"

She looks at me, her face contorting as she fights to keep from heaving. "I'm sorry."

Taken aback, I glance around at the boys who share my confused expression. "For what?"

"I need to tell you something." She drops her head and rips at the used tissue.

"Gracie." I sit down beside her, taking her trembling hands in mind. "Breathe. You're one of the best people I've met in my life. There's nothing you can say that will change that."

She sucks in breaths, one after another, until her body starts to settle. Then she wipes her face once more and shifts so that she's looking only at me.

"What do you need to tell me?"

"My father is a horrible man." Gracie swallows, and the moment hangs between us.

Numbness dances up my arms, and I brace myself for the worst.

"You're scaring me," I admit while searching her face.

"I'm your sister."

EPILOGUE

SAM

Six months later...

"Let's go," I yell from the lower bowl.

"There they go," Desmond blurts, pointing out the guys and waving frantically.

Alex skates to the glass with Kane and Mountain trailing closely behind them.

"Hey, guys," Desmond says excitedly.

"What's up, little man?" Kane greets him first and leans over the partition to do the secret handshake they spent the entire summer learning.

Alex reaches out to tousle my brother's head. "Desy. Lil Bro."

Desmond grins at that, fanboying right along with everyone else here. Other kids and fans try to get the players' attention, and they wave, but they keep their focus on Des. I watch, loving the way they've taken my brother under their wing.

"Bryden," Kai, his kid brother, screams at the top of his lungs.

"Ningwizis." *(My son.)* Bryden's mother beams, pointing as he approaches the glass. She claps her hands to her chest, eyes full of love for her son.

Mountain reaches over the partition to fist-bump Desmond

and Kai before he pulls his mother into a hug. She cups his face, kissing both cheeks.

"Your dad had to work, and Gookomis needed to rest." *(Your grandmother)* "But they are so proud of you."

"Miigwechiwi' giin ogiin." *(Thank you, Mother)*. He places a palm over the back of her hand.

And then he turns to me, and signals for me to come close. I stand to close the gap, leaning over the partition to get as close as I possibly can to him. Mountain's gloved hand hooks around my nape, bringing our mouths only inches from each other. I watch his mouth as he watches me, and then he smiles and everything around me starts to fade. Finally, he kisses me; it's soft and passionate, respectful given his mother is sitting only three feet away. I melt into him, loving how good he makes me feel. Here he is, my quiet, stoic goalie, and he's kissing me for the world to see. And when he pulls back, I miss the connection.

"I love you," he says for the first time.

My heart stops, and I read his face, finding nothing but longing and sincerity.

"I love you, too."

Mountain skates backward, his eyes never leaving mine.

"Let's go, Bobcats," I yell from the lower bowl.

If you had told me at the start of this year that I'd be cheering during an NHL game, I would have laughed in your face. But here I am, standing front and center with everyone. I've grown to love and celebrate my boys in their very first game as professional hockey players. And they look damn good out there. It's not surprising they were drafted, especially after leading the Knights to yet another national conference.

It's amazing seeing them grow; after everything we've been through last semester, they deserve it. They had the choice to play somewhere else, to leave all the fucked-up shit we discovered behind, but they stayed for me—they stayed for us. It's complicated for sure.

Navigating the ins and outs of a polyamorous relationship has had its challenges, but once we got over the initial shock of it all, everything's fallen into place. We're there for one another, helping and guiding along the way. It feels good to be loved by them, despite the glares and whispers we get from people on campus who managed to put it together that I'm with all of them. We expected the judgment, but we tune it out because the only thing that matters is that we love each other.

Fuck the world.

Fuck the opinions.

Using that money and the help of an attorney, I was able to fight for custody of my brother and win. Not that the bastard put up much of a fight.

We have our own apartment now, just a few minutes from SKU and the new school Des started this year. He's made new friends and loves his Black Panther–themed room. Though I'm almost certain he loves being *best buds* with the Minnesota Bobcats' newest star players more.

I smile at that thought as I watch them together, my heart full. None of this would have been possible without Gracie, my sister. After that bomb she dropped on me, she was able to get me access to the account my mother set up before she died. Turns out, a few months before she planned to end her own life, she went to Senator Martinez to arrange everything.

While she'd lost her battle, she wanted to make sure Desmond and I were taken care of. Not wanting Gary to have access to our money, she opened an account in my name, and every payment for the last six years went there, waiting for me to be old enough to touch it. Gary had taken enough from us; she wasn't going to let him take that, too.

Apparently, her father and my mother were supposed to end their secret relationship when everything went down with Emily's death and he got engaged, but they clearly couldn't stay away from each other, because I was born a year after Gracie.

He'd been aware of me but kept my existence a secret from his family. It would have ruined his life, everything he worked for. But he made sure my mom and I had what we needed by using the Aurelian Ltd. account to financially provide for us. That way, no one would ever find out.

But Gracie did. When she reported Jackson, the chancellor, and Mr. Kincaid, they exposed the information they had on the senator and his affair with my mother, to convince her to drop the charges. Not wanting to hurt her mother, or destroy the way she saw her father, she chose to keep his secrets and protect him. So she let it go, suffering the aftermath of what Jackson had done to her in silence, but under one condition.

She had to know me.

She convinced them to accept me into SKU and place me in her dorm. It was her all along. I was pissed at first. She's spent months pretending not to know me, not to know anything. But it eventually registered that none of this was her fault. Just like it wasn't Kane's fault.

Neither of us asked for this, so blaming her for the actions of our parents wasn't fair. And now, we're closer than we ever were before. And she's finally starting to reclaim her life. She took the video I recorded of Jackson's confession and turned it in to the police. Because of that, he will finally be charged, and my sister will finally be able to heal. Not that it will be a linear process, it never is, but she's well on the way.

Chancellor Williamsburg was arrested but released on bail in connection with the evidence we turned in. There hasn't been much development on the matter, but there is an open investigation. Which means it's only a matter of time before it blows back on every member of that club who did things to those women beyond their consent. And luckily, because the payment agreements between the victims and the club were legally binding, and due to the overwhelming amount of proof that shows these women were coerced into silence, they've been able to keep receiving funds. At least for now.

Alex kisses his mother's hand, then holds her tight. It's been a challenge for them since this all went down. Especially since Alex learned that she was aware of the things her husband had done but was too afraid to do anything. It was years after the collapse of the social club that she learned the full truth, but by then, she'd given him her life and had built a family. She'll have to own up to her complacency, but Alex knows the lengths of his father's manipulation and will always give her grace because of that.

I observe Kane with his mother, admiring the relationship they have. She seems to be doing better, so much so that we were able to bring her to watch him play his first game. She's been smiling the entire time, gushing about how proud she is of him. I've visited her every so often with Kane, and we've started to bond. She's kind to me and shares happy memories of my mother before their lives were turned upside down. It'll be a while before she comes home, but between the four of us, we make sure she has everything she needs.

Kane points at me, whispering that he loves me while Alex winks in my direction. We stare at one another for a beat, their gazes raking over my frame, love brimming in their eyes. Heat slicks my skin, and all I can think about is getting them home after this game and having my way with them. They skate off to join their teammates.

"I still haven't fully wrapped my mind around how lucky you are. They are damn fine," Evan says, breaking my thought.

When I shared with him that I'd fallen for not one but three hockey players, I expected a lot of questions, but Evan never batted an eye. He's always been open-minded like that. So long as they made me happy and took care of me, that's all that mattered to him.

I peer at him, a smile plastered to my face. Then I glance back at each of my boys.

"They are, aren't they."

The team huddles together, my three connected at the shoulders. Through it all, their bond is stronger.

And me? I'm just glad we're no longer on thin ice.

ACKNOWLEDGMENTS

Oh man! I think this is the part where I cry.

To my family, all those composition books you all brought me to write in finally paid off.

To my siblings, I love you! Thank you for always being excited for my ideas, even when you probably didn't care to hear me rambling.

To my sisters from another mister, Tiara, Markie, Brooke-Lynn, Jess, Daddy J (Jackie), thank you from the bottom of my heart.

To Josi, my friend and career wrangler, thank you for seeing my talent and standing behind it.

To Nickee, you're the MVP.

And I can't forget you, Sabrina. Thank you!

ABOUT THE AUTHOR

S. Rena (Sade Rena) is a *USA Today* bestselling author of contemporary and dark romance. Sade enjoys spinning tales that are angsty, emotional, sexy, and sometimes funny. Her characters are diverse, flawed, and—because she loves a villain just as much as she loves a hero—morally gray.

Books under S. Rena contain dark, gritty themes, high steam, and subjects that could be triggering and are meant for a mature audience (18+).

To learn more, visit:
SadeRena.com
Instagram @SadeRenaWrites
TikTok @SadeRenaWrites
Facebook.com/SadeRenaWrites

You can join her mailing list for updates at
SadeRena.com/email-list